S6

BY
GILBERT PHELPS

FICTION

The Heart in the Desert
A Man in His Prime
The Centenarians
The Love Before the First
The Winter People

CRITICISM

The Russian Novel in English Fiction
A Short History of English Literature

GENERAL

Living Writers

THE GREEN

SIMON AND SCHUSTER · NEW YORK · 1964

GILBERT PHELPS

HORIZONS

TRAVELS IN BRAZIL

CONTENTS

PREFACE

Brazil is a vast country, bigger than the United States, much of it still in the pioneer stage, without adequate roads or railways, and some of it still unexplored. To write a comprehensive book about it would demand years of study and travel. This does not pretend to be a comprehensive book, and those who know Brazil well or who are looking for a detailed guide to all the "places of interest" will be disappointed. So, too, will those who look for dramatic adventures among wild animals and naked savages. To obtain material of that kind except at a superficial level calls for finances of a kind that I could not command and lengthy preparations which would have taken up all the time at my disposal. In any case, too much has been written along these lines—often (as my Brazilian friends will agree) of a highly colored and dubious nature—and the picture of Brazil that has emerged in the minds of foreigners has in consequence tended to be distorted and unbalanced.

This book is at least based upon travels which extended almost from the borders of Venezuela in the north to the far south on the borders of Uruguay, taking in rivers, jungles (including Indians), mountains, pampas, seaports, factories, plantations, and cities old and new, and it attempts to give a picture, however partial and sketchy, of modern Brazil in its historical, political, economic and human aspects.

It is, however, very much of a personal picture—the record of one man's responses to people and places, shaped by the accidents of every day and filtered through that man's own moods, prejudices and temperament. Although I kept detailed notebooks, it is also a work of the memory, subject therefore to the molding and modifying processes of the memory. I can vouch for the truth of all that I have reported, but not always for the details or the order of events. I have also disguised certain incidents and provided fictitious names where I thought there might be a danger of giving offense.

In writing my book I owe much to the many Brazilians whom I met on my travels and who gave me information, advice, help, hospitality and friendship. In particular, I am indebted to Roberto Muggiati, of Curitiba in Paraná, and now of the Brazilian section of the B.B.C., who has read my typescript and advised me on matters of fact, spelling and accent, and to James Michie for editorial advice that was not merely helpful, but vital. I should also like to thank Joyce Eltringham, not only for her assistance in typing and getting my manuscript ready for the publishers, but also for her unfailing help and encouragement.

London, 1963   G.P.

1

APPROACHES

No journey belongs only to time and place: neither the eye that sees nor the heart that feels is a timetable or a map. Every journey to foreign lands is also a journey through the countries of the mind, and the landscapes of the one flow into those of the other. Moreover, the eye that sees and the heart that feels do not always act in unison.

As it happened I found myself, as we buffeted our way out of Liverpool in a February gale, in that state of mind in which one sees rather than feels, as the eye of the camera sees. It was as a camera that I functioned during those first weeks. If I look back upon them now I see a series of snapshots, some of them in black and white, some in color: some motionless, others pulled in strips across my face in a jerky approximation to movement, but most of them flat and two-dimensional. Even now I cannot tell when and where feeling entered into seeing, or what properly belongs to one and what to the other.

It was, for example, as a composition in color that I saw the approach to Leixões, the harbor of Oporto—a dusky blue-and-rose sky, the lights twinkling along the moles, and then as the sky deepened to mauve a huge orange-gold moon, circular behind the tracery of cranes and derricks. So it was, too, as we sailed along the soft, blurred coastline between Oporto and Lisbon and I saw the jagged purple hills, the gray-green slopes covered with dark trees, the slices of yellow, pink and terra cotta where houses showed among the foliage and the tiny fringes of beach, salt-white and smooth.

As we sailed down the Tagus another element entered. I had last come this way in September 1940 in a bumpy old Sunderland flying boat, a violent transition from the raids and blackout of London to the brilliance of Lisbon—blazing sunshine by day and that same night the outdoor cafés strung with lights, the last lights, almost, in Europe, that shuddered in the cacophony of voices, motor horns, and the wailings of *fados*—and now memory stirred my senses as I saw again the impressionistic canvas of crumbling yellow and pink buildings scattered over their seven hills and interspersed with the dark-green stripes of cypress trees, and as I stepped ashore and sniffed once more the stale wine and olive smells.

The pictures that printed themselves on my mind trembled and wavered as I saw Black Horse Square again and the Rocio, and the statue of Camões. They trembled and wavered as if old ghosts were about to materialize among the fishing nets and plaid shirts at Cascais, among the palm trees of Estoril. At Carcavelos, where my wife and our infant son had once lived, I saw the front as it had been in the past, approached by a stone path beside a private *quinta* and with its wooden shack of a beach restaurant where you could buy fish cakes made of *bacalhau* and needled with bones and where sand fleas agitated the hot white beach like rain drops—I saw these rather than the new imitation Riviera villas and the ugly multiple-shoebox hotel. As we sailed back down the Tagus and the outlines of Lisbon slowly crumbled and disintegrated, the pang I experienced had nothing to do with the present: I had made a few fragmentary contacts with a past life, and now the ghosts I had stirred into half-life sighed and turned back into their corners.

So far I had been sailing in more or less familiar waters, encompassed by a Europe that was still "home." Beyond Lisbon was for me the unknown. I paced the decks for hours. So much sky and water made me feel as if I were enclosed in a giant globe. The activities of crew and passengers were momentary agitations, as when you turn one of those glass paperweights upside down and imitation flakes of snow disturb its serenity. But sky and sea pursued their own life, and I found myself geared to their rhythms. The sea changed color hour by hour; its surface assumed an infinite variety of patterns. At night it would swirl round the prow of the ship in oily swathes, black and menacing; within a few hours it would be tumbling in hills and valleys of gray and silver, or flung about in blue folds sprinkled with white, like the insides of those blue paper sugar bags of prewar days.

The movements of the sky, on the other hand, were slow and stately. The clouds towered above the horizon like ranges of mountains, skyscrapers, pylons and generators. For hours they remained absolutely motionless. But returning to the deck after a meal I would see that the edges of a mountain peak had crumbled, a pillar had toppled, or that at sunset the black cloud that had crouched all day on the horizon now showed one flame-red corner like the lining of an opera cloak. And this cloudscape seemed to me a projection of the contours of my own mind.

At Port of Spain, Trinidad, the ship was held up by a "go-slow" among the stevedores. As it lay at its moorings, it heated up as if a row of gas jets had been lit under it. On the upper deck one was caught like a sausage between the toasting fork of the sun and the gridiron of the deck. The lights in the alleyways, left blazing day and night, turned them into long, narrow ovens. To pass along them was like running a fiery gauntlet, and when I reached my cabin it was not much better, in spite of the electric fan and the funnel-like ventilator which blew out a stream of muggy air with a roar like a furnace. As I sat at my desk, stripped to the waist, trying to write, the sweat ran down my body in rivulets and my hand stuck to the pages. When I woke in the mornings my single sheet was as wet as if I had dipped it in the bath. The bags of sugar in the hold began to melt, filling the ship with a sweet, sickly smell like that of beets cooking; it blended with that of the garbage lapping against the quay, including a dead catfish; and live catfish darted with awe-inspiring speed and ferocity at the scraps of food thrown overboard, snapping at the legs of sea gulls hovering too close. The winches, cranes, lorries, horns and stevedores, in spite of the go-slow, maintained an indescribable clatter.

But away from the docks there were intervals of tranquillity and discovery. As if I were entering a new world, I climbed down the slopes to make my first acquaintance with mahogany and teak trees, with their thick dark leaves; cacao trees, with their heavy yellow pods and, beside them, the delicate branches and the sprays of tiny orange blossom of the immortelle trees. There were palm trees of all kinds—sago-palm with untidy foliage like old sacking, fan-shaped "travelers'-trees" with protuberances on the trunks which release water when slit. I saw my first African tulip tree, its upright blossoms like Roman candles, and, near by, a row of *bucanos,* their osierlike branches (used for making bird cages) so thin that from a distance they were invisible, so that the clumps of foliage at the top appeared to float, unsupported, like the stylized clouds drawn by children. I saw, too, lime, coffee and nutmeg trees, and my first orange grove, the fruits tiny at this time of the year, like balls on a Christmas tree. A little farther on and I had entered the Garden of the Hesperides: a whole orchard of grapefruit, the fruits so perfectly rounded that they looked as if they had been copied from the plates of an old book of mythology. The pickers were on strike and scores of silvery-gold spheres lay on the ground. It was sacrilege, I thought, to apply to them such a mundane term as "windfalls"—surely they had been rolled at the feet of a bevy of Atalantas? But, to my surprise, the sight also brought back the orchard that ran the length of the back gardens of the road in which I lived as a child.

This orchard belonged to an unusual couple who lived in a house at the end of the road. Mr. F. had once been a free-lance journalist in London, was related to Gerard Manley Fenn, the writer of boys' adventure stories, and was a passionate admirer of the work of Richard Jefferies. His wife had never been to school, but she was extraordinarily well read, regularly won prizes in literary competitions or for solving crossword puzzles that specialized in bookish clues, and contributed poems to the local papers. Her conversation was witty and full of literary allusions, and as in addition she had piercing brown eyes and the suspicion of a beard she was rather a frightening figure to some of the neighbors.

It was through their orchard that I came to know them. When Mrs. F. was collecting windfalls she would stop at the ends of gardens belonging to houses where children were living and leave a few apples on top of the fence. She made a point of doing this in secrecy, but one day I heard the clanking of the buckets and was waiting for her at the bottom of our garden when she came level with it. I was invited to help. I clambered over the fence and carried the laden buckets to an outbuilding. After that I often collected the windfalls myself and in return was given periodic gifts of books and the freedom of the orchard.

It was a wonderful extension of my imaginative world. By leaping the rickety tarred fence I found myself an explorer in unknown continents. One old apple tree with crumbling bark that left a fine dust like soot on my hands and knees had a low projecting branch over which I slung a piece of carpet, so that I always had at hand a Pegasus saddled and harnessed to take me to the farthest corners of the earth. Scattered among the apple trees were several empty poultry sheds, and these became lodges along my trail, each with its secret cache of weapons, charts and iron rations—except when they were wheelhouses, holds, the cockpits of airliners, or the interiors of submarines.

But these fantasies of travel and adventure owed their satisfying concreteness to the presence of the fruit itself. I got to know the touch, the smell, the taste of every kind of apple in the orchard— knobbly Ribston Pippins with skins like green sandpaper; circular Orange Pippins with their rusty, chapped skins; the big Blenheims, swelling on either side of their stems so that they lay in the palm of my hand as if deliberately settling their weight there; a species

of Warner with vivid green skin so thin that I could cut it with
my nail and so juicy that I could put the spot to my mouth and
drink, as if from a fountain. I knew these apples at every stage of
growth and decay: coral buds, shell-pink blossoms, the bullet-hard
early fruit, fruit that yielded itself into my hand at the touch of a
finger. Above all, I knew the infinitely varied sensations of collecting windfalls—hot with sunshine in the summer, grainy with
dried mud and stuck with fluffy down and the droppings of the
ducks who shared the orchard with me; oily-wet, as if soaked in
glycerine, when the rain fell; moist and surprisingly cold, even in a
heat wave, where they had rolled among the clumps of couch grass,
nettles, dock leaves and horse-radish. There was the satisfaction of
disentangling an apple from a mesh of damp grass as tight as if it
had been woven, and finding it still clean and whole; there was the
sudden slimy cold if my fingers encountered slugs, and the thrill of
disgust when they sank into rotten fruit like balls of brown porridge. . . .

The sight of these more exotic windfalls in the orchard in Trinidad made my fingers itch; the vividness of the memories they
evoked startled me with a sense of my life as a revolving wheel upon
an unsteady axis, dipping first one, then another rim out of sight.

But now the present and Carnival ("Parade of Carnival Bands
and Individuals" as the official program described it) claimed all my
senses. As I struggled through the packed streets of Port of Spain
a steady hum was already proceeding from the direction of the
stands surrounding the track; it was echoed by another hum, like
the muttering of thunder, from the direction of the city, where the
various groups were rallying. Every now and then I heard strange,
shuddering rhythms in the distance—so strange that I tried to close
my ears to them. In the same way I refused to let my eyes dwell
on stray performers waiting to link up with their parties in the
procession—a black body daubed with red-Indian war paint, a
coffee-skinned girl shimmering in satin and silver tinsel. They lodged
like brilliant specks in the corners of my eyes and I resolutely closed
my lids on them.

The pavements and sun-baked park were thronged with crowds waiting for the processions to approach or struggling to reach the stands. The transition from the ship's world of mild English faces was almost overwhelming. There were all varieties of color and texture of flesh and hair and bone, all varieties of stance and walk and expression. Along the verges of the park were rows of stalls selling fruits as varied in color and texture as the bodies clustered round them—mangoes, bananas, grapefruit, watermelon, pawpaw. Policemen in short-sleeved gray shirts, dark-blue shorts and stockings, and peaked caps were trying to keep the crowds moving, assisted by mounted colleagues on horses, chestnut, brown or honey, their coats as glossy-smooth as the skins of the girls.

Eventually I managed to find my stand. Behind me sat a family consisting of a Negroid father, an Indian mother in a brilliant sari and a muslin head scarf stitched with pearls, and two daughters, one nearly white, the other dark brown. On my left was a Chinese woman wearing gold-rimmed spectacles, and a swarm of children of every imaginable racial type and color, the little girls with tightly braided plaits, the boys solemn in white shirts and bow ties. To my right were two teen-age Negro girls wearing sleeveless white blouses that left their plum-smooth shoulders bare, and round white hats like linen porkpies perched on top of their heads. They were sharing a few-weeks-old baby between them, with such equality of solicitude that I never discovered which was the mother. They passed the baby from lap to lap, handling it as if it had no bones or joints; it lay, like a small snake, limp and contented, across their knees.

The stand in which I was seated was made of strips of aluminum, looking exactly like giant-size Meccano pieces. The cheaper wooden stands on the other side of the track were high and narrow, like boxes of mixed fruits stood on end, and were packed with multi-colored, gaily dressed humanity. Some of the improvised awnings flapped in the breeze. One of them collapsed, and screams of laughter came from under the billowing canvas as the people beneath struggled to fix it again. Every now and then a water cart drove past, spraying the hay-colored turf, or a posse of policemen, mounted or marching, drew bursts of ironic cheering—though a respectful silence greeted a handsome hawk-nosed Inspector of Police who also rode along the track at intervals on a magnificent mount.

Then, suddenly, at the far end of the track I saw a swirl of mustard-colored dust—and for the next three and a half hours my eyes and ears were subjected to the most violent assault they have ever experienced. I meant to take notes, I meant to take photographs, I meant to follow the printed program. It was impossible. I could only sit and stare. In consequence, I cannot remember the order of the items. I cannot even remember the tune set in advance by the organizers of the carnival for each steel band to improvise upon: it penetrated deeper than my eardrums, thundering, first in one key, then in another, in the blood stream itself. It still murmurs there, like the hum of our first infant summer, or the first surf one hears breaking in childhood. It gathered up all my childhood dreams of faraway places; it piled them against the lock gates of the future.

It was not until later that I realized that the bands were competing with each other and that the hordes of performers were really subsidiary. It meant little to me when I read in the newspapers afterward that "George Bailey for the fourth consecutive time and the fifth time in six carnivals won the much coveted title 'Band of the Year,' " and that his "Somewhere in New Guinea" was a portrayal of "the law of the rare Bird of Paradise." All that I knew was that like the triumph of some Roman emperor, column after fantastic column rolled by, and that the heart of each throbbed and thundered with hypnotic music.

The core of each band consisted of oil drums, painted in blue and white or red and white stripes, propelled on wheels by excited small boys, bending double, level with the kneecaps of the drummers who walked behind them. There were frequent stoppages as the track became congested, and the ground was bumpy and uneven, but the drummers never faltered. Their expressions were glazed and trancelike; their wrists flickered like so many snakes' tongues. Weaving in and out of the drumbeats, like canaries making themselves heard above the thundering of a waterfall, were shriller notes struck from pieces of tubing, small sections of railroad track and all kinds of nondescript chunks of iron; and around the bands swirled the retinues of performers in their various costumes, swaying and dancing to the music. Sometimes they split into separate eddies of twos or threes or fours; sometimes every individual gyrated in a purely private dance; but no matter what the combinations and permutations, the apparent chaos and confusion, somehow the dancers combined into meaningful and rhythmic patterns.

Color made as unremitting an assault upon the senses as sound. The costumes were so vivid that they "hurt the eyes," so flamboyant and extravagant that they "took the breath away"—as with the language of love, one is forced back upon the well-worn clichés. But what was it that gave these costumes their extraordinary brilliance? Immense labor and ingenuity had been lavished on them, considerable sums of money too; presumably film producers are even more lavish in their expenditure, and yet the most fantastic of Hollywood "spectaculars" looked pallid by comparison.

Perhaps it was the blazing sunshine and cloudless skies, perhaps the setting of tropical trees and flowers, and of spectators as colorful, brought out the primary hues more vividly, but more than anything it was the color and texture of the performers' skins. This was particularly noticeable in items such as "Somewhere in New Guinea," "Congo Warriors," "The Black Hopi Feather Traders," where the performers exposed large areas of flesh, while letting their imaginations run riot with robes and headdresses. Half-naked bodies too provided much of the impact in "Red Indian Warriors," "The Mohawks," and "Sioux Council after the Battle of Custer" (I quote from the official program). The warriors, it is true, were mostly black. Some, indeed, had tried to paint themselves red, others had daubed their bodies in stripes of red and yellow and blue, and some had shaved their heads to produce the Mohawk tuft and had dyed the exposed parts of the scalp scarlet. But the color of their skins did not minimize the effect: as each group irrupted upon my field of vision my blood leaped more wildly than at any Western with its hordes of authentic Redskins, and as they leaped and yelled the sweat carrying the paint in rivulets all over their bodies increased the effect of savage violence.

Each band of Red Indians contained its bevy of dusky squaws (many of them with papooses) dressed in jewel-studded moccasins and brilliant feathers. Each band, too, bore in its midst at least one magnificent chieftain or chieftainess. Their costumes made no pretense at realism: they were variations upon a theme—the more exuberant the better. They walked alone, partly because they were the "Individuals" specified in the program and partly because they needed space to maneuver. Some of the feathered headdresses protruded several feet on either side of the wearers, and though they were usually giants in stature they were forced to proceed at a careful gait, otherwise a sudden breeze might have toppled them over.

Equally startling was the effect of scarlet and purple velvets, of blue, yellow, green and turquoise satins, of gold and silver brocades, against dark skins. These materials figured lavishly in items such as "Flag Wavers of Siena" and "The Stuart, the Commonwealth and the Restoration" (again I quote from the program). Here too it was fervid imaginations that mattered more than historical verisimilitude, resulting in the most exuberant interpretations of plume, ruffle, cuff, furbelow and bustle, and in a riot of color.

The weight and thickness of some of the costumes were themselves cause for wonder. There was a troop of Cromwellian soldiers —though they looked more like a cross between Spanish Conquistadors and an Ethiopian imperial bodyguard—weighed down by vast curved helmets topped by brilliant plumes, leather jerkins and flashing breastplates. "The Devil and his Sons," "Jabs from Limbo," "Remnants of Hell," "Hell's Dragnet," and other demoniac visitations, medieval in their grotesquerie, must have experienced fiery torments indeed, inside skintight garments of velvet and fur, or clamped in serpentine scales with their heads completely enveloped in horrific masks. A hundred quacking Donald Ducks marched past, the headpieces of papier mâché, the beaks operated by cords. The performers in a vast set piece entitled "Nature's Notebook" wore over their heads and shoulders huge representations of trees, plants, flowers, vegetables, beetles and butterflies. And all this, hour after hour, in a temperature of at least 85 degrees Fahrenheit.

In some cases it was the very size of the procession that overawed. Six hundred men, women and children took part in "Julius Caesar's Conquest of Gaul." As troops of Roman legionaries and hordes of Gallic warriors swept past I was stunned and dazzled by the sensation of spectacle as I had not been since I first saw Griffith's film *The Birth of a Nation*.

Hour after hour the processions swept by, shouting, yelling, dancing; and through the cloud of dust at the end of the track I saw other groups massing, when suddenly I knew that my senses had endured as much as they could stand, and I pushed my way, inch by inch, out of the stand.

That night Captain B., our oldest passenger, celebrated his eightieth birthday. The party ended about eleven o'clock, and I returned to my cabin. The champagne had completed the assault on my senses, and I felt utterly exhausted as I undressed. But suddenly I thought I heard, very faintly in the distance, the sound of a steel band, and I remembered that very soon it would be midnight and Carnival in Trinidad would be over. I got out of bed and dressed again. There were no other passengers about. The whole ship seemed asleep. The docks too were deserted, except for a few policemen. One of them tried to persuade me to return to the ship, insisting that Carnival was already over "for respectable folk" and that only the "riffraff" would be left. But I went on through the dimly lit streets, and as I drew closer to the town I was almost certain I could hear the music of steel bands and the shuffling of feet—not altogether sure, because the throbbing lingered in my eardrums anyway.

Soon I came upon groups of performers, listless with fatigue, waiting for their buses. I went down one street, then another; several people sat or lay, some of them fast asleep, in the doorways of shops or on the curbstones. The gutters were inches deep in squashed fruit, chewed sugar cane, broken Coca-Cola bottles, bits of colored paper and tinsel, and fragments of papier mâché torn off carnival masks; a blood-flecked demon's eye regarded me balefully from a heap of grapefruit skins. I turned a corner, and saw—and heard—that I had not been mistaken. At the end of the street was the tail end of a procession shuffling and swaying to the music of steel bands. I caught up with it, ran along the column to the end of the street and waited for it to pass me. It comprised the last survivors of the steel bands and a few performers whose costumes had not yet borne them down; their ranks were swelled by a number of bystanders dressed in ordinary clothes, absorbed quite naturally into the rhythms and movements of the procession. The musicians now had their oil drums suspended round their necks by cords (the small boys had departed); they looked as if they were ready to drop, but wrists flickered as tirelessly as ever. The tempo of the music had dropped: it was a threnody the drums beat out, rather than a bacchic riot, but it had lost nothing of its hypnotic power. With glazed eyes and zombielike expressions a troupe of dancers followed each band. There was none of the wild leaping and cavorting of the afternoon now; instead, an odd, snaking, shuffling movement. The girls who had joined the procession danced slightly bent at the waist, their posteriors in their tight skirts swaying like the tails of ducks: one step, two steps, waggle the hips; one step, two steps, waggle the hips—on and on, to the beat of the drums. Shoulders, arms and hands all played their part: a slow rotation of the shoulder blades, the arms bent at the elbows, and the hands dangling from limp wrists like the flippers of penguins. Their mouths lay open, as if their lower lips too were joining in the dance.

The procession began to shrink as people broke away to sit on the pavements, or as pairs of lovers retired to shop-arcades and doorways, but the ranks reformed immediately, four abreast, without interrupting the rhythmic movement of the column as a whole. Some of those who had left it were engaged in political argument; there were a few halfhearted fights, but I saw no need for the drawn batons of the police and doubt if they had occasion to use them. Once, on a deserted stretch of pavement, I was stopped by a huge Negro who asked me for money, but when I explained that I had none with me and offered him a cigarette instead, he was quite content and we cupped hands as we lit up. I was, as far as I could see, the only white man in town. I felt isolated, disembodied almost, as if I were a ghost flitting through the streets, and yet I felt contented and at peace, an observer, "a rapt watcher" (to use a favorite phrase of Turgenev's), unnoticed, perhaps unseen. Nevertheless, there were moments when, my joints and muscles twitching in response to the music, I longed to join in the dance. I did not have the courage. Instead I walked in the road alongside the procession, while the dancers regarded me blankly, too absorbed in forcing their limbs to rhythmic obedience to be aware of any intruder, corporeal or ghostly, until midnight had struck and Carnival was ended.

At sea again, and at last the old world dropped away and the new began to rise above the horizon. The movements of the ship, as hour after hour she plowed onward, held for me an air of finality. Trinidad, it seemed to me, had been a dividing line, perhaps because it had forced my eyes (for the first time since leaving Liverpool) to work harder than my memory. And memory was now an enemy I must grapple with. The familiar context of the old world had given it protective coloring; now it stood out against the blank of the unknown. In a few days' time I would be at the mouth of the Amazon and then, I knew, a new chapter must begin.

Whereas before Trinidad every new sight had lent itself to comparison with the past or with the Europe we had left behind, whatever happened now seemed new in an absolute sense, without attachments of any kind. The trade winds, for example, seemed to obey laws entirely of their own. They blew at gale force, and on the starboard deck it was difficult to keep one's feet. But they brought no refreshment. It was better than the slow roasting at the docks of Trinidad, but the heat was almost as bad. As I sat at the desk flap of my dressing table the wind rattled the doors of my cabin and blew the papers in all directions, yet the sweat poured down my body. These were not, it seemed to me, winds in any familiar sense: they were emanations of the hot, moist jungles that lay somewhere ahead.

The ocean itself provided a more tangible manifestation. On the third day out from Trinidad I was standing at the ship's rail, gazing out at the immensity of sea and sky, when suddenly it struck me that the color of the water below my eyes was oddly at variance with that of the sky above. I stared, and as I stared the color returned to its normal ocean blue. It must have been something discharged from the galley, I told myself; but another idea too had crossed my mind. I climbed up to the bridge and told the Captain what I had seen. He had seen it too, he told me quite calmly, and had logged it. He pointed to a dotted line on one of the charts, which bore the caption "Outer limit of discoloured water: 200 miles." But we were still five hundred miles away, I reminded him. Yes, he explained, sometimes, if winds and currents were in a certain direction, silt and mud and vegetable debris from the Amazon were carried out to sea far beyond the limits marked on the charts.

So my idea had been right. Those figures which as a boy I had marveled at but which had seemed too staggering to be real—the eleven hundred tributaries (ten of them bigger than the Rhine), the flow of water equal to that of twenty Mississippis, pouring out of an estuary two hundred miles across (ten times the span of the English Channel between Dover and Calais)—were at last brought home to me. I was up against natural phenomena that were not only new but on a scale vaster than anything I had previously encountered.

When, two days later, we reached the two-hundred-mile mark, the sea as far as the eye could reach had changed color. Now it was a brownish black, streaked every now and then with dark green, the greenish tinge particularly noticeable where the froth broke away from the prow of the ship, like splintered bottle glass. It was then that I remembered a story I had once read about a ship whose water supply had given out, at about this distance from land. The crew had appealed to a passing ship and had been told, "Drop your buckets in the sea!" They had done so—and found that they could drink the water.

I had noticed that we hauled a bucket on board every day for temperature tests. I fetched a tumbler from my cabin and filled it from the bucket. I held it up to the light. It was clear enough, though it contained a brownish sediment. I took a mouthful, rather gingerly, without swallowing it. It was bitter rather than salty. I would not have drunk it from choice, but if I had been dying of thirst it would have been a different matter. I was about to spit my mouthful out, then suddenly decided to swallow it; it was as if I were drinking a bitter-sweet toast to the new world I was approaching.

The advent was also registered by a notice outside the Bureau: "The ship will cross the Equator at twelve noon approximately." And at twelve noon I was again standing on the upper deck, gazing about me in awe. Surely, I thought, the skies would open, or the sea climb up in a pillar of salt? But the ship plowed on steadily, and as she was a cargo ship there were no "crossing the line" ceremonies. Most of the other passengers had crossed it before, and officers and crew were completely blasé. But suddenly I felt stirring inside me the child who used to sit on the linoleum-covered floor of the small house in Gloucester devouring those old books of travel. Our back garden was not much bigger than a cricket pitch, but I had no difficulty in transferring it to the other side of the equator; and under the inspiration of H. W. Bates's *The Naturalist on the River Amazons,* which was one of the books my friends of the orchard had given me, it was usually the jungles of Brazil that I created in imagination.

Lying about the garden were a number of old logs which my uncle, who lived with us at the time, had bought cheap but was too lazy to saw up. Gradually they became rotten as they lay half-submerged in the long damp grass, and in the process the logs assumed all kinds of weird shapes and acquired all kinds of fungoid blotches, growths and protuberances. For me these logs were crocodiles and anacondas, while one half-trunk became my dugout. In those days my life had been my imagination and it had proved sufficient and I had never believed that fantasy might pass into reality.

I hurried to the fo'c'sle head and waited for my first glimpse of Brazil. But it was not until an hour later that I picked out through my binoculars the low, sandy coastline near Salinópolis, where we were to take on board the first of our pilots. The "G" flag asking for his services was hoisted, the anchors were cleared, and the ship slowed down and began to turn—"The old man will give him a lee," one of the crew explained. High up in the prow of the ship it was excruciatingly hot, and my eyes ached as I strained to pick out the pilot's boat. At other ports I had taken its arrival and departure as a matter of course. It had been an ordinary occurrence taking place in a world that was still familiar. Now I felt I was approaching an utterly unknown world. I stood waiting, staring ahead.

The sun seemed to have shifted its position, as if to concentrate its glare more fully on the prow of the ship. My clothes did not merely stick to my body: like the shirt of Nessus they bit into it. The iron plates beneath my feet seemed red-hot. I felt as if I would fry where I stood, and yet at the same time it was sultry and oppressive. On the starboard, dark gray clouds massed, an infinite distance away and quite, quite still. I was aware of a movement under my feet as if the ship had tilted upward, and the waters of the Amazon and its countless tributaries (though we were still nearly twenty miles out) appeared to be pouring toward us in a vast, muddy-black flood.

At last, when I thought I should be able to stand the heat no longer, I caught sight of a black water beetle butting and bustling through the waves. Gradually it came closer, until I could make out the red-and-black paintwork, the word "Pilotos" on the side, and at last the man at the helm: wide-brimmed straw hat and a loose, striped shirt, like those of a Devil's Island convict, fierce blue eyes and a fair stubble on his chin. His coloring surprised me, but I felt I had made my first real contact with the raw wild Brazil of the *bandeirantes* and the *cangaceiros*.

A large Negro in a faded blue shirt appeared and threw a rope, the pilot's bag, like an old-fashioned Gladstone, went up on another, and then the pilot himself had emerged and was climbing up the rope ladder, a dapper little man with a yellow seamed face and bright eyes. He was wearing khaki trousers and shirt and an American-type peaked cap, as if he had been summoned in the middle of a game of baseball.

With the pilot on board we steamed along the coastline west of Salinópolis and entered the mouth of the river Pará, as this part of the Amazon estuary is named, though there seems some doubt among geographers as to whether it is in fact a separate river. And as we sat at dinner that night we gazed through the windows at the same expanse of water that had been our element during the past month. Yet I experienced a feeling of excitement, an awareness that as the ship throbbed we were driving deep into the body of a vast, strange country which gave before our thrust as if a knife had encountered air instead of flesh; at the same time there was a sense of immeasurable masses of land somewhere around us, of fear, even, that it might be closing like pack ice behind a whaler.

It was dark as we entered the stretch of the river Pará opposite Belém separated from the main estuary by a group of islands. Lights began to twinkle to starboard and then the headlights of cars, somehow incongruous in a tropical twilight, flashed like shooting stars along a shore road parallel to the ship, bringing the human actuality close. We passed a large grain carrier, an oil tanker, and then a towering, three-tiered vessel reminiscent of the old Mississippi steamers and known as a *gaiola* ("bird cage"), the packed passengers swinging in their hammocks like canaries on their perches and traveling perhaps thousands of miles along the Amazon and its tributaries.

The shipping grew denser; so did the lights ashore—a long chain of them now, almost like the promenade at Blackpool. Soon we were directly opposite the city. The pilot from Salinópolis went ashore and two fresh ones took his place. Slowly we edged toward our mooring place. Lights shimmered across the water like illuminated hawsers. I joined the rest of the passengers at the rail of the ship. I was possessed by a feeling of awe at the prospect of a first contact with this city of the jungle. The word "foreign" took on a new depth of meaning, and the feeling was accentuated by the presence of the familiar—harbor lights, the glimpse of a packed and lighted bus turning a street corner, a skyscraper dominating the background with neon lights of red and blue playing round its summit. Closer still and I saw that the whole harbor area was crowded with on-lookers.

I stood with my pencil poised, ready to take notes—then put it away again. It was no use trying to think about these first impressions; they could not follow prearranged tracks; they came upon one like the customers through the swinging doors of a pub, and like them they surprised by their incongruity or their ordinariness. I knew that whenever in the future I thought back to my Brazilian experiences, my first memory must be of a row of warehouses, and against them a crowd of bareheaded, brown-skinned women in pretty cotton frocks, surrounded by swarms of children—the girls in frilly frocks and white socks, the boys in white shirts and tight, short trousers—and men in short-sleeved shirts and carrying large silver-handled umbrellas. Somehow the umbrellas were the last thing I had expected.

The gangplank was secured and like a trail of ants the various officials came swarming aboard. Suddenly we remembered the warning we had received about thieves in South American ports—soap, talcum powder and potatoes being especially prized—and hurried down from the upper deck to lock our cabin doors. The boarding party were now thronging round the Bureau. We stared at them as if a capsule from Mars had disgorged its contents. It was an extraordinarily motley crowd, reminding me of those I had seen at frontier stations in remote parts of the Balkans: swarthy faces, black mustaches, crumpled dun-colored uniforms and squashed peaked caps, some tropical suits, more short-sleeved shirts. We pushed our way through to get to our cabins before they drew their cutlasses. The most ferocious-looking, a black-bearded Captain Kidd, greeted us in English public school accents—it was the agent of the shipping line. Suddenly everything was normal again: the swarthy faces creased into smiles and our pirates courteously stood aside for us to pass. We went below and locked our cabins just the same—a group of English men and women shocked by the unusual.

It was too late, the purser had decided, for the passengers to go ashore that night; but the crew were allowed to do so. I asked one of them, a Liverpool boy of about eighteen, what Belém was like. "Not much good for you first-class lot," he replied, "but it's fine for us—you can get a girl for ten bob." Wasn't it dangerous, I asked him. "That's all right," he replied, "they give us a V.D. kit." I went on to the upper deck and looked at Brazil. The skyscraper behind the harbor buildings dominated the scene. I felt a twinge of disappointment. Heat, muddle, dirt, brothels. Was this city, so romantically situated, merely another twentieth-century megalopolis? For the first time I noticed a blue star on top of the skyscraper and remembered, irreverently, that Belém was the Portuguese word for Bethlehem.

2

BELÉM

TO MANAUS

The next day was a Sunday. My fellow travelers and I sat in the dining saloon of an English ship eating an English breakfast—tables with white cloths and an array of crockery and cutlery; a typed menu card embossed with the crest of the shipping line in a silver stand; white-coated stewards with poised trays moving gingerly as if puzzled to find it more or less steady underfoot. At my table old Captain B. (who had celebrated his eightieth birthday at Trinidad) ordered porridge as he had done every morning since we left Liverpool over a month before. He was one of the "round passengers"—bound for Manaus still far away on the Amazon, and then back again to Liverpool. Eventually, I suppose, he would have to his credit nearly two thousand miles of the tropical waterways of Brazil on porridge. As an old Indian Army man he reveled in the heat; the sun penetrated every pouch and fold of his face and neck, like acids curing leather, and yet every day he looked more "Old English."

"Old English" were the whole scene and atmosphere as we sat chatting over our breakfast. It might almost have been Sunday morning in a hotel at Bournemouth—or perhaps Henley-on-Thames, for at that moment two elegant skiffs propelled by oarsmen in regulation rowing kit passed the saloon windows; and a little later a clinker-built eight paddled past. I rubbed my eyes in astonishment. At the next cup of coffee I rubbed them again: a breeze had sprung up and a sailing dinghy leaped and trembled past the windows; sunlight danced on the ripples; voices called across the water—now it might have been the roadsteads at Cowes. I took more toast and marmalade. I felt as if I had strayed into the wrong time-space spiral.

The Englishness of the scene was dispelled by the stevedores. They had stopped work and came crowding round the windows of the dining saloon to watch us eat. They were stripped to the waist. Their skins were an odd purplish-red, the result of the mixture of Negro and Indian blood. All of them had protuberant stomachs, and as the table at which we sat was against the window looking onto the afterdeck our eyes encountered, every time we raised them from our plates, a row of abnormally large navels, like portholes, or the shields along the side of a Viking ship. It could hardly have been Henley or Cowes. I swallowed my last cup of coffee, hurried up on deck and down the gangplank and at last set foot on the soil of Brazil—only *one* foot, as it seemed to me, for I was in an anomalous situation, half of me conscious that my Brazilian travels had begun, the other half still bound to the ship.

It was not as hot as I had expected of a city so close to the equator (latitude 1°28′ South, to be exact). The temperature in Belém seldom rises above 95 degrees Fahrenheit, and although it is seventy-odd miles from the river mouth it receives a surprising number of sea breezes. On the other hand, the air is never cooler than 74 degrees, and the humidity is extremely high. "The only difference here between summer and winter," one of the dockers told me, "is that in winter it rains all the time, while in summer it only rains every day."

No wonder there were so many umbrellas! What on earth, I wondered, could have led H. W. Bates to describe the climate as "one of the most enjoyable on the face of the earth"? The heat that met me the moment I stepped off the gangplank was like an oven door opening or an animal breathing in my face. I was suddenly conscious of the act of breathing, a physical effort that hurt my lungs: like a newborn babe I wanted to cry aloud.

The quayside sweated with a kind of sadness. The warehouses too seemed sad, as if the goods with which they were stacked—nuts, dyewoods, spices, fruits, skins, and a dozen other products registering themselves pungently upon the nostrils, bringing to life the geography textbook phrase "raw materials"—had suffered a degradation in being torn from their forests. The gaps between the stone blocks were filled with yellow water, steaming in the heat; a stretch of rusty, abandoned rails was overgrown with tropical weeds. It was as if the jungle had sent in its guerrillas and the harbor was reacting to its treachery in a mood more of sorrow than of anger.

I knew that Belém was no raw city recently torn from the jungle, that it had its beginnings as long ago as 1616. I knew that in the late seventeenth and early eighteenth centuries it had grown into a city that rivaled Lisbon itself, so prosperous that Portugal considered making it the capital of her colonial empire. I knew that in the great rubber boom at the beginning of our own century it became one of the richest cities in the hemisphere, with vast palaces made of marble brought from Italy and stuffed with luxurious furnishings from France and linens imported from Lisbon and London and shipped back regularly for laundering. I knew, too, that it was still one of the most important cities in Brazil's economy. Nevertheless, the impression of a jungle underground waiting to take over, or at any rate of a weary stalemate between frond and stem and spore on the one hand, and stone and brick and mortar on the other, was inescapable. It lay in the moist, fetid heat—soil, one felt, was not an essential condition for growth; foliage might spring out of the very air one breathed.

A jungle confusion seemed to attend everything about the city, including the buses. The one I boarded was patched with galvanized iron, and the whole side of another consisted of asbestos sheeting. My astonished carcass quickly told me why. The uneven granite blocks (brought from Portugal as ballast in colonial times) were hostile to flesh and machinery alike, and spinal discs soon rattled as loose as nuts and bolts. Where halfhearted attempts had been made to remove the tramlines, the holes had been left unfilled. My bus would crash into one like a runaway lift and then somehow climb out on the other side, crashing over the blocks left lying in its path. This explained another phenomenon: the position of the exhausts, which were carried out of harm's way up the backs of the buses to protrude from the top left-hand corner, like the chimneys of old-fashioned caravans.

The heat and humidity, the motion and noise, accentuated by a radio which the driver turned on full blast, somehow made it difficult to use one's eyes. If I turned them to one side, the next lurch jerked them back, as if they grew on stalks, to focus on the seat in front of me, with its torn leather and sagging canvas. In consequence I retain only a blurred impression of that first drive through Belém. I know that the skyscrapers I had glimpsed from the ship's deck by twilight had conveyed a false impression of modernity. Like jungle palms rising above surrounding scrub, they looked down upon a fantastic jumble of structures—moldering palaces of the colonial period, faced with Portuguese tiles of blue and yellow; decaying monstrosities, fluted and curlicued, of the rubber boom; bijou villas of pink and white, some of them with jazzy, modernistic projections; and wood or mud and plaster huts—all of them jammed side by side like bits of unsorted luggage. The city stretched and sprawled in all directions as if the buildings had fallen from a giant furniture van. How necessary, I thought, a *center* is to a city, for psychological rather than topographical reasons; I found myself longing for one, in order to free myself from a melancholy sense of flux and disintegration.

It was not until the bus had jerked to a stop—settling down in stages, as if the various parts were, like the limbs of a puppet, linked by strings—that the scene came into focus. We were outside a park and the pavements in front of it, crumbling and uneven, tessellated in black and white, were swarming with people, as some nearby mud flat might be swarming with the denizens of the jungle. The prevailing color of skin was that of the warm, muddy rivers. With the men the effect was one of drabness. Linen trousers, crumpled in the heat, and short-sleeved shirts, the tails hanging outside the trousers, hardly made for elegance, in spite of the silver-handled umbrellas. The moist heat makes the beard grow quickly, and daily shaving is not a common habit. How little grace there was, too, I reflected, in a sallow male forearm sprinkled with black hair, and how different were the bare arms of the women and children, smooth and rounded as jungle stems. In this part of the country there are hardly any pure Indians left, but there is a strong admixture of Indian blood, particularly evident in the women and children—in the angles of eyes and cheekbones, in the black straight hair and the way it grows round ears and temples, and in a kind of silent, secretive walk. It is apparent, above all, in the dark eyes. Looking into them, I had the feeling of making contact with a race, practically obliterated and utterly alien to us; it was as if, every now and then, a ghost appeared above a window sill.

Both women and children looked astonishingly cool; their clothes—simple but gay print dresses for the women, not-so-simple dresses for the little girls, often of muslin, cream or peach-colored, with flounced skirts and frilly petticoats, the small boys in white socks and shirts and very short shorts—were beautifully cleaned and pressed. The women and girls boasted hair styles that made those of London look dowdy. I don't usually take so much notice of clothes, but this time I could not help it: I was responding to something jaunty and defiant in the human spirit, a kind of flag-waving in the midst of tropical heat and chaos.

And these patches of color fragmented through the railings of the park and through the leaves and branches of tropical trees and slim colonnades of bamboo afforded a welcome contrast to the dabs of hot color from the food stalls massed on the pavements—orange-tinted fish cakes, pungent meat balls floating in yellow fat, dishes of a banana-colored, glutinous substance made from *mandioca* (or manioc), tanks of orangeade and *maracujá* juice, stacks of Coca-Cola bottles and popcorn in glass tanks, agitated by jets of air, like multicolored performing fleas.

It was only when I had passed through the gates that I realized that the park was a zoo. With naïve ideas of rivers and jungles ahead of me packed with wild creatures, I was at first inclined to regard this as a case of carrying coals to Newcastle. But it was impossible to remain indifferent. Fantastic shapes and colors moved behind the bars to create a slipstream of curves and stripes that belonged to an entirely new world of motion. I stared unbelievingly at pink pelicans; at tall egrets with long yellow beaks and creamy drooping plumage like silk shawls; at bamboo storks with huge top-heavy beaks, like medieval demons; at king vultures with brilliant black and ginger heads, eyes ringed in red, white and black, like a dart board, their wattles like great yellow orchids; at Amazonian parrots and cockatoos on fire with color; at tortoises and turtles, some minute like flakes of bark or toffee, others as big and flat as paving stones or chunks of slate or shale; at anteaters and tapirs that seemed to have lumbered out of nightmares; at giant rats and wild pigs; at jaguars and ocelots, vibrating with such ferocity that they seemed as if they might at any moment quiver into another dimension; at snakes whose stripes and coils assumed patterns at defiance with terrestrial geometry; and at the crocodiles—the *jacarés*—slithering unmentionably in their tanks. I felt as if a new pair of eyelids had been prized open. I was filled with a mixture of awe and elation, as if I were rejoicing in a miraculous demonstration of Nature's resourcefulness.

Then in another bus along more atrocious roads, to the outskirts of Belém, past some fine modern villas and past mansions of the rubber boom period moldering behind rusty railings and ragged palm trees, and shaded by untidy banana trees with pale-green leaves, some of them twelve feet long, drooping like green canvas over decaying verandas and balconies. We passed the airport and then off the main road and down to Icoaraci and a riverside café overlooking a beach of wonderfully clean honey sand, its edges, where the placid river waves spilled, cream-and-coffee. There I had my first *guaraná*—a pleasant drink made from an Amazonian berry and as common in Brazil as cider in England—and sat gazing across the water at the islands of Cotijuba and Tapuoca (like Icoaraci,

Indian names). They were clothed in tropical vegetation, but so low-lying that they made only the tiniest indentation against the background of water and the silver-gray skyline. Yet suddenly I realized that my eyes had registered something unique in their outlines, something entirely different from that created by any other type of foliage. I could not have described these undulations—they were so faint that it would have been impossible for brush or pencil to capture them—but my eyes knew; they knew that if I were transported in sleep to and fro across the world and awoke with a skyline of treetops in front of me, no matter how distant or blurred, I would know at once whether it belonged to the old world I had left behind or to this new one of the Brazilian tropics. I was a ship's passenger spending a day ashore, but already I had absorbed something of Brazil, and there was something stirring in this realization that the eyes were capable of independent discoveries.

We had with us a guide provided by the shipping company, a big, heavy man in a chocolate-brown alpaca suit that blended elegantly with his coffee-colored skin, with an almost spherical head with close-cropped grizzled hair, a small graying mustache and bloodshot yellowish eyes. He was a good guide in spite of the fact that he seemed tired and depressed, sitting down at every opportunity with his arms dangling at his sides. "It's the heat," he explained. "You newcomers don't notice it. It takes a couple of years for the effects to tell. If you live here year in year out, it wears you away. At my age it's difficult to keep interested—in anything." I had discovered that his name was Danim, which was also that of "the old Portuguese gentleman" who was Bates's host in the village of Nazaré (Nazareth) about two miles outside Belém. Perhaps he was a descendant, I suggested. He shrugged his shoulders: he had never heard of Bates. But our conversation had established friendly relations and I asked him to help me visit one of the roadside shacks. It would not be easy, he told me; these people resented the curiosity of strangers.

On the way back to Belém we chose a hut at random and, getting out of the bus, picked our way toward it through the mud and potholes. As it emerged from its background it lost every vestige of the picturesque. From a distance mud walls can appear neat and compact, and that is why photographs convey an inadequate impression. Close up they looked as if they had been made by children dabbling in ordure; the damp, acrid smell and the flies and wasps that buzzed round them reinforced the impression. They were pitted with tiny holes, some produced by air bubbles during the mixing of the mud, others by insects—among them the one that causes Chagas' disease, one of the scourges that harry the submerged eighty per cent of the population of Brazil. Bits of straw, used as a binding agent, protruded from the walls like chaff from dried horse dung. If I scraped the walls with my fingernail or preferably a penknife (I shuddered at the thought of direct contact), the mud would crumble away as easily as sand running down an hourglass. Palm leaves, dried to the same color as the walls, formed a damp, shaggy thatch. The over-all effect was of a terrible, hopeless drabness. My heart sank at the thought of human beings forced to live behind such walls. I felt ashamed of the shipboard comfort I would be going back to, of my full belly and of my intrusion.

Perhaps it was because my feelings showed in my face that I gained admittance, for when Senhor Danim explained what I wanted, the man, who had appeared in the doorway, at first looked angrily in my direction. He was of medium height, about forty years old, with curly black hair, a dark face with deep clefts down his cheeks, and large black eyes with an expression part deprecating, part melancholy, and part ferocious, such as I had sometimes seen in Spanish peasants or fishermen. He stared at me for a moment, then shrugged his shoulders and stood aside for us to enter. When I got inside the hut I dared not look around me. I kept my eyes lowered, as if to let them roam would be an insult. Yet somehow they took in everything. The floor was of beaten mud, damp and uneven. The windows were without glass or curtains; the walls were even rougher on the inside, bristling with straw ends and letting in chinks of daylight; light too came in through breaks in the palm thatch. In the small room in which we stood there was not a single article of furniture apart from a moldering piece of plastic sheeting covering a few square feet of the floor, on which squatted two half-naked children. Two others—a boy of about eight and a girl of about nine—clung to the skirts of a pregnant woman. They stared at us with their mouths open. When I gave the children a handful of sweets, they held them gingerly without looking at them. Their father gave me a sardonic smile and said, "I know what they are, *senhor;* they don't. I will show them later." It was as much as I could do not to turn tail and run. But somehow I forced myself to explore the rest of the hut. It consisted of a narrow passageway and, opening off it, two smaller rooms, separated from each other by rough plank partitions about breast high, as in a barn or stable. The furnishings of the first comprised four greasy hammocks; the second contained four bricks, with charcoal burning between them and supporting an old tin in which black beans were cooking, two tin mugs, two half coconuts and one knife. This completed the tally of the family's possessions—apart from a few stringy hens and a small black pig, suffering from mange, which wandered in and out of the hut.

I asked the man what they lived on. He indicated the patch of ground at the back of the hut—about ten yards square—in which he grew a few vegetables and a couple of banana trees. No, he had no other work, he said; he was a newcomer to the district, and jobs were difficult to get. Where had he come from? "From Ceará!" he replied, with an unexpected flash of pride. Why had he left? The woman spoke for the first and only time, the single word *"Sêca!"* I remembered that Ceará was one of the northern states of Brazil, subject to terrible droughts which drive refugees all over Brazil in search of work and food.

Before we left I took out a handful of notes and offered them to my host. He stared at them in astonishment, looked round him, shrugged his shoulders, and explained that he had nothing to give me in return. I had to thrust the money into his hand and close his fingers over it. He escorted us out of the hut and on to the muddy pathway outside with as much punctilio as if he had been a lord of the manor. Feeling I wanted a memento of this meeting, I unslung my camera and stepped back a few paces. He pulled himself upright, and with his left hand tried to draw the rags of his shirt across his chest. Ashamed, I lowered my camera and, running back to him, held out my hand. He looked down at the money he was still holding, grimaced, thrust it in his pocket, and then pressed my hand in both of his.

Back to Belém with a stream of lorries, jeeps, and cars loaded with holiday makers returning from the riverside beaches, past a funeral procession led by a priest, spectral-white beside the half-Indian, half-Negro mourners. The candles burned with remarkably upright flames, like the stamens of lilies, then spluttered and went out in a downfall of rain. The rain arrived as regular as clockwork at this hour, summer and winter, Senhor Danim explained, and the side roads were soon transformed into yellow quagmires. But Senhor Danim had apparently decided to take my initiation a stage further; and, slithering down first one then another of these side roads, we found ourselves among a maze of huts. Along the backwaters of the river and its smaller tributaries were other huts, built on stilts and showing signs of periodic flooding; the last high tides had left noisome mud flats, over which hovered swarms of mosquitoes, like attenuated ballet dancers. I had been inclined to doubt Senhor Danim's estimate of the population of Belém as nearly half a million. Now I saw how it might be possible. I have never seen so many human beings squashed into so small a space. The sight gave me a sense of unreasoning fear, such as one experiences in turning over a rotten log and finding it alive with wood lice. People crowded in the alleyways and on the wooden steps of every shack. Every open window disclosed rooms packed to overflowing, and across nearly every window sill sprawled naked children.

They lived in conditions which would have been appalling for animals, and yet it was the very wretchedness that threw their humanity into relief. I stared at the creatures in front of me and said to myself, Can these be men and women? And then they smiled or moved a limb, and I felt a pang of tenderness—as if in some wilderness of the cosmos I had suddenly come upon a band of fellow creatures, and indifferent to all other considerations felt only the blood pull of the species. And I asked myself if Nature's proudest handiwork was designed for this—Was it for this the clay grew tall?

These huts, however, were mostly inhabited by people who had some work. Most of them had a religious picture or image on the wall, or a calendar or a strip of colored material. Most of them had a table and a few chairs or at the worst some empty packing cases. Some had radios, and quite a number had sewing machines. A woman in one of the huts pointed to a roll of cotton print in the corner and explained that she and her daughters made most of the clothes for the family. "Soon," she said proudly, "the machine will be ours." I asked her how long she had been paying. "Only three years," she replied. But her next-door neighbor had been forced to return hers yesterday. She raised her hands in a tragic gesture, as if the sewing machine was for her a piece of equipment as essential to her human status as the first hoeing stick or the first wheel to prehistoric man.

In the hut on the road to Icoaraci it was the man who had aroused my admiration; here it was the women. Many of the children I had seen at the zoo in their Sunday best came from homes such as these. Nearly all of the girls were good to look at, their smooth brown limbs setting off their spotlessly clean frocks and petticoats—most of the latter now hanging up on nails and protected by sheets of newspaper. How they managed to keep them so clean was beyond my comprehension, for there was no running water in the huts and outside there were only the muddy pools and channels. Their hair was the greatest miracle of all, and now I saw how it was achieved; in practically every hut I saw girls with their hair in curlers—but curlers made of plastics in pink and blue and green and yellow, so that the heads of their wearers looked as if they were surmounted by buds.

It was dark when I returned to the ship. A few hours later we had swung away from Belém harbor. I stood on the upper deck and watched the row of lights recede. I did not move until, leaving the harbor behind, we had anchored a mile or so offshore to await the morning tide. My preliminary contact with the mainland of Brazil was over; I was once more a British passenger on a British ship, absorbed again into its small, intimate world. But before I went down to my cabin I strained my eyes through the tropical darkness until I was able to distinguish behind the skyscraper with its blue star of Bethlehem the faint, uneven fringe of jungle vegetation, a fraction darker than the sky, and remembered that it had become meaningful to my eyes. I remembered, too, the refugee from Ceará, the naked children on the window sills, the girls defiant among their squalid shacks, and I knew that these had already worked their way into my imagination, that they constituted motifs that would recur again and again and that—for good or ill—they were inextricably woven into my picture of Brazil.

I had thought that my first contact with the Amazon, five hundred miles out at sea, had already adjusted my vision to its scale and scope. I had not yet come to realize that to be born and bred on a tiny island necessarily meant a limitation of horizons. I had to learn that as far as the seeing eye was concerned not only Britain but the whole of Europe was a miniature. In the days that followed my eyes were forced to take in vaster and vaster perspectives, until I began to feel that the circumference of the actual was not only approaching that of the imagination itself, but was about to out-distance it. Was this not bound to affect the operations of the inner eye itself? I asked myself. Would not the boundaries of the one, like an expanding universe, fly before those of the others?

I had studied the maps and read the books, but they were mean-ingless when I found myself face to face with the facts. Even with the aid of ruler and compasses I could not visualize them in advance. I knew, for example, that we were heading for the Narrows, which separate the southern point of Marajó Island from the mainland, but fixated still on my puny English scale I had envisaged this as the equivalent, say, of a trip from Portsmouth to the southern end of the Isle of Wight, or from New York to Oyster Bay on Long Island. I saw a shore line in front of me and thought it was Marajó. Then I realized it was merely one of the islands off Belém. Beyond was open water with no land in sight, and I thought that for some reason we were heading back for the open sea. An hour later I again saw land ahead and—by now thoroughly confused—imagined we were heading for the opposite shore of the estuary, forgetting that this was over two hundred miles across. It was, in fact, Marajó Island, and I had to make a fresh adjustment to the word "island." It had nothing in common with my homely conceptions. Marajó was as big as Wales, or Switzerland, or Belgium. I watched it from the upper deck in the company of a new acquaintance, an elderly little man with a bald head and a flat nose pitted with blue marks, like tiny enamel inlays, who had joined the ship at Belém. Like me he was bound for Manaus; after fifty-odd years in the export trade in various parts of Brazil, he was going there to spend his retirement. He had been born in the state of Amazonas, of an English father and a Brazilian mother. It had not occurred to me that anyone would live in so remote a spot from choice—in our arrogance we assume that we are the only ones who know what the word "home" means. He pointed out to me, beyond the fringes of high reeds, the herds of humpbacked cattle (mostly a cross between zebu and local strains). As we passed the frequent narrow waterways, or *igarapés*, busy with canoes, he told me of the teams of oxen which, farther inland, plod along the beds of these channels, up to their ears in water, drawing the larger boats after them. Together we watched the stretches of jungle coming down to the water's edge, the clusters of huts, the occasional settlements and logging stations with their white churches and red-tiled roofs.

No one, though, not even my new acquaintance, seemed to know exactly where the Narrows began. According to my map it was as soon as we had rounded the southeastern tip of Marajó, but in fact for a considerable distance beyond this point the passage widened out, and for me the experience of the Narrows really belonged to the network of channels between the sizable town of Breves to the southwest of Marajó and the headland of Antônio Lemos on the southern mainland, where we swung sharply west again and into the mainstream of the Amazon.

Each of these channels was dotted with islands in so intricate a pattern that, as the ship twisted and turned, I lost all sense of direction. One moment we would be charging straight at what appeared to be a continuous line of land, the next it would reveal itself as a necklace of islands and we would be passing through one of the gaps. Some of the islands were low-lying, covered with curly vegetation, so that from a distance they looked like green poodles. On others, tall jungle trees came right down to the water's edge, creating the effect of man-made palisades, and sometimes stragglers, their trunks half submerged, waded out into the water. In other cases the palisades were fronted by tangled scrub, like rolls of barbed wire. But when I looked closer I saw that layers of vegetation, of varying heights, were ranged one behind the other: through my binoculars they stood up flat and sharp-edged as if I was looking at a peep show or a stage set. There was little of the riot of color I had expected. I picked out a few yellow mimosa-type blossoms, but for the most part I was aware only of a single color, though one that was represented in every imaginable shade and intensity: it was green that flowed and rippled and cascaded around me, so that I felt as if we were sailing through an element, a new entity almost, of greenness. Now at last I felt that I was caught up in this new element, that my eyes were forced open upon a world as new as if it had just been created.

Other islands towered above us, tall and circular like hilltop forts; others had minute beaches of smooth fawn-colored sand, which turned to coffee as our wake touched them. Some were large islands, as big, say, as Manhattan (and Gurupá, beyond the

Narrows, is more than fifty times that size), others as big, perhaps, as Lundy or the Isle of Wight, others no bigger than armchairs, yet every bit as lush and green. What was more, many of these were floating islands, some mere mats of marsh vegetation, others composed of dense tangles of bush, others with several inches of soil; these last might eventually anchor themselves to the river bed if the roots of their infant trees struck deep enough, but might just as probably be obliterated at the next tide. Any one of the tufts and scraps of vivid green—undulating in the wake of the ship and looking like those pieces of artificial grass one sees on fishmongers' slabs—might be an embryo island. I was filled with a sensation of simultaneous growth and dissolution; I felt as if I were in one of Nature's more frantic workshops or forcing houses. Or was this what the world was like when it was in process of creation?

Sky, water and weather were in an equally amorphous state. As we approached the Narrows it was an English sky above us—gray, piled-up clouds with patches of blue. Later the sky turned black and rain fell steadily; later still we sailed into a Manchester drizzle driven into our faces by a surprisingly chill wind, and the ship had to slow down almost to a standstill. In between these spells the sun glared down mercilessly, and even when it retired behind clouds one was conscious of a withdrawn, incubating heat. The water changed—now yellow, now olive green, now chocolate brown—according to the movements of the sky above and the mud and silt beneath, and our pilots told me that they knew all the gradations of color, steering by these as much as by their charts.

I had expected to see all kinds of wild life. For a long time I scanned every mud flat we passed, until my Anglo-Brazilian friend, who spent most of his time pacing the upper deck, his gnomelike head cocked to one side as if, for him at any rate, the warm, sticky air was worth sniffing, stopped at my side, gave a bark of laughter and said, "It's a good job you saw them in the zoo—you won't see the *jacarés* here!"

"There aren't any crocodiles?" I asked, surprised and disappointed.

"They have more sense. When I was a boy parts of the Narrows teemed with them. But there's too much shipping now; they got out of it years ago."

"Where have they gone?"

"As far along the *igarapés* as they can get. You might search for months nowadays and not see a single one. It's much the same with the other animals."

It was hardly what the travel pamphlets, lavish with pictures of crocodiles, monkeys, cockatoos and anacondas, had led us to believe, I told him. He gave another bark of laughter.

"I met one of the shipping agents who wanted to put plastic crocodiles on the mud flats!"

He was quite right: there were no crocodiles here and all I saw of other animals was the flat snout of a manatee as it nibbled a piece of floating vegetation, though one of the pilots assured me that many of the floating islands carried capybaras, pacas, peccaries and snakes, and that monkeys lived in the dense forest of the larger islands. Neither did I see many birds; there was an occasional bright flash of tail or wing tip at the water's edge, and when we passed close to an island—and sometimes we were so close that I could watch our wake breaking on the shore behind me—there would be a scurry among the undergrowth. At dusk, too, the old man stopped his pacing, looked at his watch, seized my arm and pointed. A flock of birds rose from the trees on one of the islands, flew across the narrow channel and disappeared among the treetops of the island opposite. "Parakeets," he told me. "They cross here at exactly the same time, year in, year out. They've been doing it ever since I can remember." But if he had not told me I would not have known. They had flown too high for me to distinguish either shape or plumage. The sea birds, terns and sea gulls among them, which accompanied us through the Narrows—and far beyond—were far more in evidence, as far as we ship's passengers were concerned, than the birds of the Amazon.

Insects were a different matter, though it was their size rather than their numbers that startled—a huge black dragonfly, for example, that whizzed under my nose like a miniature jet, an outsize moth with wasplike stripes on its body and orange underwings which I found in my cabin, and a black-and-white butterfly so big that at first I thought it was a swallow. On several occasions I felt a stab on wrist or ankle and found a small gush of blood where the motuca fly (which looks like a bluebottle) had bitten me, but I found that travelers' accounts of its effects had been exaggerated.

It was human beings who seemed the real denizens of the jungle. There were occasional collecting stations for the products of the jungle—nuts, seeds, sisal, piassava fiber, skins and rubber among them—and these contained one or two solid-looking buildings. But more characteristic were the huts, single or in small clusters, standing at the water's edge, most of them perched on stilts, as a precaution against the fantastic rise of the river. Some of these huts belonged to fishermen who catch ocean-going fish (sharks, tarpons, sawfish and swordfish can be found two thousand miles along the Amazon), as well as fresh-water natives such as the *pirarucu*, which can measure eighteen feet in length and weigh three hundred pounds, and a giant catfish, some nine feet long, called the *paraíba*. On one island I saw fishermen laying traps for the huge electric eels, which, my Anglo-Brazilian friend told me, are shipped to Columbia University for radiation-research purposes. A week before, one of the barrels had become electrified and hurled four men to the ground.

Small clearings stood at the backs of the huts, but as most of these were constructed of interlacing palm leaves they seemed outgrowths of the jungle, so that often we would round a bend to hear excited voices calling out to us before we could distinguish either huts or people. Then on the small landing stage we would catch the flash of women's print dresses and a moment later we would see the dark-skinned naked babies in their arms and the swarms of children, the color of the river and of the dried palm thatch.

The children would come out to meet us in canoes, darting out from every creek and every landing stage. The canoes were high and narrow, the paddles had wide clumsy-looking blades, like ping-pong bats or the lids of water butts. They were wielded with incredible dexterity by mere infants, the boys usually naked, the girls in print frocks tucked up above the knees. They swept along the side of the ship, shouting and waving. Some of the passengers threw them fruit or chocolate, which they scooped up as neatly as storks transfixing fish. But the old Anglo-Brazilian explained that it was empty beer cans they prized more than anything else—to be used as utensils or converted into oil lamps. We raided the bars and the galley and soon dozens of empty cans littered our wake, the canoes bobbing perilously beside them. They sought the wake of the ship in any case. I watched one naked tot, no more than three years old, alone in a rickety canoe, nonchalantly riding the highest waves. For these children the canoe was an extension of their bodies, like an extra limb, and many of them are adept in its management before they can walk.

Some of the nineteenth-century travelers—Bates, Wallace and Edwards among them—have written of the "equable" nature of the Amazonian climate. Personally, I found that after a few weeks of the moist, sticky heat I began to experience the kind of lassitude Senhor Danim had commented upon in Belém. It was the uniformity of the temperature that was the real strain: merely to contemplate a whole year in the same key filled me with despair. How could one live, I wondered, without the lowering and raising of tension that the changing of the seasons brings? What kind of life would it be in which there was no winter with its partial hibernation of body and spirit, no summer fullness or autumnal unwinding, and, above all, no spring awakening?

The canoes were still rising and falling around us as sunset fell—a sunset that began with gray, smoky clouds streaked with lemon and blue and then plunged into umber and orange, turning the ripples behind us to silver and bronze and the still backwaters to gold. It was only when the tropical night descended, leaving swathes of oily blackness behind us and turning the outlines of vegetation sharp and black, in spite of their exuberance, like cardboard cutouts or hedges trimmed by topiarists, that the canoes disappeared, and then voices, in answer to our siren, called to us across the water and a myriad tiny lights (as the wicks in the beer cans were lighted) sprang up all around us.

When we reached the main Amazon, three days out from Belém, there was the same pattern of islands and embryo islands; but they were spread out now and on a different scale. The only thing I had ever seen remotely like it was the Fen country in England when the dykes had burst, but for the comparison to make sense I had to multiply it a thousandfold. Often I found it impossible to tell which were the banks of the river and which were chains and clusters of islands. We would approach what at first sight I took to be layers and terraces of jungle, only to find as we got closer that it was ranks of islands lying one behind the other. Or again I would see ahead of me what looked like the wide embracing arms of a harbor with still water between, and find that it was a pair of crescent-shaped islands with a narrow opening between the farther tips.

In other places the floating scraps of green stretched as far as the eye could reach, looking like a gigantic version of one of those "skeleton pictures" in children's books in which you have to join the letters or numerals until the design is completed. Here, too, the floating islands were often of considerable proportions. Between Prainha and Monte Alegre, for example, one of our pilots, a cheerful, stocky man with black hair and mustache as curly as the jungle vegetation, pointed out Faraday Island (about as big as Lundy) and showed me the dotted lines on his charts that marked its varying positions: it had moved over a mile in the last twelve months.

Canoes still came out to meet us as we threaded our way through the strings of islands, and when we were in open water we could see them plying to and fro on the still water parallel to the banks, like cyclists on the bridle path of a motorway. Larger canoes shaped like sampans were floating homes with fires blazing in braziers or on heaps of bricks. Motor launches packed with half a dozen families chugged past. There were covered canoes loaded with rolls of cloth and bristling with household utensils, like river versions of the old mobile shops at home. Once, too, at dusk, as I stood on the upper deck watching the darkening waters (the river at this point was nearly five miles across), I saw a canoe glide past, almost scraping the sides of the ship, propelled by an old, old man with a white stubble on his chin, wearing steel-rimmed spectacles, tattered singlet and trousers and a squashed peaked cap, with all his worldly possessions piled up behind him. He paddled silently, his bare feet stretched out in front of him. He glanced up as he passed and gave me a toothless grin.

But the river had also become a great inland waterway. Now we passed other ships, including *gaiolas*—the spaces beneath the hammocks crammed with luggage, hens, pigs and goats. There were oil tankers, and big square-prowed timber carriers, and once, amid a blare of sirens, a dilapidated tramp steamer of five thousand tons passed us on its way to Rio de Janeiro.

The dimensions again overawed. There was the astonishing depth of the river along which we—a ship of nearly nine thousand tons—were charging, in spite of the frequent twists and turns, at full speed, and the knowledge that though Manaus, for which we were bound, was itself nearly a thousand miles from the sea, other ocean-going vessels of up to four thousand tons could go yet another thousand miles beyond it, to Iquitos on the borders of Peru, where the river is still one hundred and twenty feet deep. There was the sense almost of shock with which, as the river broadened out to the dimensions of a small sea, one realized that vast tributaries were pouring into it: the Tocantins (along which Bates had made an expedition); the Xingu, the upper reaches of which (where some of the few surviving Indian tribes live unmolested) are still marked "unexplored" on the map; the Tapajós, which turns the Amazon blue for several miles, and the Madeira, three thousand miles long and with ninety tributaries of its own. "Madeira" is the Portuguese word for wood, and the river received its name from the tree trunks which it rolls along its course and out into the Amazon. Almost opposite the point at which it joined us, a log caught in our propellers with such a thud that I thought we had run aground.

And all of these rivers were navigable for ocean-going vessels, which had at least thirty thousand miles of waterway open to them. Lighter vessels had far more, and it was possible, the old Anglo-Brazilian told me, to sail the equivalent of twice round the world without once leaving the Amazonian system.

The landscapes (as distinct from the riverscapes of water and islands) became more varied and spacious. Sometimes vivid-green marshes stretched as far as the eye could reach, and (one of the pilots told me) in seasons of heavy rain, when the river sometimes broadened to a width of three hundred miles, would stretch over an area the size of Texas. At other times we would sail for hours together beside Constable-like green meadows scattered with farmsteads, herds of horses or of black-and-white cattle, and clumps of tall trees that looked like elms. Then again we would pass apparently interminable stretches of jungle trees: Brazilian chestnut, rubber, *babaçu*, loaded with nuts, *carnaúba*, rich in wax, gigantic *cieba*, the umbrella-shaped *capirona*, calabash, with pale-green gourds the shape and size of rugby footballs, jacaranda, banana, palms of all shapes and sizes, and the *embaúba*—remarkably like silver birch from a distance and so distinctive that the pilot used some of the clumps as navigational points. Near Parintins, settled by Japanese immigrants, we passed fields of rice and jute busy with workers in coolie hats, and above them rose hills covered with groves and densely cultivated valleys. Sometimes we saw ranges of smoky-blue hills in the distance, and sometimes the banks of the river rose in cliffs of pink and gray.

The skyscapes too were sometimes oddly Constable-like in appearance: blue skies with high cannon-puffs of white and gray, like the skies above Lord's cricket ground on a sunny afternoon. Then suddenly the clouds would swell to enormous size, coiling and twisting into the shapes of Egyptian mummies, and then again, as twilight approached, shrink just as suddenly and race away with the speed of shooting stars until they grouped above the horizon in clots and wisps of black and brown and purple, leaving a pale-blue, empty sky above. It would be blue still when the stars began to come out, so bright that they imprinted themselves upon the light like sparks struck from flint. Sometimes at night the moon was so big that I was half frightened that it was about to crash onto the deck, and so bright that it was impossible to look directly at it, while the forests turned an ashy white as if gripped by an English hoarfrost. And one afternoon without warning turned, for the space of half an hour, into night, while summer lightning leaped and blazed behind the fringe of jungle trees, like the flashes of distant gunfire or a huge *son et lumière* display.

Palm-thatch huts still clustered at the water's edge, but there were also numerous small settlements each with its church and a nucleus of red-roofed buildings, as well as farmsteads with straggling outbuildings, and sometimes a rough football field. There were also sizable towns. On the northern shores, for example, were Prainha, Monte Alegre and Óbidos, perched upon high red cliffs, which H. W. Bates described as "one of the pleasantest towns" on the Amazon, where the river for a while returns to a channel only six thousand feet across and where (nearly six hundred miles from the sea) the tides of the Atlantic are still strongly felt. On the southern bank was Santarém on a headland near the junction of the Tapajós and the Amazon, a city with docks, warehouses, an impressive waterfront, a city square with some solid stone buildings and a cathedral. Parintins was on the same side of the river as Santarém: on the other side, again perched high on cliffs, safe from the annual flood, was Itacoatiara (beautiful Indian name) with its sawmills and log booms.

The approach to Manaus, another hundred miles beyond Itacoatiara and our fifth day out from Belém, was grand and panoramic. Where the Rio Negro joins the Amazon there is an astonishing line of demarcation—on the one side the yellow of the Amazon, on the other the grayish black of the Negro. And so to Manaus itself, some ten miles along the Negro.

And now as we tied up at the floating harbor, constructed, like that at Liverpool from which we had set out, to accommodate the tremendous rise and fall of the tide, realities of quite a different kind intervened. I had forgotten with what comical rapidity the human mind can revert from the grandiose to the petty. One moment my spirit, or so I thought, was extended across the interminable spaces of water and forest or soaring through the jungles and canyons and mountains of cloud, the next it had tumbled among the minutiae of departure.

So far my contact with Brazil had been partial and protected: the ship had been my vantage point and my home, and that home a floating extension of the one I had left behind. Now I found myself, while the ship's bells sounded that beloved routine which had cocooned me for the past month and while passengers bustled past upon concerns in which I no longer had a part, in the middle of my cabin surrounded by clothes and half-packed cases. What, for one thing, was I to do with my winter clothes? My Amazonian friend advised me to keep some of them, warning me that when eventually I reached the south of Brazil the weather might produce some unpleasant surprises. But in this heat such eventualities seemed impossibly remote, and as most of my travels would be by air the problem of weight, which for some reason I had hitherto ignored, loomed before me. I saw all my money disappearing in excess charges. I saw myself stranded with three heavy suitcases in some godforsaken spot, my tropical clothes (which I had acquired with such pride) in rags, a sweaty stubble on my chin. I couldn't close the cases, I couldn't find the keys, I couldn't find my camera, and I couldn't find my passport and disembarkation papers, and then, when I was about to step onto the gangplank, customs officials made me open the cases and the contents spilled around my feet.

But at last the formalities were completed, my porter had gone off with my luggage, I had said goodbye to my fellow passengers, and I was walking down the gangplank. I stepped on to the moldering planks of the floating harbor. I was conscious of the ship at my back, with its Union Jack, its white-coated stewards and old Captain B. and his breakfast porridge, but with every step I took it seemed to recede a thousand miles and I did not dare turn round. It began to rain. I had no umbrella and my raincoat was in one of my cases; but I was past caring. Soon I was setting foot on Brazilian soil— both feet, for this time there was no British floating home to return to. In front of me was Manaus, with its moist cobbled streets, its swarming market place, its piles of fruit and fish rotting in the gutters, its fantastic opera house in the background. The rain stopped; the sun blazed. I crossed the road, dodging a jeep which squirted muddy water up my trouser leg. Suddenly I stopped and stared. On the top of every building were black shapes with outspread wings, like gargoyles on a Gothic cathedral. I stared at them for a good five minutes before I saw one of the shapes move and fold its wings. The other gargoyles followed suit. They were *urubus,* or Brazilian vultures; after rain it is their custom to hold out their wings to dry, like motionless black umbrellas. It was, at any rate, an exotic reception committee. I could hardly complain now that the scene was too English.

3

MANAUS
AND BEYOND

I crossed the road, stepped over a gutter running with muddy water and found myself in a bedraggled *praça*. Along the pavements, part uneven blocks of stone, part mud, was a string of stalls selling the sort of goods you find on English fairgrounds or in the cheap-Jack markets of small North Country towns —combs, hair nets, ball-point pens, plastic wallets and purses, imitation jewelry, key rings, and tins of talcum powder. The people round them were closer to the Indian than those I had seen in Belém, but their physical condition and their appearance were worse—both men and women mostly squat and stunted, with brownish-yellow, seamed faces, and dressed in drab, sweat-stained clothes. The walls of the two-story buildings opposite were scabbed with damp; torn election posters fluttered from them, and political slogans were painted on every available surface; the iron balconies were dilapidated and rusty; many of the windows were broken. To my right was a precipitous, narrow street crammed with small shops with high, narrow windows and with doorways from which protruded rolls of cloth and linoleum, hammocks, hardware, cheap clothes and clusters of sandals like bananas on their stalks. The atmosphere was that of a Turkish bath.

I left the pavement and climbed up a muddy bank into a

so-called garden. The spectacle of the sparse, uncut grass, each blade apparently dipped in yellow mud, the overgrown flower beds, the ragged palm trees, the chipped stone seats, and the hollows in lawns and paths crammed with all kinds of gourds, skins and shells and singing with insects, formed such a despairing contrast to all that I associated with the word "garden" that I could have wept. I found one of the less objectionable-looking stone seats, swept it free of twigs, leaves and bits of mortar and sat down. A lizard darted out of one of the cracks; half a dozen stray dogs crept close and lay down, looking at me half hopefully, half cautiously; their tongues lolled, their ribs rose and fell; the bitches licked their teats, black and hard like gutta-percha and distended by the heat. I felt as if I had come to the fag end of the world, and of my own spiritual resources. I was alone as I had never been alone before.

It was my eyes that once again came to my rescue, suddenly taking in what was apparently a tiny segment of green leaf, scurrying past my foot. I looked closer and saw scores of these animated green bits, like miniature markers on a golf course. Bates's description of the sauva ants had stuck in my memory since boyhood, but I had not expected to see them in the middle of a busy city. I got up and saw that there were, in fact, two columns of these large, reddish-brown insects with their shiny, protuberant heads— one column carrying the green segments (like sceneshifters in a theater), the other hurrying back in the opposite direction. They had worn a runnel through earth and grass, like the impression of a miniature cart wheel. It took me to the very edge of the *praça* where a tree leaned over one of the busiest stalls. One column of ants was mounting the trunk, disappearing among the branches; the workers of the other column were descending with the pieces of leaf they had bitten off held in their jaws. Fragments of leaf fell at the foot of the trunk, and other ants were waiting there to collect them. The tree was already half denuded. I accompanied the returning column. I had to walk the whole lengh of the *praça* before I came upon a series of large mounds. Ants were busy at work on top of them, mixing the bits of leaf with the granules of earth which they had brought up from the soil beneath, preparatory to covering the domes over the entrances. I didn't attempt to explore the galleries themselves. I knew from Bates that these were often of astonishing extent. He tells of sauva ants in the state of Rio de Janeiro which had excavated a tunnel under the bed of the river Paraíba at a place where it is as broad as the Thames at London Bridge. But it was not the natural history that I was interested in at the moment so much as the evidence of this other life going on, busy and preoccupied beside my own. In the same way, I told myself, the forces of renewal were stirring somewhere inside me, irrespective of either accident or will.

I left the *praça* and ventured my Portuguese on the first passer-by I saw. It was a half-Indian girl of about nineteen; like many of the women of Manaus her figure was spoiled by a squareness of the hips (creating a curious effect as if she were sitting down as she walked), but she was more comely than most, with black silky hair tied by a ribbon and with white teeth flashing against a dusky skin. I asked her the way to my hotel; she understood my Portuguese and offered to take me there. She chatted gaily as we walked along, every now and then prodding my arm with her forefinger, very carefully as if she were selecting the spot. Later on I was to learn that this charming gesture was a commonplace in Brazil; at the time I was extravagantly grateful for it. The hotel, surprisingly, was new, solid and eight stories high. I entered the reception hall, with its red-leather couches, potted palms and porters in smart beige uniforms. I presented my passport, signed the register, and was escorted to the lift and to my room. It was a large room, with air conditioning, electric fans, a parquet floor and good modern furniture. Beside the bed, hooks of galvanized iron, like meathooks, were let into the wall for those who had brought their hammocks with them. I had not yet learned that in this kind of heat the pressure of a mattress against the body was almost unbearable. The window looked out on to a steep, narrow street. Opposite was a half-finished block of flats. The lower floors were already occupied; the topmost one bristled with girders, in between which lay upturned wheelbarrows and bags of sand and cement that had split open. The money for finishing the block, the waiter who brought me a bottle of iced beer explained, had given out three months before, and there was no telling when work would start again.

On either side of the block of flats were older buildings, stuccoed in moldering pinks, greens and yellows, the upper parts inhabited, the lower parts mostly shops. As I watched, the latest shower of rain stopped. The umbrellas of the shirt-sleeved passers-by were closed. The vultures with heavy, clumsy movements once again placed themselves on top of the roofs and held out their black, rubbery wings, looking like obscene parodies of the imperial eagle.

The dining room of the hotel was on the eighth floor. The side facing the harbor was open and I chose a table near the iron balustrade. I ate my first cutlet of *pirarucu*, or Amazonian codfish, well cooked and tasty, and my first plate of *palmitos*—the hearts of a species of palm tree delicious with olive oil and vinegar. A strong wind sprang up, surprisingly chill. It fluttered the tablecloths and most of my fellow diners retreated, but I stayed where I was; I could see the lights of the ship and with a pang I remembered my vacant place at Captain B.'s table.

In fact, my farewell to the ship was followed by anticlimax. It was still there two days later, and reunited temporarily with my old shipmates, I became a tourist again. Together we visited the famous opera house, the Teatro do Amazonas. It stands on high ground, almost in the center of the city, looking down on the red roofs, the floating pontoons of the harbor with its clusters of shipping, the wide expanse of the Rio Negro and, beyond, the dense tropical forests. From accounts I had read in England I had expected to find it in a state of decay, but the structure was in good repair, and its most bizarre feature—the vast dome, covered with green, blue and gold tiles—had been freshly cleaned, so that it glittered like a mound of jewels.

The opera house of Manaus is a symbol of one of the most horrifying chapters in the history of nineteenth-century capitalist exploitation, a fitting subject for the author of *Nostromo* and *The*

Heart of Darkness. It is a folly, a thousand miles up the Amazon, built to commemorate a scramble for riches as wild as the gold rushes of the Yukon and the Klondike, and the amassing of huge fortunes founded upon the enslavement and torture of thousands of Indians and the debt-bondage of thousands of "poor-white" *seringueiros,* or rubber tappers, not much better off than the "expendable" Indians themselves.

When Bates visited Manaus—or Vila da Barra do Rio Negro, as it was then called; the new name, taken from the Manau Indians, was not used until 1856—it was a small township of about three thousand inhabitants built on the site of the old Portuguese outpost of São José (founded in 1669 by Francisco da Motta Falcão, one of the greatest pioneers of the Amazon country). But as the demand for rubber grew—and between 1842 and 1910 the Amazon was producing more than three quarters of all the rubber used in the world—the town expanded rapidly and became perhaps one of the wealthiest the world had ever known and one of the most expensive. All kinds of luxuries, including caviar and other foodstuffs, clothes, tapestries, furniture and grand pianos, all imported from Europe, literally cost their weight in gold. Diamonds were imported from Minas Gerais in central Brazil and Manaus became one of the world's chief diamond markets. The rubber barons built palaces with marble from Italy and furnishings from France even grander than those in Belém. Families traveled annually to Europe. The first electric trams to run in South America were those of Manaus— with ten miles of track—and it also had one of the first telegraph and telephone systems.

It was in this atmosphere of boom (to be followed with dramatic suddenness by bust) that in 1896 this remote city of about 55,000 people—it is now about 150,000—set out to build from materials mostly imported from Europe, and at a cost of two million pounds, one of the world's most lavish theaters with a seating capacity of nearly two thousand, paying out astronomical fees to induce famous performers—including Sarah Bernhardt, who once played Racine's *Phèdre* here—to make the long journey along the Amazon.

To my disappointment, however, none of the plaques commemorating the visits of these foreign performers bore the name of Pavlova, and the guides who showed us round had never heard of her. One more of the innumerable tall stories about Brazil had been exploded, I told myself. So, too, was the claim, which I had seen in several books and magazine articles, that the interior of the theater is now given over to bats and spiders. The stage and dressing rooms were in a shabby enough state: the theater is used for performances only about six times a year, and then mostly by schoolchildren's choirs or amateur dramatic societies. The most recent plaque referring to a performer from Europe was dated 1936, announcing that Bidú Sayão, the distinguished Brazilian operatic singer, *cantou neste teatro* ("sang in this theater"). But most of the interior was in good repair: electric lighting had been installed, making use of the fine original chandeliers and candelabra, and workmen were busy on maintenance work.

The theater contained, in addition to stalls and orchestra pit, four pillared balconies faced with gold, the lowest of them a parterre devoted to sumptuously appointed boxes, particularly that in the center, which was reserved for the governor and had the coat of arms of the state of Amazonas emblazoned on the front. The domed ceiling was sky-blue, populated by pink angels. The foyer (its terrace overlooking the city and the river) and the saloons were decorated with wall paintings depicting river and jungle scenes, trees wrought in bronze and copper, and pillars, doorways, window embrasures and imitation draperies of Italian marble, cream, pink and coral. Here, too, I saw my first examples of furniture made of Brazilian woods, especially jacaranda—elaborately carved chests, settles, and great chairs that needed two men to lift them.

I knew the ship was sailing on the night tide, but when next morning I looked out of my bedroom window I was not prepared for the shock as my eyes registered the gap in my field of vision: it was as if the ship had been blown out of the water. This time, though, I welcomed the desolation. Dumped down here, a thousand miles along the Amazon, the ties with home were stretched to breaking point, and with every turn of the ship's engines they became more attenuated.

And as the days went by, to my astonishment I began to experience an odd feeling of "belonging." In spite of the humid heat and the rain, the usual squalid agglomeration of shacks and the general air of decay, Manaus was a city that engaged the interest and even the affections. At first the shops had struck me as unutterably dreary; now as I added oil stoves and lamps, iceboxes and refrigerators, guns, jackknives, fishing tackle and bicycles to the tally they seemed a fascinating index to the life of the region; they were not shops in the usual sense, but trading posts such as one associated with the old frontier towns of the American West.

More solid shops were to be found on the main boulevards, the only parts of the city to be lighted at night, for the electricity supply here, as everywhere else in Brazil, was quite inadequate. Here were to be found the few restaurant-bars where the businessmen of Manaus consumed their *cafèzinhos,* the little cups of jet-black coffee which Brazilians treat with as much reverence as we do our cups of tea. And along these boulevards, too, came the schoolgirls to window-gaze on their way home from afternoon school. In their uniform skirts, of gray, fawn or royal blue, with snow-white blouses, short white socks and black patent-leather shoes they looked as bandbox neat and fresh as American drum majorettes. Every afternoon they came out at the same time like a cloud of butterflies over a swamp, and there was never a speck of dirt or dust on blouse or toecap and never a pleat out of place. It was the prettiest sight in Manaus, and it was also a mystery. I had not yet learned that flashes of perfection against the muddle and squalor were part of the pattern of Brazil.

They were also remarkably nubile and sophisticated schoolgirls. Make-up was expertly applied; hair styles, eyebrows and eye-slants would have done credit to the fashion magazines of Paris; the white blouses were well and endearingly filled. I have never seen so many Lolitas together in one place before. The old hands of the European colony watched my reactions and chuckled. Tales, tall, romantic and horrific, involving fathers, grandfathers and uncles and the various methods of obtaining satisfaction while maintaining a technical virginity were bandied about the places where they gathered.

One of these was a shabby little bar near the barracks, on the site of an old Manau Indian cemetery. It was a favorite haunt of the employees of the Harbour Company, still British-run, though the concession was nearing its end. We used to meet there to drink an excellent lager-type beer (most of the Brazilian brewers are of German descent) and to shout gossip at each other above the noise of brawls between the soldiers from the barracks and their prostitutes, which sometimes irrupted through the swinging doors like a scene from a Western.

Many of the Europeans were married to Brazilians. There was in particular the wife of one of the bank managers, a woman of outstanding charm and beauty, with black hair and brilliant black eyes, whose looks and carriage reminded me of the women of Castile, but also struck a chord closer at hand which I could not at first identify. I asked her where she came from, and she uttered the word "Ceará" with something of the same pride I had heard on the lips of my refugee near Belém.

It was in the company of the bank manager and his wife that I visited the club (a regular feature, I was to discover, of Brazilian life), situated on the outskirts of Manaus among jungle trees, where members sometimes went snake-shooting. Through it flowed an *igarapé*, which had been dammed to form a swimming pool, and for the first time I swam in the warm, yellow water of Amazonas. In the bar the merchants and businessmen of Manaus congregated in their bathing trunks to talk about the prices of jungle products. A tall hatchet-faced Swede complained that nowadays one had to go farther and farther into the jungle to find the best trees. An American in a floppy linen hat told me about a form of rubber used in the manufacture of chewing gum. A mountainous German with scars on his forehead and left cheek—inflicted, it was rumored, by fellow countrymen just before the war because of his anti-Nazi views—promised to show me how Brazil nuts were prepared for export.

And the wealthiest member of the community, an elderly Jew from Syria with the physique of an athlete, did handstands on one of the bar stools.

One afternoon I hired a car and set out to look for the Tumúra Falls, whose beauty had been praised by Bates. The road was surprisingly good, but the forests on either side appeared wild and impenetrable. My driver, a young man with an oval Indian face and oddly shaped teeth, like the pegs in a cribbage set, grinned sardonically. "The jungle! The jungle!" he kept saying, peering at my reflection in the mirror. When I winked, his face fell. He explained that many of the tourists he had driven along this road had gone back to their ship convinced that they had been in imminent danger from jaguars and anacondas. My Amazonian acquaintance on the ship, however, had taught me to be skeptical, and in fact when I looked closer I saw that beyond the first fringe of greenery there were a number of small clearings. We stopped opposite one of these, followed a path for a few yards and came upon a hut.

A tall woman, with high cheekbones, black wiry hair tied at the nape of her neck, and a skirt falling to her ankles was apparently waiting for us. As soon as we stopped she picked up a round object lying at the foot of a nearby tree. It was like a gourd in appearance (though with a barklike exterior) and about the size of a melon. She placed it on a bench outside the hut, picked up a machete, and took careful aim. The object split open and to my astonishment scores of Brazil nuts cascaded out. I had not known before that they grew, packed close together like the segments of an orange, in this tough outer shell. The woman took one of the separate nuts between her finger and thumb and again raised the razor-sharp machete. I shuddered, but with a few deft strokes she removed not only the shell but the husk as well, and proudly handed me a smooth, milky nut.

When we left the main road for the track that led to the Falls we found that it was inches deep in mud, rutted and furrowed by timber lorries and strewn with boulders and the roots of trees deposited by the last floods. For nearly two hours I was hurled from side to side. The strap to which I was hanging broke; when I tried to cling to the ashtray it came away in my hand and the cigarette ash turned to a gray paste as soon as it touched my sweat-soaked trousers. It was a saloon car, the windows would not open, and I felt as if I was being roasted alive. Then suddenly the driver turned the car at the bank to the right of the track, crashed over it and, by some miracle avoiding collision with the trees, bumped and lurched his way to a halt in a small clearing overlooking the stream, a tributary of the Negro, which at this point broadened out to about fifteen yards. I got out of the car and twenty yards farther along came upon a small fall, so even in its flow that it looked as if a bead curtain had been stretched across the river. The main falls, my driver explained, were still ten miles farther on, but there was no need to worry, the road would surely improve.

While he was filling a bucket of water for the radiator I walked back along the bank of the stream in the other direction. I had heard the sound of voices, and rounding a bend I came upon a small stand of gray pebbles and opposite it a calm stretch of water in which two women and several children were bathing. The children were naked. The water turned their bodies an ocher color. The little boys faced me unabashed; the girls, even the tiniest, crouched down and cupped their hands over their genitals. The women were wearing clinging stockinet bathing costumes which must have survived from the 1920s; they made their clay-colored bodies look like the cloth-draped figures in a sculptor's studio.

I turned my back and climbed up a slope toward a hut I had glimpsed through the trees. It was unoccupied, though in quite good repair. It was constructed entirely of palm leaves—the walls closely woven out of small young leaves still retaining a greenish tinge like new-mown hay, the roof of shaggy older fronds. When I went inside it was like entering one of the "dens" which, as a boy, I used to build out of bits of sacking and the branches of the elderberry tree that grew at the bottom of our garden. With one half of my mind I used to know that a sneeze or a cough would blow the walls away; the other half would feel completely cut off from the outside world and gloriously self-sufficient as if I were enclosed by walls of granite. The light filtered through these walls in the same way, and the air had the same smell, cool yet slightly musty as if it had been kept in a phial. No ordinary huffing and puffing would have blown these walls down, though; and I was just admiring how firmly and neatly the ends of the palm leaves were fastened and how tough and compact was the framework of slender poles—bound with piassava fiber, without the use of a single nail or screw—when I caught sight of a faded notice. I approached it and saw it was headed in thick type by the word BOUBA! Literally this means "a small ulcer," but I had also been told that it was used to denote a form of plague.

I didn't really stop to read the rest—probably it was merely some routine notice from the health authorities—but I jumped to the conclusion that it meant that the hut had been evacuated because of the visitation of the disease. The friendly shelter was transformed into a noisome hovel, and I turned and fled.

I was almost glad to be bouncing up and down in the car again. The road, however, did not improve, and three miles farther on the car came to a stop in soft yellow mud. We could not go forward and we could not go back, but, the driver assured me, a timber lorry with chains on the wheels would be coming back from the Falls shortly and would give us a tow. We settled down to wait. The driver spread his arms across the steering wheel, rested his brown cheek on them and began to snore; his hair was so black that every now and then, like the coat of a badger, it glinted white in the sun. I got out and sat on the running board. I was wearing sandals, and the mud oozed over the soles; when I shifted them the mud baked hard, tightening the skin. The sun blazed down. My forearms, which I had thought were by now impervious, turned a fiery red and I was glad to put my linen jacket on again.

On the road it was absolutely still, and in the stillness I became aware for the first time of the jungle, which began directly behind a high bank to the left. The noises my ears picked up were small ones—sighs, whisperings, rustlings, an occasional whistle, and from time to time an odd bubbling cough. But I was aware not so much of these separate sounds as of the jungle itself as a pervasive presence. Heat—only it wasn't just heat but something that possessed all the senses indiscriminately—came beating from it like a green thundercloud in spite of the humidity and the masses of vegetation, bringing back a vivid memory of the first time when, searching for a lost ball, I had plunged my hand into a compost heap and found to my astonishment that the center of the wet, steamy mass was as hot as an oven. I remembered that I was far from human habitation and, according to my friends in Manaus, here undoubtedly wild animals and snakes still abounded. But it was no panther that came screaming out of the jungle, merely a cloud of tiny insects. I felt a score of bites, and then a second later each bite flared up as if it had contained a minute charge of gunpowder. I retreated to the car.

The leather of the seat was agonizingly hot. The driver was still asleep. When two hours later I woke him up, he opened his eyes slowly and his Indian ancestors looked out at me, mournfully and suspiciously. It was several minutes before he took in the situation, shrugged his shoulders and announced that the timber lorry must have passed before we arrived. I pointed to the jungle; he nodded and we got out of the car. We climbed the bank and began tearing at the brushwood and the branches of the nearest trees. We carried them to the lane and arranged them under the back wheels of the car. We had to bring half a dozen armfuls before the wheels would bite. As soon as they had passed over the brushwood and branches, I pulled them out from under the car and carried them behind the wheels again. A few feet at a time we reversed down the lane until at last we found a gap in the bank and a small clearing of reasonably dry ground, where we were able to reverse.

We arrived back in Manaus caked in mud from head to toe. We stopped at a restaurant-bar and drank a quart bottle of beer apiece; no one paid any attention to our appearance. But back in the hotel, the Austrian manager, in a silvery-gray alpaca suit, raised his elegant eyebrows. When I tried to raise mine in return I felt the cracking of dried mud.

When I stood under my shower the next morning I saw that my face, back and arms were covered with fiery red spots. I remembered the notice in the abandoned hut, rushed back to my bedroom and examined myself in the mirror. There was no doubt about it, I had *bouba*, whatever that was; I was going to die a grisly death—in Manaus of all places. I made up my mind to dash to the airport and, hiding my spots somehow, get a passage back to England so that I could die on my native soil (I had a "home" after all, I decided). Then I remembered the insects that had bitten me. I returned to my shower; the cold water started the spots itching again, but the following day they had disappeared.

The harbor area was one of my favorite haunts. I would cross the road from the *praça* (where the sauva ants still toiled as preoccupied as if they belonged to another dimension and we humans were mere irritating phantoms) and make my way along the narrow pavement leading to the dock gates. Often I would go by way of a narrow alleyway which led down to the water's edge. It was crammed with stalls, their projecting canvas roofs meeting overhead. The weird fish of the Amazon lay on marble slabs; there were stalls loaded with fruits, exotic in color and shape, though for the most part disappointingly insipid in flavor. There were nuts, sandals, cooking utensils, Indian baskets and mats, turtles, tortoises and comatose hens. There were stalls with trays of black beans and *farinha de mandioca*—the rough flour made from *mandioca*, frequently sprinkled over one's food, looking and tasting like sawdust. At one stall a half-Indian boy stood with a woolly monkey on his shoulder; behind him were ranged cages containing other monkeys and odd marmoset-like creatures, whose names I did not know, and in a large cage a *maracajá*, or wildcat, licking itself clean of the human taint, every now and then raising its head so that its eyes flashed in reddish-gold points. The next stall was gay with the blues and reds and yellows of parrots and cockatoos. Another stall, its sides festooned with dried herbs, was covered with brown-paper packets, canvas bags, tins and pillboxes containing remedies and balms for every imaginable disease (including *bouba,* no doubt), all manufactured from plants of the Amazon, many of them from age-old Indian recipes.

I would leave the market and approach the harbor gates, skirting piles of brownish-black lumps that looked and smelled like the offal of whales and which had baffled me until someone told me that they were "biscuits" of raw rubber. Inside the gates I would have to make my way through vultures as numerous and almost as sluggish as the pigeons in Trafalgar Square. On my first visit I bore down on one of them, as big as a Christmas turkey, that stood directly in my path; when I was almost on top of it, it flopped to one side, wriggled its rump and broke wind with a sickening stench. After that I gave the vultures right of way. I asked one of the harbor guards why no one shot them; in a shocked voice he explained that they were much too valuable as scavengers.

When I had negotiated the vultures I would make for the Alfândega, or Customs House, a ponderous, castellated building of orange stone that reminded me of the old St. Pancras Station. Whenever I entered the hallway and looked at the plaque commemorating its opening in 1908, I was struck by the thought that here was a monument not only to the grand period of Manaus but also to the really solid achievements of the Victorian era; for the Customs House was prefabricated in England, shipped from Liverpool across the Atlantic and along the Amazon to be assembled stone by stone and girder by girder under the supervision of British engineers. British engineers had also installed rolling stock, steam cranes, and the aerial haulage gear, operating, sixty years later, as efficiently as any of the modern machinery, and under the main quay I saw a network of girders bearing the date 1902, furry with rust but still holding out against the ravages of the climate.

On my first visit to the warehouses my nostrils caught a smell that brought back memories of the grocer's shop at Carcavelos in Portugal and when I entered I saw the *bacalhau*—dried codfish imported from Norway—hung from the rafters like pieces of starched canvas or the pelts of small brown animals. In other warehouses were drums of pressed paper from Finland; crates of dried milk from the United States—gifts to combat malnutrition, but, so rumor had it, passing at ever-increasing rates of profit through half a dozen middlemen until it reached the hotels and restaurants; sacks of flour and crates of beer from the south of Brazil and sacks of coffee beans from the state of Paraná dyed in various colors to confound the smugglers.

There was one large warehouse in which was encapsulated a segment of the frantic past, before the Englishman Wickham had smuggled out to Malaya the rubber plants that eventually brought the Brazilian rubber boom to a disastrous end. Columns of porters were bringing the "biscuits" of rubber from the lighters at the double, pushing their heavy trucks before them as the loose boards of the pontoons and the arched spaces of the warehouse shuddered and groaned, and swearing at anyone who looked like getting in their way. I had to weave and dodge until I reached the far end of the warehouse where, aloof from the turmoil, an official stood beside a scale with a ledger at his side. The porters tipped out their loads and raced back the way they had come. Other workers, wielding grappling hooks, yanked at the "biscuits" (roughly oval in shape, like gigantic black bobbins) as if they were handling sides of bacon. A man armed with a machete neatly sliced each "biscuit" down the middle, and I saw a groove, like the bore of a gun, passing through the center. This is caused by the pole upon which the *seringueiro* drips the liquid latex he has collected from the rubber trees, revolving it like a spit over a fire made from the nuts of the *uricuri* palm, the smoke from which contains creosote, an effective coagulating agent. Gradually the ball of rubber becomes larger, though it takes several days to reach the size and weight (about a hundred pounds) of those I saw in the warehouse. These "biscuits" are cut open before weighing to make sure that the *seringueiro* hasn't embedded a stone in the center to increase the weight; it is a stratagem that is still practiced, though nowadays the punishment isn't a flogging, usually fatal, with a whip made of tapir hide, as it was in the days of the rubber boom.

One day one of the harbor officials, a large, good-natured Englishman with a wilting R.A.F. mustache, took me on a tour of the
harbor. We climbed down the ladder of one of the pontoons. Un-
derneath, among the drums supporting it, were canoes in which
whole families, gaunt and half-naked, were living, and once again
I heard the ominous word "*sêca.*" We boarded the Harbour Company launch and threaded our way through the river traffic, past
the governor's boat, a two-tiered floating hotel, and past long, narrow canoes (some with outboard motors) that wobbled under
towering cargoes of green bananas. Soon we were in the midst of a
floating city. The narrow lanes of muddy water were dense with
moored craft, some like miniature houseboats, some on rafts made
of planks, but mostly built on logs chained together. Some were
roofed with red tiles and others with corrugated iron, but more common was a shaggy, untrimmed palm thatch. On roofs, landing
stages, window sills, and along the banks of the river itself, laundry
was spread out to dry. The landing stages were crammed with
chicken coops, pigs and goats. Children swarmed everywhere and
one naked tot squatted over the water at stool. A woman lay in a
hammock suckling a baby. A girl in a bright-orange frock was fishing with a homemade rod and line.

It was Bates who had declared that the term "a nation of shop-
keepers" ought by rights to be applied to the Brazilians. This floating slum bore him out, for every few yards was a bar-*cum*-store,
usually with a refrigerator operated by a small dynamo, and customers drinking at the counter or seated on the minute foredeck.
There were grocers' shops, radio-repair shops and shops that sold
ice, fishing tackle, cheap clothes and scrap; there were shops that
sold paraffin and there were petrol pumps. There was a surprising
number of chemists' shops, and near one of them I saw a hospital
launch provided by the city authorities. Occasionally we passed
houseboats of gayer appearance—their verandas painted white,
their doors bright blue, with curtains and flower boxes at the windows, like the houseboats moored along the Thames at Hammer-
smith. Our boatman winked and asked if I would like him to bring
me back at night: they were floating brothels.

We made now for the northeastern side of the harbor. I began to trail my hand in the water, until the boatman shouted a warning: we were opposite the city slaughterhouse and this stretch of water was a favorite haunt of the tiny, ferocious *piranhas*. My companions exchanged horrifying stories of the speed of their onslaught. A cow which had escaped from the slaughterhouse and plunged into the river had been reduced to a skeleton in five minutes; passengers who had trailed their hands in the water as I had been doing had lost their fingers. Even more traumatic were the stories of a barbed eel that would burrow its way into the orifices of the body and of the equally ghastly operations that had to be carried out on those who had been its victims.

Our destination was a floating factory for preparing Brazil nuts, to which my German acquaintance of the club had given me an introduction. It consisted of an old lighter chopped in two, the halves joined by a gangplank. Long narrow canoes, loaded with sacks of nuts (already taken from their outer cases), queued up for unloading. On the upper decks rows of women and girls wearing broad-brimmed straw hats and short-sleeved blouses which set off their yellowish-brown skin were working behind what looked like long counters. As we approached they waved and giggled. We drew up at a small landing stage in between the two halves of the lighter. There was a minute office, like the cab of a bulldozer. The clerk, who was making entries in a ledger and wearing a green shade like a croupier, was expecting us. He explained that the overseer, "Didi" (at least that is how the name sounded), was on his rounds, but a few minutes later the heads of the women and girls on the decks above us, which had been turned inquisitively in our direction, suddenly bent over their task. We heard a deep voice roaring exhortations and the movements of the girls' hands sped up like a sequence in Charlie Chaplin's *Modern Times*. A short, round figure, dressed in pink pajamas, the jacket open to reveal a barrel chest and a protuberant belly covered with a mat of curly hair, appeared at the top of the ladder above us.

He shinned down with remarkable agility and shook hands with a quick, hard grip. The clerk came running with a tray bearing three *cafèzinhos*. He drank his in a single gulp. The girls had to be kept up to the mark, he explained; unfortunately, he was without his foreman, who had been taken ill—"nut dust in the lungs"—and sent to a sanatorium in São Paulo. I asked him about his name. "Didi" was a nickname, he explained; his real name was Saeed. He was a Syrian; there were many Syrians in the northern states of Brazil. He had been in Amazonas since he was fourteen, and now he was a Catholic and married to a "real Brazilian."

When we had finished our coffee he led the way to the upper deck. We passed along the rows of operators and I saw that the long counter behind which they were standing was divided into sections by strips of wood about two inches high and that they were combing the nuts to and fro with pieces of curved wood in order to remove the bad nuts and loose bits of bark and dirt. When we passed over to the other half of the lighter we saw a further process of sorting and cleaning in wire trays. Wherever we went Didi shouted and shook his fist, and the noise of the rolling of the nuts rose from a rattle to a roar.

Now Didi pointed the way below. As we descended a smoke-laden blast smote my nostrils so painfully that it felt as if someone had punched me. I thought there must have been a fire, then I recovered enough breath to look around me and saw that scores of men and girls were arranging nuts in ridges with the help of long rakes. The roof was so low that I had to stoop. There was a row of naked electric bulbs along the roof, but their light barely penetrated the pall of smoke and nut dust. The electricity was generated from a diesel engine at one end of the hold; a rotator, in which the nuts were put through yet another drying process, was operated by an ancient steam engine. I had to shout at the top of my voice to make myself heard; but as soon as I raised my voice I began to cough and splutter and my lungs felt as if they were being sandpapered.

Didi now led the way through a doorway to another compartment, where the heat was so intense that it was as much as I could do to keep on my feet. Here, too, human beings were working—

small, dark-skinned, taciturn men, naked except for swimming trunks, on their hands and knees intently combing the ridges of nuts to and fro. Even Didi was affected. "Now you see why I wear these," he said, flapping at the jacket of his pajamas.

It was like wandering through the pages of a novel by Dickens— conditions in many of the smaller Brazilian industries, especially in the north, are still at the mid-Victorian stage. On the other hand, the state of Amazonas enforces a seven-hour day and there are regular breaks: as we resumed our seat on the bench, for example, a motor-boat carrying urns of coffee arrived, and the girls came running from the upper deck. The difficulty, Didi thought (his bark was worse than his bite), lay in circumstances beyond the control of normal legislation. Many of his girls lived far outside Manaus; even those who were near bus routes or who could make the journey by motor launch or canoe had to leave home at four o'clock, while many had to walk as many as fifteen miles, setting out as soon as dawn began to break. In addition, their diet was deficient in essential vitamins and they were often so weak when they arrived that they broke down and wept.

One day I got up at dawn myself. I made my way through the deserted docks to one of the landing stages. On the bench outside a small customs shed were seated a woman in a yellow cotton dress, with a child about four years old; a young man in dungarees and a blue short-sleeved shirt, carrying a transistor radio; a little old man with a skinny, wrinkled neck, dressed in a singlet and greasy black trousers; and the owner of one of the *fazendas* (farmsteads) for which we were bound, who had spent the night in a hotel of Manaus—a rather resplendent figure in a suit of white ducks, wearing a wide-brimmed straw hat and carrying an umbrella with a silver handle in the shape of a dog's head. His jacket was open, revealing a revolver with an ornate butt in a leather holster. A black pig, its rear legs hobbled, and several bundles of hens, their legs tied together, looking like feather dusters, occasionally blinking their eyes and emitting feeble squawks, also lay on the landing stage.

The diesel-powered milk boat arrived; the passengers scrambled aboard; the pig, squealing lustily, and the half-dead hens were dumped into the stern, and we cast off. It was still dark and our lights were switched on. A breeze sprang up, driving the rain into our faces, and the canvas side sheets were lowered. The farmer was engaged in an altercation with the young man in dungarees; they talked so fast that I couldn't follow what they were saying, but at any moment I expected the older man to draw his revolver. The canvas sheets completely blocked the view, and with the prospect of a nine-hour trip in front of me I began to wish I had stayed in bed. But an hour later the breeze disappeared, the rain stopped, and the canvas sheets were rolled up. We were close to a small island; lights flickered on a long sampan-type canoe lying close inshore. Our launch swung sharply to larboard and the young man and the farmer stopped their arguing. The canoe was a smuggler, the skipper explained. "Best to give them a wide berth."

The sky began to brighten; our lights were switched off. By the time we reached the junction of the Negro and the Amazon the sky was a vast silver-gray expanse. Close up, this meeting of the rivers was even more astonishing than it had been from the deck of the ship, and the dividing line showed even more distinctly. The Rio Negro in this light was almost coal-black; the Amazon beyond was as yellow as if it lay a few inches above sand—whereas, in fact, it was deep enough to carry ocean-going liners. Even more dramatic was the suddenness with which the water churning in our wake changed from the appearance of old-fashioned black toffee splintered by the confectioner's hammer to that of honey. As we sailed into the Amazon the yellow water was suddenly broken by the tumbling and leaping of a pair of dolphins, and a moment later the passengers crowded the rail to gaze down at a huge white, shadowy form cruising just below the surface—a *peixe-boi* ("cowfish," or manatee).

Soon we were chugging down one of the small tributaries of the Amazon. The banks looked as if some cosmic collision had mixed up the opposite ends of the world; English meadows came down to the water's edge, the red-roofed farmsteads might have belonged to

Somerset or Devon, and black-and-white cows stood sheltering under trees whose leaves and branches glistened with raindrops—but the trees were the palms and bananas of the Brazilian tropics, and a board above the main paddock bore the legend: "Fazenda Hildebrando Marinho."

As we drew abreast of it a green-painted canoe put out toward us. The launch slowed down. The hatches over the hold slid back to disclose aluminum containers resting on blocks of ice. The canoe came alongside; a boy in a tattered straw hat caught at our gunwales; another lay back nonchalantly on his paddle, holding the canoe steady. The boy in the straw hat handed up four milk churns; the man in the hold seized them, poured their contents into the containers, and then hurled them overboard, without a glance to see where they landed. As the boy in the canoe deftly caught the last of them we were already gathering speed. So it continued, hour after hour, as we threaded our way through an intricate network of channels. As one after another the containers in our hold were filled the man in charge pushed them to one side and shoveled blocks of ice around them, and the sweet smell of fresh milk blended with the diesel fumes.

The larger farms—many of them with handsome stone houses set in groves of mango trees, with gardens filled with flowers that looked like stocks and hollyhocks—had collecting stations thatched with palm fronds and moored at the water's edge. Here we also took aboard butter in wooden casks and big square cheeses. At one of them the old man in the singlet disembarked, and at another the young man in dungarees, shouting a last insult at the farmer, who caressed the butt of his revolver and brandished his silver-handled umbrella.

Occasionally, too, we stopped at floating stores. At one of them a large marmalade cat slept on the counter in front of a row of Coca-Cola bottles. Another boasted a lavatory, open to the river, with an ornate green chamber pot below a board with a hole cut in it. At another the woman and her child were embraced by an old man with a bald head and steel-rimmed spectacles. At another we slowed down for our skipper to throw onto the counter a bundle of newspapers; the man at the wheel had miscalculated the distance and as we picked up speed the prow of the boat tore away a plank and showered us with bits of palm thatch.

Sometimes it rained and grew dark. Then, five minutes later light, like strips of aluminum, would streak the gray sky, a rainbow would appear, somehow incongruous behind banana trees and palms, and the tropical sun would blaze as confidently as if it had never been obscured. We passed a radio repair shop, more floating stores, a floating bar, then *mandioca* plantations and an open shed with a large circular cauldron in which the *mandioca* was converted into *farinha* (the roots looking like large horse-radish). We passed men cutting *cipó* reeds, for weaving into baskets, women spreading laundry on the banks, and naked children glistening in the rain or steaming in the sun.

By late afternoon the farmsteads and stores had thinned out. The man in charge of the milk containers closed the hold, stretched out along the rail and closed his eyes, like a performer on a tightrope. A canoe appeared from a creek, the farmer with the revolver shook hands all round and clambered into the canoe, which disappeared as silently as it had come. There was no sound now apart from the chugging of the launch. The clumps of bananas and palms came closer and jungle trees ranged behind them. The reeds grew denser, leaving only a narrow channel, and from the reeds rose moor hens, ginger, black, or black-and-yellow, and weird-looking ducks, and geese with red-and-yellow wings like giant dragonflies. A little farther and I saw my first egrets in flight—long and graceful like animated skeins of silk—and, even more beautiful, a pair of flamingos flying with necks curved like a capital S. Farther still and we were in a stretch of water which from a distance looked like a green-paved colonnade. It was covered with the circular leaves of the victoria regia lily, each one three to four feet in diameter, vivid green speckled with red, flat as a pancake except for a raised brown rim which was as firm and regular as if made of baked clay. It was not the flowering season; there were only a few white blossoms, still tightly closed, like peony buds; but the sharp spikes below the water scraped the bottom of the boat.

Half an hour later the scene changed again. The jungle trees had receded, the banks were wide and shelving, and suddenly on one of the mud banks fifteen yards or so ahead I caught sight of two dark shapes. As we drew abreast one of them stirred into violent motion and splashed into the water with the flick of a powerful tail. The other lay motionless; perhaps it was sleeping, perhaps it was dead. Neither of the shapes, to tell the truth, had been very large, but there was no doubt about it: I had at last seen *jacarés* in their natural habitat.

Back in Manaus I found that another English ship had arrived. About four thousand tons, she was bound for Iquitos, another thousand miles up the Amazon (or the Solimões, as it is called in its upper reaches). There was a delay in loading cargo and for several days she lay alongside one of the floating piers. She was so placed that she caught whatever breezes might blow off the river and her ventilation system worked perfectly. Most of her crew were on shore leave, and for me and my friends she represented an oasis of peace and cleanliness. The skipper, a large, rawboned Irishman, would greet us stripped to the waist, his huge torso burned brick-red, and take us to his cabin lined with pitch pine, with chintz cushions on the settles and chintz curtains at the portholes. The chief engineer, a short, tubby Yorkshireman with round, innocent eyes, was an authority on the brothels of Brazil, discoursing with astonishing particularity upon regional distinctions and characteristics.

"*Never* go knocking in ————," he told me one day, naming a town in central Brazil. "When the first mate and I were there a couple of years ago we took a couple of whores with us in a jeep to a restaurant about ten miles out of the town. On the way back my girl shouted out, 'Stop.' So we stopped. And she got out, whipped up her skirts and squatted in the roadside—didn't even bother to get out of the headlights. When she'd finished she began to get back into the jeep. 'Hold on a minute,' I said. 'Aren't you going to use any paper?' 'Paper?' she says. 'Whatever for?' 'I've got to go to bed with you,' I told her, 'and I've paid two thousand cruzeiros for it!' 'Oh well,' she says, 'I didn't know you were such a *cavalheiro*. If we pass a pump I'll stick my tail under it; if not I'll give you a fifty-cruzeiro discount!' Now what do you think of *that*? No, whatever you do, don't go knocking in ————."

"And Manaus?" I asked.

"There's only one place in Brazil with more knocking-shops than Manaus, and that's Iquitos. Ah, Iquitos!" (and his eyes grew round and moist). "But Manaus is all right. Especially the Shangri-la. That's a really *decent* place. You could eat your dinner off the girls at the Shangri-la."

He may have been right in placing modern Manaus below Iquitos, which is famous throughout Brazil for its beautiful women, but it must be a comparatively recent development. In the days of the rubber boom, Manaus probably had more brothels to the square mile than any other city, and prostitutes from all over the world flocked there. The red-light district was internationally famous, and what began as a district eventually extended through practically the whole town. It is said that the police records for 1911 showed that 64 per cent of the residences of Manaus were brothels of one sort or another.

Another drinking companion, an elderly, gentle little German who had been in the timber trade in Manaus for over thirty years, also mentioned the Shangri-la a few evenings later and offered to introduce me.

I had assumed that we would merely get into a taxi and drive there. But that, I was informed, was how "greenhorns" approached the matter. He took me first to a shabby little café off the main boulevard, led me past the counter and into a room at the back. Along one wall was ranged a row of tables and chairs, where several men sat drinking beer. A group of women and girls sat on a bench along the opposite wall. The men scrutinized the women, and the women pretended to be unaware of the fact; they chatted gaily among themselves and from time to time combed their hair in front of a mirror placed in the center of the wall behind the bench. An occasional smile or nod was exchanged, but the men and women did not speak to each other. It might have been a "hop" in the parish hall of an English village—except that a urinal, which badly needed disinfecting, was placed at one end of the room, behind a narrow board which revealed heads and shoulders, legs and feet.

We sat down at a table and ordered beer. The women were of all shapes, sizes, ages and color combinations. A half-Indian girl of about sixteen wore a brown gingham frock and black hair down to her waist. A neat little Negro girl, with gold fillings in her dazzling-white teeth, wore a neat brown skirt surmounted by a vivid orange jumper. A statuesque blonde with shoulder-length hair wore a long skirt with a low-cut black blouse stitched with *diamantes*. An older woman, aged about thirty, wore a heavy, clinging dark-blue dress, shot with gold and silver threads.

But when I got up and made to walk across to her, my companion pulled me down again. "You shouldn't speak to them *here*," he said. "It's not usual—the first time. She will have noticed you. You will meet her at the Shangri-la."

A moment later, however, another woman came into the room, glanced in our direction and immediately sat down next to my companion. "We have known each other for twenty years," he explained; "it is a different matter." And he smiled tenderly at the woman—a dyed blonde, with a thin, haggard face and heavy make-up. She had been born in Yugoslavia, she told me. I tried out my few words of Serbo-Croatian, but she shook her head. "I left Zagreb when I was twelve," and she added, with a grimace, "It is a long time ago." She turned to my companion. "Excuse us," she said, and began to tell him eagerly and at length about an argument she had had that afternoon with the hairdresser.

Half an hour later she looked at her watch and got up. *"Até logo"* ("Until later"), she said. The other women too were collecting their handbags and gloves. Without another glance at the men they left the room, and the men went on sitting behind their beer. It was not until two hours later, after we had dined in a nearby restaurant, that my companion hailed a taxi, and we set out for the Shangri-la.

It turned out to be an open-air restaurant with trelliswork walls, tables with white cloths, waiters in dinner jackets and an excellent dance band.

We found a vacant table and ordered a bottle of whisky. The Yugoslav woman appeared and sat down next to the little German. They smiled at each other and resumed their cozy conversation. The band was playing a cha-cha. On the crowded dance floor above us the little Negro girl in the orange jumper, her white-and-gold teeth flashing, was dancing energetically with a young English sailor. The statuesque blonde was in the arms of a distinguished-looking Brazilian in a white suit. The half-Indian girl in the gingham frock was standing hopefully at the foot of the dance floor. I could not see the woman in the blue dress, until my companion, breaking off a detailed account of a recent illness (which the Yugoslav woman was following with wifely solicitude), murmured, "To your right." I saw her then, through the haze of tobacco smoke, sitting at a table with several other women. In the café in Manaus she had avoided my eyes; now she raised her glass and gave me a demure smile. I pushed my chair aside and stood up.

"No, no, that is not the way," my German friend told me. "You must wait a while."

I sat down again and poured out another glass of whisky.

"But won't somebody else . . . ?" I asked.

"But no!" he cried, shocked. "She has seen you. She knows *you* have seen her."

I looked over at the girl in the blue dress. She smiled and went on unhurriedly with her dinner. I couldn't understand what was happening. Perhaps I was mistaken? Perhaps these women were perfectly respectable citizens? Perhaps I had unknowingly committed some *gaffe* and mortally offended the girl in the blue dress? I began to scrutinize some of the other girls, but they quickly looked the other way: the fact that I had already exchanged smiles with the girl in the blue dress had apparently marked me out.

At last I ventured to interrupt the tête-à-tête at my side. "I should like to dance with that girl," I said.

The little German sighed. "You are very impatient."

"Well, what do I do?" I asked. "Shall I go and ask her?"

"It is *not* the best way," he replied.

"Then what in God's name *is* the best way?"

"Do not worry," he replied. "Metka will go and invite her to join us." The Yugoslav woman got up and went over to the other table, returning a moment later with the girl in the blue dress. I stood up and held the chair for her. She bowed and sat down. I saw her face clearly for the first time. It was small and pointed; her skin was of a beautiful pale-copper, almost olive-green, color; her eyes were deep and dark, her hair jet-black and silky; there was a faint black line on her upper lip; her mouth was small and slightly turned down at the edges. The melancholy of her expression I recognized as that of the Indian, and by a curious intuition I knew exactly from what part of South America her Indian blood derived.

"You come from Peru," I said.

She gave a quick smile, revealing small, very even, white teeth. "Yes," she said, "I was born over the border in Peru, but as a child I lived in Iquitos."

We climbed the steps to the dance floor. I took her in my arms. She danced superbly; by the subtlest of pressures she made my body follow the rhythms and soon I was dancing with ease and self-forgetfulness. We danced hour after hour, and I was oblivious of the heat and humidity. I admired her dress. "A sailor bought it for me," she said, "in Rio de Janeiro." She shrugged her shoulders and gave a wry smile. "I thought he was going to marry me." Had she been married? I asked. "I had a husband once," she replied, "but he left me." She paused, then added, "I have three children. When a woman's husband leaves her here, there is only this she can do."

This was the first reference she had made to her profession. She seemed perfectly content to go on dancing, and for my part I wanted nothing more than this pressure of a woman's body and personality against mine. But I was worried: by monopolizing her all this time I felt that I had entered into an unspoken contract and that I was keeping her from other customers. But when at last I muttered, "Is there somewhere we can go?" she stopped smiling and looked straight into my eyes. I felt I had behaved crudely and brutally. She took my hand and led me off the dance floor and round to the back of the restaurant, where there was a long palm-thatched building. An old woman sat in the doorway. She held out her hand. "Fifty cruzeiros—for the room," she said. I paid her. The girl took my hand again and led the way inside. The building was divided into cubicles. She tried the doors of several, but they were locked. The girl squeezed my hand. At last we came to a door that was unlocked and went in. The only furniture in the cubicle was a low, rickety bed. There was an uncurtained window filled by a swelling tropical moon. Light came through the thatched roof.

We held each other as if we were still dancing. Her body was as flawless as her face; her breasts were large and firm. We forgot the laughter, moans and creakings coming from the other cubicles.

When eventually I got out of the bed I did so clumsily; there was a rending noise and one of the struts collapsed. She kicked up her legs and shook with silent laughter, then put out her hand and drew me back into the lopsided bed. Her arms came tightly round the nape of my neck. We lay together until the old woman came knocking on the door. I called out that I would pay her again and she went away. Again I put my arms round the slim, dusky body. The bones of her pelvis were very pronounced and they left a bruise which I felt for days afterward.

When we left the cubicle and went into the corridor the little Negro girl was coming out of the next cubicle, adjusting her orange jumper. She flashed a smile at us. Hand in hand we returned to our table in the restaurant. My German friend and the Yugoslav woman were still discussing their illnesses. We drank a glass of wine, and then climbed back onto the dance floor. As she put her hand on my shoulder she gave a quick movement and pressed her body closer.

We danced until the cocks began to crow, and there were only half a dozen couples left on the dance floor; among them were the Negro girl and her sailor and, as we passed close, the girl, with an affectionate, conspiratorial smile, leaned away from her partner and pinched my buttocks.

It was six o'clock when we woke up one of the taxi drivers and drove back to Manaus. When I paid the girl, the money passed between us like an honorable gift. I had thought that such contact was finished for ever. I had thought I was possessed only of eyes, a brain and a notebook. I had come to collect "experience" like a naturalistic novelist compiling a dossier, and out of the most unlikely and unexpected circumstances I had discovered that I was still a feeling human creature.

4

FROM MANAUS
TO SÃO LUÍS

The group sitting near my departure bay consisted of two girls in blue frocks, an older woman with a baby crowing in spotless white on her lap, and an old, old man in black coat and trousers and a black stiff-brimmed hat and with a face so wrinkled that it looked as if it had been tattooed. They were the first pure-blooded Indians I had seen. The old man (the only one who spoke Portuguese) was in charge of the party; he tended them with touching solicitude, bringing them cups of coffee, stroking the baby's cheek, checking tickets and supervising the weighing of bundles. They were returning to one of the Salesian missions along the Rio Negro, he told me, after a visit to the regional headquarters of the order in Manaus. The women had never seen "a big city" before, but he often came. He had been adopted by the Fathers as a boy, and educated by them to be a teacher and lay reader. Now he was old but, he added proudly, he still "helped the Fathers in their work." When the loudspeaker announced the departure of our flight, he beckoned to his charges. They smiled at him timidly; they had that passive, slightly smug look you see sometimes on the faces of cripples or orphans in the better-run institutions.

The plane was an old Catalina amphibian. It was crammed with parcels, packages, cardboard boxes, sacks of mail, crates of beer, drums of petrol and paraffin, several sewing machines, outboard motors, and bicycles, half a dozen hencoops and four small, silky goats. As we took off we lurched and swayed like the gondola of a balloon.

I had just unfastened my safety belt when the stewardess summoned me to the captain's compartment—and I remembered that I had met a Brazilian Air Force pilot in one of the bars in Manaus who had told me that the pilot of the Catalina was a friend of his and had promised to let him know that I was traveling.

I made my way along the plane and entered the compartment. The pilot was a black-haired, stocky young man with a serene expression and capable, beautifully manicured hands. The compartment was a glass dome quite separate, it seemed, from the rest of the plane; it hung, suspended in space like a car on some gigantic fairground wheel. Below the land was still dusky, scattered with slivers of water like the smashed fragments of a mirror. Manaus was barely distinguishable: a huddle of buildings hugging the riverbanks, so that for a moment I had the illusion that I was looking down at the original settlement, and that the cluster of lights on the outskirts of the city were jewels beckoning to El Dorado. Then the plane wheeled and climbed above a bank of cloud.

When we emerged again it was broad daylight, and I was looking down at a square of brown water. It rose toward me like the palm of a hand thrusting into my face, and before I had realized what was happening there was a smack and a bump, water streamed past the windows, and then everything was still except for a gentle, rocking motion. Ashore I saw the white church of the village of Carvoeiro, with blue doors, surrounded by a cluster of stone buildings and palm-thatch huts. A canoe was waiting for the plane; two of the mailbags and some of the cargo were loaded into it, and five minutes later we were airborne again. We stopped at two other villages; at one of them our Indian passengers went ashore, at another I caught a glimpse through a fringe of jungle trees of a church with a spire and a square tower and a group of white-robed Salesian Fathers. The fourth stop was Barcelos, once the capital of the Rio Negro.

When Alfred Wallace visited it in 1850 (it took him a week by canoe from Manaus) it was practically deserted, and he described the "lines of the old streets" as "paths through a jungle, where orange and other fruit trees . . . mingled with cassias and tall tropical weeds." But now the jungle has been cut back and Barcelos is once more a sizable village.

Beyond Barcelos was nothing but the endless panorama of jungle, crisscrossed by brown ribbons so straight and regular that for a moment I forgot where I was and thought they were macadamized highways—until I realized that they were waterways and that the green blobs, looking from this height no bigger than Brussels sprouts, were tree-clad islands. Masses of low-lying clouds swirled round the curly tops of the jungle trees until they themselves seemed tinged with green and it was difficult to tell where one ended and the other began; I would not have been surprised, as the plane banked and turned, to find it was fleecy green above and fleecy white below. From the air the movement of the water as it lapped on the white sandy beaches could not be detected, so that each island looked like an emerald in a silver filigree setting, touched with bronze and gold at the edges, and the sandbanks were like flat brown fishes. The river widened and swelled as we advanced; its surface grew concave and then was lost to view in the distance in a bank of white cloud, as if it had poured over the edge of the world.

When eventually we reached Tapurucuara and I had clambered out of the plane onto the pontoon to which it was moored, I was conscious of a miracle: I had been transported to another world. The sky between the wisps of cloud was a vivid blue; the river danced and sparkled; the far bank was an indistinct smudge of green; it was hot and moist, but the air was surprisingly clear and the bustle of unloading merely emphasized the spaces and the silences. I felt as if, like a character in a Wellsian fantasy, my body had been dissolved into its separate particles and reassembled at the ends of the earth.

I had only discovered at the last moment that the plane was

making its monthly journey on this particular day and I had no introductions and no idea how the mission would react to my arrival. My heart sank as I watched a long canoe emerging from an *igarapé* to the left of the shelving beach. It was poled by an Indian dressed in a singlet and dungarees; a man in the habit of the Salesian order sat in the stern; a black mongrel dog stood on the prow, barking furiously. Another canoe, with an outboard motor, also emerged from the *igarapé,* passed the first canoe, and reached us ahead of it. A burly Brazilian, with a brick-red face, and a white stubble on his chin, jumped onto the pontoon. He was wearing a faded khaki shirt, with the buttons missing, and linen trousers of the same color tucked into leather boots. Two knives in leather sheaths, one short, the other as long as a bayonet, hung from his belt. He had blue eyes with the kind of twinkle that leaves one in doubt whether it comes from benevolence or ferocity. He was followed by five Indians who, under his supervision, began to unload drums of petrol and other cargo from the plane. All of the Indians were short—no more than five foot three or four—but they were sleek and well-fed, with satiny, copper skins. They were dressed in singlets or T-shirts and dungarees; their feet were bare. Two of them wore their jet-black hair in Indian fashion, combed down from the crown into a circular fringe almost touching the eyebrows.

The other canoe had now arrived. The dog jumped onto the pontoon and, still barking excitedly, began to dash round sniffing at the bundles and packages and at the legs of the new arrivals. When I tried to pat him he backed away, growling and baring his teeth. The priest jumped onto the pontoon, revealing a pair of ancient gray-flannel trousers under his habit, and seized the dog. The dog screwed round his head and licked his master's hand. The priest looked at me curiously and held out his hand. He was a stocky man of about thirty, his face almost lost in a black, bushy beard. He told me that his name was Brother Antônio, smiled and assured me of my welcome; his teeth were white and even. He looked like a character in one of Tolstoy's short stories—a younger version, perhaps, of one of the old men whom the Bishop in "The Three Hermits" visits on the isolated island on just such a remote, silent stretch of water as this.

The smaller canoe was loaded with supplies for the settlement. The rest of us, including the other Indians, piled into the canoe with the outboard motor. It was more like a dugout than a canoe, and so overloaded that, as the motor started, water began to trickle over the gunwales. We crawled along, the motor spluttering, the canoe shuddering. A petrol drum, too big to be stowed in the stern, was placed across the gunwales, protruding several inches on either side; two Indians tried to hold it steady, but every now and then it nearly rolled out of their grasp; the dog stood in front of it, head down, growling and barking. When we reached the entrance to the *igarapé*, overhanging branches and bushes threatened to knock us into the water. The big Brazilian (who was a kind of factotum to the mission) and Brother Antônio reacted to these hazards with roars of laughter. The Indians were silent and expressionless.

We drew up at a landing stage and scrambled onto it. The mission was some fifty yards back, hidden behind a shelving bank. It consisted of a long, solidly constructed two-story building, with a gateway leading into a quadrangle, paved round the sides and with a few dusty-looking fruit trees growing in the center. The path along the far side was roofed over, giving a cloister effect; a row of rooms opened onto it, their glass-fronted doors hooked back; and as we approached I heard a sound for which I should, I suppose, have been prepared but which was somehow the last thing I had expected in this remote outpost—the sound of children chanting their lessons. Brother Antônio led the way toward one of the classrooms. Another of the Brothers stood behind a tall desk to the right of a blackboard, upon which was written a religious text in Portuguese. About thirty children were seated behind regulation desks. They stood up as we entered, staring at me curiously. They ranged in age from about eight to twelve. They were clean and apparently well-nourished, dressed for the most part in shorts, sandals, and singlets or striped T-shirts. About four of them were white, among them a boy with startlingly fair, cropped hair. The others were Indian or near-Indian.

The teacher came from behind his desk; he flushed when Brother

Antônio introduced me, and he muttered in English, "Let us go outside." We went out into the cloister. He spoke to me again in English, but in so curious an accent that I had difficulty in following him.

"You must forgive me," he said. "I call myself Brother José, but I'm an Irishman—from County Clare. But it's so long since I spoke English that I've nearly forgotten it."

"You can still read it, though," Brother Antônio said, slapping him on the back, and he gave him a letter from the bundle he was carrying. They tore open their letters excitedly, exchanging items of news as they read them. Brother Antônio's letter was from a sister in São Paulo, Brother José's from his mother in County Clare, a widow of eighty, "but still hale and hearty, praise be to God."

Another priest came hurrying across the quad, a tall, lean man, with a bald head and a gray beard spread out on his chest. He held out his hand toward the bundle of letters, caught sight of me, and hesitated. Brother José tucked his letter into his belt, and introduced us. Brother Marcio clasped my hand. "So glad! So glad!" he said, in the most impeccable English public school accent. He chuckled. "No doubt you are surprised, but if you listen carefully you will know my country of origin!" And he rolled his r's for my benefit. "Yes," he said, "my father was a Hindu, my mother an English-woman, but I haven't seen either India or England these forty years. But I sometimes get letters from relatives"—and he looked at the bundle in Brother Antônio's hand. When Brother Antônio shook his head he sighed. "Ah well, next month perhaps." Turning to me, he again shook hands. "So glad!" he repeated, "so glad!" and hurried away.

We left the mission buildings, skirted a cemetery with plain wooden crosses, and took a path through tall jungle grasses. The view to right and left was uninterrupted save for patches of scrub. As everywhere in Amazonas the sky seemed of abnormal extent, dappled with the characteristic clusters of small gray and yellow clouds, like bouquets, and apparently at a vast distance; it was only at the skyline that the indentations of jungle trees were apparent, but ahead of us, directly beyond the Indian village, dense jungle began and continued almost uninterrupted to the borders of Venezuela and beyond.

The village comprised some dozen huts built round a compound. Most of the huts consisted of a palm-thatch roof built over poles with crosstrees at either end; three of the sides were open, but lengths of rush matting, which could be lowered in wet weather, were rolled up against the eaves. Goats, hens and dogs wandered in and out, and the floors were of beaten mud—but each hut contained tables and benches of unplaned timber, as well as the low-slung, very deep hammocks, which the Indians prefer to the more tightly stretched variety. Bunches of bananas and other fruits, vegetables, and various gourds were tied in neat bundles to the crossbeams at either end of the hut; so, too, were various pots and cooking utensils, rush mats and baskets, all of them of pleasing native design. In one of the huts I saw a bow and in another a blowpipe, though these were apparently for decoration, and I saw no arrows or darts. The length of the blowpipe—about six feet—astonished me. Later I handled one of them in a Salesian museum of Indian arts and crafts. It was beautifully fashioned and balanced, with raised wooden sights, but so heavy that I had difficulty in raising it to my lips, and when at last I managed to blow down it, the dart—a piece of sharpened bamboo flighted with a tuft of some kind of fiber—trickled out at the end. Yet the little Indians of the jungle use the blowpipe singlehanded and pick off small birds and monkeys from the tops of the tallest trees. What was worse, the fat, jolly nun in charge of the museum, who rushed round at the double, enthusiastically beating drums, twanging bows and even leaping in and out of hammocks, raised the blowpipe to her mouth with ease, and a moment later the dart struck the door at the far end of the room with a thud, and when I went to pull it out I found I had to exert all my strength. After several attempts, though, I got the knack of it: the raising of the blowpipe depended upon the correct placing of one's second hand, and then one had to give a short, sharp puff, and the dart (which had to be sharpened each time) would shoot out with terrific momentum.

The children in the Indian village were naked, but the Brothers had seen to it that the adults were properly clothed. The women wore long print dresses and had their hair gathered in wedge-shaped knots at the nape of the neck, fastened with slides or combs. A young man, dressed in the usual denims and striped T-shirt, joined us. He moved as if his body had no connection with them, standing in front of us (barely reaching our shoulders), his long brown arms dangling, his legs apart, and balancing on his hips. He looked as graceful and timid as a gazelle. He regarded me and Brother José warily; at Brother Antônio he flashed a brief smile. "This young man," Brother Antônio said, "is spending his second day at our mission. Only yesterday he was as naked as the day he was born." How had he reached the mission? I asked.

"Why, I brought him in myself!" And he described how at intervals, he would set out by canoe with his dog, teaching and preaching in the Indian villages. He had returned from one of these expeditions, which took about a fortnight, only yesterday and had brought several Indians with him. This newcomer was restless at present, he explained; he might settle down, but it was just as likely that he would go back with him on the next trip, or even make his own way home. Brother Antônio was a little doubtful himself on the question of clothes. "In the jungle," he said, "they are the cleanest people imaginable, but they're not used to clothes and don't always wash them properly; the clothes trap germs and they get diseases, especially tuberculosis." He shook his head and sighed. "With them tuberculosis and clothes seem to go together."

By now Brother José was speaking English fluently—with a thick Irish brogue; but he still had difficulty with his enunciation. "It's my teeth, or rather the lack of them," he told me. "The Portuguese words don't seem to mind, but the English ones want something to knock against." He opened his mouth and pointed: his front teeth, between the two canines, had been recently extracted. "Praise be, they've gone," he said, "for they gave me the agonies of the damned!"

"Who took them out for you?" I asked.

"A saint!" he replied fervently. "Come with me and I will show her to you." And he led the way to a stone building a little distance from the mission. We entered a tiled hall and knocked at a door. A woman's voice called out, but so softly that I could barely catch the words. Brother José opened the door, and I found myself in a small dispensary smelling of disinfectant. Jars and bottles were ranged on the shelves. A cupboard with a red cross on the door and an image of the Virgin on top stood in one corner and near it a sterilizer. Behind a plain deal table strewn with dishes, trays and surgical instruments stood a nun, so tiny that at first I thought she was a child, until I looked into her face and saw that she was about thirty years old. "This is Sister Agatha," Brother José said in an awed voice, as if still marveling that this frail creature could have pulled out his teeth, and the two exchanged a look of tender complicity, as if the operation had constituted a bond.

"I have brought you a visitor, Sister, all the way from England," Brother José said.

"You have come to see my hospital?" she said, a spot of color touching her cheeks. "I am a nursing sister," she explained as she led the way out of the dispensary. "I studied in Lisbon. I was going to qualify as a doctor, but it was decided that I was needed here." She opened the door of the women's ward—a square room, very clean and simple. The windows were open, and there was no netting: mosquitoes are not troublesome in this part of the Negro. The ward contained six truckle beds; only one of them was occupied—by an old Indian woman, who was sleeping peacefully.

The men's ward was larger. One of the beds was occupied by a half-caste, who sat bolt upright against the pillows, his eyes glittering, his mustache a sharp line against his gaunt face. An Indian boy of about thirteen was swinging in a hammock, nursing an arm swathed in cotton wool and bandages; a bed, with the sheets turned back, stood near by, in an attempt apparently to lure him into it.

"In this climate," Sister Agatha said, "hammocks are cooler; but it is not easy for nursing." She accompanied us to the door of the hospital and gave me a hand no bigger than a butterfly and so light that I didn't at first notice when she withdrew it. "It has been interesting for me," she said. "Thank you, Brother José, for bringing the *senhor* from England to see our hospital." She stood in the doorway and watched us as we walked back to the mission.

The girls' school was separated from the boys' by a high gray-stone wall. Brother Antônio and Brother José conducted me through the postern; the Mother Superior—a tall, plump woman, with a round pink face and round gold-rimmed spectacles—was waiting for us. She was holding the hand of an Indian girl, about four years old, in a frilly dress, who kept looking up into her face, then chuckling as she elicited a smile. These, the Mother Superior explained, were the first clothes the child had worn; both her parents had recently died and Brother Antônio had brought her too back with him from the jungle the day before; the nuns would bring her up now. The poor child still felt lost and frightened, but she would soon get used to it—and the Mother Superior bent down and kissed the child's forehead. The child smiled, put her thumb into her mouth and began to suck.

The Mother Superior led the way to one of the classrooms. As we entered the girls rose to their feet—just as the boys had done—but in addition they chanted in unison, *"Bom dia!"* The Mother Superior and the teacher—a pale-faced nun in her early twenties—exchanged pleased glances, then looked quickly into the faces of Brothers Antônio and José. "You see," Brother Antônio said, realizing what was expected of them, "the sisters are better disciplinarians than we are!" The two women flushed with gratification.

It was with the same air of innocent competitiveness that I was shown the laundry, in which about twenty Indian girls were working, the staff dormitories, with their rows of hammocks, and the dining room, with its spotless stone floors, scrubbed wooden tables and benches, and aluminum plates and mugs scoured until they looked like silver. But the sight of their own kitchen, with its air of feminine order, seemed to make the women uneasy. They peered into the rueful faces of Brothers Antônio and José. On one of the tables were ranged bowls of oranges peeled with sharp knives so that enough of the pith remained to keep them fresh. The women rushed over to these bowls, and, uttering little cries of solicitude, began thrusting oranges into the hands of the Brothers. Then, remembering that I was the visitor, they fetched two brown paper bags and filled them with oranges and Brazil nuts, placing on top of them half a dozen tiny live turtles, like flakes of green slate. I took the oranges and nuts (I was still eating my way through them a week later); the turtles, regretfully, I had to leave behind.

With a bag under either arm, my haversack on my shoulders, and accompanied by Brother Antônio and his dog, I left the mission and made my way in the direction of the landing stage. The sun beat down, the blue of the sky flickered with heat, but suddenly two umber-colored clouds were racing toward us like bombers. Overhead they swelled, shutting out the sun; a gust of wind nearly bowled me over, and the placid surface of the river was broken as if somebody had attacked it with a chopper. "It's the *trovoada*," Brother Antônio cried, "we often get it about this time." And, gathering up his habit, he raced toward a large canoe that was propped up on its side some twenty yards away. Before we reached it the rain came pelting down with such force that my cheeks stung as if someone were hurling gravel at them. The three Indians who had been caulking the canoe had already taken shelter. They moved up to make room for us. They had taken off their T-shirts and were sitting on them (presumably to keep them dry); their bodies, reddish-brown like a briar pipe, were smooth and absolutely hairless.

It was still raining five minutes later when I had to set out for the plane. My companion, however, insisted on seeing me off, and the Indians came too (leaving their T-shirts under the canoe). By the time we reached the pontoon Brother Antônio's habit was so heavy that he had difficulty in clambering out of the canoe. As I climbed into the plane my brown paper bags split and oranges and nuts cascaded on to the pontoon. The Indians, assisted by the dog, rushed to and fro retrieving them. They handed them up to me, one by one. I was the only passenger. The other seats were piled high with cargo. My own seat was hemmed in by plastic bags filled with water of the Rio Negro in which swam tiny iridescent fishes (for export to aquariums all over the world) like clippings from a peacock's tail. As the plane taxied away from the pontoon I caught a last glimpse of Brother Antônio's beard beaded with raindrops before the floats sent the water streaming past the windows to blot the scene, too, out like an abrupt dissolve in a film.

Everybody had told me that I must see the Amazon from the air. So I flew back to Belém. To my surprise I found I had grown weary of immensities. I was aware of them out of the corner of my eye, but I had to leave them to their own element. In any case, flight over the Amazon is notoriously unpredictable and about a hundred miles from Belém we ran into a violent storm. I was caught in the toilet, hurled backward and forward until I thought I would crash through the fabric of the plane, and my overriding emotion was that I didn't want to die with my pants down. And when eventually I emerged, smoking a pipe, against all the regulations, and trying hard to display English *sang-froid*, the riverscape was hidden in a white, impenetrable fog.

With the idea of "getting closer" to Brazilian life, I decided to try the second-class hotels of Belém. They were indescribably dreary, with poky entrance halls and reception cubicles littered with broken chairs and dusty papers. I was shown a bedroom in one of them: it contained three unmade beds, the gray sheets screwed up, revealing greasy paillasses beneath; cockroaches scuttled along the baseboards, and there was a reek of stale sweat and cheap brilliantine. The proprietor, though, had made a mistake and the beds were already booked. To my relief the other hotels were full too, and I made my way to a "first-class" one. It boasted a Palm-Court-type orchestra, while an air-conditioned bar created the illusion of cosmopolitan sophistication. The majority of the guests were Americans, technicians working for the Brazilian government on various schemes of development. Some of them were sitting disconsolately at the bar, drinking whisky and throwing dice. At a table near by, a domestic crisis was developing: a pretty woman of about thirty complained in a high-pitched, quavering voice that she couldn't stand "this goddam place." She was so drunk that her husband, a dour-looking man with grizzled, close-cropped hair and rimless spectacles, had to keep propping her up in her chair like a ventriloquist's dummy. Three boys, with crew cuts and Hawaiian shirts, and two girls in Alice-in-Wonderland dresses, ranging in ages from about twelve to fourteen, were bent over empty ice-cream dishes pretending to be absorbed in the task of scraping up the last drops.

On my right two men were talking in broken English. One of them, a giant with ginger hair and a neatly clipped ginger mustache, took out a cigar case from the breast pocket of an elegant suit and held it out to me. I took a cigar and he lit it for me. "Dutch," he said. "I'm Dutch myself. My friend is a Swede." The Swede, plump, with straw-colored hair, grinned. "English is our only common language," he explained. "Neither of us know it well." We talked and drank; there was nothing else to do, and everybody seemed to dread the thought of the cheerless corridors and bedrooms upstairs. The Swede settled down to steady and morose drinking, contributing nothing further to the conversation. The Dutchman talked non-stop. He owned timber concessions, he told me, on an island near Amapá. He worked there for about six months of the year; the rest of the time he lived with his wife in a luxury flat in Rio de Janeiro. It was hard work on the island, but he had a comfortable stone house, plenty to drink and dozens of servants. It was worth it: his wife had everything she wanted, a Cadillac, several racehorses, everything; they belonged to the best clubs in Rio; he had just brought off a deal with the Pakistan government for supplying hardwood for railway sleepers; soon he would be able to retire and he was only fifty-three. Fortunes were still to be made out of the forests of Amazonas, but not much longer, because there was no systematic replanting. He was still talking when I left the bar. The American was helping his wife into the lift, his hands under her armpits; the children stared at her speculatively. I wished I could have helped; but I could think of nothing to say.

At five o'clock in the morning the Dutchman knocked on my door. "Come to my island with me," he called out. "The plane for Amapá leaves in half an hour." But I decided to stick to my itinerary, and in any case there were loose ends I wanted to tie up in Belém. For one thing, I was irritated by my failure to find any evidence of Pavlova's visit to this part of Brazil. The legend was that she had danced in the Teatro do Amazonas at Manaus, but that apparently was incorrect. The idea had struck me that the books might have confused this theater with the opera house in Belém—also built during the rubber boom. Sure enough, after a few minutes' search I found a plaque announcing that "Anna Pavlova worked in this theater"; and it was dated March 1918.

I had been given the address of the two surviving daughters of one of the old rubber barons. I found the house, a vast mansion faced with Portuguese tiles of blue and yellow. An iron balcony ran the length of the house, supported on iron pillars; balcony and pillars were red with rust. The garden in front was a wilderness of ragged palms and giant banana trees. I tried the rusty gate, but it was padlocked. I peered through the bars and the tangle of leaves and branches and caught sight of two very old ladies, in long black dresses with lace "chokers" at the throat, sitting on the gloomy veranda. When I rattled the gate they got up and tiptoed into the house, closing the doors behind them. On the other side of the road, behind rusty railings, was another stretch of tangled wilderness; it had once been part of the old ladies' park; the main road had been cut through the middle of the estate.

I was more successful with an introduction to a descendant of one of the early French settlers, a tall, lean man, with a gentle, lined, face. He proudly drew my attention to his Dulwich College tie: he too was one of the survivors of the rubber boom, when it was common practice for the children of the wealthy to be sent to Europe for their education.

He took me on a visit to the governor's palace. The hall and the

wide, curving marble staircase leading to the first floor were
thronged with petitioners: small farmers from the interior, dressed
in ancient suits and with unshaved chins, and sad-looking women
with thin, yellow faces, some of them in widow's weeds, some of
them attended by swarms of children. They sat on the stairs or
leaned against the walls. Clerks and officials moved among them,
forming a startling contrast with their clean-shaven faces, glossy
hair, black suits and snow-white shirts and collars. My guide was
recognized and we were told to ascend the staircase; the petitioners
stared with a mixture of awe, envy and resignation. We entered an
anteroom, where those at the head of the queue sat on chairs ranged
round the wall. A secretary—young, bland, with watchful black
eyes and impeccable manners—ushered us to another waiting room.
It was magnificently furnished, but rain or humidity had penetrated one corner and there were fungoid patches on the wall and
ceiling. Several prosperous-looking gentlemen, wearing neat dark
suits, with jeweled pins in their ties and with pink, glossily manicured hands, sat in a semicircle with dispatch cases on their knees.

We were ushered into the governor's presence. He was a stocky
middle-aged man, with that air of having just left the hairdresser
and manicurist in order to be poured into an expensive new suit
which seems to belong to all Brazilian politicians. So, too, does the
charm: Brazilian politicians must be the most charming in the
world.

When we left, a fresh batch of businessmen had entered the
waiting room. As far as I could see, the petitioners in the anteroom
beyond and on the stairs had not altered their positions.

São Luís is the capital of Maranhão, another of the northern
states, about twice the size of England and Wales. I went there because I had been told that it was the finest of the old colonial cities,
where I would hear the best Portuguese in the whole of Brazil, and
because as the home of many of the country's leading writers it has
been described as "the Athens of Brazil."

It was, though, the mules and donkeys, carrying panniers on

either side of their cruppers, that first struck me after weeks spent in areas where the only form of poor man's transport is the canoe. They also played their part in my disillusionment. For as soon as the baskets are broken they are discarded, and no attempt is made to remove them. I found them everywhere, trodden into the mud, sodden and disintegrating. They littered the public gardens, where the blades of grass, alternately parched by the tropical sun and flooded by the rains, grew long and spindly. They surrounded the statues (including that to Gonçalves Dias, Brazil's greatest lyric poet) and they choked the fountains. The Athens of Brazil! Yet it need have been no more than a pardonable exaggeration: São Luís was the ruin of a city, which might have been the most beautiful in Brazil. In the noisome slums the ghosts of what had once been imposing colonial mansions still shimmered through, and there were fine relics of the earlier French and Dutch occupations (the Dutch were not finally expelled until 1644). The policeman who directed me to my hotel assured me that, not so long before, everything had been newly cleaned and groomed in honor of a visit by Jânio Quadros, then President of Brazil. "The climate—it is the climate," he told me. "It ruins everything." But why, I asked, were there no municipal gardeners or refuse collectors? He shrugged his shoulders. "It is *politics!*" He uttered the word as if it were, like the climate itself, one of the forces of Nature.

The noise in the city center was deafening: the trams, linked in pairs, ground and rattled; the decrepit buses lurched over the potholes; and the traffic roared and hooted continuously. From every direction, and almost drowning the din of the traffic, loudspeakers blared out dance music and political exhortations. The central square was packed with shabbily dressed men, sitting on the crumbling stone seats, reading newspapers, or gathered in groups talking politics. Shoeshine boys, some of them no more than seven years old, all of them pale and dirty, moved in and out of the crowds. Beggars, many of them cripples, were everywhere; a legless man propelled himself on a homemade trolley.

I arrived on a Saturday, and Saturday night treat was dinner in the airport restaurant. I was driven there by the representative of one of the English shipping lines—a stocky and cheerful Scot. His Brazilian wife was a handsome woman with auburn hair. She wore a sleeveless frock revealing beautifully bronzed arms and shoulders, and also strips of surgical dressing under her armpits where boils had recently been lanced. In this humid heat—and in the absence of fresh green vegetables—boils were a common complaint, she told me, but in the dry season the climate was healthy enough, and there were excellent beaches a few miles away where one could swim and sunbathe.

On the way a tremendous storm broke, lashing the windows of the car and nearly bowling it over. The windshield wiper did not work, and the engine coughed and sputtered. Anywhere else the car would have been relegated to the junk heap; here, it was practically worth its weight in gold: in Brazil, even in the prosperous south, a car is a precious and expensive possession.

The airport restaurant was crowded with middle-class families. The chicken was tough and the wine (from the vineyards of the south) an indifferent imitation of a German Hock. But there were clean linen and cutlery on the tables, the waiters wore dinner jackets, and there was air conditioning.

On the way back the rain stopped, a huge yellow moon suddenly appeared, silvering the fronds of the babaçu palms, and the night became noisy with a curious whooping and whistling from a local species of frog. When we entered the municipal center a transformation had taken place. The pavements were lit by flambeau-shaped lamps; there were lamps, too, on the curving balustrades that bounded the steps leading up to the cathedral. The dim light softened the façades of the buildings and obscured the chipped masonry and moldering plaster. It might have been a square in Venice; the beauty behind the squalor emerged like a ghost materializing.

We sat down at one of the tables outside my hotel, which stood on a corner facing the cathedral, and ordered beer. A group of Americans joined us. One of the men was a gigantic Texan, with an ugly crumpled face and an engaging grin. "Hello, Joe!" he cried, clapping my companion on the back. "Pleased to meet you, Joe!" he said when I was introduced. He addressed everybody within hailing distance by the same name. He was a seismologist, he told me; the other American was a geologist. Like their fellow countrymen in Belém they were on loan to the Brazilian government under one of the schemes of American-Brazilian economic collaboration. They were vague about their work—it was, I suppose, something to do with oil—though they offered to take me to their camp in the interior; after thirty miles or so the roads became impassable, but they had solved the problem of transport by using a tractor.

A swarm of shoeshine boys descended. Each carried a box of his own design and each was eager to demonstrate the small variations he had invented—a curved cup to hold the heel of the customer's shoe; a "secret" drawer containing a spare brush; or a scraper that could be raised or lowered. On their hands and knees they set about their work with intent, solemn expressions, vying with each other in the brandishing of brushes and in the cracking noise, as loud as pistol shots, they could make with the strips of cloth they used for imparting the final polish.

When they had gone, grinning at the size of their tips, the Texan banged the table with a fist the size of a football. "Aren't they *ever* going to do anything about these kids?" he demanded. "Do you realize, Joe"—addressing me—"that nearly all of them sleep rough? Their parents are dead, or scattered God knows where, looking for work."

"Is it as bad elsewhere?" I asked.

"Wait till you get to Ceará!" he said. "It's worse there—far, far worse. Those kids just don't have a chance. And there's so little you can do to help. It's so big that it makes you want to sit down and howl. Joe, tell him about that pal of yours in Itapipoca."

"Itapipoca is in Ceará," one of the other Americans explained. "This pal of mine was another geologist. He used to get his shoes cleaned by the same kid every morning. He noticed that this kid was looking peaky, and when he questioned him he found that he was scared stiff that he had tuberculosis. So he paid for him to go into a hospital to be examined. A few days later he came up to him, grinning all over his face. 'It's O.K., *senhor*,' he said. 'It's only V.D.!' "

The young men at the tables around us were still arguing politics. When I went to bed at midnight I was lulled to sleep by the rise and fall of their voices.

I got up at six o'clock—to the same sound; perhaps the debaters had never gone to bed. I left the hotel, passed the governor's palace, outside which two sentries stood, and reached the end of the *praça*, which is bounded by a balcony overlooking the estuary. A row of *urubus* stood on top of the stone balustrade. The water was low (the rise and fall of the tide here is one of the sharpest in Brazil) but a number of small sailing ships scuttled to and fro in the strong breeze, looking from this distance exactly like *sauva* ants. A small island lay about a quarter of a mile offshore. "It is Bonfim," a soldier told me. "The lepers live there." I could see a cluster of buildings and a jetty with people moving about on it. "It's very close, isn't it?" I asked. The soldier replied quite calmly, "Yes, *senhor*, it is very convenient for those who have relatives there. Sometimes, though, the lepers come here. It's not *official*, of course, but sometimes the fishermen bring them over. They are lonely on the island, and they don't get much to eat."

I climbed down the lane leading to the waterfront, picking my way over heaps of rubble (which included the broken head of a statue) and slipping on the refuse. The bandstand was a still grace-ful skeleton: the original roof had fallen in and had been patched with sheets of corrugated iron. It was packed with refugees from the *sêcas*. Some of them were still asleep on palm-weave mats, others in hammocks slung from the pillars at varying heights and forming a crisscross pattern like that of cobwebs in a loft. Others were beginning to stir, rolling up their mats or hammocks. A Negro woman, heavy with child, her lips ashen, stood motionless, leaning her forehead against one of the iron pillars.

Several dilapidated motor launches crammed with passengers,

the Sunday best of the girls making bright dabs of color, were putting out from the harbor. A paddle steamer was moored a few yards offshore, its decks a complicated network of hammocks, many of the passengers still asleep. The streets near the harbor were steep and narrow. There were holes where the granite blocks had been removed to prop up sagging doorways; these holes were filled with a mash of orange and banana skins, fishbones and the usual bits of palm-leaf basketwork. Many of the eighteenth-century Portuguese tiles, or *azulejos,* had been hacked out. Mud had collected in the cracks, and small palm trees looking like cabbage stumps had taken root and were sticking out at impossible angles. Larger palm trees grew out of the debris that had collected on the flat roofs. In the narrowest streets the iron balconies practically touched. They were crammed with an assortment of livestock, including hens, turkeys, pigs, goats—in one case even a donkey, his tail hanging through the railings. On the edges of some of the balconies vivid Amazonian parrots perched; on others black-faced monkeys, the ends of their long tails curled like question marks. In the appalling red-light district the balconies were crowded with prostitutes taking their Sunday morning airing. One of them, a child of no more than twelve, dressed in a faded silk dressing gown and bedraggled swansdown slippers, waved to me; another of the girls slapped her arm.

On my way back to the harbor I passed two other prostitutes. Their cheeks were round, the flesh above the necklines of their low-cut blouses had the plumpness of childhood. They were holding hands and swinging their arms. Every now and then they darted to the harbor wall and pointed excitedly to something that had caught their attention. I could see nothing but muddy water and dilapidated canoes propelled by ragged, unshaved *caboclos:* it was a mirror image of the squalid streets behind me. The clean, wide sea seemed leagues away.

Farther along, a group of laborers in wide-brimmed straw hats were unloading bunches of green bananas from a flat-bottomed boat. A beggar came out of a doorway and held out a hand. I gave him a twenty-cruzeiros note and he mumbled his thanks. I noticed that his other hand, which he held half concealed under a piece of sacking, was misshapen, like a ham bone, but it wasn't until a few seconds later that its significance struck me. The laborers, seeing the expression on my face, burst out laughing. "Don't worry, *senhor*," one of them said. "The police will send him back to Bonfim!" I had touched a leper. I expected a recurrence of the kind of panic I had experienced after reading the notice about *bouba* in the woods near Tumúra Falls, but pity and horror had cured me of hypochondria.

When I passed the bandstand again the hammocks had been rolled up. Several men were sitting on upturned orange boxes; a group of children were kicking a cardboard box; the pregnant Negro woman was trying, without the aid of soap, to wash a dirty rag of clothing in the equally dirty water of the gutter.

Outside the hotel the political discussions continued, like the repeating groove of a gramophone record. When it rained the tables were carried into the hotel lounge; when the rain stopped, they were carried out again. Girls in pairs walked up and down in their Sunday best. Families promenaded. A vast blue American car driven by some Brazilian *nouveau riche* in a Palm Beach suit, with a fat, bejeweled wife at his side, the children in the back in showy clothes with patent-leather shoes, passed and repassed, driving slowly so that everybody could see and admire. Other cars drove to the hotel, stopped for a few minutes, then drove off again; they were back before long, having made another circuit of the few passable roads.

After lunch I visited one of the residential suburbs. This was on higher ground, removed a little from the steamy heat of the estuary. Here were white villas and bungalows; men in white linen suits wandered round their well-kept gardens; their wives and daughters sat at the open windows manicuring their nails. My own host was a dental surgeon, his son a doctor, and two of his daughters were studying at the city's College of Social Services. We sat round a brass-topped table on the veranda, drinking coffee.

There was a piano in the drawing room behind us, and a glass-fronted bookcase.

In the evening the cathedral's congregation overflowed the doors. At first I thought those on the top step of the *praça* were merely onlookers, until they too knelt down. There was a power failure before the service was over; the interior of the cathedral was lit only by the candles on the altar; the choir, in the midst of singing an anthem, faltered and then stopped.

After the service the tables outside the hotel filled again. Inside the hotel a small orchestra was playing Latin-American dance music, interspersed with European numbers of the Twenties and Thirties. The pavements were packed with onlookers attracted by the music. On the fringes of the crowd beggars and refugees stood staring. Shoeshine boys sat on their boxes waiting for customers. A boy in shorts, his left leg amputated above the knee, the stump smooth and white, hopped among the tables, holding out a tin. The Americans arrived in their jeeps. A mulberry-colored Cadillac, driven by a chauffeur in a uniform of the same color, drove up and parked at the curb. Two beautiful Lebanese girls with ivory-colored skins and sleekly coiffeured hair sat in the back. A young man with stooping shoulders came out of the hotel, and the girls held open the door for him. "That's the brother," the waiter said. "He's a well-known pederast. His sisters adore him." "Joe," the Texan said, "have you tried *cachaça*? It's Brazilian firewater—but it's good with lemon." My watch had bubbles of moisture inside the glass. I found it had stopped an hour before. The leather strap had practically disintegrated anyway, so I put it in my pocket. The power came on again, and the cathedral opposite was flooded with light. The interior looked bright, orderly, clean. A few old women were still kneeling at their prayers.

5

CEARÁ

In Fortaleza, the capital of Ceará, it was the sea that pulled me first. I entered from the landward side, but at once I felt the mud under my feet gritty with sand blown in from the beaches of the Atlantic. At last I began to feel that I had emerged from the green-and-brown whirl of Amazonas. The air I breathed was sticky not only with tropical moisture but also with brine. The sea permeated the sky. The streets told you at once, as they always do in a port, that they would lead you to the sea.

They took me through a city of startling contrasts. Gaunt and ragged figures from the interior stood at every corner. They had the same black eyes and curly hair, and the same fierce, finely cut features of the refugee I had met near Belém—the distinctive Cearense face, racially the result of the blend of Portuguese and Indian bloods, with only a slight Negro admixture. But there were fine houses, skyscrapers and hotels, and American limousines threaded their way through the narrow streets. It looked more like a twentieth-century city than any of the others I had seen. There were few relics of the past, though the city (now about the size of Bristol) grew up round the Dutch fort which the Portuguese conquered in 1655—*fortaleza* is the Portuguese word for fortress.

The shops were also better stocked than any I had seen so far, especially with cotton goods (the cotton is grown in Ceará) and the beautiful, silky hammocks which are famous throughout Brazil.

I continued through a maze of alleyways, past shacks with the words CASA FAMILIAR ("family house") chalked or painted on the walls to distinguish them from the brothels and to preserve the inhabitants from annoyance, and on to the waterfront and the roar of the Atlantic. There was no harbor. The ships lay at anchor a quarter of a mile offshore. The cargoes were unloaded onto lighters, slowly and laboriously because of the heavy swell. Passengers slithered down an almost perpendicular gangplank into launches.

At the end of the pier was a flight of black, dripping steps, every now and then submerged by the waves. The launches arrived and, bobbing violently, maneuvered toward the bottom step. The passengers began to jump, in frantic fits and starts, as if they were abandoning a sinking ship. The younger ones came first, scrambling out of the way of an advancing wave. Then, when the water had swirled back, they spread out their arms to receive the women, children and old people. Somehow they all landed without falling into the sea. A short, almost spherical priest gathered up the skirts of his habit and to the applause of the audience leaped so vigorously that he almost landed on top of the pier.

I could see no sign of the lighters. A stevedore explained that they were bound for Mucuripe Point, some four miles to the east. The quay wall in Fortaleza was unfinished and could only deal with ships drawing up to twenty-one feet. Sometimes a ship had to wait at anchor for as long as a fortnight before the lighters could discharge the cargo. He pointed to the piles of timber stacked all over the harbor area. "For the cranes," he said. "They are still operated by steam. Is it not strange, *senhor,* when you remember that Fortaleza is a big port, where the liners from Europe and America call?"

I made my way to the Barra do Ceará—the largest of the beaches—where the rollers thundered behind a glittering screen of spray.

High up on the beach among seaweed, fishing nets and piles of rubbish were flimsy huts built of driftwood, sacking and hammered-out petrol cans. Small boys, dressed in rags, but happy in the presence of the sea, rolled in the soft, white sand. Then, catching sight of a group of fishermen hauling in a net, they dashed off to help. I followed. The fishermen stood behind the net, waist-deep in the water, spray breaking over their heads, while the rest of us hauled at the ropes. It took nearly an hour to drag the net clear. As soon as the men had finished their sorting the boys made a dash—but were held back until two old women, their bare feet and ankles knotted with veins, had shuffled forward and taken their pick of the remaining fish. Then the boys hurled themselves into the net, shrieking, laughing and tumbling over each other. They emerged holding tiny silver fishes, still wriggling in their fists. They raced up and down the edge of the breakers, brandishing them, until suddenly they lost interest. Soon the foreshore was littered with dead and dying fish. The fishermen gathered up their net and plodded back into the water.

Near by a *jangada* was coming in to land. The triangular sail of patched cotton was lowered, and three men hauled the boat away from the combers. Their chins bristled, their eyes were red with salt, and there were patches of brine on their forearms. Their clothes and tattered straw hats looked as if the elements had reduced them to the point of disintegration, like the wrappings of mummies.

The *jangada* was pulled clear of the tide. It was made of logs of the *pau jangada*, or "raftwood tree," a very buoyant, feather-weight timber similar to balsa. There were six of these rough logs, each about twenty feet in length, fastened together with wooden pegs, the outside logs tapered at one end to form a rough prow. They all looked alike to me, but one of the crew, pointing to the two outside logs, which he called *mimburas*, explained that they were quite different, in weight, texture and buoyancy, to the two next to them, the *bordos*, and also to the two in the center, the *meios*. I sat on the wooden bench aft, which he called the *banco do govêrno* (literally the "seat of government"), and he placed in my hands the long paddle, shaped like a cricket bat, which fits into a hole cut into the timbers and serves as a rudder. There was another raised bench in the center of the raft, on which rested the lowered sail, operated by a single rope; another forward with a hole in the center for the mast. Fishing lines, hooks, baskets, and other pieces of equipment were securely tied to the center bench— it is not uncommon for a *jangada* to be overturned in heavy seas, though like a lifeboat it usually rights itself. A water jug and a tin box containing *farinha* were also tied to one of the benches. I asked the crew how long they had been at sea. "This is the third day, *senhor*," they told me. Later I learned that this was nothing out of the ordinary. Fishing expeditions lasting a week were not unknown, and these flimsy craft sail far out of sight of land whatever the weather, with a lantern by night and a white rag by day to warn ocean-going ships of their presence.

The *jangada* has its place in Brazil's national mythology, and I found miniature replicas on sale not only in the cities of the northeast but as far away as Rio de Janeiro and São Paulo. When, in 1850, further importation of slaves into Ceará was prohibited, the owners hoped to sell their Negroes in Rio de Janeiro and São Paulo. The only method of transportation between shore and ship at that time was by *jangada*. But, led by their chief, Nascimento— known as *Dragão do Mar* ("Dragon of the Sea")—the *jangadeiros* refused to carry the slaves. Abolitionists in Rio de Janeiro sent for Nascimento, and he and his *jangada* were carried in triumph through the streets.

It was dark when I set out to return to my hotel. I paid off my taxi (new and American) in the center of the city and walked the rest of the way. Lights streamed from the skyscrapers. Colored bulbs played round the cinemas. The *praças* were well lighted. Opposite one of them was an arcade crammed with eating stalls— including one displaying the Stars and Stripes and a placard announcing "Hot Dogs." I sat on a high stool and ordered a cup of coffee. I suggested to the man who served me that there was apparently no *Falta de luz* in Fortaleza. I had touched on a sore point, for he leaned forward and seized me by the arm. *"Senhor, I come from Macaiba in Rio Grande do Norte. We were three years without electricity, senhor, three years, and all because a piece was missing from the diesel plant. The mayor kept promising to buy it. For three years he was promising!"*

"And what happened?" I asked.

"It was election time, so of course he bought it." And he uttered a phrase I was to hear frequently in the northeast: *"Sua Alteza o Voto"* ("His Highness the Vote").

On my way back to the hotel I found myself in a dark side street. I had gone only a few yards along it when I tripped over a bundle. It stirred and muttered. It was a boy of about eight. He was using a stack of newspapers as a pillow. I bent down and shook him by the shoulder, but he was breathing heavily and I could not awaken him. I counted ten other such bundles, some on the pavements, others huddled in doorways. Some of them were newspaper boys, others had shoeshine boxes beside them. When I reached the hotel I questioned the night porter. He shrugged his shoulders. "There are hundreds such, *senhor*. They are the orphans of the *sêcas.*"

"But this child," I said, "I could not waken him: perhaps he is ill."

"No, *senhor*, it is alcohol, or perhaps *maconha* [marijuana]. There are many addicts."

"Is *nothing* done?"

"The police do their best. But they can't see to everything."

"And the government?"

"There used to be a Society for the Protection of Beggars. It has several hostels. But it closed last year."

"Why?"

"The money gave out."

In the hotel lounge a television set, the first I had seen, was showing a noisy commercial. The only viewer was a tall, thin man in a crumpled linen suit, with a Groucho Marx mustache. When he saw me, he switched off the set. "I've been waiting for you," he said in English, "and so has a bottle of whisky." I sat down beside him. The bottle of whisky was three-quarters empty, but it was Scotch and there was a bucket of ice.

"The manager told me that a fellow countryman had arrived. Lucky devil, coming from England. Are you staying in Brazil?"

"No."

"Lucky devil, going back! I haven't been home since before the war." And he launched into an account of English life in the 1930s, so dated in tone and content, so full of turns of phrase that no one at home would dream of using any more that as I listened to him I had the sensation of having slipped the last thirty years off my shoulders like a many-caped overcoat.

He was now, he explained rather vaguely, something "in the export trade." There had been a time, he said (finishing the bottle of whisky), when he had dreamed of making a fortune and "buying a little place in Sussex." But what chance was there in this country for an honest man? And he glanced at me challengingly out of bloodshot eyes.

"You can't get anywhere here without bribery and political influence," he said. "Have you seen the guns?" Then, when I looked puzzled, "You will, you will! All the politicians here are gangsters. There's a murder a week. A deputy was shot only last month —not far from this hotel. Politics are big business. Votes are bought and sold—I could tell you exactly how much it costs to become a state deputy and a federal deputy—and as soon as a man has been elected it's grab, grab, grab! Federal funds disappear. So do private grants. So does American aid. There are so many rackets that an honest businessman like me hasn't a chance. Smuggling, for example. Take this whisky"—and he mournfully shook the empty bottle—"ten to one it's contraband. Whisky, radios, cars—they're smuggled from state to state. Then someone tips off the Customs, they make a raid and eventually hold an auction of the confiscated goods; the hotels and clubs bid for them and get them at cut prices. It's all perfectly legal—unless you're a poor bloody foreigner." He lapsed into gloomy silence. I took the opportunity to escape.

The next day I set out to find the British consul. Following the hotel porter's directions, I walked down several narrow streets and past a jumble of small stores and warehouses, but I could see nothing remotely resembling a consulate. Then suddenly I came upon a square yellow house, with a Union Jack painted above the doorway, set in a small, dusty garden. The door was open, and I saw a hall parlor crowded with people. As I opened the garden gate two small white dogs darted out of the house, prancing and yapping. No one moved inside until I had rung the bell. Then a man got up from a basket chair and threaded his way through the furniture. He greeted me with an old-fashioned bow, at the same time crooking one arm; the noisiest of the dogs jumped and settled down against his chest. The other yelped in falsetto protest. The man was slim and elegant, with gentle brown eyes and carefully brushed hair. He was wearing a long-sleeved shirt and a pair of flannel trousers, both of that deep cream color that one associates with prewar tennis parties on an English vicarage lawn.

"You are the British consul?" I asked.

"Oh no, that is my brother. Please come inside." His English, too, had an old-fashioned sound.

The parlor was stuffed with Victorian furniture; the wallpaper was the gravy-brown of ancient boardinghouses at Folkestone. Highly colored portraits of the Queen and Prince Philip held pride of place on the walls; there were numerous other photographs of members of the royal family. Hedged in by horse-hair chairs and sofas were a filing cabinet and a desk with a telephone and a typewriter. A dark-haired, broad-shouldered man was seated behind it, discussing with two Brazilian businessmen various matters connected with a shipment of *oiticica*. He stood up as I entered and shook hands. His English was even quainter than that of his brother. Meanwhile, two elderly ladies, in long black dresses, their hair in buns, were chatting in Portuguese, seated in easy chairs with their backs to the rest of the room. They had glanced round briefly when I entered, but then resumed their conversation as if neither I nor the other occupants of the room existed. But a few minutes later the consul's brother conducted me round the backs of the old ladies' chairs and introduced us: one of the ladies was his mother, the other his aunt; both were Brazilians and neither spoke a word of English. The father, now dead, had been an English businessman who had settled in Fortaleza. After a few polite exchanges I was escorted back to the "consulate" and the ladies resumed their conversation.

An invisible curtain divided the little room in two: visitors might or might not be formally conducted into the ladies' presence; under no circumstances must one half of the room acknowledge the existence of the other, and to address the ladies (who were only a few feet away) when one was in the operational half was a breach of etiquette. Even the dogs respected the division: they came to the door when visitors arrived but returned to their mistresses' laps as soon as the visitors had been admitted.

I explained that I wanted to get into the *sertões*, the interior of the state. The consul took me to the governor's son. The governor himself was occupied with affairs of state. The son was being groomed in public-relations work. He was only seventeen and in his first year at the university, but he already had the politician's gravity and aplomb. He had traveled widely with his parents both in Brazil and in the United States. He spoke excellent English, with an American accent. He was intelligent, surprisingly well-read for his age, and he possessed charm and good looks. Obviously he has a brilliant future ahead of him. Sometimes the prospect seemed to daunt him and he would become anxious and depressed, as if he longed to escape from premature responsibilities. He drove me (very fast and efficiently) through Aldeota, the smart, residential suburb of Fortaleza. The square white bungalows with porches and verandas, and the two-story Spanish-type houses were set in beautifully kept gardens of flowers, cactus plants and palm trees. The governor's house was modest in size—"people would criticize if he had too big a one," Carlos commented—and guarded by two soldiers in steel helmets.

We came to the Náutico Atlântico Cearense, famous as the most luxurious club in Brazil. It was a staggeringly hot afternoon: the tennis courts were deserted, and even the bathers in the huge swimming pool—the finest in Brazil, where Olympic swimmers train—had been driven into the shade, though a few children in the charge of Negro nannies splashed about in a smaller pool. In the gardens petals wilted, and leaves and twigs crackled. Only the lizards reveled in the heat. I had always regarded lizards as secretive creatures; the species here were as big as baby crocodiles and instead of darting or slithering they ran about on their hind legs, leaping about and fighting like quarrelsome puppies.

We retreated to the bar. It opened into a ballroom with magnificent cut-glass chandeliers and a balcony with marble pillars. A projection room was built into the back of the balcony for cinema shows. The lounge was filled with leather wing chairs; inlaid chess tables were ranged round the walls. Waiters in smart uniforms tiptoed over the thick carpets.

I told Carlos what I wanted. "Leave it to me," he said. "My grandmother lives in the country. I will write to her."

This was better than I had hoped. I knew that Carlos's grandmother was the widow of a famous figure in Ceará's recent history, who had been known as "the last of the Colonels." The Colonels had been so called because they had, like medieval barons, commanded private armies and ruled over huge properties, granted in most cases by the Brazilian emperors in return for services rendered. The old Colonels had disappeared, but their descendants still control thousands of voters, who are not only dependent on them economically but, in spite of the droughts and the poverty, are often actuated by a blind feudal loyalty.

We left the club when the heat had eased. A few yards from the entrance was a cluster of the usual squalid huts with the usual swarms of naked children. I caught Carlos's eye. "Yes, it is terrible, terrible!" he said, and suddenly he was confiding that he didn't want his ready-made career; he wanted to get away from Ceará; he would like to go into the diplomatic service. "That's how I can best help my country!" he cried. I am sure he was sincere, and he will make an excellent diplomat.

He kept his promise; and a few mornings later, just after dawn, I climbed into a jeep provided by Carlos's father and driven by one of his retainers, a taciturn man with a lined face and grizzled, curly hair. The road leading out of Fortaleza was the worst I had encountered, with huge cracks and crevices. Then it joined a good asphalt highway. At first there was a good deal of traffic, mostly jeeps, wagonettes and lorries. Gradually they gave way to carts, donkeys, flocks of goats, and an occasional horseman. The highway petered out, and for several miles we bounced and skidded on a scatter of loose rubble. Then came another good stretch, and for the next sixty miles or so the surface was tolerable, bad, or downright atrocious; it all depended, my driver explained, on the finances of the municipality concerned and on the honesty of the officials and contractors.

We were now in the *sertões*. To my surprise, the vegetation was lush and green. It consisted mostly of a kind of brushwood, or *carrascos*, and tall plants called *caatingas* (some of them thirty feet high) with ugly-looking thorns and spikes, but also with plentiful foliage which makes excellent forage for the cattle. But the soil was red and sandy, and when it rained I saw how quickly it drank up the moisture. The average rainfall in the state ranges between eight and twenty-four inches and when the *sêcas* come they can last for two or three years. After a month or two without rain, my driver told me, the vegetation withers with astonishing rapidity. The cattle grow thin, and bloodsucking bats descend and weaken them still further. The animals gnaw at the dead trees and then they drop and die in their thousands. The first of the "retreaters" leave their homes. The number swells, until the roads are hidden in clouds of red dust. During a normal *sêca*, he told me, fifteen to twenty thousand families emigrate; in a bad year it will be as many as a hundred thousand. Yet, when the drought ends, somehow the news penetrates the far corners of Brazil and thousands make the long trek back home.

We stopped at a roadside bar with open sides and palm-thatch roof. The floor was of beaten mud, the benches and tables of unplaned wood. The men who sat at them were swarthy, unshaven and fierce-looking; some carried revolvers, the rest knives. They stopped talking as soon as I entered, turned round in their seats and stared. I said, *"Bom dia,"* and they still stared. I sat down and they continued to stare. My driver leaned his chin on his fist and grinned. A huge fat woman came from behind the bar and stood over me. My driver introduced me as a visitor from England. "And a friend of the governor?" the woman said unsmilingly. She sat down beside me, and laid her hand on my arm. *"Senhor,"* she said, "you should know that there are people only a few yards away from here who are dying of starvation. They have nothing, absolutely *nothing!"* I told her that I had eyes in my head and tried to use them. She clapped me on the back, and her vast bosom heaved with laughter. The others continued to stare, and when the woman brought me some bread and cheese and a bottle of beer a pretty girl of about fourteen, suckling a baby, and five small children clustered at the end of the bench, their eyes following my every movement, until my driver, seeing my embarrassment, banged his glass on the table and they retreated.

The men turned their backs and resumed their meal. A boy of about ten, accompanying himself on a concertina, began to sing songs of the *sertões* in a clear, sweet voice. After every song the men applauded enthusiastically. But when I took out my pipe and tobacco—a false move, for a pipe was a rarity in Ceará and the only other person I saw smoking one was a wrinkled old granny in the market at Fortaleza—the singing and the talking stopped and again everybody turned and stared. The woman again came from behind the bar, and carefully examined my tobacco pouch and its contents. Then she caught hold of my left wrist, studied my watch (the British consul's brother had got it repaired for me), and asked me where I had bought it, where I had bought my haversack, my wallet, and practically every garment I was wearing, and how much they had cost. In the meantime, I continued to smoke. I had got used to the staring. It was not meant to offend, and each man as he left the restaurant turned toward me and bowed or laid his hand on my shoulder as he passed.

We drove on, hour after hour, through the *sertões*. In the blazing

sunshine huge butterflies hovered like Chinese lanterns. A dead
sheep at the roadside was attended by an army of *urubus*. We began
to climb. Gradually the landscape became barer and wilder. *Carrascos* and *caatingas* gave way to tall spiky cactuses; they quivered
against the vivid blue of the sky, every needle white and distinct.
Jagged rocks and boulders broke through the red skin of the soil.
Higher still, and we were passing through canyons of stark rock;
we might have been in the deserts of Texas or Arizona except for
the political slogans painted on the rocks. Then at the very top of
the *serra* the jeep broke down. The driver swore, picked up a bag
of tools, got out, and opened the bonnet. I too descended; there
was nothing I could do to help, so I set off down the road. I found
a flat rock at the roadside and sat down. There was not a soul
in sight. I could see the road winding for miles among the rocks
and cactuses. On the slopes behind me a riderless donkey was
picking his way through the loose stones; the clatter of his hoofs
and the distant tapping of my driver's spanner were the only
sounds. But a moment later there was a rumble of thunder, and
drops of rain as big as pennies began to fall. I hurried back to the
jeep. The driver was trying to mend a connection with a rusty bit
of wire. It did not look promising, but when he pressed the starter
the jeep shuddered into life.

Two hours later we entered a small town. Apart from a well kept
praça and a cluster of handsome villas, it was stark and cheerless. Goats and small black pigs wandered along the pavements and
in and out of the open doorways.

While the driver was looking for a mechanic I entered a shop,
part chemist, part general store and part café. The tablecloths were
dirty and thick with flies, and when I raised my glass of beer flies
settled round the rim and at the corners of my mouth.

We drove on again, through a number of squalid villages, past
miles of fields planted with cotton, and several new reservoirs
(earnest of the government's efforts to combat the *sêcas*). Then
once again into wild country, deserted except for an occasional
horseman. One of these had stopped beside a cairn of stones

surmounted by a rough wooden cross. He placed a branch of some flowering shrub against it, took off his hat, crossed himself, then rode on. It was the grave of a child, my driver explained: the *sertanejos* often buried their children at the roadside so that passers-by might pay their respects and pray for the souls of the departed. I must remember, he told me, that Ceará was not only the "Wild West" of Brazil, but also the most devout state in the country. Had I not heard of the great Padre Cícero?

It was hardly possible to visit Ceará without having heard of him. His story is one of the most fantastic in the whole fantastic history of the region. It began in the 1870s when a fanatical young priest, Cícero Romão Batista, from the seminary in Fortaleza, settled on the *fazenda* of Joazeiro, in the valley of the river Cariré in southern Ceará, an oasis of tropical vegetation in the midst of the *sertões*. During the drought of 1877–79—one of the most terrible of all—he organized the digging of wells and the planting of *mandioca* and *maniçoba* to feed the refugees. The *sertanejos* hailed him as a man inspired by God. Then some years later the "blessed" Maria de Araújo, a member of his congregation, fell to the ground with a trickle of blood running from her mouth at the moment the Padre was administering the Sacred Host. There were skeptics to argue the physical basis of the incident, but at first both medical and ecclesiastical authorities were impressed, while to the *sertanejos* it was an undoubted miracle of transubstantiation, and in their eyes Padre Cícero was a new messiah, especially as the "miracle" occurred again and again. Devotees from all over Brazil flocked to the site, built a large new church for the Padre and transformed the tiny hamlet of Joazeiro into a shanty town that eventually numbered some fifty thousand inhabitants. When the Church authorities decided to expel the Padre he proclaimed Joazeiro a municipality and appointed himself mayor. When Maria de Araújo died his own position was unaffected and she became the patron saint of the movement.

His followers were divided into two main sects. The "blesseds" wore long black cotton habits with a large cross on the back and strings of rosaries, charms and little bags containing relics round their necks. Like the friars of medieval Europe they professed chastity and wandered through the countryside living on the charity of the credulous. The other group were called the "penitents." They were extreme fanatics who let their beards grow, practiced flagellation with *chicotes*—whips with brass studs fastened to the thongs; I was shown one of these later in Fortaleza—and wore leather belts peppered with tacks next to the skin.

This was the period when bandits controlled large areas of the *sertões*. The term "bandits" needs some definition, for they were at one and the same time ruthless robbers, symbols of a very real popular unrest, and on many occasions the allies of feuding "colonels," or politicians. Many of the bandits were also adherents of Padre Cícero. Joazeiro became one of their headquarters and the most notorious of their chiefs, Virgolino Ferreira da Silva, self-styled "King of the North" and popularly known as Lampeão ("The Lantern"), was lavishly entertained there by "the Messiah." At the same time feuding Cearense politicians secretly supplied him with funds and munitions.

With the encouragement of these powerful allies, in December 1913, Padre Cícero expelled the legal authorities from Joazeiro and proclaimed one of his henchmen governor of Ceará—and he in turn proclaimed Joazeiro the new capital of the state.

The official governor in Fortaleza dispatched an army against the rebels. When they arrived they found that fifty thousand of the Padre's followers, men, women and children, working day and night, had in a mere six days erected a rampart round Joazeiro three leagues in circumference, six feet in height, with sloping inner walls and loopholes for rifles and cannon.

Several expeditions of state troops were unable to penetrate it. Its defenders, convinced that their "messiah" had received divine assurance that all who fell in his cause would rise again in three days, fought like demons, and a "holy war" on his behalf developed, until eventually an army of his followers, augmented by thousands of bandits and vagabonds eager for plunder, marched to the outskirts of Fortaleza itself, sacking towns and villages in their path, sparing only churches and sacred images.

A new governor was eventually installed in Fortaleza, but the politicians who had backed the Padre were mistaken in their assumption that he would become their tool. According to some authorities, he was for some years "the most powerful man in Brazil," and until his death in 1934 he dominated the *sertões*. Before he died he was reconciled with the Church, and bequeathed a fortune to the Salesian order, on the condition that it should establish a school in Joazeiro.

The school has never been built, but there is a statue of Padre Cícero in the central *praça*, and pilgrims still pray before it and place flowers and religious relics.

The road became even worse, until I was convinced that we would have to turn back. Then, just as I was beginning to feel that my body could not tolerate another jolt we came to the top of a rise and there in the twilight below us was a miracle—a city of white buildings set among dark trees, so unexpected that it looked as beautiful as a miniature Mecca in the midst of the desert.

There was indeed an Arabian Nights unreality about the next few hours. We entered an avenue shaded by palm trees, and stopped in front of a handsome modern white house. I passed through a wrought-iron gate into a garden bathed in the light of flambeau-shaped lamps set at intervals on elegant standards. The floor of the porch was paved with jade-green tiles, the walls tessellated in the same color. I rang the bell; the heavy wooden door, decorated with diamonds of wrought-iron, opened. A manservant took my haversack. A housekeeper led me through a hall inlaid with Brazilian woods and dotted with basket chairs on iron frames and easy chairs of tubular steel, their seats and arms made of strips of rubber in green, blue and coral. I followed the housekeeper up a curving stone staircase with white-painted iron balustrades. She showed me into a bedroom. The apricot walls were soft with diffused lighting; Persian rugs lay on the parquet floor; the furniture was luxurious and modern; the vast bed, under its arched mosquito net, was covered with a silk bedspread.

The bathroom was equally luxurious. The water in the paneled porcelain bath was hot and scented. The Turkish towels were as thick as fleeces. By the time I returned to my bedroom the change of clothing I had brought in my haversack was laid out on a chair, the dirty clothes had been taken away, and my shoes shone like mirrors.

I dressed and made my way downstairs. The housekeeper was waiting for me in the hall. She explained that Dona Isabel was away at one of her ranches and was expecting me there the next day; in the meantime I was to treat her house as my home. I was conducted to the dining room, where I sat alone at the head of a long table. A meal of soup, steak, eggs, beans, vegetables, salad and chicken arrived. Two servants waited on me. I was offered wine or beer. I chose beer; it was ice-cold, and through the door leading to a kitchen which might have figured in an Ideal Home exhibition, I saw a refrigerator reaching almost to the ceiling. Every time I drank, my glass was refilled: I never seemed able to fit in a really long swig, and I began to fear the consequences of this method of drinking.

Two visitors joined me for coffee. They had been asked by Dona Isabel to see that I had everything I needed. One was a doctor, about thirty-five, charming and cultured, wearing a particularly fine short-sleeved embroidered shirt (in Brazil jackets are worn only on formal occasions). The other was a broad-shouldered, good-looking young man of about twenty-six, with a Roman nose and dreamy eyes, who had studied English in the United States. He was in business, he told me, with his father and brothers—they dealt in *mamona, oiticica* and cotton—but his passion was teaching, and for the next hour he talked about it with the kind of enthusiasm one associates with the educational idealists of a hundred years ago. It might have been the youthful Tolstoy in his pedagogic phase, and this semifeudal state with its extremes of poverty and wealth, its primitive hutments and its unexpected pockets of culture and luxury inevitably brought to mind the Russia of the late nineteenth century. Whenever I was with Maximiliano I had the feeling that I was in the company of one of those young idealists that people the pages of the Russian novelists. He made me, a teacher *manqué*, feel unutterably blasé; but before I knew what was happening I had allowed him, my fatigue forgotten, to drive me to a *Cultura Inglêsa* which he had organized in this unlikely spot, and I found myself giving an impromptu English lesson to a class of young men and women who had been thoroughly infected by his enthusiasm.

It was late when I returned to my luxurious bedroom. I opened the window and looked out. The white buildings shone in the tropical moon; the shrubs and palm trees in the garden threw long black shadows. I climbed into the bed, with its foam-rubber mattress and cool sheets. But I soon regretted opening the window: I had cause to remember that even the Cearenses speak of the Sobral mosquito with awe. My handsome net was no match for it.

When I came down the next morning I stepped into the garden for a breath of air. As I did so, two men who had been squatting on their haunches on the porch got up and disappeared round the corner of the house. Several others were lurking in the garden, and when I went to the gate I saw a whole row of them sitting on the pavement outside with their backs to the garden wall. Was Dona Isabel's house, I wondered, besieged by bandits? I hurried inside. "Who are all those men?" I asked the housekeeper. "Why," she replied, "they are Dona Isabel's people." Later, while I was eating my breakfast, I heard the sound of voices, and when I went to investigate I found that there was a second and larger kitchen, in which at least twenty of "Dona Isabel's people" sat eating and drinking.

Maximiliano had taken the next day off to accompany me to Dona Isabel's *fazenda*. A large estate wagon was waiting for us and we got in next to the driver. Two of Dona Isabel's retainers squeezed in beside us—riding with women just was not done—and Dona Isabel's cook, her personal maid and several other female dependents rode in the back. The maid, a plump girl of about twenty-five, pulled back the glass panel and begged the driver to hurry. She had a basket on her knees filled with various odds and ends which her mistress had left behind, and she kept lifting the cloth to check them, muttering and shaking her head.

A few hours later, after negotiating roads even more atrocious than those leading to Sobral, and after fording several streams, we entered the *fazenda*, drove past outbuildings, corrals, stables, bunkhouses and a cluster of palm-thatched huts, and at last drew up in front of a long, one-story ranch house with a veranda. An elderly woman stood on the porch. The maid scrambled out of the back of the van and ran ahead of us. She stopped in front of her mistress, scrutinized her carefully for a few moments, and then put her hand up to her mistress's hair and removed a bit of dried leaf. Dona Isabel bent her head, a quizzical smile at the corners of her mouth, and patted the maid's arm. The maid, her face glowing, ran up the steps and into the house. Then Dona Isabel turned and held out her hand. Her eyes were humorous and very shrewd. She was dressed in a faded black dress, the neck fastened by a safety pin.

While the cook, attended by a swarm of helpers, prepared lunch, Maximiliano and I set out for a swim in a nearby pool. One ferocious-looking retainer carried our towels, another a tray with various drinks, and a third was in reserve. I felt like a bandit chief surrounded by his bodyguard.

When we reached the pool a group of farmworkers with hoes and spades over their shoulders came hurrying over. As I undressed they kept up a running commentary upon the whiteness of my skin (though I had been proud of what I considered a very un-English tan) and the "golden color" of my hair. When I turned my back to pull on my bathing trunks they laughed in a pleased, gentle way. "The Englishman," they cried, "he has embarrassment!"

I climbed on top of the concrete dam and looked down. The water was a brownish-yellow color. I dived—and it was like plunging into warm tea. Even in the middle, where one could feel the current around one's ankles, it was not cool enough to refresh, and when I climbed out I felt sticky and languid.

One of the retainers stepped forward with a towel. It was hardly necessary: within a few seconds the sun had sucked up the drops of moisture from my skin. Another retainer poured whisky into glasses, and then to my astonishment took his long, broad-bladed knife from its sheath, cut open a coconut, and poured the milk on top of the whisky. It was, Maximiliano assured me, a great delicacy. I pretended to enjoy the sickly mixture.

Back in the ranch we sat down to a meal consisting of eggs—fried, scrambled, and mixed with black beans and cheese—chicken, fried and stewed, chunks of goat meat, and the very sweet sweet-meats for which the northeast is famous. The room was very simple, the plank walls whitewashed and hung with trade catalogues, family portraits, and photographs of horses and cattle. Dona Isabel talked about her travels in Europe with her late husband, about cattle and horses, and about the superstitions and traditions of the *vaqueiros* (or cowboys); she was well-informed, ironic and witty. Maximiliano launched into another enthusiastic description of the joys of teaching. A maid stood behind each of our chairs, plying us with food and filling our glasses. Dona Isabel's maid fanned her mistress with a fan made of woven palm leaves. A grizzled old man kept the dense cloud of flies at bay by waving a large leafy branch. Other retainers stood in the doorways and at the open windows, watching every swallow and every mouthful.

The *sesta,* too, was a public affair. It was taken in hammocks slung across the veranda, while women and children clustered on the steps. But the combined effects of an enervating swim, whisky and coconut milk and the huge meal had rendered me oblivious to scrutiny and I fell into a deep sleep.

I awoke to the chattering of excited voices and the barking of dogs. A group of horsemen was approaching. They stopped in front of Dona Isabel and raised their whips in salute. They were dressed from head to toe in leather: riding boots with big, clumsy spurs; trousers reaching to the thighs; a wide, studded belt giving the effect of a waistcoat or cummerbund; a kind of frock coat fastened high at the throat; and a curious hat, roughly triangular in shape—

each item blackened and worn but as hard as a board. Their small, shaggy and very skinny horses were also fitted out with leather on chest, knees and quarters. They looked like the stragglers from some medieval army, or a band of Don Quixotes mounted on their Rosinantes.

Their leader, an old man with a lined and weather-beaten face, each crease sprinkled with white, and eyes that had once been fierce but now merely twinkled, dismounted stiffly and climbed the veranda steps. He bowed to Dona Isabel and they talked for a few moments, eagerly and confidentially, like old friends; the old man's attitude was gentle and protective, as if he were addressing a young girl.

Horses were brought for Maximiliano and myself, and we followed the *vaqueiros* into the bush. I now saw the point of the leather clothing, for when the *vaqueiros* caught sight of a steer they charged full tilt through the clumps of *caatingas* jagged with thorns and spikes. Soon they had rounded up about a dozen steers. They drove them through the bush and into the open. Each man now chose a steer, galloped after it and then, leaning low in the saddle, seized it by the tail. With a sudden twist he threw the animal to the ground, leaped off his horse and as quick as lightning fixed the tips of one of the steer's horns into the ground or bound its eyes with a piece of cloth. The old man surpassed them all in speed and dexterity. Normally, I suppose, the steers would have been branded at this stage. On this occasion, after a perfunctory examination, they were released and allowed to run back into the bush; the exercise, I suspect, had been laid on for my benefit. But everybody enjoyed it. Old men, women and children came crowding out of their huts to cheer, dogs barked, the horses whinnied, and the *vaqueiros* themselves yelled until they were hoarse.

Later, Maximiliano and I went riding with the old *vaqueiro*. For several hours we wound our way along the courses of streams (which in time of drought disappear completely), up and down thickly wooded slopes and through the tangled masses of spiky vegetation. Red, furry butterflies, as big as bats, brushed our faces, strange birds darted out of the undergrowth, and once my horse shied and looking back I saw a snake with beautiful zigzag stripes, which the old *vaqueiro* called a *coral;* it was, he told me, one of the deadliest in Brazil.

He spoke of his life on the *sertões*. He had seen some terrible *sêcas*, he said; many of his friends had lost their lives, but, heaven be praised, he had had a good master and he and his family had never starved. There were tears in his eyes when he spoke of "the Colonel." "He was the champion of the poor," he cried. "I would have done anything for him. *Senhor*, he needed only to say to me, 'That man is my enemy,' and I would have killed him!"

He tapped the knife in his belt. Then the light faded from his eyes. "There were many bandits in those days," he muttered. Again I had the feeling of being in touch with a vanished piece of history, a way of life with values and loyalties utterly unfamiliar to me. Two hundred years ago perhaps there were clansmen in the Scottish Highlands who would have understood.

Back in Sobral I watched Dona Isabel hold court in her study, listening to complaints, settling disputes, doling out charity. Then she drove me round the town in the big, heavy wagon. Beyond the residential belt, and by daylight, the town was hardly the magical place it had seemed on my first arrival. There was, it is true, a well-kept *praça*, and trees with feathery foliage and rows of cactuses were planted along the center of the main street. There were schools, a seminary, a modern hospital, a home for destitute old people, churches ("too many," Dona Isabel commented) and, inevitably, a club with fine swimming pool and ballroom, but also the usual squalor, the usual smells, the usual potholes in the roads. Strings of donkeys were loaded with small round barrels, like brandy kegs. They contained water for sale: even in a wet season water was a precious commodity.

Dona Isabel made no attempt to hide the ugly facts. She pointed out deficiencies, made caustic comments about "crooked politicians," and took me into several of the ramshackle huts. In most of them women and children were hard at work weaving straw hats from the long narrow leaves of the *carnaúba* tree. In one of them Dona Isabel borrowed the razor-sharp knife and demonstrated, with great speed and dexterity, how the leaves are split to make the strands of straw. The woman of the house, her mother, and three daughters ranging from ten to six, watched and applauded. The woman told me that she was able to make three or four straw hats a day: her mother and the girls managed an average of two each. They were paid twenty cruzeiros a hat—about sixpence.

Several naked children, too young to help and covered with flies, squatted on the mud floor. A baby girl of about six months, with a pretty oval face and big solemn eyes, had suffered some accident at birth and her navel protruded like a large pear. Dona Isabel patted it with her hand and sharply (and in clinical detail) questioned the mother as to how the deformity had taken place. The woman accepted the scolding with a good-natured shrug.

Straw hats, as well as baskets, handbags and other articles, were also made in a small factory. The manager, who showed me over, told me that these were exported all over Brazil, and even to Europe. Here the girls worked an eight-hour day, earning the equivalent of two shillings to half a crown. There were, too, factories for preparing *oiticica* and *mamona*. Huge circular piles of them, shaped like gas containers and covered with tarpaulins, stood in the yards. There was a railway, but the tracks were practically hidden by weeds, and goats and pigs grazed between them. Most of the produce was carried by lorries, and in view of the state of the roads between Sobral and Fortaleza, much of it was taken to the small port of Camocim to the north.

On the journey back to Fortaleza the *serra* seemed even more beautiful, with its bare crags and its tall cactuses with their scarecrow arms, and a gray sky like a battleship. Pigs, goats, horses, donkeys and cows wandered along the roadway. As it grew darker these became more dangerous—and more mysterious. A donkey would suddenly appear in the headlights, his coat transfigured, silvery, like a model in a Christmas tableau. Cows would loom up unexpectedly, regarding us out of eyes like golden pools as we skidded and swerved to avoid them. A mare stood in the middle of the road, giving suck. And all the time swarms of insects streamed and glittered like flak.

Soon we were passing lines of workers trailing homeward in their tattered straw hats with their hoes and spades across their shoulders. They included boys no more than ten years old. There are laws about the employment of children and education acts on the statute books, but like so many others they mean little in practice.

Then the workers were home and had changed into clean clothes and were sitting outside their huts while their womenfolk bent over their sewing by the light of candles placed on upturned boxes. As it grew darker these twinkling lights sprang up all around us. Candles or oil lamps were lit, too, inside the huts, until even they took on the warmth and magic of home.

Gradually the road emptied of traffic; the long-distance lorries drew into the side and the crews lit campfires beside them. At last our jeep was in sole occupation—except for the cattle. They had bedded down for the night and our progress was reduced to a crawl. Then at last the lights of the roadside bar streamed out to meet us. The fat proprietress welcomed us with gusts of laughter. The habitués shook hands. The boy was playing his concertina and the warm darkness vibrated with the wild and poignant songs of the *sertões*.

6

RECIFE TO RIO

If I had been compiling a guidebook instead of sending my eyes, like those of a snail, along the winding track of accident, I would have chosen not Fortaleza, but Recife and Salvador (or Bahia) as my representative cities of the northeast. They are more important economically, and much more up to date. But accident intervened—in the form of a lobster Thermidor which I ate on my last evening in Fortaleza. I had not been more than a few hours in Recife—time enough to feel intimidated by the clanging of streetcars and the pedestrians scuttering to and fro to the winking of traffic lights, by the towering skyscrapers with the long queues waiting for their lifts—before I began to feel sick and dizzy.

When eventually the doctor arrived, he was a crushed-looking little man in down-at-heel shoes and a suit made of sailcloth so stiff that I could imagine him climbing in and out of it as with a space capsule. He diagnosed food poisoning, took the necessary steps, gave me a pill, and departed.

When I began to recover, the main difficulty was diet. Fortunately, I discovered the merits of *maracujá* juice, and quite unexpectedly a Brazilian newspaperman whom I had met in London years before and who had somehow discovered that I was in Recife arrived on the scene, took charge of my diet—and inevitably talked politics. He believed that Jânio Quadros, the president who had resigned so dramatically and unexpectedly a few years before, had represented a "last chance" for Brazil and that corruption had worsened everywhere since. "Fidelismo," he said, had many supporters in the northeast; to them Castro was the only politician in the Latin-American world who had shown that he understood the basic economic difficulties, and who had taken decisive action to combat them. When I murmured the word "Communism," he shrugged his shoulders.

"When things are as bad as they are," he replied, "the label's irrelevant. The word 'Communist' doesn't mean much here. A lot of good Catholics call themselves 'Communists,' and plenty of crooked businessmen and politicians with fortunes salted away in the Swiss banks use the same label, because they think Communism might be a good band wagon to jump on. What counts here is the program, and the honesty of the people who are carrying it out. Whatever his faults Castro *is* honest and sincere."

He himself was a follower of Francisco Julião, the moving spirit behind the Ligas Camponêsas (Land Leagues) of the northeast. The word "revolution" had no terrors for him. "We are used to it in Recife," he said. "We have been in the forefront of practically every revolutionary movement in Brazil's history. We were the first city in South America where a General Assembly was held, the first city in Brazil—over two hundred and fifty years ago—to advocate a republic. We were the first city to win our freedom from Portugal—some months before the rest of Brazil. In 1911 we threw the government out. And it was from here that the revolutionary troops marched on Rio de Janeiro in 1930."

"And you think history will repeat itself?"

"I think there is going to be a revolution, and I think it will start in the northeast—in Recife."*

Eventually the little doctor told me I could get up. As he was

---

* As it turned out he was wrong—and the revolution when it came was of a very different kind. It remains to be seen whether his miscalculation was a lasting one. G.P.

packing his bag I asked what I owed him. He whispered an astronomic fee, glanced at me quickly, and quartered his figure. "We have no National Health Service here," he muttered as I paid him.

"Recife" is the Portuguese word for "reef," and the city is not in fact on the mainland, but is built over an undersea barrier reef on a number of islands and peninsulas linked by bridges. The nickname "Venice of Brazil" is an exaggeration, but parts of the city were remarkably reminiscent of Copenhagen, while the road facing my hotel, with its row of stalls on the pavement with their green canvas sides, even possessed a touch of Paris; but instead of books and prints, they sold miniature *jangadas,* tiny leather replicas of the saddles and hats of the cowboys of the *sertões,* and clay figurines, full of humor and character, forming a portrait gallery of regional types as vivid as Cruikshank's illustrations for Dickens. They included a figurine of Padre Cícero's ally, the bandit Lampeão.

To the northeast, Lampeão is a combination of Ned Kelly, Dick Turpin and Robin Hood. It was as a Robin Hood that he envisaged himself, claiming that he robbed and killed in order to avenge the murder of his brother by the police and the exploitation of the poor by "crooked politicians." His troops or *cangaceiros,* dressed in leather, well-armed and disciplined, terrorized the *sertões* for twenty years, and by 1926 they were attacking and occupying many of the towns. Sometimes they would descend without warning. Sometimes Lampeão would send a telegram to announce his intention so that the rich could evacuate their properties and avoid bloodshed. One town prepared a huge *churrasco,* or barbecue, for his entertainment; this saved it from pillage, but Lampeão exacted lavish tribute from the merchants and bestowed equally lavish alms upon the poor. A few years later he was "advising" a number of mayors, giving interviews to the press on his ideas of government, and threatening to march on the capitals of the northeastern states in order to "straighten out certain governors," and it was not until 1938 that the authorities succeeded in disposing of him.

There was a revival of interest in Lampeão as the result of the Brazilian film *Os Cangaceiros* based upon his exploits. As far away as Belo Horizonte in the state of Minas Gerais I came upon a van containing a "Lampeão exhibition." It contained a number of photographs of Lampeão, of his family, and of the woman with whom he lived, herself a kind of "Annie-get-your-gun" bandit, and a remarkably lifelike wax model of "Lampeão." He stood there, six feet in height, powerful of build, dressed in leather trousers and jacket, with bandoleers across his chest (which in life never contained less than ninety pounds of cartridges); a rifle was slung over one shoulder; his belt was stuffed with knives, a sword and two revolvers; about his forehead, below a leather hat with the front brim pinned back, was a double band of golden sovereigns; on his left hand he wore a ring with a huge ruby; at his throat hung a cross of diamonds and tightly rolled scrolls of paper prayers, which, he had believed, would bestow upon him a *corpo fechado* ("closed body"), immune to the bullets of his enemies. He had been blind in one eye, and the waxwork effigy has captured its fixity; both eyes were large and almost colorless, and the effect of cold ferocity was heightened by rimless spectacles.

The harbor of Recife (sailors usually call it Pernambuco, after the name of the state) was a very different affair from the whimsical improvisation of Fortaleza. It could accommodate ships drawing up to thirty feet, there were seventeen piers, and the equipment was among the most efficient and up-to-date in South America. It is also the closest port to the European continent, and through it flows nearly all the sugar, cotton, coffee, and tropical fruits of northeastern Brazil.

The general pattern of an increase in the civilities of life as one traveled south maintained itself. There were miles of "superior" avenues in the suburbs, with fine gardens behind wrought-iron gates and expensive skyscraper flats close to the center of the city. There were smart dress shops and *boutiques,* and there were jewelers specializing in the gems of Minas Gerais.

There are many relics of the Dutch occupation (which lasted until 1654), particularly of the seven-year governorship of Maurice of Nassau (later Prince of Orange), who landed in 1637 with a brilliant entourage, including painters, a botanist, a naturalist, a poet, and an architect who was set to replanning the town. Most of the sixty-odd churches, lavish with wood carvings, belong to the seventeenth century, and one which I visited, Espírito Santo, had served as a Calvinist church during the occupation. Some miles outside Recife I saw a plaque inside one of the churches to commemorate "the heroes of the first Battle of Guararapes," where the Brazilians had defeated the Dutch, an occasion annually re-enacted in pageant. The churches of Olinda, the old capital of the state— very beautiful with its narrow, winding streets, perched on a hillside among coconut-palms and banana trees and overlooking a vivid blue segment of the Atlantic—are limpid with blue-and-white Dutch tiles. And in the little riverside village of Igarassu (which contains Brazil's oldest church, built in 1535) I saw an old Dutch house, converted into a museum which contained a collection of Dutch muskets, cannon balls and coins, and a print of Admiral Henry Cornell Lonck, who had captured Recife and Olinda in 1630.

Most of what I knew about the history of Pernambuco I had learned from the writings of Gilberto Freyre. I visited him in his beautiful colonial house on the outskirts of Recife, set among trees and shrubs, with balconies, verandas and balustrades, massive urns trailing creeper and blossom, the walls inside and out decorated with Dutch and Portuguese tiles.

The house was filled with relics of the period of the sugar barons. In the study (which was lined with books in calf bindings, among them the best collection perhaps in existence of the works of eighteenth- and nineteenth-century European travelers in Brazil), I sat on one of a set of huge armchairs of jacaranda, the backs and seats of Singapore cane, the arms and legs elaborate with carvings of Brazilian fruits, animals and birds. My host caressed them lovingly; he spoke enthusiastically of "the native tradition" and the need for modern Brazilian artists to return to it. He talked about the old sugar plantations with their traditional pattern of mill, church, *senzala* (slave quarters) and the *casa grande* itself, part fortress and part manor house, with its gigantic salons and kitchens, its private chapel, and its innumerable rooms which housed the vast families, the poor relations, the hangers-on and the numerous guests. The sugar barons (many of whom were ennobled in fact by the Brazilian emperors) often ruled over properties bigger than the kingdoms of Europe; they established a culture unequaled in the rest of Brazil and similar in many respects (including, of course, the economic basis of slavery) to that of the nineteenth-century Russian manor or of the plantation house of the Southern states of America before the Civil War. The wealth derived from sugar provided all kinds of luxuries—damasks, satins, brocades; rubies, diamonds and emeralds; furniture from famous European workshops and from native craftsmen (such as the chairs we were seated on at that moment); porcelains from Goa and Macao; crystals, silverware, gold plate; and books, paintings and musical instruments. It was not a matter of mere ostentation as with the *nouveaux riches* barons of the rubber boom; a genuine aristocratic tradition emerged, and it produced, in addition to much cruelty and vice, many of Brazil's best administrators, jurists, essayists, novelists, poets and musicians.

It is Gilberto Freyre's view that this culture owed many of its characteristics to the Negro slaves. These were imported not only as laborers in the fields and mills and as "house serfs," but as mining experts, herdsmen, metal and leather workers, manufacturers of textiles, soap and other products, as barbers and bleeders, and as musicians and entertainers. Most of the slaves in the northeast were Mohammedans, and among them were teachers, preachers and prayer leaders who could read and write Arabic. Some Brazilian historians have argued that the rising of the slaves in Bahia in 1835 was as much the rebellion of a superior culture against the domination of an inferior as a revolt of slave against master.

Although the record of the slaveowners of northeastern Brazil was no better, as far as oppression and cruelty were concerned, than that of their counterparts in the Southern states of America, there were important differences in the relationship between master and slave. Because of the lack of white women a Negro woman would often become the *dona da casa*. The children of a *senhor* by his slave mistresses were in many cases treated as full members of the family, eating at the same table as the legitimate children, and in the more cultured households, sharing the same tutors. Usually they would be provided for in the master's will, or at least they and their mothers would be granted their freedoms. As on the old plantations of the Southern states, Negro women were the wet nurses and nannies and frequently trusted assistants and housekeepers. The black *tia* (aunt) occupied an honored position in the *casa grande,* and was treated by the slaves with the same respect and obedience as the *senhora* herself. When old and trusted slaves died, they were buried with the same rites and solemnities as members of the family. The consequence of all this was that antagonism between white and black was, on the whole, less severe than in the Southern states of America, and there is no overt color bar in Brazil today.

The decay of this aristocratic culture was set in motion by the discovery of beet sugar and by the abolition of slavery. It followed a pattern remarkably similar to that in the Southern states of America after the Civil War. The more enterprising of the sugar barons got out while the going was good, emigrating to the coastal capitals and playing a vital part in their rapid expansion. The majority stayed on, but, deprived of slave labor, they could no longer cultivate their vast properties. As in Georgia, they were gradually forced to rent or sell larger and larger tracts of land. The new tenants and owners were themselves for the most part ousted by the new *usinas* (factories), which employed the traditional land-grabbing methods, including intimidation by armed bands of bandits. The *casas grandes,* like the mansions of the old plantations of the South, gradually fell into decay and their owners lapsed into much the same kind of decadence.

I visited one of these *usinas,* passing through mile after mile of young sugar cane—like English meadow grass in June, but the green a little paler. Scrollwork above wrought-iron gates announced the name of the *usina*—that of the *casa grande* it had replaced. The employees lived on the site; the managers in smart, well-built bungalows, the workers in tumble-down outhouses.

In the factory yard, dried sugar canes, as lifeless-looking as sticks of firewood, were shoveled into crushing machines: the cracking and splintering of the sticks made as much noise as the clatter of the cogwheels.

The foreman, a gentle old man with a lame foot (he had caught it in one of the machines when he was a young man), took me up a series of narrow ladders and through a bewildering network of galleries and monkey-walks festooned with scalding pipes. Down in the entrails, men were clearing the bits of stalk from various cogwheels; others, with oil cans in their hands, lay on top of hissing engines and boilers. The miracle was that behind the portholes of the boilers liquid sugar leaped and bubbled, while fifty yards farther on it was as granulated sugar that it came pouring out of the funnels. It was shoveled into sacks, and the sacks were sealed and stamped with the name of the *usina*. A stream of men, stripped to the waist, their bodies glistening with sweat and dappled with white sugary patches, were heaving the sacks onto their shoulders, setting them against the napes of their necks, then trotting and staggering to the waiting lorries. The old foreman was at pains to reassure me that nowadays the *usinas* were state-subsidized and state-inspected. In the old days they had been even more ruthless employers than the slaveowners. He had some scarifying tales, handed down from his grandfather, of the bands of *cabras* (men of mixed Negro and Indian blood with a small admixture of white) employed by the *usinas* in their attacks on the plantations and by the surviving "sugar gentry" in their attempts to protect them.

In Bahia (or Salvador), the most beautiful city in Brazil, the heat was drier, the light clearer. The airport had the air of being on the edge of carnival—which was probably true, for Bahia has an almost continuous succession of religious and popular festivals as well as an annual carnival, frowned upon by the authorities because of its blatantly pagan character. The airport lounge was crammed with kiosks selling bangles, earrings, necklaces made of dried beans, and black dolls dressed in Bahian costume—miniature replicas of the statuesque Negro women who stalked about with baskets on their arms. The costume consisted of a vast tentlike skirt in brilliant colors rolled over an array of heavily weighted petticoats, a low-cut white blouse with short, puffed-out sleeves, over which is thrown a multicolored silk shawl with a long, glittering fringe, a bandana on the head, and a battery of heavy gold rings, bracelets and charms. The baskets contained souvenirs and various Bahian delicacies, including *abará*—a savory cake made of black beans smothered in a peppery sauce, palm oil and shrimps and wrapped in banana leaves—and various *doces* (sweets) made of honey, sugar and *goiabada* paste. But the *turismo* had a gay, relaxed air about it. My Negro taxi driver laughed uproariously and threw his cab about as if we were on a Dodgem track as he drove me from the airport, through colonnades of bamboos arched overhead, through avenues of wilting coconut palms and banana trees, and tracts of blackened and still smoldering undergrowth (there was a *sêca* both in Pernambuco and Salvador) past dazzlingly white bungalows and houses, with every now and then glimpses of palm-fringed beaches, some of them with shanty towns built almost to the surf line.

Salvador is built on what is virtually a cliff face, and is divided into two halves. My hotel was in the Upper City. It was square and white and ultramodern; outside, shaded by palm trees, were scattered white-painted iron chairs and tables, curly and fluted. In the entrance hall was a long curved reception desk in strips of multi-shaded Brazilian woods. The ceiling was of midnight blue, and a whole wall was devoted to a rising-sun motif in brilliant yellows and ochers. On the first floor was a lounge with a huge curving window, a bar at one end and clusters of chairs and tables islanded among bamboo screens, potted palms, and parrots and cockatoos in cages shaped like Chinese lanterns. The cuisine was famous for its Bahian dishes, lavish with palm oil and spices; and the waitresses wore Bahian costume.

In the *praça* facing the hotel I saw my first buttress-root tree (which the early naturalists loved to describe), rising on exposed, spreading roots arched so high that a man could walk under them, like a castle on top of its vaults. As the long twilight deepened, from roots and branches alike, outsize bats emerged with a flapping like that of wild ducks. A Negro woman crossed the *praça*, balancing on her haunches, carrying a huge bundle of washing on her head. A group of Negro youths, their beardless faces smooth as grape-skins, lounged against a palm tree, whistling to passing girls, who flashed smiles and twirled their skirts.

The lines of the old colonial houses, with their curved eaves, frilled cornices, and wrought-iron grilles disclosing colonnaded gardens, seemed in perpetual motion like the waving of branches or the flowing of water. Blank walls, where buildings had been pulled down, were exuberantly frescoed. The walls of cafés, bars, and night clubs were populated with *bandeirantes*, Negro dancers, gods and demons, mules, donkeys and green and yellow fruits on scarlet backgrounds. The flamboyant modern buildings blended perfectly with the old colonial ones and with the setting of bamboo, palm, mango and cactus. The Teatro Castro Alves, for example, was like a white cliff molded by the sea. And outside it was a fantastic giant figure, gaunt, bearded, the feet clumsy, earth-clogged, the arms raised in a travesty of crucifixion, or like those of a tortured spirit striving to haunt its tormentors. It is the work of Mário Cravo, a sculptor of Yugoslav origin. The subject is Antônio Vicente Mendes Maciel, better known as Antônio Conselheiro ("Coun-selor"), another of the strange, fanatical products of the *sertões*. As a child, Antônio had lost his father in one of the interminable clan feuds of Ceará. As a young man, according to one of the legends, his wife had been raped by an official, and after shooting her and her seducer he had taken refuge in the *sertões*.

Another version has it that his mother, hating her daughter-in-law, told her son that his wife was unfaithful and persuaded him to return home unexpectedly one night: when he did so he saw a dark figure lurking near the window, fired at it and then, enter-ing the house, shot his wife as she lay sleeping—to discover afterward that the figure outside had been his mother and that he had killed her too. What is certain is that he was ultimately arrested for double murder, but released for lack of evidence. This, however, was after Antônio had spent fifteen years in penitence and self-mortification, during which he had emerged as a kind of Savonarola of the *sertões*, preaching that suffering and sorrow are the only paths to salvation, and prophesying that the world would come to an end in the year 1899. His release by the police was accounted another miracle, and his following grew rapidly. When he traveled in the *sertões* the inhabitants, carrying crosses and banners, flocked to meet him. When he rested in the shadow of a tree on the outskirts of one town, it was credited with magical properties, and its leaves were collected as an infallible remedy for every distress of body and mind. When the church of a priest who had dared criticize him collapsed, the Almighty Himself was supposed to have intervened.

He began to dabble in politics, announcing his hostility to the new republic and receiving the secret backing of disgruntled politicians and of those who provided arms to both sides, eventually leading his followers to Canudos in the state of Bahia, an old cattle ranch which he transformed into a fortified holy city, which was, he declared, a steppingstone toward heaven itself. His followers, or *jagunços* (another of the words applied to the outlaws of the *sertões*), attacked settlements, villages and towns. Successive government expeditions were defeated, and it was not until 1893 that Canudos was captured and Antônio Conselheiro and most of his followers killed.

But the grotesque statue seemed quite out of place in modern Bahia among the strings of colored lights in the *praças* and the sounds of Bohemian parties in the high-ceilinged rooms of colonial houses, converted into studios, their walls vivid with modernistic paintings. It seemed even more incongruous when I passed it the next morning in sunshine so brilliant that one could not bear to look at the white walls, on my way to the university, where I was to lecture on (of all things) Virginia Woolf.

Like most Brazilian universities, its public face was impressive: there were fine staircases, lecture rooms and assembly halls, but libraries, study rooms and laboratories were crowded and inadequate. Most of the professors and lecturers had to supplement their stipends by teaching in the high schools; it was hardly surprising that they complained that they had no time for research.

They complained, too, of intimidation by the nucleus of Communist-inspired students, and before my second lecture a deputation of very embarrassed young men and women came to me to explain that their union—which was dominated by this nucleus—had banned all lectures. As I left the university buildings a young man caught up with me, and introduced himself as a member of the students' union committee, deputed to convey their apologies. They had decided to strike, he explained, because the university authorities had just appointed a professor of history of whom they disapproved on academic and ideological grounds. Their own nominee, paradoxically, was a Jesuit priest.

Freed from my lecture, I made my way down the steep, cobbled streets called *ladeiras* ("ladders")—there are also two lifts—to the Lower City, past strings of donkeys led by Negroes in wide-brimmed straw hats and striped cotton suits like pajamas, groups of nuns in habits of black or white, and young seminarians in round black hats and ankle-length coats. Bahia is known as the "city of churches," and at least twelve churches are outstanding examples of baroque architecture. The cathedral, for example, built of Lisbon marble, has a sumptuous high altar, sculptured and gilded by João Correia, and the most beautiful sacristy in South America; and the Church and Convent do Destêrro has a two-hundred-years-old silver tabernacle and a gold and jeweled "Sun of the Holy Sacrament" made by the goldsmith Boaventura de Andrade. The presence of these works of art by some of the greatest of the Portuguese and Brazilian craftsmen gives Bahia something of the feel of Florence. The *solares,* or private palaces, of the old Bahian aristocrats—such as the Solar do Saldanha (now a college) built by the Guedes de Brito family, with its fine eighteenth-century door of sculptured stone; the seventeenth-century Solar do Sodré, where Castro Alves, the poet, died; the mansion of the Calmon family which contains a collection of European and Oriental china, fans and antique furniture—reinforced the impression.

The Lower City was a maze of crowded streets, jammed with traffic, flanked by vast modern commercial buildings and banks and warehouses crammed with cacao, tobacco, piassava fiber, castor-oil nuts, coffee and sugar. In the harbor, two or three miles offshore, was an old circular fort, with two palms, almost identical, sprouting from its center, looking like a set for a *Beau Geste* film. The bay was breath-taking—thirty miles square and one hundred and eighty-two miles in circumference, dotted with red and white sails, enclosed by low wooded hills and streaked with as many shades of blue as the sea at Barbados. The full name is Bahia de Todos os Santos (All Saints' Bay) which was conferred upon it by Amerigo Vespucci when, under the flag of Manuel I of Portugal, he first cast anchor there on All Saints' Day, November 1, 1501. The city itself was founded in 1549 as the first capital of the colony of Brazil; and it is still regarded as the cultural capital. The original name of the city and of the state was Salvador. Officially it is still the approved name, but the citizens prefer to call themselves *Bahianos*, people of the bay.

What I was looking for, however, was information about the *candomblés*—religious ceremonies evolved by the Negro slaves who had been forcibly converted to Christianity, and containing a fusion of Christian, totemic and fetishistic elements. But these follow a strict calendar of their own, only partly related to that of the Church, and there were no "sacred days" for some time. But a Negro taxi driver told me of a *capoeira* meeting, speaking of it in the same breath as a religious cult and as a "method of fighting with the feet" which had once been tremendously popular, with public contests and championships, but which was now apparently banned by the authorities—except in "the safe form" practiced in Vicente Pastinha's Academy.

That evening I set out to find it and, after a long search through a warren of alleyways, came upon a rickety stairway leading to a long, low-ceilinged room with bare floorboards. A group of young men were lounging about in the center of the room. A cloth of yellow and black, crudely embroidered with odd-looking musical instruments and figures locked in combat, was pinned against one of the walls. In front of it, on a wooden bench, sat several young Negroes, one old one with high cheekbones, white eyebrows and a bald head ridged and veined like one of those model craniums you see outside a phrenologist's booth, and one white youth of about twenty with soft brown eyes. They were holding instruments similar to those depicted on the back cloth—curved bows decorated with yellow and black ribbons, tambourines, gourds filled with dried nuts or leaves, drums, and curious funnel-shaped iron prongs.

Wooden benches were ranged round the walls. On one sat a row of wide-eyed pickaninnies. A handful of spectators was scattered among the others, most of them black (about fifty per cent of the inhabitants of Bahia are Negroes—a far higher proportion than anywhere else in Brazil). Placed to one side were a few straight-backed chairs, on which sat a party consisting of several well-dressed white men and women, and a large, bland Japanese in a pin-stripe suit. They were talking with a little old man with a brown face, thin white hair and a white handlebar mustache, dressed in a singlet and a pair of grubby linen trousers fastened at the ankles by bicycle clips.

Hanging on the walls were a number of framed photographs, yellow and faded, showing groups of spectators in frock coats and top hats surrounding pairs of men dressed in what looked like long woolen pants, facing each other warily or caught in various gyrations, legs flying. The feet were shod in heavy iron-tipped boots: it was evident why *capoeira* in its original form was regarded by the authorities as a dangerous sport. There was also a series of paintings in grays, greens, blacks and yellows, depicting the various positions and maneuvers, the black figures stunted and out of proportion, the backgrounds of palm trees and turreted castles crude and childlike, but with a kind of wistful, Douanier Rousseau quality. Pictures of melodramatic villains carrying knives, clubs and revolvers, being astounded and discomfited by the flying feet of *capoeira* adepts, were painted on posters and embroidered on strips of cloth. The captions extolled the virtues of *capoeira;* surely, they demanded, this "ancient sport practiced by our forefathers," this "more-than-sport," this "training of body and mind," this "unsurpassed method of self-defense which inculcates the highest moral qualities" and which "is one of the glories of our Bahia, our Brazil," must not be allowed to fall into disuse? In the corners of paintings and posters alike, the words "Vicente Pastinha" were inscribed in laborious capitals.

As I was studying one of them the little master himself came over. "You must not think," he said, with an anxious glance in the direction of the Japanese, "that *capoeira* is merely an imitation of judo. I have explained to the Japanese consul over there—he is a judo 'black belt'—that any similarities are quite accidental. *capoeira* is purely African: the slaves brought it to Bahia many, many years ago." He looked at me quickly. His mustache seemed to droop; in his eyes was the hurt, sad look of the devotee of a dying craft.

"Of course," he said wistfully, "we can't show you *capoeira* as it *used* to be. But you will see." He clapped his hands and two young men in singlets, their feet bare, looking rather sheepish, stepped forward. I found a vacant chair near the Japanese. The rest of his party were members of the Swedish and Norwegian consulates; they looked bored and skeptical. In the chair on my right was a plump middle-aged man with eyes for nothing but the pale-faced youth in the orchestra.

The two young men bowed formally, then began to circle each other. The orchestra struck up; the bows were banged with sticks, the funnellike instruments were struck with small iron bars. The pale-faced young man was operating one of these. "He is a folklorist from the state university at Rio: he's writing a thesis on the music of Bahia," his plump friend informed me. The instruments, rhythms and arrangements, he explained, were traditional to *capoeira* and had much in common with those of the *candomblé.*

The contestants were now circling round more rapidly, making sudden feints and flourishes with their legs, every now and then standing on their hands and flashing their heels like a pair of horses. The movements were strictly formalized and more like dance steps than serious attacks. They were not very well executed and there was a good deal of aimless hopping and shuffling. I began to feel sorry for little Senhor Pastinha.

But suddenly the music took on a more urgent beat, and the master himself stepped into the center of the room, bowing to the scattered applause from his pupils and from his fans on the benches. He beckoned to a Negro who had not yet taken part in the performance. "This," he said, turning to us, "is my most promising pupil." The pupil overtopped him by a good eighteen inches. They made their formal obeisances and began their circling movements. At first it was quiet enough, but a new purpose and a new grace had entered into the proceedings. The maneuvers became more complex and subtle. A whole series of attacks and counterattacks was demonstrated: these stopped short at actual throws, but the potentially deadly nature of some of them—if one envisaged the heavy steel-tipped boots—became apparent. The chattering in my part of the room stopped. The Japanese judo expert began to look interested.

So far the tall Negro had appeared to be having the best of it. But now Vicente Pastinha exploded into action; his little body wheeled and cavorted like a lighted Catherine wheel. His opponent was quick and skillful, and he did his best to keep up with him, but soon he was made to look a clumsy amateur. Time after time the old man tripped or threw him, catching him and lowering him gently to the ground before he came to harm, or trapped him in a lock betweeen ankles, knees or thighs, turning toward the audience to pat joint or muscle in order to demonstrate how easily he could have tightened the hold, or described a series of cartwheels round his bewildered opponent, or darted, swift as a lizard, between his legs. For a good thirty minutes it continued, while the music beat faster and faster, until at last the tall Negro, gasping and sweating, shook his head ruefully and stood back. The music stopped; everybody clapped and cheered; pupil and master embraced. The old man turned to the audience and gave a courtly little bow, then he stood upright, head up, shoulders back, and twirled the ends of his white mustache. His eyes shone.

The Japanese hurried forward and shook his hand. Senhor Pastinha fetched a manuscript book filled with black silhouette drawings of the moves and countermoves, each carefully and lovingly annotated. He produced another book and asked us to sign our names, then he shook hands and escorted us toward the door. It was only when we reached it that one of the pupils succeeded in attracting his attention and indicated the upturned tambourine he was carrying. The old man looked at it with distaste. He turned aside while his pupil passed it round for our contributions.

Rio de Janeiro at last. Everything was moving, changing, flowing. The trams clanged louder and lurched more dizzily than anywhere else in the world. The stream of ultramodern cars raced along highways that looked as if they had only been finished yesterday; and mounds of yellow earth stood near by, where entirely new roads were in the process of construction. Whole hills had been flattened or hurled aside to make way for them, with such speed that their shadows still seemed to haunt the places. Another hill had been hollowed out to make the Botafogo tunnel, linking the center of Rio and Copacabana, magical by day and night with its constellation of lamps, flush with the vaulted roof, and the cars and lorries thundering through at breakneck speed. I had nightmares of being involved in a breakdown in that tunnel; but once, when a friend was driving me through at eighty miles an hour, a tire burst, and he quite calmly proceeded to change the wheel. A Negro free-lance mechanic, in dungarees, the pockets bulging with tools, appeared as if out of the bowels of the earth and offered his assistance. I stood on the narrow sidewalk, flattened against the curving wall, deafened and battered by the roar of the traffic.

Buildings grew obsolescent as one looked at them. Those of ten years' standing already had the air of ancient monuments; five years imparted the patina of maturity; new ones swarmed with life before the mortar was dry. One had the feeling of a population rushing from one building to another, as if in retreat before an advancing army. The skyscraper hotels of Copacabana ringed the bay like segmented white cliffs, so close to the beach that they seemed to receive the spray of the surf; suddenly glimpsed on a dark night, they looked like an array of grumbling, hovering ghosts. But even these became dated almost as I watched. I visited one famous hotel still resplendent with marble floors, deep carpets and massive chandeliers, but the long sun-bathing chairs round the swimming pool, which—if the photographs I had seen just before leaving England were anything to go by—had recently been occupied by the internationally famous and beautiful, were now mostly empty.

My own hotel, it is true, was brand-new, magnificent with wood paneling, stone stairways, and purple tiles, standing one block back from the bay, but rising above its front-rank neighbors to survey its whole fantastic expanse. But the gleaming rind of Copacabana was a thin one. The street in which the hotel stood was close to being a back street; twice a week it became a market, a kind of Petticoat Lane, crammed with stalls so that the debris of fruits and vegetables drifted into the foyer, to the horror of the commissionaires in their coffee-and-chocolate uniforms. Near by were scores of small shops and cafés and rows of newspaper kiosks, dusty and bedraggled *praças,* narrow pavements tessellated in tiny black and white chips, dirty and crumbling. The gutters and the circles round each ornamental tree were piled with mud and refuse, and many of the apartment houses went without water for months at a time.

Some of the most palatial hotels, too, lacked water. The sky-scrapers have shot up and the concrete and asphalt have come pouring out of the old city like a stream of lava (only thirty years ago Copacabana was a desolate stretch of barren sand; today it has a population of almost half a million), but the facilities linking the two have never caught up. There are places in downtown Rio where the wooden water pipes of colonial days are still in use. In Copacabana, though, the swimming pools are kept full, the fountains go on playing, and the taps work. At first I was puzzled when late at night I came across tankers outside the big hotels with hoses like anacondas stretching across the pavements, until I realized it wasn't petrol that was being pumped through them but water.

At night, as I sat on the terraces of the hotels or restaurants on the Avenida Atlântica, under striped umbrellas on poles with gilded spear tips, the shoeshine boys came swarming, so that I half imagined I was back in São Luís or Fortaleza—and indeed many of the boys were refugees from the northern *sêcas*. And long before it was even discreetly dusk the prostitutes, mostly colored, pretty and smartly dressed, accosted one with astonishing directness, grabbing with unerring aim at the front of one's trousers. The first time this happened to me I was with a Danish journalist whom I had run into at one of the bars. As one of the girls pounced he let out an agonized yell: "Leave my —— alone!" The fact that he had used English (of idiomatic exactitude), rather than his native tongue, struck me helpless with laughter.

By day the center of restless movement was the curving three-mile expanse of beach. By the time I had stood for five minutes at the pavement's edge, among the swarms of holiday makers in shorts and white peaked jockey caps, in bathing costumes and dressing gowns, and had then dashed through a gap in the traffic, my senses were already racing. Once on the beach, I could sit down on my patch of vacant sand, hiring, if I wished, a striped umbrella and a length of straw matting. Sit was what I usually did, for there was not much comfortable bathing and less swimming: the waves broke with such force and at such a height and beyond them the under-tow was so fierce that as a rule one was exhaused by the time one got into deeper and smoother water. The first time I attempted it, I had some difficulty in getting back. When I reached my towel, a Japanese lifeguard as wide as a barn door, wearing bathing trunks and a peaked baseball cap, was waiting for me. He pointed to the top of the beach, where for the first time I noticed a lifesaving station with a flag flying from the top of it. It was meant, the Japanese explained, to be a warning that today the currents were troublesome. I might have drowned, he said rather wistfully, eyeing me from top to toe as if to calculate the distribution of my weight.

Vendors of Coca-Cola, fruit drinks, ice cream, and especially of maté, kept in large drums strapped to the back and served cold in plastic containers, plodded to and fro in the soft white sand, raucously crying out their wares. The sunbathers lay in their floppy straw hats and bikinis, their limbs gold, brown, yellow or black. There were little pockets of family life, heated quarrels and arguments, courtships, gossiping, and family conferences. Sometimes a Negro mother suckled a baby, sometimes a child defecated in the sand while its parents hastily plied its toy spade. Sections of the beach were roped off: they contained gaily striped pavilions and stretches of sand where young men and women played football. There wasn't enough space for full-size pitches, so the game consisted of kicking the ball in the air and then keeping it there, passing it from person to person until the last one made a shot for the makeshift goal. Watching the speed, dexterity and ball-control, I could believe the stories I had heard of world-famous footballers who had been first spotted on the beaches of Rio and Copacabana. It was now, too, that I first heard the words *Copa do Mundo* ("World Cup"), uttered with passion and awe. Cup-fever had started.

But it was the back cloth that was the real source of the sense of flux and change. The whole landscape seemed in process of eruption: hillsides crumpled and folding, peaks and crags protruding at impossible angles, fissures and gullies scooped out as if by lava, islands looking as if they had that moment risen from the bottom of the sea, and everything smothered in a vegetation so dense that it looked like a covering of vivid-green volcanic ash just fallen from the sky. This background accompanied me wherever I went in Rio. It tugged at the senses so that it was impossible to cross a road or board a bus without moving more convulsively than usual. On the beaches the limbs of bathers and footballers chimed with the crests of the waves and the craggy outlines of the islands and mountains as in some frenetic ballet.

You try to get close to the back cloth. You never succeed. It recedes as you approach, disclosing fresh resources of fold and peak and hollow. The contact remains purely visual. My first attempt was an ascent of the Corcovado ("Hunchback"). It is a rocky peak of 2,300 feet, on top of which stands the gigantic figure of Christ (the work of a French sculptor and a Brazilian engineer) a hundred feet high (a hundred and twenty if the plinth is included), and weighing over a thousand tons.

The little electric train edged its way upward, stopping at several tiny stations, and passing shacks perched on ledges of rock as perilously as Charlie Chaplin's hut in *The Gold Rush*. Jungle vegetation tumbled around us: coconut palms and giant banana trees, each leaf big enough for a hammock, creepers like green waterfalls, and at the side of the track flowers like magnified scarlet pimpernels. And then, quite unexpectedly, a drizzle began to fall and a thick mist descended. It turned the trees into ghosts. They emerged, very slowly and gradually as we approached, their leaves and branches quivering like the components of a mobile.

As we approached the summit the shadowy outlines of the gigantic Christ appeared, the outstretched arms just visible, the head completely obscured. By now the rain was lashing down. It was bitterly cold, and shivering in our summer clothes we crowded into the restaurant at the base of the steps which lead up to the statue. Usually the view of Guanabara Bay and its skyscraper fringes is one of the most impressive in the world. Today, looking downward, nothing was to be seen but the white mist; it was like being stranded on a lighthouse.

But I was determined to see the Christ of Corcovado, and I dashed out into the rain and began to race up the steps, ankle-deep in the swirling rivulets, hoping to get to the statue and back again before I got too wet. But the steps were steep and there were far more of them than I had expected. By the time I reached the terrace at the summit I was soaked to the skin. I looked over the balustrade. The outlines of trees came floating toward me like fish in an aquarium; there was no sign of Rio. I went to the foot of the marble-faced plinth. A row of floodlights were directed upward; in their beams I caught a glimpse of folds of drapery and, very dimly, the vast outspread arms (ninety feet in span and each weighing eighty tons) and the upturned hands (each of which could carry a cluster of men). In spite of the floodlights the head was still invisible.

At the bottom of the steps a small riot was in progress as a crowd of soaked and shivering passengers struggled to board the train. The conductor refused to budge until some of the passengers had dismounted. Half a dozen men hanging out of a car at the front of the train got off, and, as it slowly moved off into the mist, got on again at the back. The rest of us waited.

At last another train arrived and we were crawling back through the mist. It was evening now, and the lights of Rio had been switched on, but it was not until we were halfway down that a few yellowish blurs appeared. Suddenly the mist began to clear. The outlines of streets and squares appeared, milky and luminous. Then a whole firmament of lights sprang out as the last threads of mist dispersed, brilliant as if a duster had just been passed over a display of jewels. Brilliant too were the drops of dew picked out by the lamps of the train, while the vegetation flowed round us like the "green rain" of a fireworks display.

Back at the terminal there was nearly another riot, this time among the "organized" parties of tourists. The coach drivers had grown tired of waiting and had departed. The guides decamped in a panic the moment the train stopped. It was still pouring rain, and there were no taxis. I splashed my way through the muddy streets in search of the bondes as Brazilians call their electric trams (because the English company which had originally run them had financed them by an issue of bonds) and at last reached my hotel. I suppose even now I could not really claim to have seen the Christ of the Corcovado.

The cone-shaped stub of rock known as the Sugarloaf I visited in brilliant sunshine. The ascent began in the Praça Adalberto Ferreira, in a cable car which rose giddily above a cluster of skyscrapers. From the top I had my first complete panorama of Rio de

Janeiro—fold upon fold of peak and rock and island like rumpled bedclothes; slopes bare and brown, or awash with blue-green vegetation; hilltops sprinkled with buildings, their roofs glittering in the sun; deep clefts and gullies down which houses, pink, white and blue, straggled among the masses of foliage. Guanabara Bay was absolutely still—the ships like flies stuck in flypaper; the islands like the backs of dolphins; the old forts like toys; Niterói, on the eastern shore, the capital of the state of Rio de Janeiro, a collection of dolls' houses. The planes on the runways of the Santos Dumont Airport looked like the flies made by fishermen; at first I could not believe my eyes when one of them rose into the blue air, then flashed in the sun with a drone no louder than that of a dragonfly. Copacabana and Ipanema were like painters' canvases, the skyscrapers slabs of white paint. All around mountains and crags, jagged and angular, seemed to converge upon the beaches, to gather at its edges like restless icebergs.

Having seen Rio de Janeiro from above, I had to see what it looked like from the sea. It was early on Easter Sunday when I set out for the harbor (the old cabdriver greeting me with the words "Christ is Risen," like a character in a Russian novel). At this hour the leaves of the palm trees were edged with sunlight, as if they had been cut out of tin foil. Islands and peaks were soft, dusky blues against the pale sky. The Sugarloaf was insubstantial gold, as if crumbling away or just created. The figure of Christ on top of the Corcovado no longer had the stance of crucifixion; it looked as if it had indeed just risen.

The steamer was crowded. The deck tilted as everybody crowded to the rail to watch the receding skyline of Rio, its skyscrapers soon reduced to scale as the background of mountain and jungle overshadowed them. Then I had eyes for nothing but the bay itself, nineteen miles across and ninety miles in circumference, roughly triangular in shape, with a bottleneck at its apex leading into the Atlantic Ocean—through which the Portuguese navigator Gonçalo Coelho sailed on January 1, 1502. It was his custom to name every place after the saint on whose feast day he discovered it. There was no saint for the first day of January, and assuming that the bay was the mouth of a great river, he called it Rio de Janeiro—"River of January."

The island I was bound for was Paquetá. The scores of tiny beaches were packed with sunbathers and picnickers. Tired businessmen in floppy shorts and baseball caps cycled resolutely along the promenades, while their womenfolk drove in little horse-drawn cabs (cars are not allowed). The main centers of tourist attraction were the *quinta* with the rock known as the *Pedra da Moreninha* celebrated in one of Brazil's best-loved novels, *A Moreninha* by Joaquim Manuel de Macedo (a combination as potent to Brazilians as *San Michele* and Axel Munthe once were to Europeans); and the Solar del Rei, one of the refuges of John VI of Portugal when he fled to Brazil after Napoleon's invasion of his country (a moldering colonial mansion, darkened by files of towering *coqueiro* trees, its rooms full of royal relics and its stables of ancient carriages).

It was, in spite of the crowds, the most beautiful island I have ever seen. The interior was a mass of vegetation including *flamboyant* trees, their leaves as delicate as fishes' skeletons, stimulated to such exuberant growth by the balmy climate of the island that their branches coiled and twisted into arabesques and figures of eight. There was a profusion of palms of every description and— one of the islanders' proudest boasts—bougainvillaea in three colors: coral, purple and white. Brightly plumaged birds and flame-colored butterflies were everywhere. The coastline was indented with innumerable boulder-fringed coves; the sea was warm and calm and I was able to swim out until the outlines of Rio and Niterói came undulating across the water, like transfers in a cup of water.

I caught the last steamer back to Rio. Again the decks were packed. The steamer rolled and lumbered. It was forced to take a circuitous route, passing through clusters of rounded knolls with tiny trees growing on them like candles on top of a birthday cake. Sea gulls settled on the mast. The wind blew the smoke from the funnel straight into our faces. A Negro family, father, mother and small son, dressed in their Sunday best were standing next to me. Father and mother were flirting enthusiastically; every now and then the boy whimpered and banged his head against his mother's stomach.

The mountains behind Rio, dusky in the twilight, stood out more dramatically than ever. Gradually the skyscrapers, glinting in the setting sun, came into their own. The Negro took out a large comb and pulled it through his son's woolly hair, and then with touching solicitude began to clean out his wife's ears with a grubby handkerchief.

7

BEAUTIFUL
HORIZONS

The road switchbacked over a series of ridges, rising to nearly three thousand feet above sea level, and as regular as the ribbed sand of the seashore. There were few trees: most of them had been cut down years before by the first miners to fire their furnaces, and the dark-green turf was scarred by patches of rock—rusty red, gray-blue and salmon pink. The sun was beginning to sink. The stream of long-distance lorries was thinning out; a number of them had pulled into bays where the hillsides had been scooped out for ore, the drivers cooking their evening meal or already asleep. Suddenly the sun dipped lower to reveal not one but half a dozen sunsets, red, blue, gold and silver, behind what appeared to be half a dozen distinct horizons.

The phenomenon has given the capital of the state of Minas Gerais its name—Belo Horizonte ("Beautiful Horizon"). Seventy years ago it was little more than a village; thirty-five years ago its population was still only fifty thousand; today, with over three quarters of a million inhabitants, it is a city of arrow-straight roads, three-story white buildings and stolid white skyscrapers like inverted shoe boxes. The beauty is in the name and the setting. The city is a center for exploration, not a theme for exploration in itself.

My first journey was dictated by the enthusiasm of the British consul, a distinguished amateur archaeologist, who wanted to show me some Indian rock paintings in the area of Lagoa Santa, where Dr. Peter Lund discovered many fossils and prehistoric artifacts, and the primitive human skull known as Lagoa Santa Man—now, I believe, regarded with some doubt by the experts.

The site was hidden in wild and beautiful countryside. To reach it we drove along a narrow track, until the grasses and weeds met above the roof of our car. Then we climbed out and continued on foot. "We should be wearing boots and leggings," my companion told me, "and we ought to have a machete. Look out for snakes." He led the way, laying about him with an elegant walking stick he had taken from the car. I followed, curling up my toes inside my sandals. Bates, I told myself, would have shown more foresight. I certainly felt that I was in Bates country. Butterflies in their hundreds rose before us: saffron-yellow and lime-green; big ones, like the Red Admirals at home, with black scarlet-tipped wings; small ones, black or cream, like bits of confetti; and an even smaller one, with red wings spotted with black, no bigger than a ladybird. Insects swarmed round our heads in a vibrating gauze. The undergrowth stirred and crackled.

We entered a wood of black, almost leafless trees, their branches gnarled and twisted and festooned with creepers. The cliffs, which lay beyond the wood, kept it in semidarkness. There were no butterflies here, but moths, furry as rabbits or big and rubbery like bats. Cobwebs stretched between the trees. I ran full tilt into one of them; it was as tough as a hammock and I struggled to break free as if I was caught in a nightmare. A little farther on, as I cautiously skirted another, I saw a spider crouched at the center: it was as big as a golf ball and vivid-green in color, more like a lizard than a spider. The ground was pitted with the burrows of armadillos. The shadowy shapes of marmosets and monkeys darted among the topmost branches of the trees.

At last we broke through. Tall grasses, purple-flowered weeds not unlike foxglove, and wild tomatoes no bigger than cherries but delicious in flavor grew at the foot of the cliffs. The rock face was reddish-brown in color, smooth and firm except where the roots of the *gameleira* trees, which clung to every available ledge, had found their way along the cracks in the rock, widening the cracks as they went and forming a series of handrails, which the Indians had once made use of. The overhanging summit was dense with foliage. When I trained my binoculars on it I saw what at first I took for leaves thrown upward by a gust of wind, but which a moment later I realized were flocks of vivid-green parakeets.

The Indians had long ago been driven from the state or been exterminated. But they had left their mute witnesses. A ledge, about three feet high, at the base of the cliff, which they had used as a bench, was worn marble-smooth. The earth in front was soft and grainy from the ashes of countless fires. I had only to find a piece of wood and dig down a few inches to find several "nut-cracker" stones with indentations scooped in them—though this doesn't imply any considerable antiquity and the site was probably no older than the fourteenth or fifteenth century A.D.

All I could see of the paintings were several blobs a few feet above the "bench" and in niches and caves about twelve feet higher up. But we filled two tins with water from a nearby stream; and as soon as we had climbed up and splashed the water over the rock face a whole range of colors—brown, yellow, gray, blue, maroon—sprang out, astonishingly bright and fresh. There were geometrical designs, and also lively representations of deer, armadillos and wild pigs, and in one of the niches a fine picture of a deer in flight with an arrow stuck in its back.

Minas Gerais—literally the name means "general mines"—is the richest in minerals of all the Brazilian states. The patches of red earth and salmon-pink rock glitter as the sun picks out the flecks of quartz and mineral. The streams too have a reddish color. The early prospectors used to work them for gold, damming them into sections and washing the exposed sand in flat pans. Some fifty miles from Diamantina (the center of the diamond beds) I saw a group of *garimpeiros*—as the free-lance prospectors are called—still doing so.

Gold is also mined. I visited Morro Velho, reputedly the deepest gold mine in the world (more than a mile and a half). For many years it was managed by an English company, but now it has been taken over by the government. The chief engineer was American, but a few of the English staff remained; one of them showed me the remains of a typical English clubhouse and an overgrown field where he and his colleagues had once played cricket.

The Brazilian "Captain of the Mines" fitted me out with overalls and a miner's helmet, introduced me to a visiting French engineer, and led the way to the cage. It was my first descent into a mine of any kind, but I was too proud to admit it and my companions jumped to the conclusion that I was an old hand. I was hard put to it to conceal my panic as I crouched in the cage. My eardrums felt as if they were splitting and I gasped for breath. I was convinced that a saboteur had cut the cables. The two minutes and forty-five seconds it took to reach the first level, 1,900 feet below, seemed an eternity. It takes an hour to make the full descent.

We went from gallery to gallery, the sliding doors closing behind us with an ominous clang. Sometimes we were ankle-deep in mud, sometimes in dust. We crammed ourselves into a tiny flat truck, like a builder's wheelbarrow, and hurtled downward at an impossible gradient, my heart in my mouth as I found myself beginning to slip over the edge. We climbed down a shaft, hanging on to a crazily wobbling length of iron piping. The *capataz* and the French engineer, moving as easily as if they were taking a holiday stroll, were deep in conversation and gradually I fell behind. I had to bend double and, whenever I forgot, cracked my helmet against the roof. Once I slithered the whole length of a steep tunnel filled with loose rubble. I was hardly aware of the solid, stocky miners around me, their limbs and faces covered with dust, many of them Spaniards from Asturias, the only miners who can work for any length of time at such depths. My lungs felt clogged with dust, and my ears were numbed by the clatter of trucks and machinery. My reactions slowed down; I was continually misjudging the speed of approaching trucks and hopping out of the way only just in time. Once I got out of line as we passed a machine that was gouging out chunks of rock and hurling them into the waiting tubs, and a piece of rock, missing my left eyebrow by a hair's breadth, struck the front of my helmet. When at last I stood under the hot shower at the surface I found that I was covered with dust from head to foot and that the skin had been removed from both my ankles. Outside the air seemed icy-cold.

Beyond Morro Velho the country became more precipitous: swiftly flowing streams, small waterfalls, and a swirling mist, like the Highlands of Scotland, though foundries were still tucked away in the valleys, with heaps of crude ore—iron, bauxite or manganese—stacked outside them.

Farther still, and the population thinned out. Ahead lay a line of blue hills, smooth and clean-cut, like a landscape by Derain. And then suddenly against this background, spread like a series of garlands over a rocky hillside, 3,400 feet above sea level, the white spires and towers of Ouro Prêto, the old capital of Minas Gerais.

Its history began in the late seventeenth century when a group of *bandeirantes* from São Paulo discovered some small black grains which, when ground, were found to contain gold of the finest quality: hence the name Ouro Prêto ("black gold"). Various gold rushes followed, together with battles between the miners from São Paulo and Portuguese settlers to whom the king in Lisbon had made grants of land. In 1720, the year in which Minas Gerais became a separate region, independent of São Paulo, Ouro Prêto was still one of a number of mining settlements (which were given the over-all name of Vila Rica de Albuquerque) no more flourishing than the neighboring Ouro Podre ("poor, or bad, gold"), which in spite of its name included some of the richest miners of the region, living in stone houses, and possessing a labor force of some four thousand Negro slaves. When, however, a newly appointed Captain General imposed crippling conditions on the collecting of gold in order to divert the bulk of it to the royal coffers in Lisbon, a revolt broke out among the miners of Ouro Podre. It was savagely put down, Ouro Podre was burned to the ground and the site prohibited in perpetuity. Local inhabitants were oddly reluctant to visit it. I found a taxi driver who consented to take me to the foot of the steep hill, now known as Morro da Queimada ("Hill of the Burned"), from which I could see a ragged line of blackened stones against the skyline; but he would accompany me no further. When I struggled to the top I began to understand why: the surroundings were impregnated with that sense of doom you get in the pass of Glencoe. The ruins were extensive—cobbled streets overgrown with weeds and grasses, piles of charred timber and debris, foundations of houses and remnants of walls. I stood inside one square of blackened stones; it was a small garden of wild flowers, but if ever a place was haunted this was it.

With the disappearance of its rival, Ouro Prêto had, by 1725, become the chief of the mining settlements. In order to prevent as much as possible of their gold reaching Portugal the miners lavished it on *festas* in which their costumes and the harness of their horses scintillated with gold and diamonds, and on the religious processions in which friars carried damask banners fringed with gold and the priests wore vestments so stiff with it that they could stand up by themselves—as I saw in the sacristy of Nossa Senhora do Pilar, the parish church of the old town.

The city added one more page to the annals of Brazil's history, toward the end of the eighteenth century, with the plot of the *Inconfidentes* ("rebellious ones") led by Joaquim José da Silva Xavier, an ex-dentist known to every Brazilian schoolboy as Tiradentes ("tooth puller"), who stayed to face the music when the rest of the conspirators fled, was hanged, drawn and quartered—and thereafter regarded as one of the great martyrs in the struggle for Brazilian independence.

But, apart from Tiradentes, the city's main claim to interest from about 1738, when the governor's palace was started (it is now a school of mines), is the great period of building, which made use of the quartz from the nearby mines, and lasted until the 1830s. In this period Ouro Prêto took shape as Brazil's museum and showpiece, and then more or less stood still. For historical and sentimental reasons, it was made the capital of the state, but its geographical position made further expansion impossible, and in 1897 the capital was transferred to Belo Horizonte. In 1933 Ouro Prêto was finally encapsulated in its golden age when the federal government proclaimed it a national monument.

The town in consequence has that timeless, slightly unrealistic air you get in university towns from the juxtaposition of antiquity and youth. The comparison which most readily springs to mind, in atmosphere and situation, is Coimbra, in Portugal—the same steep, cobbled alleyways, with donkeys picking their way along them, attended by bent old women dressed in black, the same sleazy taverns and restaurants frequented by students.

There was only one unequivocal touch of modernity: the Grand Hotel, designed by Oscar Niemeyer, the architect of Brasília. The eighteenth century absorbed it without difficulty. It was no more part of the living present than the bridges, fountains, statues, terraced gardens and balconies, the colonial palaces and public buildings, the two-story houses, or *sobrados,* faced with tiles or carved stone, with wrought-iron balconies and arched wooden doors—and of course the churches.

I have never seen so many churches crammed into so small an area. The oldest was built in the early years of the eighteenth century, the chapel of São João Batista, built by the first prospectors of a gray claylike iron ore called *canga;* but most of them belong to the same sixty or seventy years that saw the emergence—and arrested development—of the city as a whole, when the various religious orders crowned every ridge and hilltop with convents and churches and competed with each other in lavishing upon them gold leaf, carvings, murals, tile paintings, crystal, gold and silver ornaments, and images adorned with diamonds and solid-gold crowns. Nossa Senhora do Pilar, for example, contains nearly a thousand pounds of gold and silver. My own favorite, though, was Santa Efigênia, because of the legend attached to it which ascribes its foundation to "Chico Rei," an African chieftain, who together with the whole of his tribe was captured by the slave traders. His wife and all his children except one died crossing the Atlantic. With his surviving son he was sent to work in the mines of Ouro Prêto. Somehow he managed to save enough money to buy his freedom and then went on working and scheming until he had succeeded in emancipating first his son, then all the surviving members of his tribe and finally those of another tribe related by kinship. Together they formed a kind of confederacy ruled over by "Chico Rei," discovered a rich gold mine and, choosing Saint Iphigenia as their patron saint, erected a statue to her in a small chapel which later formed the nucleus of the church. I hope the story is true. The wizened little Negro caretaker who showed me over certainly believed it, claiming descent from "Chico Rei" himself and proudly pointing to a stoup in the entrance in which, he declared, the Negro women used to wash the gold dust out of their hair so that it could be used to enrich their chapel.

But most people go to Ouro Prêto to see the work of Antônio Francisco da Costa Lisboa, whom Brazilians regard as their greatest artist. He is better known as Aleijadinho, or "Little Cripple." The son of a builder and architect who built or designed many of the churches of Ouro Prêto and one of his African slaves, Antônio in his forties contracted an appalling disease—probably leprosy or tropical *bouba,* according to a doctor I met in Belo Horizonte. He lost his toes and had to move about on leather pads fastened to his knees. Later his fingers, too, atrophied, and crazed with pain, he hacked them off with his sculptor's chisel. His most famous works were executed with his instruments strapped to his wrists. The disease spread to his face, and to avoid frightening people he had himself carried to his workshop at dawn and stayed there till it was dark.

There are few churches in Ouro Prêto without some of Aleijadinho's work, even if it is only a font or a lavabo of soapstone (his favorite material).

His best work, though, is a landscape with figures. It is at Congonhas, a small town some fifty miles from Ouro Prêto, breathtakingly beautiful in a saucer of swirling green, blurred and shimmering at the edges and backed by a range of dusky-blue mountains. As I arrived, the evening sun flared like a sheet of tissue paper; the white quartz of the houses scattered among the trees blazed and spluttered; the helmets of the miners streaming out of the little station looked like polished silver. And on a hilltop, placed at intervals round the walls of the Sanctuary of Senhor Bom Jesus stood twelve gigantic figures of the prophets, carved by Aleijadinho when he was turned sixty, long after he had lost the use of his hands, rich in detail and gesture, gazing, calm and impassive, across the valley.

From a distance the buildings of Brasília seemed temporary disturbances, denting the skyline like sand that has drifted into dunes. At dusk the lights twinkled like the naphtha flares on some vast fairground or caravanserai, and the beams from the skyscrapers cut the darkness like searchlights on an improvised airfield.

The "pilot plan" was designed for a population of half a million, and in view of the fact that it wasn't until 1956 that Novacap, the public corporation in charge of the project, really started its work, the progress has been fantastic. Most of the tens of thousands of tons of building materials had to be transported to the plateau by lorries, and the roads themselves had to be hacked out of the jungle. I met a construction engineer who had worked on one of these. He spoke of the experience with awe, remembering giant trees which had broken the teeth of diesel-driven saws, a jaguar attacking the camp at night, and a bulldozer hurled over in collision with an anaconda. When I was there the population was reckoned at forty thousand, and by now it has probably doubled.

Yet Brasília was a ghost city—more weird than that indeed, for the magnificent shells lacked even the warmth of lingering spirits; there weren't enough bodies to generate them; they were lost in the immensities of stone and concrete.

The town planners of Brasília are particularly proud of their road system. "Only city in the world without crossroads," the souvenir guide declares. It was true: there were three great loops or "trefoils" on each branch of the trunk roads, and three underground passages. In addition the trunk roads were divided into five lanes of traffic.

The result was that everywhere I saw cars hurtling away from me, but too far off to see the drivers: for all I knew, the vehicles might have been set in motion by somebody pressing a button. I longed to catch another driver's eye, to wave my hand. I longed for the smell of exhausts, for hooting of horns and grinding of brakes. I even longed for the tangle of traffic lights and traffic jams. But there was no tangling in Brasília.

There wasn't even the sensation of going from one place to another. I felt as if I were perpetually driving through Brasília, never that I was *in* it. On my first evening I was invited to dinner by the British minister, and the Danish minister and his wife, who were staying at my hotel, offered to drive me there. We felt as if we were trapped like rats in a Watsonian maze, and when we missed our way it took us over an hour to find the underground tunnel that put us back on the right road.

Brasília has been the official capital since April 1960, but the ambassadors have been reluctant to move in. The Chileans had built their embassy when I was there, but it was still half-staffed. The Japanese and the Yugoslavs had nearly completed theirs, and most of the other countries had laid the foundations or at least drawn up the plans, but most of the ambassadors themselves were still in Rio, represented in the new capital by ministers living in temporary bungalowlike structures.

It was, though, only a matter of time, the American minister assured me. "Rio's impossible as a capital," he said. "Imagine trying to administer the United States from Miami!"

It was the Brazilians themselves who were dragging their feet, the Danish minister explained. The President had his official residence in Brasília, but he took every opportunity to get away from it. Deputies and senators crowded the airlines back to Rio or São Paulo whenever there was a recess. Most of the ministries had only skeleton staffs in Brasília. Those who could, clung to Rio; and whole departments were fighting ingenious delaying actions. Civil servants who had been forced to make the move complained bitterly, and weekend commuting between Rio and Brasília was common. "The two good things about Brasília," a popular adage ran, "are the climate and the plane out."

This too, the American minister insisted, was a passing phase. "It will take a few more years," he said, "but there are sound political reasons behind Brasília. It's an attempt to offset the traditional hostility felt toward Rio de Janeiro by cities such as Recife, São Paulo and Pôrto Alegre. For hundreds of years people have been agitating for a new unifying center for the federation. Eventually this will become a real capital."

"And a real city?" I asked.

"Ah, that's another question."

My hotel was the most luxurious I had stayed in: swimming pool, entrance hall as big as a railway station, a lavish use of Brazilian woods, and bedrooms with bath, shower, radio and air conditioning. But its very luxury had a kind of horror yawning beneath it. The shops with their expensive jewelry and tourist goods clustered round it like houses round a medieval cathedral threatened by flood or siege. The guests sat on the thickly upholstered settees like the characters in one of those spooky plays of the 1930s where millionaires who are dead but don't know it sip wine and clutch cigars on liners or in airport waiting rooms with a nagging suspicion that everything isn't as it seems.

I found it impossible to sleep. There was none of the clangor of Rio; on the contrary, I was conscious of the vast spaces and silences of the plateau and of the complete absence of that muffled beat which belongs only to cities that have been lived in for a long time. But the thinness of the medium accentuated every sound—a typewriter clattering somewhere in the hotel, the distant whine of a car, and a group of workmen on a building site chattering all night. I stood at my bedroom window and gazed upon the wide, empty avenues illuminated by lights on curved stanchions; they were like brightly lit greyhound tracks, whose occupants had inexplicably melted away. Then for a time they were blotted out as gray-and-orange clouds massed overhead and thunder rumbled in the distance. But by three o'clock the clouds had disappeared, a cock began to crow, a pale-blue sky, merging with the lake, stretched across an incredibly wide horizon, so clear that a cluster of stars still shone brilliantly overhead. The surrealist outlines of Brasília's buildings emerged: the two "cups" of the parliamentary buildings, the towering H-shaped skyscrapers of the administrative offices between them, and close to the hotel the curved upper reaches of the cathedral, like a cluster of boomerangs, the underground nave still unfinished. Cars began to hurtle along the distant highways, then to collect outside the government buildings. Two coaches emerged from the white fortresslike bus station with its unexpectedly angled fly-overs. So far I hadn't seen a single pedestrian.

I found some of them picking their way among the mounds of raw earth, peering about them like the survivors of a nuclear explosion. Others wandered, wide-eyed and openmouthed, among the architectural showpieces, as if they had been suddenly set down on one of the planets.

The best of these buildings are exciting because they don't remind you of anything at all, but force your eyes to entirely new and unexpected adjustments. Above all, this applies to Niemeyer's masterpiece, the President's palace—Palácio da Alvorada ("Palace of the Dawn")—with its floors of Brazilian woods and of marble, a huge ramp lined with bronze leading to the first floor, walls of glass, polished brass and marble, pillars faced with polished aluminum, a veranda paved with black marble running the whole length of the building, and huge white curving pillars like the jawbones of whales.

But the *people* of Brasília? "Brasília will be a city living under the sign of discipline, order and logic," an official brochure of 1960 written in English announces, "since all its elements contribute to reinforce these principles." The residential blocks, separated from each other by strips of earth some twenty yards wide, are grouped in *super-quadras*. These "super blocks" are intended to be self-supporting, with their own shopping centers, crèches, schools, hospitals, swimming pools, and playgrounds.

The swimming pools and playgrounds had plenty of life, taken over by the enthusiastic and noisy young, but even they seemed to be in temporary occupation, like the members of a Sunday school outing. The skyscraper apartments were more like Shredded Wheat factories than homes. How could you feel at home with an address like "Quadra 108, Block 4"?

The next day I went to Cidade Livre, the shanty town some sixteen miles outside Brasília. It had originally been set up by Novacap as an encampment for the architects, engineers, businessmen, politicians, civil servants, and the armies of workers engaged on the construction sites in Brasília: they had to live somewhere, for the plateau then was practically a desert and the nearest towns were hundreds of miles away. Shops of all kinds sprang up; temporary hotels, restaurants and tourist agencies, newspaper and airline offices, warehouses and banks were built. At one time there were thirty hotels ("of the most different kinds," as one of the earlier brochures put it) and thirty-five boardinghouses ("of an inferior type"). Even so, there was a mad scramble for accommodation; astronomical prices were charged for tiny wooden rooms, and the hallways of the hotels and boardinghouses were packed. The brochure also listed "two markets, nine hundred stores of several types, two cinemas, twenty-five drugstores, forty dentists, twenty physicians, thirty lawyers and seven gas stations."

As the skyscrapers went up in Brasília the architects, engineers, politicians, administrators (and presumably the lawyers) moved in. Originally the idea was that the rest of the population would follow in stages and that Cidade Livre would be disbanded; the land strips had been leased for four years only, and theoretically the leases expired at the end of 1960. But new influxes of immigrants swarmed into the vacant buildings and lots. When I was there at least fifty thousand people were living in Cidade Livre and more were arriving every day.

Many of the banks retained their wooden premises and the hotels and boardinghouses, with their high-sounding names like Hotel Monte Carlo, Pensão Nossa Senhora de Fátima, were still flourishing. All that had happened was that the clientele now consisted mostly of the carpetbaggers, the commercial travelers, the small clerks, the tradesmen prospecting for businesses, and the families of foremen and minor technicians on the building sites of Brasília who were biding their time for vacant shacks or for opportunities of building them.

There were already shacks of every description. Some were gaily painted, with flowers in window boxes; parrots or cockatoos perched on the sills, and cheap furniture graced the insides. Some had their walls papered with cutouts from colored magazines; others were content with sheets of newspaper. Even Cidade Livre had its gradations, for there was a "lower end," where the huts were built of bits of rotting wood and rusty tin and were hemmed in by towering heaps of refuse. An old crone smoked a clay pipe. A trio of mangy dogs had set upon a monkey, who cowered against the wall of a hut and then, chattering hysterically, flew at his tormentors and dispersed them, yelping. A tiny tot, naked except for an outsize pair of Wellington boots, was howling lustily, a pacifier still clamped in his mouth. Two soldiers, very drunk, their uniforms creased and dirty, staggered out of a brothel. Farther on I met a pair of neat young military policemen; they told me that they were on their daily rounds looking for deserters, but I didn't let on about the soldiers. A group of schoolgirls, spotless in white blouses and dark skirts, listened to our conversation.

Some of the shops were quite extensive wooden structures—the Armazém Horizonte (Horizon Store), for example, which sold dry goods of all kinds. There were bicycle shops, dress shops, hairdressers, barbers, even small jewelers' shops. There were open stalls, selling fruit, Coca-Cola, hot meat balls and *farinha,* household utensils, and new and secondhand clothes. At one stall a man was painting secondhand shoes white, at another a score of women bent feverishly over sewing machines, making alterations and repairs and running up lengths of material while their customers waited. Girls sat in chairs in the open air, having their hair curled with ferocious-looking tongs. There were rows of monkeys and parrots in cages. The skulls of oxen denoted the open-air butchers and slaughterhouses. Crowds queued outside an asbestos cinema. There was a continuous coming and going of long-distance coaches and dilapidated buses, taxis, and little open horse-drawn *calèches*.

Every few yards was a bar. I went into one labeled "Bar Cearense." When I told the proprietor that I had visited Ceará he insisted on paying for my beer. Yes, he told me, he had been "a refugee of the *sêcas*," but he was not one of the romantics who yearned to return; for the first time in his life he and his family had enough to eat. "Brasília, city of the future!" he cried, waving his hand toward the swarming crowds and shacks of Cidade Livre.

Many of the bars carried the additional title of *boite*—literally "box," the Brazilian idiom for "night club." As dusk fell these were lit up by fairy lights or acetylene flares, and girls in dance frocks of orange and green taffeta stood at the open windows. The traffic from Brasília increased—taxis, jeeps and expensive limousines. Those who had once been forced to live in Cidade Livre were returning eagerly and of their own free will. But it wasn't the *boites* that drew them as much as a longing for contact with the noisy, dirty and intensely vital swarms of humanity.

São Paulo squatted with solid assurance. Its beauty, as with Manhattan or Chicago, was that of a city landscape in its own right. The skyscrapers had grown out of concrete, not out of jungle. The taximan who drove me from the airport outdid any inhabitant of Chicago in civic pride. "See that skyscraper?" he would shout, turning round and escaping collision by a last-second twist of the wheel. "It was opened last week. That one—it wasn't here six months ago. And over there—you see?—it's quite a decent-looking building, isn't it?" Then, with another haul at the wheel, "It's coming down. Not good enough for São Paulo. They're putting up another skyscraper." When we reached the residential areas: "Do you know, *senhor*, that a new house is completed in São Paulo every minute?" And a little later: "London's big, *senhor*, but we're catching up fast. When I came here, ten years ago, the population was only two million. Now we're over five million."

Yes, he agreed, there was poverty, but I wouldn't see any tumble-down shacks in São Paulo: the poor lived in good, solid cellars. Most of them anyway came from the north—"as you can see, *senhor*," he said, and he pointed to a lorry we were skirting. Standing in the back, with no support but a rope fastened down the center, were about thirty men, gaunt with fatigue, the color of their skin indistinguishable for the layers of red and yellow dust.

"They've traveled like that for two thousand miles," the taxi driver said. "They sell their last possessions for the fare, and they arrive here penniless. I'm sorry for them, but they spoil our city. They are barbarians; they don't know anything about machines, so what use are they, *senhor*, in a place like São Paulo?"

The foreman in one of the steel mills I visited (ores from Minas Gerais and the last word in electric furnaces) shared his doubts. "*Senhor*," he said, "these northerners, they only understand bananas and monkey nuts. We try to employ them, but they can't even learn how to use protective clothing." He himself was of German origin, and according to him the elite of the workers in São Paulo were of European stock.

All the same, several of the big firms have training schemes for immigrants, and practically every region of Brazil is represented. When I visited the Willys-Overland plant (which produced Brazil's first motor engine in 1958, and which now manufactures both Jeeps and saloon cars) I met *mestiços*—a mixture of Negro, Indian and white—from Amazonas, *mulatos* from Pernambuco, *mamelucos* (half Indian and half white) from Ceará and Rio Grande do Norte, and pure-blooded Negroes from Salvador working in the sheet-metal workshops and on the assembly lines.

They had no cause to regret that long trek by lorry. The factories were working three eight-hour shifts a day, seven days a week, there was a forty-eight-hour week, and overtime was paid at an additional 25 per cent. Many of them were earning six times as much as the basic minimum of the north—which they would have been lucky to get anyway. When I watched the workers leaving the spacious, airy factories with their clinics and their canteens, crowding into the fleets of buses or into their own Jeeps, bound for suburbs of decent villas and bungalows, it was difficult to believe that I was in the same Brazil in which I had seen men and girls sweltering among the Brazil nuts in the rotting hold of an old lighter or squatting on the floor of ramshackle huts making straw hats for a few cents a day.

São Paulo is cosmopolitan in quite a different way from Rio de Janeiro. In Rio people of all nationalities meet and mingle, but it is a shared visual and imaginative experience and a shared atmosphere that hold them. People go to São Paulo because that is where the center of economic gravity lies. It is the largest industrial city in South America and when you are there you feel that you are in the world of international industry and finance. By comparison, Rio seems thoroughly Brazilian and almost parochial. It is in São Paulo that most of the foreign capital is invested. In the motor industry, for example, Volkswagens, Benzes, Simcas, Alfa-Romeos and Fords are assembled. As far as I could see, Britain's motor industry wasn't represented by as much as a sparking plug.

The smart Jardim Paulistano suburb has the cosmopolitan bourgeois comfort you can find anywhere from Tokyo to Berne, from Detroit to Sydney. I stayed with an old friend, the widow (half Russian and half English) of a former English Professor of Statistics at the university. It was a beautiful house with a garden and a lawn, and an annex at the back, where the Negro maid lived. When I took the children to school, with their shining English faces and their Portuguese textbooks in their satchels, the saloon cars were backing out of the garages and the wives were waving goodbye from the windows. When I returned an hour later they were hosing their gardens, or snipping off the dead flowers, or having coffee with each other, or strolling and chatting through the nearby self-service store. An elderly couple sat on the porch of one of the houses, the woman with her knitting (the first I had seen in Brazil), the man in a black skullcap, wearing steel-rimmed spectacles and reading a German newspaper. When I asked the way, I was quite likely to be addressed in German, or in Italian, or in Swedish.

The racial cross section was repeated in every quarter. In the center of the city I saw newspapers in practically every language, many of them published and printed in São Paulo. I dined in Russian and Yugoslav restaurants to the accompaniment of balalaikas, in Hungarian restaurants to gypsy music, and in Portuguese restaurants to the singing of *fados*. There were kiosks where one could stand and eat Portuguese fishcakes of *bacalhau*, Syrian *kebabs*, and *rissoles* made of meat and buckwheat, Chinese chop sueys, and Japanese snacks of dried squid and seaweed.

There were districts almost entirely populated by Japanese, and many of the shops selling crockery, toilet goods, small furnishings and ornaments were run by them. I bought several fans, ashtrays and paper-knives of exquisite Japanese workmanship, though those who made and sold them were second- or third-generation Brazilian. During the war, however, they had reverted to ancestral loyalties. When the news of Japan's defeat was announced, I was told, they refused to believe it. They were shown newspapers, but they dismissed them as enemy propaganda. They were shown newsreels of the surrender of the Japanese Army but somehow managed to persuade themselves that they were really doctored pictures of American troops surrendering to the Japanese. When emissaries were sent out from Japan itself they were still not convinced, and it was not until a member of the imperial family came to Brazil and explained what had happened that they would face the truth.

The presence of tourists from the luxury liners docked at nearby Santos added to the cosmopolitan atmosphere. Most of them came to see the snakes. The Butantã Institute was founded in 1902 by the state of São Paulo for the preparation of serums, for research work into the nature of venoms, viruses and bacteria, and for the study of poisonous creatures—scorpions and spiders, as well as snakes—and it is the only establishment of its kind in the world.

The snakes, some horribly active, others comatose, lying in heaps on the grass like monstrous droppings, or hanging from the branches of the trees like some disgusting trailing fruit, were housed in a series of enclosures. Inside each enclosure was a number of low, domelike structures with slits at ground level, covered with heavy lids, and inside these, scores of other snakes slept and digested their unmentionable meals. A sickly-sweet smell hung over the whole park.

Every now and then a keeper, wearing leather gaiters and armed with a pole with a prong at the end, would step over the wall into one of the enclosures. Some of the snakes paid no attention, some came hissing round his ankles, and others glided out of the slits of the small blockhouses as inquisitive as terriers. The keeper lifted the lid off one of these, plunged in his pole and deposited a seething mass on the grass. As an encore he thrust his pole into the branches of one of the trees and pulled: a dozen snakes fell with a thud at his feet. Another keeper used the toe of his boot to provoke the dry-leaf skirr of a rattlesnake, and another prodded at a long, flat snake which time after time reared and struck at his gaiters with incredible speed and ferocity.

The climax came when a keeper seized a snake with his bare hands and squeezed its neck until the jaws gaped. With a pair of pincers he indicated the two main fangs (there was a third spare one), then very carefully drew aside the pellicle of flesh, soft and pink like an orchid, and squeezed again; we could see the glistening drops of venom shoot into the test tube which the keeper held in his other hand. After this the huge scorpions and the giant, furry spiders scuttling obscenely up the walls of their cages were an anticlimax.

Most of these creatures are sent to the Institute by hunters and settlers in return for phials of serum, indispensable for survival in the interior. In some years, one of the officials told me, as many as fifteen thousand snakes are sent in. They are needed, for even this total, he explained, would yield only about two quarts of venom a year from some ten thousand extractions, and by the time it was dried this would have been reduced to a bare pint.

Almost as horrific as the live snakes were the thousands of skeletons, stuffed skins, and bottled snakes in the museum, and the dummy human arms and legs, showing in mottled technicolor the effects of various types of bites. One room was devoted to a display of statistics illustrating the output of the Institute and the results of its products. A notice proclaimed: "Butantã has saved millions of lives with its medicines. Brazilians, be proud of your Butantã."

Paulistas also had cause to be proud of the collection of paintings bequeathed to the city by Senator Assis Chateaubriand Bandeira de Mello. I was introduced to it by a friend of the senator's, a slim, elegant woman with the pale oval face one associates with Spanish beauty and a string of names just as cosmopolitan-sounding as his. The approach was not propitious, by a crowded lift to one of the upper floors of an ugly skyscraper shaped like a radiator. But the galleries were beautifully appointed and the extent and variety of the collection startled. There were canvases by Titian, El Greco, Velázquez, Goya, Daddi and Mantegna. In another room were pictures by Rembrandt, Frans Hals and lesser-known Dutch masters. There were several Constables and Turners and numerous French Impressionists, including two fine Degas nudes, a Gauguin self-portrait, several Van Goghs and Cézannes, and a Picasso of the "blue period."

But beneath the cosmopolitan culture, the hum of the factories, the frantic building lurked fears and doubts. I was taken to lunch at the Automobile Club—very English with its leather wing chairs, its newspapers and periodicals, its ticker tapes and indifferent food. The group at our table consisted of "top people" of São Paulo— industrialists, bankers, descendants of the old Imperial nobility—and it included an elderly little man with brilliant eyes who had been a minister under the presidencies of both Getúlio Vargas and Juscelino Kubitschek. They were worried because Brazil had resumed diplomatic relations with Russia. "We too are now in the Cold War," one of them said. "Never again will Brazil know true independence." They were bitter in their denunciations of Jânio Quadros (then fighting an unsuccessful battle to make a comeback as governor of São Paulo), whom they had originally supported as President because they believed he would stamp out corruption. They were worried about the shortages, the strikes, the inflation, the flight of foreign capital. They even questioned São Paulo's own prosperity. The dizzy rush of building and installation went on of its own momentum, they said, but the boom had no really solid financial foundations.

My host, tall and distinguished in beautifully cut clothes, with German and French forebears, drove me after lunch along the Via Anchieta, the magnificent highway (named after one of the two Jesuit priests who founded São Paulo over four hundred years before) which links the city with Santos, its seaport and the largest coffee-exporting center in the world. "Where does the so-called great future of this country lie?" he demanded. I mentioned the "untapped mineral resources" the newspapers talked about. "But the world already has ample mineral resources," he replied, "and Brazilian iron isn't of the best quality."

"Timber?" I suggested.

"The best trees have been chopped down and the distances are too vast to make reafforestation feasible."

"Agriculture then?"

"The soil is bad, and there's too much single-crop economy; if world demand for coffee falls off, for example, our whole economy will collapse."

"Cattle?"

"We've plenty of cattle, certainly. More in fact than Argentina; but you've eaten Brazilian steaks . . ."

Like everybody else in this frame of mind, he was eager for a scapegoat. It was the Syrians he had cast for the role as far as São Paulo was concerned—they were the modern usurers, he declared, who were swallowing up everything. And then suddenly he said, "I'm tired of living on the edge of a precipice. It's boom now, but inflation gets worse every day. Eventually imports will have to be cut back, then industry will slow down and there will be massive unemployment. Boom and the Syrians today, tomorrow slump, and the day after tomorrow the Communists. Yes, I would like to get out while there's still a chance, and start life again, in the U.S.A. perhaps, or in Europe—yes, in Europe."

We had stopped the car halfway between Santos and São Paulo

and climbed to the top of a knoll overlooking both cities. Mountains in the background were as wild and jagged almost as those behind Rio de Janeiro. The pylons, factory chimneys and oil refineries of São Paulo might themselves have been mountains. The air was very clear and the lights of the two cities swarmed below us to left and right. Beyond the wide, curving bay of Santos the ocean horizon was just visible.

8

PARANÁ

Paraná is nearly as big as Britain—with an Atlantic seaboard, a high central plateau, and to the north a region of tropical rivers and forests, some of them still unexplored, which reaches out to the borders of Paraguay and Argentina. It is the newest of the Brazilian states, splitting off from the "Capitania" of São Paulo in 1853. The western part of the state was originally occupied by Spanish Jesuits who collected the Indians into large villages, later destroyed by *bandeirantes* from São Paulo (a sad day for the Indians, who were massacred in their thousands). But Paraná was too far away for easy colonization. Most of the permanent settlements were in the eastern part of the state; they spread slowly and they were not rich enough to justify the importation of slaves in any numbers. Up to 1940 a large portion of the population consisted of German, Polish, Ukrainian and Italian immigrants. Then came the coffee boom, and hundreds of thousands of Brazilians both from the north and from some of the southern states (especially Rio Grande do Sul) poured into Paraná. In consequence it has the rawness, the diversity, and the energy of a pioneer state, combined with the problems of a boom economy.

"Muitos problemas, muitos problemas" ("many problems") were practically the first words which the governor—likable, immensely

able and tipped in some quarters as a future President of the Re-public—addressed to me. As one of his schemes for "promoting" the state of Paraná he had reanimated the Tourist Department and established a highly efficient public-relations system, and in fact I came as a semiofficial guest of the state. Youthful, dapper, slightly balding at the crown, with a neat black mustache and dressed in the usual dark "politician's suit" and a beautiful pair of black hand-made shoes, he received me in the study of his palace, in the new civic center started in 1953 to mark the centenary of Paraná's statehood, then left unfinished after two successive frosts had affected the coffee crops.

"Here is one of the problems," he said. He handed me a photo-graph. It showed a group of men armed with rifles, knives and re-volvers. "They are land squatters. You can hardly blame them. In the interior there are sometimes as many as seven titles to one piece of land. But we have to do something about it. Law and order must be maintained. You will learn some of the other problems for your-self."

As I left the anteroom a clerk handed me a typed document written in English. It stated "some of the other problems" with remarkable frankness. A section headed "The Socio-economic Situation" gave the following statistics: "Infantile death-rate: 155 per 1,000 live births. People served by running water: 18%. People served by sewerage systems: 7%. Hospital beds: 1.8 per 1,000 inhabitants." Another paragraph pointed to "the coffee boom, triggered by the geographical expansion of the coffee-growing area of São Paulo" as the great turning point in Paraná's his-tory, as a result of which the population had risen from not much more than a million in 1940 to well over five million today. A sec-tion headed "General Outlook" contained the warning: "It must be remembered that the coffee market is unstable and lives in constant oversupply." It was followed by the terse statement, "The solution: to diversify the economy"; and an outline of policy which read: ". . . to create the necessary attraction so that internal and external investment capital will be directed into the sectors with better conditions for development; to direct public investments into those sectors that represent the bottleneck of the development process, like power, roads and others."

Curitiba, the capital of the state, was settled by the Portuguese in the seventeenth century. Now it is a city of over half a million inhabitants, with ranks of skyscrapers, remarkably regular and all of them chalk-white so that from a distance they look like cliffs smoothed and diced by wind and sea. The older buildings are nineteenth-century, Central European in style rather than Portuguese. The Prefecture, for example, with its stone balconies, arched windows, pointed eaves and central tower surmounted by a dome might have been a *rathaus* in one of the provincial towns of Germany or Austria.

The churches, of no particular architectural interest, reflected the cosmopolitan nature of the population. In the center of the city were Lutheran, Baptist, Presbyterian and Adventist churches, as well as a large Jewish synagogue. Tucked away in the side streets I found a mosque, a Positivist temple, a temple of Pythagoras and a half-completed Rosicrucian temple.

The men wore suits and trilby hats as they drank their *cafèzinhos* ("we are bolstering the economy," one of the habitués told me as he drank his sixth cup) or walked up and down in the street outside, discussing business or politics. This itself was a small thread in the changing texture: from now on as I went southward I was to find that nearly every town had one street set aside for this purpose; the custom probably originated in the *corso* of Italian cities and was introduced by Italian immigrants.

In the northwest the aboriginal inhabitants of the state are still to be found. There was great excitement in the university's Department of Anthropology because of a report just brought in by the pilot of a plane who had been flying over the dense jungles of the Serra dos Dourados, and had seen the smoke of Indian fires. But there was more to it than that. In 1950, a young anthropologist explained, the pioneers were trying to reach the extreme north of Paraná, but had found their way blocked by the high ridges of the

Serra dos Dourados. They were forced to turn south, and were eventually able to ford the lower reaches of the Ivaí River and to make use of an old track used for driving cattle into Paraná from Mato Grosso. The result of this diversion was that the Indians of the Serra dos Dourados remained completely isolated. Later on, several expeditions of surveyors prospecting the territory with a view to extending the coffee-growing area reported the existence of an unknown tribe of Indians. The Federal Bureau for the Protection of the Indians also dispatched expeditions; but the tribe was elusive, and even when Brazilians began to settle in the area it was only rarely that they caught glimpses of them.

Then in 1955 a severe frost delayed the ripening of the palm trees, upon which the Indians are largely dependent for their food; driven by hunger, a group of them approached the nearest *fazenda* for help. The foreman treated them well and intelligently, and with his help officers of the Protection Bureau were able to make contact with them and to establish not only that they belonged to a hitherto unknown tribe, known as the Xetá, but that anthropologically they were of the greatest interest because, with their absolute freedom from contact with white men or semicivilized Indians, they were still living a nomadic Stone Age existence, their weapons and tools made entirely of stone or animal bones, their diet consisting, apart from the tender stems of the palm trees, of wild honey, jungle fruits, the larvae of bees and beetles, together with some river fish (though they have no knowledge of the fishhook) and the occasional tapir which they catch in skillfully constructed traps, as the hide is too tough for their arrows to penetrate.

Photographs of these Indians were displayed in the Department of Anthropology. They were naked except for loincloths woven from plant fibers. Men and women wore necklaces of dried fruits or the teeth and bones of animals, and also earrings and head-dresses of feathers. Their lower lips were pierced and deformed by ornaments made of resin. They had no pottery, and their only receptacles were the shells of nuts and fruits. Their only furniture consisted of palm-weave baskets and sleeping mats, and their huts were temporary affairs of twigs and palm leaves. One photograph showed several women carrying their babies fastened to their hips by bands of palm leaves, and another showed them on the march carrying their belongings in baskets fastened to their foreheads by bands of the same material, while the men, armed with bows and arrows, guarded them.

It had, however, been suspected that there were other members of the Xetá still in the jungle who had never seen white men or been seen by them. A year before, there had been reports of the discovery of abandoned camps and of the smoke of fires rising above the trees. Then all trace had once again been lost. And now this new report from the pilot of the plane.

The Department of Anthropology was in the old university. High up on the outskirts of the city a new one was taking shape, designed to hold four thousand students and specializing, as befitted a pioneer state, in mechanical, constructional and hydraulic engineering.

One of Brazil's greatest engineers, Teixeira Soares, had in fact achieved his most spectacular triumph in Paraná. When in the 1860s the idea was first raised of linking Curitiba by rail with Paranaguá, the state's main port, on the other side of the mountain range called the Serra do Mar, Belgian, French and Italian engineers, in turn, were invited to consider it, and in turn, they pronounced it to be impracticable. Eventually the job was given to Teixeira Soares and after surmounting fantastic problems he succeeded in building a railway, which was opened in 1888.

It is one of the most remarkable railways in the world. When I traveled on it I could certainly see the point of view of those Belgian, French and Italian engineers: it *was* impracticable, and theoretically it ought not to have succeeded. The journey began equably enough, in a train pulled by a red-and-yellow diesel engine, through meadows in which cattle grazed, past a lake steaming in the morning sun, fringed with reeds on which the dew still glistened. But soon we were among the foothills of the Serra do Mar in a wild country of woods and tumbling streams. And then as the mountain range loomed up in front of us we were curving, plunging, twisting, at every imaginable gradient and angle. The track crossed gorges so deep that their extremities were lost in mist and the vegetation came swaying out of it like seaweed from the bottom of the ocean. It passed behind waterfalls, over streams in which were embedded boulders as big as houses, crawled like a centipede up and over mounds of rock and coiled so closely round some of the mountains that, looking out from the front part of the train, I could see the rear car far below and apparently quite detached, and when I made my way to the back there above me was the red-and-yellow engine toiling away, it seemed, in the opposite direction.

Sometimes we plunged deep into the bowels of the mountains, and where the rock had proved too hard for tunneling, Soares had built iron platforms curving round the flanks of the mountains. One of these platforms, at a dizzy height, was built on iron pedestals sunk into stone piers, themselves embedded in the mountainside; another described a tremendous double loop to disclose the track below like gleaming snakes. And everywhere the vegetation came crowding round the track; the graceful wands of bamboo, with leaves at the end like bits of green rag; the biggest banana trees I had seen, with clumps of fruit like yellow-gloved hands—and, rising above them all, the giant Paraná pines.

The descent into Paranaguá was anticlimax. Away from the plateau, tropical heat and tropical squalor returned. The only bright spot was the town's solitary skyscraper, called the Coffee Palace, which had a restaurant on the top floor, overlooking the steaming waterfront. It was run by an Austrian and his Italian wife. Their daughter, a pretty girl of nineteen with honey-colored braids, talked wistfully about the limitations of life in Paranaguá for a girl who had been born in Europe. One day, she confided, she hoped to go to Curitiba—or even São Paulo. It was very gay in São Paulo, was it not?

There was one good eighteenth-century church, São Francisco das Chagas, the oldest in Paraná, and another famous throughout the state for its reported miracles. A wooden building near by sold wonder-working relics and contained an astonishing collection of objects deposited by worshipers and pilgrims who presumably hoped that they would work on their behalf by sympathetic magic. There were photographs of newlyweds and newly christened babies and marble effigies and busts of loved ones. Several shelves were filled with crutches, spectacles and surgical appliances. Most bizarre of all were the plaster casts of legs, arms, hands, hearts, livers and other organs, many of them luridly carved and painted to depict the diseases or deformities from which the owners of the originals were suffering.

The smell of coffee was everywhere. Warehouses lined the waterfront, and practically every suitable building had been converted into a warehouse. The sacks were stacked to the ceilings. Some of them had been stored for a considerable period, and the beans were beginning to deteriorate. The main topic of conversation was coffee, and much of it had an undertone of anxiety. It was essential, everybody was agreed, to search for new markets. "The Japanese are our most promising new customers," a coffee broker told me. "We must change their drinking habits." "Perhaps," another added wistfully, "we shall soon be friends with the Chinese, and we shall be able to change *their* drinking habits?"

It was a relief to get away from coffee and into the maté warehouses—which before 1940 had taken precedence—and to taste my first *mate-chimarrão*. I had drunk maté once before, as an undergraduate after reading Joseph Sheridan Le Fanu's famous story "Green Tea," but I had brewed the leaves in an ordinary teapot—and had been sadly disillusioned by the absence of any of the esoteric revelations Le Fanu had led me to expect. But in southern Brazil (and in many other parts of South America) the leaves are toasted and ground into a powder (*mate-chimarrão* in fact means "without sugar"). The fine powder is placed inside a small calabash or *cuia*. Boiling water is poured on top of it, turning it into a thick green paste. The liquid is then drawn through a silver tube (*bombilha*) with a spoon-shaped strainer at the end to prevent the powder getting into one's mouth. When I first arrived in Paraná and saw people sucking away at the silver tubes I thought that they were smoking oddly shaped pipes. In southern Brazil the habit indeed is almost as common as smoking. For my part I couldn't see the attraction. When I tried it, the liquid shot into my mouth, scalding hot and very bitter, and a good deal of the powder came through in spite of the strainer.

The use of maté derived from the aboriginal Indians. It was found that the Xetá of the Serra dos Dourados, for example, drink a beverage of maté leaves, slightly toasted, ground, and mixed with cold water. When the Department of Physiology at Curitiba University analyzed a specimen, they found that besides containing important mineral salts it was rich in Vitamin C. Like cats who seek out couch grass when they are sick, primitive men instinctively discover the plants their bodies need—and perhaps it was the same instinct that led white men, in this region where fresh vegetables are almost nonexistent, to copy the habit.

The whole region of Paranaguá is rich in Indian associations. The eighteenth-century Jesuit College has been converted into a Museum of Archaeology attached to the University of Paraná, and its main task is investigating the numerous *sambaquis*—ancient Indian shell mounds or midden heaps—which yielded many primitive artifacts and in some cases the remains of human burials, probably several thousand years old. I saw posters all over the countryside calling for information about new *sambaquis* and warning people that it was illegal to interfere with them.

It was, however, the road to Ponta Grossa that played the biggest part during this stage of my travels in Paraná. Ponta Grossa itself— a town of about fifty thousand inhabitants and a center for maté, rice, timber, tobacco, cattle and jerked beef—I never set foot in. Too many distractions intervened. Sometimes it was the echoes of Europe—children with fair hair and blue eyes, wearing smocks; old men wearing caps with hanging earlaps; carts with steep, gaily painted sides, and the horses with polished harness and rosettes fastened to their heads; chalet-type bungalows with steep-pointed eaves; churches with long spires, or square, wooden churches with separate towers, built by Polish settlers; and once a village of Italian immigrants set among vineyards.

Sometimes all I wanted to do was to follow the pines. There were hundreds of square miles of them. Their numbers were calculated at eight hundred million, though the recent forest fires must have thinned them out. They are of a very distinctive type (*Araucaria angustifolia* is the botanical name), with broad, straight trunks about ten feet in diameter at the base, but slender-looking because of their height—two hundred feet and more. The trunks are quite bare and then toward the top the branches stretch out on either side, apparently identical in number and length, and either curving upward so that the trees look like giant candelabra, or curving downward so that you feel that if you uprooted them you could stand them on end. Much of the building in Paraná is of pine wood, and there are many paper mills. In the more isolated regions of the plateau the pines also shelter the best of the maté bushes, and from December to August teams of men, taking food and cattle with them, set up encampments in the forests in order to pick the maté leaves and prepare the *tatacuas*, or curing grounds.

On the next occasion it was a distraction of a different kind. I was accompanied by the guide whom the Tourist Department had appointed to help me—a young man with an Italian name and a clever Italian face. We had headed into the Serra de São Luís, a country of tumbling rock-strewn streams with a Dartmoor gray-and-pearl sky. Rocks of pink, cream, ocher and gray erupted through the thinning turf; gradually the landscape grew wilder and barer. Then against the skyline rose what looked like the ruins of an Inca fortress-city. Close up, my bewilderment increased, for surely these were the remains of early medieval walls, towers, keeps, ramps and buttresses? On top of one battlement I even saw a row of gargoyles.

It was "Vila Velha"—but an "Ancient City" made by Nature, not by man. Erosion had worn away layer after layer of soil and softer stone, exposing the ancient rocks, grainy with fossilized marine plants and sea shells, and molding them into the shapes of walls and buildings. In the open spaces were single formations of rock in the shapes of giant anvils, cromlechs, thrones, tortoises and altars. The most spectacular had acquired traditional names, such as the Chalice, the Camel, the Sphinx. Some were grouped in circles and avenues, like the sarsens of Stonehenge; others rose in spires, needles, obelisks, and pillars like twisted candlesticks; others swelled out from slender columns into huge bossed heads, like giant knob-kerries; and there was one vast escarpment, ridged and furrowed like a petrified waterfall. The coloring of the rocks was as variegated as the sandstone cliffs of Alum Bay in the Isle of Wight. The rocky flooring of the lanes and avenues was striped in red and yellow, or streaky brown like polished crocodile skin. Where sandy soil had collected at the foot of some of the formations, or high up in their hollows and ledges, stunted trees and bushes had established themselves. The "battlements" were surmounted by rows of palm trees, their fronds like the banners and plumes of an occupying Saracen host.

When I next took the road to Ponta Grossa I was in search of Russians. In Curitiba I had been told of some thirteen hundred Old Believers—the sect that had refused to accept Peter the Great's Church reforms and as a result had suffered persecution ever after —who had recently been settled on a tract of land in the Ponta Grossa area as Paraná's contribution to the World Refugee Year. Their ancestors had left Russia in the eighteenth century, wandered from place to place in Central Asia, returned to Russia, and then left again, on the outbreak of the Revolution, for Manchuria. Revolution had caught up with them again, and after a number of abortive attempts at integration the Chinese People's Government allowed them to go to Hong Kong. From there the World Council of Churches arranged for them to be flown to Paraná, the first group in May 1958 and the second some fifteen months later.

I could find no one in Curitiba who knew what had happened to them since. Occasionally, I was told, a jeep had driven in containing strangely dressed, bearded men (the Old Believers do not shave), but they spoke no Portuguese, kept very much to themselves and, after buying the provisions or equipment they had come for, left immediately. I discovered that the name of the colony was Santa Cruz, but I couldn't find anyone who could tell me where it was—apart from a vague "on the road to Ponta Grossa." Then I met a White Russian—a former Guards officer who had escaped from Russia in 1918 and eventually emigrated to Brazil—who had also heard of the Old Believers and was longing to see Russian faces again. Together we set off along the road to Ponta Grossa.

It proved a complicated business. Nobody knew the way to Santa Cruz. One old shepherd repeated wonderingly, "Russians? With beards?" and stared at us as if we were mad. Those who had heard of it had only the vaguest idea where it lay, and we were misdirected a dozen times. Eventually we found ourselves in Palmeira, a little logging town, sleepy in the afternoon sunshine. Here too the word "Russians" produced bewilderment, but the beards did the trick: we were given fresh directions, but were warned that the settlement was not easy to spot. "The bearded men" discouraged visitors, and their village was well-hidden. We must look out for a barred gate; there were many barred gates, but this one had an advertisement for Casas Pernambucanas stuck on it.

There were, in fact, several such gates—the advertising campaign of Casas Pernambucanas, Brazil's biggest chain of stores, must be one of the most enterprising in the world. We chose the most se-curely fastened and drove over rough, bumpy ground in the direc-tion of a clump of trees. The stretch of rough ground had obviously been left for purposes of concealment, for about fifty yards farther on we came to fields of crops, very regular and well tended, and a track surfaced with chips of stone. There was not a soul in sight, and we were about to turn back when suddenly we came upon a woman standing at the side of the track. She wore a dress down to her ankles and an embroidered pinafore; her head was wrapped in a scarf; she had a broad, homely face, burned brick-red by the sun. My companion leaned out of the window and called to her in Rus-sian. She stared at him unbelievingly.

Another mile, and we were in a Russian village—a wide street of beaten earth; compact wooden huts on either side, each with a tiny yard enclosed by railings; curtains or strips of lace at the windows; smoke coming from the chimneys. A small boy in a scarlet blouse and a fur cap was cracking a whip. A little girl of about two, bundled up in skirts, pinafores, head scarf and long boots, so that she looked like one of those circular Russian toy dolls, was tottering unsteadily down the center of the road. The only other person in sight was a tall man with a ginger beard, wearing a blue blouse, belted and hanging over his trousers, who came out of a cow shed a little farther down the village street, regarded us sternly and called out something to a nearby hut, from which, incredibly, came the soft, liquid sound of a Russian choir.

We made for the hut, stopped outside it—and almost immediately were surrounded by about twenty young men. They too wore blouses, with square embroidered necks and embroidered belts. Some had Brazilian straw hats on their heads, but most of them wore Cossack caps or went bareheaded, their straight hair tow-colored and growing low over their foreheads. All of them were bearded, some with fine bushy growths, the younger ones with the merest wisps, like camel's-hair paintbrushes. They closed round the car. My companion spoke to them in Russian, asking to be directed to their *staretz*. But the sound of their own language had the opposite effect from what we had expected. They drew closer and their expressions were far from friendly.

I remembered the recent resumption of diplomatic relations between Brazil and the U.S.S.R., and it occurred to me that these young men might think we were from the Soviet Embassy in Rio de Janeiro, sent perhaps to spy. I mentioned my suspicion to my companion. He spoke to them again. When he had finished, one of the young men went inside the hut and returned a moment later with two older men: one a fat man in a blue blouse, with a jet-black beard and a mouthful of gold teeth; the other a tall, elderly man, thin and stooping, with a straggling white beard, wearing an old gray suit over a blue blouse. The older man spoke to us: "Our *staretz* is in Ponta Grossa on business. I am one of the elders. This is my younger brother; he too is an elder. We have few visitors here—

and you are speaking Russian. We want only to be left alone to practice our religion in the ways we have been taught. What is it you want?" My companion launched into another speech. My Russian wasn't good enough to follow, but obviously he convinced them of our *bona fides*, for the young men hurried back into the hut— from which the sound of singing, to the accompaniment now of a balalaika, was still proceeding—while their elders held open the doors of the car for us to descend.

They led us into the hut. "We are celebrating a betrothal," the older man explained. "Also it is a day of rest in our religion; that is why you see no one working, except the cowherd." The hut was solidly built of planks of Paraná pine. On the walls were icons and religious pictures. There was a huge Russian stove in which wood was burning, and the atmosphere was stifling. About thirty young men and women were seated on wooden benches, or on the beds, which were fitted into alcoves, with the curtains drawn back; curtains and bedspreads were gaily embroidered. The elders introduced us to the betrothed couple: a shy, fair-haired boy of about nineteen in a satin blouse, and a pretty, ruddy-cheeked girl wearing a red head scarf, a flowered frock and green apron.

The church at the center of the village was a plain wooden shed. Inside was an equally plain altar. For some reason the carpenter must have made it longer than usual, for the very fine altar cloth only reached halfway; the rest was covered by odd lengths of embroidered cloth. On top of the altar were candles in rather battered candlesticks together with a pair of snuffers, a large Bible fastened with a gilt clasp, and a number of icons and holy pictures. Most of these were obviously of recent workmanship, but one icon and one small painting, the treasures of the community which had accompanied them and their forebears in all their wanderings, belonged to the mid-seventeenth century. A little old woman, bundled up in dark clothes, with a black cloth round her head, placed two candles in front of one of the images, then stood muttering her prayers and crossing herself. On a side table was a huge parchment book of psalms, open at the psalm of the day, the words in ancient

Cyrillic characters and the musical notations executed by hand; it was a recent copy of many copies, the original of which had been lost, no one knew how, centuries ago. The copying of this book and of ancient Bibles, like the painting of holy images and pictures and the art of embroidery, were important spare-time activities, the elders explained, that had been handed down from generation to generation.

From the church the old man took us to his own home. The plank floor had been recently scrubbed and was protected by bits of sacking. Two beds, set in alcoves, were covered by patchwork quilts. Working clothes hung on hooks. Here too was a huge Russian stove. There was even an old grandfather sleeping on top of it. It might have been the set of a Gorky play. The elder's wife was a plump, big-faced woman, with black skirts round her ankles and a woolen cloth over her head, fastened round the neck like a cowl. She showed me her kitchen. The smell of baking came from an earthenware oven. Carrots, onions, turnips, swedes and other vegetables one doesn't often see in Brazil were scattered over a stone-topped table in readiness for the stewpot. Other pots and pans, scoured until they shone, were ranged on a shelf.

Back in the living room we sat on heavy wooden chairs—homemade, like the huts themselves—while the two elders told us about their lives and problems since they had arrived in Paraná, and children peered in at the windows and doors. Things had been hard at first. The World Council of Churches had provided them with agricultural machinery, including tractors, plows and seeders, barbed wire, tools, seed, fertilizers and insecticides, as well as horses and carts. In addition, each family had received a cow and a clutch of hens. But they were facing unfamiliar conditions. In Manchuria there had been hunting and fishing; here they had to subsist entirely by agriculture. They had set to work plowing the land, working in shifts twenty-four hours a day, at night using the headlights of their tractors. But the land was poor and the wheat they had first sown had been a failure.

At this point the elder's wife bustled in and placed on the table a plate of freshly baked oaten biscuits, mugs, and a jug of some cloudy, orange-colored liquid. The elder filled the mugs. I raised mine to my lips; it had a pleasant, sharpish taste. I drained the mug, and the elder refilled it. A glazed look had come into the eyes of the Russian from Curitiba; he was staring into his mug. *"Kvass!"* he murmured. "After all these years!"

I felt almost as moved as he did. *Kvass* was one of those trigger-words—like *troika,* or *droshky,* or *babushka*—which summoned up the whole fictional world of pre-Revolutionary Russia. I never dreamed that I would drink my first glass in Brazil, in Paraná, somewhere on the road to Ponta Grossa.

The elder and his brother took up their tale again. After the failure of the wheat crop they had been successful with corn, oats, beans—and above all with a species of "dry rice" (rice, that is, that does not need to be puddled), which they had brought from Manchuria. Proudly they informed us that out of their profits they had already bought fourteen new tractors, three combines and four lorries. Now they were in a position to acquire additional land. The problem here was a contractual one. The banks were reluctant to lend money to the community as a whole; they wanted the signatures of individuals, and the private ownership of land was contrary to their religious principles. At this moment their *staretz* was in Ponta Grossa discussing the problem. I asked what they would do if the banks persisted in their attitude. Perhaps, they said, they would come to some arrangement whereby the land would be legally divided between the elders, each acting for a group of colonists, so that a series of separate contracts could be drawn up. But they were not happy about it.

I questioned them about education, knowing that by Brazilian law all children domiciled in the country had to be educated in Brazilian schools. At the moment, I was told, the Paraná education authorities were sending teachers to the colony to teach the children Portuguese, but they also had a school of their own, where the elders taught Russian and the traditional arts and crafts—and, of course, the tenets of their own religion. Over the centuries they had isolated themselves almost completely from the outside world and they saw no reason why they should not continue to do so. Marriages with outsiders were discouraged. Yes, there had been quite a number of marriages since their arrival (and, as I had seen, there was soon to be another one), but they had all been within the community or with members of the other settlement (the second group flown over by the World Council of Churches), which was some five miles away.

They had no anxieties on the score of their religion—there is no state church in Brazil (though the bulk of the population is Roman Catholic), and in religious matters it is probably the most tolerant country in the world. Their creeds and forms of worship, they assured me, had remained unadulterated over the centuries. I gathered that religious services occupy practically the whole of Sunday and much of Saturday, that they celebrate two Lents a year, that there are a number of days of complete fasting, and that a strictly vegetarian diet is observed every Wednesday and Friday. But they were certainly no flint-faced ascetics. The two elders, for example, were enjoying their *kvass* as much as I was.

The day was hot, the stove made the inside of the hut like a furnace, and I was very thirsty. It was a pleasant drink, which seemed to me quite innocuous, and I drank a good deal of it. Eventually my companion suggested it was time we left. I agreed, but for some reason which I could not comprehend nothing happened. I saw the old man looking at me, his eyes twinkling; his long white beard stirred as he began a rumbling laugh deep in his chest. I stared at him in horror. My legs would not move. My companion offered me his arm, but the elders insisted on helping me to my feet themselves. It was astonishing: the top half of my body felt perfectly normal, but my legs hung loose as if they were filled with sand. By the time we reached the door I was able to take a few tottering steps, but it was supported by two elders of the Russian Old Believers that I made my way back to the car.

Early one morning I found myself on the private airfield of Curitiba. The governor had put one of the state's planes at my disposal, an American Skywagon four-seater monoplane. It looked no bigger than a tandem as it was wheeled out of its hangar on to the runway.

The pilot arrived, a young man of about twenty-eight, with a fresh complexion, white, even teeth, close-cropped fair hair, and wearing, not the pilot's outfit I had expected, but a smart summer suit of dark-gray alpaca. Like the young guide of the State Tourist Department, who was to accompany us, he had an Italian name. Under his hands the plane took off as casually as if it were a fly rising from a tablecloth.

Three hours later significant streaks began to appear in the hill-sides—the first signs that we were approaching the *terra roxa*, the reddish-purplish soil of the coffee country. At first the plantations were quite small. With their plants set in regular rows, the tops of the bushes circular green bosses, they looked like so many solitaire boards. Beyond Assaí (a town of thirty-two thousand, of whom 80 per cent are Japanese), the full extent of the coffee boom struck home. The plantations extended now as far as the eye could reach, on and on over hills and valleys and up to the horizon and then, as the plane approached, on to yet another horizon. There was the same astonishing appearance of regularity—like vast armies on parade. Here and there, however, the lines of bushes, particularly on the hillsides, curved and swirled in order to guard against erosion—for all these hundreds of square miles represent the bulldozing of the natural landscape of pines and jungles and there are fears that the frantic haste with which it was done may one day have disastrous consequences. Now, too, instead of homesteads there were whole towns, the buildings, streets and squares as symmetrical as the plantations themselves, like so many Welwyn Garden cities.

The largest and most remarkable of them is Londrina, the center of the whole vast industry. The coffee plantations advanced to its very edge, like ranks of green-helmeted ants. Then suddenly they gave way to mile after mile of warehouses, beyond which towered the skyscrapers. The airfield was one of the biggest in Brazil, ranking third in the number of passenger flights, I was assured by a stocky, broad-shouldered man with a mop of grizzled hair and the eyes of a fanatic, who ran an air-taxi-hire service and was a friend of my pilot. He showed us his hangars and his workshops, where spare parts were ranged in shelves, neatly labeled so that he could, he boasted, undertake almost any repair to almost any type of plane at a moment's notice. His bungalow was itself not much more than a shed, so close to the airfield that the red dust raised by propellers and exhausts swirled round it, and the baby in the pram outside was coated with it. But a luxury American limousine was also parked there.

"Come to Londrina—and make a fortune!" he urged us. "There are unlimited opportunities. Don't worry what kind of business— *any* business will succeed here. That's my advice: raise every penny you can lay your hands on and bring it to Londrina. You will be rich in three years—I promise it."

The atmosphere of the whole airport was one of frantic, pioneer excitement. Private planes arrived continuously, and farmers from the interior, their boots caked inches thick with *terra roxa,* clambered out of them. Others arrived in taxis, in cars, or on horseback, after visits to their plantations on the other side of the city. The sheds were crammed with crates of goods and equipment.

The redness was everywhere—on the floor of the airport lounge, on the tablecloths of the restaurant, in the pages of the telephone directories. A child sucking a lollipop had red stains round his mouth. The urinals oozed red mud. It was the same in the city itself. The gutters ran red, the pavements and the boulevards were red, and the flowers and the grass and the Flamboyant trees of the central *praça* were streaked with it. The walls of the buildings were splashed with it up to four feet from the ground. Even the upper reaches of the skyscrapers had taken on a pinkish tinge, and in the bedroom of my hotel, eight floors up, I found the freshly laundered sheets still showing traces of it. By the time I left Londrina my skin and the leather of my shoes were alike engrained. For weeks after, whenever I washed my hair the water was a reddish color, and even now, after many cleanings, I find streaks of red in the cuffs of the trousers I was wearing. Most astonishing of all, when the rain fell, that too was red from the particles of dust in the atmosphere and my shirt was spattered with polka dots.

In the rain the modern gloss of Londrina was quickly washed away to reveal the pioneer settlement beneath. The streets were covered with a film of mud, the side streets in the suburbs were quagmires; the skyscrapers seemed temporary visitants and the rows of wooden bungalows the reality.

The city jail might have been some calaboose in the Klondike, though its squalor, no doubt, was characteristically South American. Our pilot was a friend of the chief warder. When we arrived he was in the main office, talking to a woman in a ragged shawl with three children, ranging in age from seven to two, all of them barefoot, their feet and legs caked with red mud. They had been working, she explained, on one of the coffee plantations, but now the crop was gathered, they had nowhere to go, and her husband had absconded with the takings.

The chief warder made out free travel passes which would take her and the children to a village near Paranaguá where they had relations. "God knows what *they'll* say," the warder added, "when they turn up without a *cruzeiro*. God knows the state they'll be in when they get there. They've only had one meal in three days, and that's the one we've just given them."

He led the way out of the office into a slimy exercise yard not much bigger than a handball court. Two men in their underpants, with blankets over their naked shoulders, were trotting round and round, looking up at the sky and taking in deep gulps of air. It was easy to see why, when we entered the cell block. The plaster walls of the corridors were cracked and pitted, and smeared with filth. The floors were littered with scraps of dirty paper; as the heavy door clanged shut they stirred, then settled again, creating an atmosphere of appalling desolation, as if one were stranded for eternity upon an abandoned railway platform. The stench assailed the nostrils as if acrid fur had been pressed over them. One cell, about as big as an average pantry, contained three women with tangled black hair, who stared at us sullenly; an unemptied toilet bucket stood in the middle of the floor. In the same corridor were other cells crammed with men detained for preliminary questioning. I counted fifteen in one of them. They sat on the edges of their bunks or on the floor, staring in front of them. Three of them had torn out the pages of an old magazine which they repeatedly passed backward and forward. It was by no means uncommon, the warder told me, for a prisoner to be detained a year before standing trial.

In one cell, two youths of about nineteen, handcuffed together, kept up a continual clamor, pressing their faces to the bars and every time we passed shouting out the names and addresses of friends and relations, begging us to get in touch with them, protesting their innocence. The chief warder regarded them impassively. When I asked why they were handcuffed, he shrugged his shoulders. "They attacked one of my officers." In another cell a man lay on a bunk, shivering violently. I asked what was the matter with him. "Ague," the chief warder replied.

"Shouldn't he see a doctor?"

He shrugged his shoulders again. "It's common in prisons. He'll probably get over it." He was not a cruel man; he merely regarded the conditions as natural and inevitable. When I ventured a criticism, he regarded me with astonishment. "But prisons aren't supposed to be nice places!" he said.

In another corridor the cell doors were open and the "trusties" sat chattering on homemade stools. When the evening meal arrived, they tugged at our arms when the warders' backs were turned, and demonstrated the thinness of the soup—gray in color, with bits of macaroni floating in it; apart from a piece of bread there was nothing else—by lifting their spoons and letting the contents trickle back into the bowls.

One prisoner stood out from the rest, a gigantic Negro dressed in spotless dungarees and singlet, with a smooth, gentle face. The chief warder politely asked his permission to show us into his cell. The rough plaster walls were stippled with blue paint; there were pin-ups cut out from magazines, and pictures of palm trees and blue seas, crudely but vividly painted on squares of brown paper; there was a mattress on the bunk, and the blankets were stacked with military precision. "Oh, yes," the chief warder agreed, when we were out of earshot. "He's a superior type; we all respect him. And of course a man doing life deserves his privileges."

"Life?"

"Yes: he's done ten years so far."

"What was his crime?"

"Double murder."

As we left the prison the two young men were still banging their handcuffed wrists against the bars and shouting out that they were innocent. Perhaps they were.

Londrina's night spots were notable for the furious gaiety of the customers and the amount of money that was being thrown about. The establishment to which our friend of the air-taxi service took us was situated in a network of muddy roads on the outskirts and was crowded with men with bulging wallets, many of them in boots still red from the plantations. Any one of the tips given to waiters and cloakroom attendants would have fed the woman and her children I had seen at the police station for a week; the presents lavished on the girls would have kept them for a couple of months. Nearly everybody was drinking Scotch whisky, contraband and very expensive. The waiter looked down his nose when I ordered my favorite Brazilian drink—*cachaça* with lemon; they had none on the premises and had to send to a "lower-grade" establishment to get some. The girls were young, fresh and expensively dressed. They came from all parts of Brazil in search of the pickings and, according to a blond nineteen-year-old of German origin from Rio Grande do Sul, in the hope of capturing a coffee baron as lover or husband. Some came from other South American countries: there was a Paraguayan beauty, for example, tall, willowy, with an ivory-colored skin and jet-black hair piled up and sloping back, so that she looked like the ancient Egyptian Queen Nefertiti.

While the money and the whisky flowed, our host took out an envelope and demonstrated how his business had doubled in the last six months. His younger brother, shouting at the top of his voice and banging on the table with his glass, insisted on paying for everything, including girls whom no one wanted or who kept the arrangement dark so that they could collect twice over. He too urged us to settle in Londrina. "This is the life," he cried. "I have a wife, three children, and two mistresses—and I adore them all. I have two cars, a fine house and money in the bank. I tell you, this is the most exciting city in Brazil—it's the city of the future, the city of opportunity!"

It is certainly a remarkable phenomenon. The population when I was there was nearly 150,000; six new houses were completed every day; it was the fourth-largest banking center in Brazil, surpassed only by Rio, São Paulo, and Santos. And yet in 1924 it was no more than an idea in the minds of a group of British businessmen in London who sent out a team of technicians to investigate the possibilities and then after negotiating concessions with the government of Paraná formed the Brazil Plantation Syndicate. The first tract of land was bought toward the end of 1925, but it was not until July 1929 that the clearing of the site began. A year later came the first settlers. I was shown a list of them. It included names like Stassiak, Kernkampf, Ferrari, Larsen, Razgulaef, Frohlich, Rottman, and Ohara (Japanese, not Irish). The names of the British pioneers were there too; and in 1930 the link with London was perpetuated when the site was officially christened Londrina. But the Syndicate, along with so many other British assets, disappeared during the war.

Still closer to the pioneer stage was Maringá, fifty miles to the west of Londrina, only begun in 1947 but already containing 45,000 people and planned to hold five times that number. Here most of the roads were still raw red earth, and most of the houses were of wood, and the men, for the most part, wore wide straw hats or Stetsons, bush shirts and boots. But the wealthy nucleus already had their creature comforts well organized. The mayor treated us to the only really outstanding meal I had in Brazil, in a handsome hotel set in a grove of cactus, bananas and palms. Afterward he drove us in his American car to the Country Club, first requisite of the Brazilian well-to-do, hacked out of the jungle and containing the usual tennis courts, swimming pool, ballroom and cinema—and in addition a notice announcing, "Sunday: Bingo." Western civilization reached out to us even here.

Like the governor of the state, Maringá's mayor stressed the importance of diversifying the economy. In his area cotton, beans and other crops were grown, as well as coffee, and oil was extracted from *mamona*. But for a long time to come, he admitted, the fortunes of all these new cities would rise or fall on coffee. The far-sighted recognize the dangers of overproduction. The speculators keep up the wild scramble. As we headed southwest from Londrina we looked down upon a panoramic battle between jungle and coffee. At first, nothing but jungle as far as the eye could reach; then, equally extensive, coffee plantations; then again the jungle; but smaller plantations still bit into it, and every now and then we flew over large areas devastated as if by shellfire, still smoking and scattered with the blackened corpses of trees.

Gradually, however, the jungle took over. As we approached the River Paraná, which forms the boundary with the huge state of Mato Grosso, we entered what must be some of the wildest and most beautiful country on earth. The river is the fifth-largest in the world, 2,750 miles in length, fed by hundreds of tributaries, and scattered with islands with white, fan-shaped beaches, almost as numerous as those of the Amazon. In its upper reaches it is known by the Indian name of Paranaiba, or "Great River Full of Cata-racts." This is because near the junction of Paraguay and the Brazilian states of Mato Grosso and Paraná the valley becomes a chaos of precipitous rocks, gorges and canyons and the river thunders down them (more than thirteen million cubic feet every minute) in a series of cataracts called the Sete Quedas—though the Sete (seven) is used for euphony rather than accuracy, for the number of the falls varies according to the rate of flow.

Below the Sete Quedas, as the river, incredibly deep now, charged southward, the forests, whether we were flying over Paraná, Mato Grosso or Paraguay (and we weaved backward and forward like a dazed bird) ranged deep, silent and boundless. The trees crowded right up to the towering riverbanks—palm, pine and *ipé* in rose or golden flower, and in front of them a narrow border of bamboos like ostrich plumes. There was no break in the vegetation: nothing but an occasional black hollow.

It was nearly an hour before we came upon the first house, in a small clearing on the Brazilian side of the river. From then on a house appeared every few miles. There was, too, an occasional logging station and once we saw a small boat emerge cautiously from a creek and make for the Paraguayan side of the river—probably a smuggler. Then we were approaching the new International Bridge (the biggest single-arch concrete bridge in the world, and all of it Brazilian-made, the engineers boast) which links Brazil and Paraguay.

Later on, we crossed this bridge. There was the usual business of passports, currency and customs, though eventually I suppose it will be simplified, as the plan, still under negotiation between the two governments, is to give Paraguay access to the port of Paranaguá on the coast of Paraná. A village of shacks had sprung up on the other side of the bridge. A store was crowded with Brazilians buying goods in short supply across the water, particularly toilet requisites, cans of American beer and cut-price bottles of whisky. There was a landing stage at the river's edge where a paddle boat, which travels along the Paraná River as far as Buenos Aires, was taking on passengers. A long-distance bus was setting out for Asunción, a thirteen-hour journey. The people were the usual mixture of white, Negro and Indian. Only the soft, floppy straw hats of the laborers and the gold earrings and Spanish combs of the women told us that we were in another country.

Now, however, we flew straight on along the course of the river, sweeping west in a wide curve to meet its tributary the Paraguay (itself a vast river) at the dividing line between three nations— Paraguay to the west, Argentina to the east, and Brazil protruding into the angle formed by the junction of the two rivers. A few miles below this junction another river, the Iguaçú, which rises near Curitiba and flows south and west for five hundred miles, collecting the waters of over thirty tributaries as it goes, also joins the Paraná. And as we headed up the Iguaçú we saw in the distance, above the treetops, a billowing white cloud, and above the vibrations of the plane we could hear the roar of the Foz do Iguaçú, one of the world's greatest waterfalls—half as wide again as Niagara (more than a mile across) and thirty to forty feet higher, though Iguaçú's descent, unlike Niagara's, is broken by a ledge.

We flew below the treetops along the river and straight at the falls. They came hurtling over a vast horseshoe of rock. The white cloud revealed itself as foaming water bursting from the "Devil's Gorge," the most spectacular of the cataracts, at the point where the northern arm of the river hurtles through a narrow canyon and down in an uninterrupted drop of two hundred feet. Within an ace, it seemed, of our plane being caught up like a matchstick we banked sharply, turned, and flew back at another of the falls, sweeping down this time in a vast, cream curtain. We repeated the operation (altogether there are twenty-three separate falls, divided by barriers of rocks and boulders) until sight and hearing, and the sense of wonder itself were exhausted.

The Hotel of the Cataracts, more Spanish than Brazilian in style, had spacious pillared halls and thick white walls. But they weren't thick enough to shut out the roar of the falls. It haunted us until we left the hotel and found our way through the woods—on the alert for the *onças* (a generic term for all wildcats, but applied especially to the panthers) which still haunt them, though this is now a national park, with paths and bays and an observation tower overlooking the falls. The moon came out just as we reached them. Its light seemed to slow them down. They came out of the blackness in dense columns, as if the night were a gigantic wounded tree from which a milky sap poured eternally; they pounded on the rocks below with immense slow-motion deliberation; the roar seemed quite separate; the illusion was of absolute silence.

By day, there was nothing slow-motion about the falls: they hurtled down as if the skies had been torn open, and the earth shuddered. Movement and sound worked together with disconcerting effect. The one filled me with a kind of mad exhilaration, the other deadened my sense of reality and of danger. Between them they drove us to get as close to the falls as possible, and we began clambering over slippery rocks and tree trunks scoured and polished as smooth as glass, until we were at the very edge of one of the steepest falls. Its sheer volume nearly toppled us over, and when I put out my finger a fraction of an inch it was practically carried away. Then, dripping with spray and perspiration, we scrambled back to the shore, made our way to the head of the falls, past the observation tower and a hunting lodge (from which parties hunt the *onças*) and then began another perilous climb across the upper river. At the point where the water plunged downward it seemed to bend over in a thick oily coil like a giant python.

Amongst all the frantic motion and clangor there were islands of astonishing calm. Only a few yards higher up, the river swirled lazily; within a few feet of a boiling mass of water were still pools clouded with insects; on the small islands at the foot of the cataracts grass and wild flowers waved, and the island of San Martin, which dams back the waters, sending them tumbling and foaming on either side, was crowned with dense forest, dark and silent. The cliffs, too, thrusting through the dense jungle which surrounded the whole valley, were still and impassive, except for the parakeets, extraordinarily numerous and as active as grasshoppers.

It was as if the Garden of Eden and the mouth of Hades had been brought into juxtaposition. The trees were bigger, more beautiful, and more bewildering in their variety than anywhere else in Brazil. Palms, bamboos, vines, creepers and shrubs clung to every islet and ledge. Wild begonias and numerous varieties of orchid grew in profusion. There were butterflies, cream, gray, fawn, and black-and-white; strangely elongated scarlet butterflies; giant butterflies, black, peacock-blue, green and gold; and butterflies with thick, downy wings like brown velvet. The birds were as numerous and almost as variegated, and I saw swallows darting

through the spray, or spiraling down the currents of air, to nests
built right behind the walls of water, while dozens of rainbows
arched above the columns of spray.

To see the falls from the Argentinian side we had to cross the
river Iguaçú itself. The point of embarkation was some ten miles
downstream. This strip of territory between Portuguese and Spanish
America, so similar in climate and vegetation, so different in habits
and traditions, had an individual tang of its own. The farmhouses
were of wood, most of them with orchards of orange trees, the
fruits, smooth and remarkably symmetrical, like the decorations
on Christmas trees. In the meadows, horses outnumbered cattle.
Most of the horsemen wore black Spanish-type hats with stiff
crowns and brims, fastened under the chin with a leather strap;
the saddles were placed on top of sheepskins dyed a vivid ginger.
The rather Mongoloid features of the Indians who originally inhabited the region were much in evidence. An unfamiliar feature
was the squares of leveled earth devoted to a game called *bocha*.
I asked one of the players to describe it to me. I couldn't follow
his complicated explanations properly, but I gathered that it was a
kind of cross between bowls and skittles, that it takes three days
to complete a match and that it is Basque in origin.

There was great excitement as we passed one copse. Men were
beating the undergrowth with sticks, others armed with rifles stood
near by, and every dog in the village was barking its head off. An
onça had just been spotted.

The little town of Iguaçú was very much of a frontier outpost, with horsemen trotting down a wide earth road, Wild West
saloons with swinging doors and horses tethered outside, and open
stores with goods spilling onto the pavements.

To reach the boat we had to scramble down a steep and muddy
bank with the aid of a few inadequate toeholds. An old woman,
incredibly wrinkled and dirty, wearing a navy-blue dress down to
her ankles, head scarf and shawl and carrying a huge sack, was
stuck halfway. Her daughter and two grandchildren were trying
to help her, but they were also loaded with bundles. I took the

sack, while my two companions helped the old woman. I slipped just before reaching the motorboat and had a muddy seat to my trousers for the rest of the day.

The boat, loaded to the gunwales, chugged laboriously across the river. A boy in a black Stetson collected the fares. I was seated next to a man wearing a striped shirt and trousers, like pajamas, and a floppy straw sombrero. He too was carrying a large sack. When I asked him what it contained he grinned and said, *"Muamba!"* ("loot"). The customs officers, he explained, turned a blind eye on small-scale smuggling, especially if one "kept them sweet." With bigger items you had to be more circumspect, and he launched into a story, which, judging by the delighted laughter and applause, everybody else in the boat had heard half a dozen times before, about a priest who had tried to smuggle a Cadillac across the river on a homemade raft, which sank in midstream.

Puerto Yguazo, on the Argentinian side, left only a few random snapshots in my memory: frontier police with uniforms and gestures more elaborate than those of their Brazilian counterparts; men of a different build, burly, with big mustaches, wearing stiff leather riding boots, on sleek black horses or driving estate wagons; stores where we bargained for magnificent leather goods, including cases shaped like Gladstone bags with sides made of natural cowhide, glossy black-and-white or brown-and-white; radios blaring Spanish music; atrocious coffee and interesting liqueurs; an old woman in her front garden, with iron-gray braids down to her buttocks; a *quati*, a lynxlike animal which abounds in the nearby forests, prowling in a cage with its tail stuck up like a poker—and another *quati*, tame as a Siamese cat, on a leash held by a pretty half-Indian girl with gleaming black braids, very chic in an emerald-green blouse and tight slacks. I remember that the poinsettias were of special brilliance, that the oranges were almost transparent in the sun, and that the cicadas were the loudest I have ever heard.

We couldn't get as close to the falls as on the Brazilian side; on the other hand, we had a panorama of the whole fantastic scene—cliffs, valley, forests, river, and the innumerable curtains of falling water. From this distance the roar was muted, but the colors came into their own. Orange clouds were reflected in the still water of the upper river, but the cataracts changed their color combinations —white, brown, rose, blue, and yellow—with every minute shift of cloud and sun, as if someone were operating an intricate system of floodlights. The green of the jungle frothed everywhere, as delicate as the plumes of spray.

When we flew over the falls the next day the weather had changed. The coloring had become almost monochrome; the cataracts again seemed slow and stately, as if they were about to turn into glaciers; the upper river looked not merely placid but stagnant.

9

GOING SOUTH

It wasn't a large town, but I have no sense of direction and I could not find my way back to the hotel. I saw two Negroes looking into the window of a delicatessen, where sausages of all shapes and sizes, cheeses, meat pies and jars of gherkins and pickled cabbage were displayed. Next door was a china shop which sold steins with metal lids. I asked the Negroes if they could direct me to my hotel. They looked at me and replied in German.

Following their directions, I walked down the main street. It was in perfect repair; the pavements were freshly swept. In the butchers' shops women wearing aprons and with their hair in buns were scrubbing down the marble slabs. The women's dress shops sold dirndl skirts and Tyrolean belts; there were bookshops selling German classics, and music shops with busts of the German composers. I passed elderly, almost circular men, wearing berets too small for them, young women in smart summer frocks, their bare arms biscuit-colored and flecked with gold, young men with closely cropped fair heads and serious clean-shaven faces, tieless but with the top buttons of their sports shirts carefully done up.

In the houses off the main street old ladies in long black dresses, and wearing steel-rimmed spectacles, sat in rocking chairs on their porches regarding the passers-by over their knitting or neeedlework.

Most of the houses had bell-shaped eaves and steeply pitched red roofs. There were no skyscrapers, but a number of new square concrete houses with long, rectangular windows, looking like Swiss or Austrian chalets. The new cathedral, of warm-colored granite, with slender white pillars and narrow, elongated arches, had been designed by an architect from Munich. When I entered a restaurant I sat on a high-backed settle of varnished pitch pine and was served by a bland-faced German-speaking waiter with a meal of Wiener Schnitzel, salad, and lager in a stone tankard.

I was not the victim of a hallucination that had jumbled together the two ends of the world. I was still in Brazil. But (in spite of those two Negroes) Blumenau, in the state of Santa Catarina, is to all intents and purposes a German city.

I suppose I might not remember it with the same affection if I had visited it before the war. "There were Nazi rallies here," a German-American, who had lived most of his life in Blumenau, told me; he had joined the United States Navy during the war and returned to Blumenau after it. "But now we don't ask questions. The past is the past."

I asked him how the authorities had reacted. "The federal government passed a law in 1938," he explained, "establishing Portuguese as the sole teaching language in all Brazilian schools; theoretically, German was only allowed in the fourth or fifth grades. But it wasn't very strictly enforced until Brazil came in on the side of the Allies. Then the authorities went to the other extreme. Anyone speaking German was liable to be clapped into jail. The only people they caught, though, were old folk from the interior who don't speak anything else!"

I found it difficult to believe that any of the kindly, hospitable people I met in Blumenau had ever been convinced Nazis. Surely not that jolly, rubicund business executive, a Mr. Pickwick in a tropical suit, who gave me whisky and soda in his study and proudly presented me with a romantic novel which his mother had written? Or his wife, dark-haired, Viennese-looking, dressed in smartly cut navy-blue slacks, a sculptress and potter who had built her own kiln and studio at the back of the house? Not, I knew, the tall, gentle Swiss who invited me to dinner in his old-fashioned house, with its books and flowers, its armchairs with chintz covers and cushions; or his youthful-looking fresh-complexioned wife proud of her home cooking and her housekeeping.

What was certain was that the citizens of Blumenau, like all the German immigrants in Brazil, clung more obstinately to their racial identity than any other group in Brazil, except the Japanese. There was, it must be admitted, a touch of racial superiority. "The north is a colony of the south—and, what is more, a colony that doesn't pay," one businessman told me, and when on the outskirts of the city I saw a group of palm-thatch huts with their usual ragged inhabitants, the honey-blond young woman who was driving me laughed apologetically and remarked, "These are our 'natives.'"

Older people in Blumenau shook their heads and complained that the younger generation, though they could still speak German, could no longer write it correctly, and that their culture was gradually dying out. But to me Blumenau seemed an astonishing instance of the persistence of national patterns under unlikely conditions. As I stood at the spot on the banks of the River Itajaí where, in September 1850, the first seventeen German immigrants landed, pioneers of a colonizing scheme organized by Dr. Hermann Blumenau of Rudolfstadt in Thuringia, I saw low-lying, swampy ground, a tangle of palms and banana trees, and a landscape blurred with tropical heat. The immigrants must have felt that they had been set down in darkest Africa. But I only had to look at a photograph taken just after their arrival—stern-faced men with Chester Conklin mustaches and watch chains across their waistcoats, capable-looking women in mutton-chop sleeves, with their hair in buns and cameos at their throats, sturdy blond children in sailor suits—to understand the kind of stock from which most of Blumenau's citizens have sprung.

Not that German organization was everywhere in evidence. "Falta de luz" was a common cry even here; at every spring tide the river overflows, flooding the lower part of the town, and nobody seems to do anything about it; and there were beggars in the streets and orphan shoeshine boys outside the cafés.

The factories, though, wouldn't have disgraced Adenauer's Germany. My Swiss friend was welfare officer with a firm that manufactures a variety of goods, specializing in textiles and pottery. He took me to one of the biggest factories, beautifully situated on a hillside and set in a small cultivated forest, which included a nursery for seedlings.

Outside the factory, hundreds of bicycles were neatly stacked in sheds with grooved concrete stands. Workers and their wives were buying vegetables and groceries in the co-operative store. In the factory bank, other workers were depositing their savings or the bonuses they receive on their own shares in the business. There was a health center in charge of a doctor and uniformed nurses. Near by was a crèche, each cot draped in white muslin, the babies plump, well cared for and spotlessly clean. The canteen was light and airy, with freshly scrubbed tables and benches, and with waitresses in white caps and overalls behind the service counters.

My Swiss friend had to visit the widow of a former employee in connection with her pension. We entered a garden gate and climbed a steep, concrete path, the garden on either side a patch-work of vegetable plots. The house was solidly built, with timber crisscrossing the red brick—such as you see in Saxony or Pomerania. The wooden porch was crammed with potted plants. A plump, middle-aged woman came to the door, wiping her hands on her apron, flustered by our unexpected arrival, apologizing for the state of the house. In the living room she rushed round picking up muddles, flicking at the furniture with the corner of her apron. Two blond, crop-haired boys, of about six and eight, one of them with a squint, were seated on the floor playing with a box of toys. She pointed to one of the family photographs hanging on the walls, and said, "That was my husband; he was a carpenter at the factory; he died six years ago. But," she added proudly, "he had paid for the house."

An old lady, dressed in faded black, wearing steel-rimmed spectacles tilted forward because she had somehow cut the bridge of her nose, came bustling into the room. "That was my son she was talking about," she said. "He was a good lad—looked after his family. *That* one"—and she nudged me, pointed to the boy with the squint, and dropped her voice to a sepulchral whisper—"*that* one never saw his dad. You know—born two months after."

In the kitchen a stewpot stood on a slow-burning stove. Shining pots and pans were arranged on racks. The shelves were crammed with jars of jam and preserved fruit. There was a refrigerator in one corner. The old woman rushed round opening cupboards and drawers, delighted to show us everything. She threw open the back door and practically pushed us into the yard. There were hens in a small coop. Ranged round the yard were rabbit hutches. "We sell the fur—and eat the meat!" the old woman cried, cackling with laughter. At the far end of the yard was a tool shed. An old man, bent and knotted with arthritis, was laboriously planing a length of wood. "My husband," the old woman announced, "used to be head fireman at the factory. He's making another rabbit hutch. We'll need it soon!" She cackled again, and the spectacles nearly fell off the end of her nose. She led us back into the house, chattering about her plans for the future. "We're going to keep bees," she said, "and perhaps a few ducks." It was clear that she was the driving force of the household. Her daughter-in-law had the bewildered overgentle look of a woman who has not yet got used to the loss of her man.

One day the American's wife and sister-in-law drove me (the car, of course, was a Volkswagen) into a countryside of mixed farming, with small holdings and farmhouses of brick and timber. We picked one of the farmhouses at random, pushed open the gate and ascended a muddy path. An old woman, thin and wrinkled, wearing a threadbare black dress, her hair tied up in a scarf, her yellow, veined feet bare, with a dirty bandage tied round one ankle, came to the door and peered at us suspiciously. One of the girls addressed her in German. The old woman beamed, and talking excitedly (with a Pomeranian accent so thick, the girls told me later, that they could barely understand her) led the way into a long farmhouse kitchen with raftered ceiling and stone-flagged floor. Two of the walls were roughly plastered, the others were of white-washed planks. On the walls hung family photographs, and a number of texts and mottoes. One of them, in silver tinsel on black velvet, announced: *"Der Herr segne unser Haus"*; another, embroidered on brown canvas: *"Wer auf Gott vertraut hat wohl gebaut."* There was also a framed certificate announcing that Rolf Krutzsch had once served "with distinction" in the Brazilian Military Police.

"A long time ago," Frau Krutzsch commented. "He's eighty-five now, and I'm only two years younger myself." She pointed to a cuckoo clock on a shelf. "I was thirteen when an uncle in Germany sent that to my parents. It seems a long time ago, but the clock keeps ticking, and so do we." Both she and her husband, she told us, were third-generation Brazilian, and their grandparents had been among the first batch of German immigrants. She showed us round the farmstead. There was a vegetable garden with red cabbages, a poultry yard with chickens, geese, and several of the curious-looking Brazilian ducks. The stock was very small—a couple of horses, five cows and half a dozen pigs. There were a few fields of *mandioca*, maize and corn. It was difficult to see how they lived, but the old woman insisted that they had all they needed and had "a little bit put by" for when they were too old to work. She spoke as if it was still a remote contingency, and her skinny frame looked as if only the weather could wear it away.

Longevity, it appears, is common in Santa Catarina. A jolly, red-faced woman in another of the *colônias* we visited told us that both her parents had lived into their late nineties. (The average life expectancy in the north, by the way, is thirty-three years; in the south it is about sixty.) This was a far more prosperous holding, worked by the woman's husband, brother and two sons. The inside walls were plastered and freshly distempered. The living room was well furnished with a couch, armchairs, a dresser stacked with crockery, and a table with a handmade lace tablecloth. Here too there was a cuckoo clock, German texts embroidered on cloth, and framed family photographs, among them a wedding group with the bride's veil forming the border.

Behind the house was an orchard of lemons, tangerines and bananas in which a sturdy girl of about twelve, dressed in a Tyrolean blouse and skirt and with her fair hair in braids, was seated on a swing. My companions eyed her speculatively. I remembered that my Swiss-German friends had told me that when the ladies of Blumenau want a maid they drive into the interior, confident that on some obscure farmstead such as this they will find a good, strong girl of German stock, imbued with the domestic virtues of fifty years ago. They had found their own maid in this way—incredibly strong and hard-working and, though her father was Brazilian, still speaking the dialect of an obscure corner of Pomerania from which her mother had originated.

On the way back to Blumenau we came upon a disused cemetery. I wandered round it studying the headstones. *"Hier ruhet in Gott,"* they announced—Bertha Conrad, Johann Dumke, Conrad Glau, Heinrich Schmidt, and scores of other German immigrants. The cemetery had not been used since 1912. It had been nearly pressed out of existence by encroaching palms and banana trees, and tropical grasses and flowers grew over the graves.

Southward by plane, over downs scattered with herds of grazing cattle and studded with clumps of pine trees. Bagé, Bemvindo, Vacaria, Caxias do Sul—the plane came down at all of them. The airports were so much alike—bumpy runways, wooden waiting rooms, a cluster of estate cars and horsemen outside—that I can't remember which one it was where I encountered the gypsies.

I know that there was a half-hour delay, and that I strolled out of the airport and, after about five minutes, came upon a cluster of tents on a patch of waste ground. In front of them were a lorry, several jeeps and a campfire with a cooking pot suspended over it, tended by a group of women with long, dark faces, their black hair fastened in double-looped braids, wearing long flowered skirts and aprons.

I approached the first of the tents, a big, square, marquee affair, with the flap nearest me hitched back. When I entered I saw that it was divided into sections by curtains. The section in which I was standing contained two double beds covered with patchwork quilts, a table with crockery and cooking utensils, and the leather seats from the lorry.

I was just about to leave the tent when the curtain facing me parted and a young woman entered. She seemed not in the least surprised at my presence, and immediately caught hold of my hand and examined the palm. "You have had food-poisoning," she said, "and are still suffering from pains in your stomach. I will take them away from you." She laid her hand on my stomach, then took mine and laid it on her own. "Now the pains will go," she said. She examined my palm again and recounted my various ailments, physical and psychological, actual and imaginary with astonishing accuracy. "But do not worry," she said, taking a crucifix from round her neck and knotting it in a handkerchief. "You are unhappy in love, but you will make old bones."

I glanced at my watch and saw that it was time to return to the airport, so I took out my wallet and gave her a hundred-cruzeiros note. She put out her hand and prevented my returning the wallet to my pocket. "How much money have you?" she said. I thought for a moment, and cautiously halved the amount. "Give me your money," she said. "I will take it to the other women and we will say special gypsy prayers over it—and I promise you that some stroke of fortune will double it before you leave Pôrto Alegre." (I had not, incidentally, told her that this was my destination.) Before I had time to reply she had snatched the wallet out of my hand. I tried to take it from her. She backed away, put her free hand on the crucifix which she had put back round her neck, fixed her dark eyes on me and said, "*Senhor,* I swear to you on this crucifix that I am not lying, and that I will do what I have said."

I looked at my watch again; the plane would be leaving in ten minutes. "I must go now," I said. "Give me my wallet." She slipped to one side of me, pulled at a cord and the open flap descended; it made the tent seem menacingly confined. The girl clasped her crucifix again and broke into a torrent of speech which I could not follow and which must have been Romany. I lunged forward and managed to catch hold of a corner of the wallet. She kept a tight hold of the rest of it and started to wail—and I could have sworn she was weeping real tears. I began to feel a brute and even to consider whether she might not be speaking the truth, but another look at my watch and I panicked. I remembered saying to her in my halting Portuguese, "*Senhora,* I may be doing you an injustice and I hate to hurt you, but I can't understand what you are saying and I have to go. Please forgive me." And this time I tugged really hard so that she staggered and the wallet came away in my hand.

She began to wail louder than ever. The curtain at the far end of the tent parted and three men entered. Wringing her hands, the girl turned to them, her eyes round and tragic, and poured out her story. One of them looked at me and shaking his head spoke to me, more in sorrow, it seemed, than in anger, but again in the language I couldn't understand; and when, thoroughly alarmed now that I might miss my plane, I made for the flap of the tent they stood in my way. I was apologizing profusely as I rushed forward and, as if I were charging through a rugby scrum, hurled them aside, fumbled with the flap and dashed outside. I heard angry voices behind me, and when I looked over my shoulder the three men were giving chase, the girl bringing up the rear and screaming throatily. I've never run faster in my life, and when I approached the main road my pursuers dropped back. I didn't stop running till I reached the airport. I had to continue my rush across the tarmac and only just reached the plane in time. I found that between my gasps I was laughing. I had an "adventure" of the kind I used to dream about as a boy. The bother was that I still half believed that the gypsy girl had been speaking the truth. Perhaps if I had let her take my wallet she really would have doubled the contents? After all, the pains in my stomach had gone.

In Rio Grande do Sul I found pockets of German culture as concentrated as in Blumenau itself. São Leopoldo, a city of about eighty thousand inhabitants with leather, furniture and metal-lurgical works and a Protestant church with a knobbly Gothic spire was the first of the German colonies there. Novo Hamburgo, as the name implies, was another of them and even deep in the "Serrana" zone, close to Caxias do Sul which is the center of the wine country and predominantly Italian, I came across German farmsteads and also a chalet-guesthouse-*cum*-sanatorium honey-combed with cozy little rooms packed with elderly ladies reading German magazines and newspapers and with barely a square inch free of wooden plaques bearing mottoes encircled with flowers, coats of arms of German cities, pictures of the Rhine, cuckoo clocks, steins and ornate clay pipes.

Between 1817 and 1865 no less than sixty-seven groups of colonists settled in Brazil, eighteen of them in the south. They included English, Danes, Belgians, Poles, Italians, Swiss, and even Icelanders and Mongols, in addition to the Germans. But whereas most of the other colonization schemes died out, the Germans con-tinued to arrive, concentrating on Rio Grande do Sul. It was here that Nazi doctrines took the firmest hold. In Pôrto Alegre, the capital, I was shown an essay in the 1937 *Annual of Brazilian Literature* declaring that Catholic Brazil would one day acknowl-edge Hitler alongside Christ, Buddha and Mahomet as a manifesta-tion of the Godhead, and an article in the *Quarterly Journal of Inter-American Relations* that divided the million or more German-Brazilians into two classes—the *teuto-brasileiros* (those born in Brazil) and the *Reichsdeutsche* (those born in Germany)—and claimed both as true German citizens because "a German remains forever German in the national sense."

São Leopoldo was the scene of a famous Brazilian novel by Vianna Moog, *Um Rio Imita a Reno* ("A River Imitates the Rhine"), which aptly pinpoints the prewar situation. The hero is a Brazilian engineer from Amazonas, who comes to São Leopoldo and falls in love with the daughter of a *teuto-brasileiro*. Her parents, horrified at the prospect of a "mixed marriage," promptly lock her up, only to discover eventually that they have Jewish blood in their veins and to turn thankfully to their Brazilian future.

Pôrto Alegre is a large skyscraper city of over half a million inhabitants, dramatically situated on a peninsula projecting into a lagoon. It was founded in 1740 and settled by families from the Azores. One of the central squares has recently been renamed Largo da Resistência Democrática—an interesting comment on the political temper of the state, for when in August 1961 after Jânio Quadros's sudden resignation the Federal Assembly tried to curtail the powers of his deputy, João Goulart, who automatically took over the presidency, his fellow Rio Grandenses threatened revolt, and the new name commemorates the success of this threat.* Rio Grandenses are notoriously hot-tempered, perhaps because the original Indian tribes of this region, the Charruas and Minuanos, were among the fiercest in South America.

The state has a long history of warfare. Spain and Portugal fought back and forth across it for over a century. The most serious of the Indian revolts, often with the support of the Jesuits, broke out here. The Uruguayans invaded it to forestall Portugal's own ambition of annexing their territory. Here in 1864 Paraguay opened her five-year war against Brazil. The Rio Grandenses themselves were often in revolt against the central government. The "Ragamuffins' Rebellion," which broke out in 1835, lasted for ten years, and both in 1930 and 1937 they came close to declaring themselves an autonomous state.

The political crisis of 1961 had, I found, exacerbated student discontents. The University of Pôrto Alegre is one of the most impressive in Brazil and boasts a magnificent theater, complete with orchestra pit, which seats over a thousand and presents plays, concerts, and film shows (there was a season of Soviet films when I was there). The Students' Union, however, was demanding a third of the seats on the administrative body. They had set out their case in a lavishly produced booklet, distributed free to all students. Where had the funds for this production come from? one of the professors

---

* The threat does not seem to have been repeated during the more recent crisis in 1964 which lost Goulart the presidency—so far, at any rate. G.P.

demanded. He told me that three of the students in the School of Philosophy had been there for ten years (there is no time limit in Brazilian universities), devoting themselves almost exclusively to the affairs of the Students' Union.

The center of Pôrto Alegre's social life was the Rua dos Andradas, a broad thoroughfare which began at the tip of the peninsula and split the city down the middle. The best shops were there or in the numerous arcades opening off it. Traffic was not allowed and the whole thoroughfare was thronged from morning to night, mostly with men arguing and gesticulating in small groups. For once the main topic of conversation was not politics— but football. The merits and deficiencies of every member of Brazil's team and every aspect of the game was discussed with a purehearted passion and analyzed with an objective realism that, applied to the country's economic problems, would have solved them long ago. *"A Copa do Mundo! A Copa do Mundo!"* was the cry one heard everywhere. I can't remember what stage the world competition had reached, but I know that England was still in the running, and whenever I joined one of the groups of debaters they would regard me warily, eyeing me from top to toe as if measuring, by proxy, the potential opposition. And I would draw myself up as if I did.

The effect was somewhat marred by the fact that I was wearing a borrowed overcoat, several sizes too small for me, for the *minuano* was blowing, an icy wind (presumably named after the Minuano Indians) that comes straight from the Andes. Both men and women were wearing *palas*—wide strips of woolen cloth, a kind of cross between a scarf and a shawl—or woolen capes, or *capas*.

On one of the coldest afternoons, I stayed in the hotel and went into the dining room for tea. A party was in progress, at a long table stretching across the center of the room, in honor of the beauty queens of Rio Grande do Sul. A waiter obligingly brought me a program with my tea and toast, and as I ate I studied the names of the competitors and tried to identify them. The ivory-skinned, full-bosomed beauty with pouting lips was, I decided, Senhorita

Namat Habbab of the Sociedade Libanesa (Lebanese Society). The blonde next to her must be Nieva Terezinha Kopper, and that black-haired girl with a diamond necklace was undoubtedly Yana Capeletti. The two girls sitting in the places of honor were the retiring queens, Maria Helena Rudiger, a chestnut-haired statuesque beauty, and her successor, Maria Arismende of Jaguarão, a small cattle town in the interior. She was a lovely nineteen-year-old, tall blonde, with a long, slender neck, a tender expression and cream-and-carmine complexion. I turned to the program. "*1.67 de altura*," I read, "*57 de pêso, 98 de busto, 58 de cintura, 98 de quadris, 56 de coxas, 22 de tornozelos*." Somehow the vital statistics seemed much more romantic in Portuguese.

The next morning, as I was collecting my bill in the hotel foyer, I saw her again. She was being interviewed by a newspaper reporter with a bald head and an unshaven chin. She had a beautiful, gentle voice. She caught my eye, recognized me and blushed.

To Pelotas across a flat countryside with grazing cattle, fields of rice and sugar cane, and pools ruffled by the *minuano*. It ruffled health and temper too. Pelotas, the second-largest city in the state (with a population of over a hundred thousand) and an important center for agricultural machinery and produce, was no more depressing than most cities of its size in Brazil, but the discomforts irritated more than usual.

The *minuano* didn't discourage the mosquitoes, and I had to lard myself with Cox's Insect Ointment before going to bed. I was told of an American lady in Pelotas who took a tin of Keating's Powder with her whenever she went to the cinema and sprinkled the seat and the area round it before sitting down. Washbasin and *bidet* lacked plugs, and I had to stuff them with toilet paper. There was a fireplace in the hotel lounge, but it was only for decoration. "Open fires cause flu," the manager told me.

It was a relief to get out of Pelotas and on to a road bordered by palm trees (which persist right down to the borders of Brazil and on into Uruguay) and groves of orange trees (a touch of frost, the locals said, improved the flavor). And a few miles to the west the *pampas* began.

At first glance the impression was of interminable grasslands, the monotony relieved only by an occasional reservoir shaded by a clump of eucalyptus trees. Close up were richness and variety of the kind that Chekhov describes in his story "The Steppe." The green of the grass alternated with the paler green of young rice and the orange-gold stubble (which makes excellent cattle fodder) from the harvesting of the year-old rice; the alternation of grass and rice is the classical pattern of cultivation in this part of the Brazilian *pampas*. It was not "dry rice" like that which the Russian Old Believers were growing in Paraná. Hence the reservoirs which had puzzled me at first, for I already knew that the lives of the *gaúchos*, unlike those of the *vaqueiros* of the *sertões*, were not overshadowed by the fear of drought. Close up, in fact, the *pampas* were nothing like as flat as they had appeared from a distance; on the contrary, they were broken by deep trenches and ridges, and these twisted and curved in order to facilitate flooding for the rice crop. In addition, the knobbly towers and minarets of giant anthills were scattered everywhere, and this miniature landscape of ridges and anthills was as rich in bird life as any of the jungles.

The *quero-quero* birds, long-legged, with a kind of coif at the back of their heads, and known to the *gaúchos* as "the sentinels of the *pampas*," rose round my feet wherever I walked. The name *quero-quero* ("I want, I want") is a remarkably accurate reading of its call. There were yellow-breasted birds, thrushlike birds with orange throats, and black-and-white-striped birds like miniature badgers. There was a tiny brown robinlike bird with a red breast, called locally *sangue-de-boi* ("ox's blood"). A neat little gray owl built its nest on the ground among the ridges and its mate dive-bombed me if I ventured too close. I also saw a gray, mottled hawk on a concrete fence post: it was one of the few posts that were not occupied by a strange shape, like a beehive and itself as hard as concrete—the nest of the ovenbird.

The *gaúcho* huts were as much natural outcrops of the landscape as the anthills, which in fact contributed to their construction. I watched two laborers shoveling the soft, sifted earth from one of them into a wheelbarrow, wheeling it to a house that was under construction and spreading it over the floors. "The ants do half our work for us," they explained as they began pounding. "This makes the best mud floors in Brazil."

The walls, too, came from the *pampas*—from peatlike mud mixed with cement and rice stubble, sometimes faced with lime but mostly left rough and bristling. All of them were a good two feet thick to keep out the *minuano*. The roofs too were several feet thick with a thatch made of rice stubble. The better houses had wooden ceilings, but the one I spent most time in was open to the rafters. Loose boards instead of glass covered the windows, through which the wind moaned and whistled, and a rough iron chimney pushed through the thatch to carry away the smoke—or rather a portion of it—from an open fire burning on slabs of stone. The living room was furnished with rough, handmade wooden table and chairs and a glass-fronted cupboard. On a shelf were an alarm clock, several oil lamps, and a battery radio, on the walls a calendar, a religious print and a cow's horn filled with ferns. Empty olive-oil tins containing cactus plants were nailed outside the house. There was a shed stacked with logs, rice husks and corncobs; there were chickens, several pigs and half a dozen dogs.

By Brazilian standards this represented comparative affluence, and it was reflected in the attitude of the inhabitants. My hostess, a big-boned, weather-beaten woman, chattered away with a freedom and self-confidence utterly different from the crushed taciturnity of the women of the north. Her husband extolled the life of the *pampas*, revealing in the process little compassion for his less fortunate countrymen. "We're not nut-and-banana men here," he would say; "we eat men's food. *Senhor*, I never start the day with less than two kilos of good mutton or beef, with a *cuia of chimarrão* to bring out the flavor."

But he hardly lived up to the romantic picture I had carried round in my mind since, as a boy, I had seen Douglas Fairbanks in the silent film *The Gaucho*. He was, it is true, wearing the traditional loose baggy trousers, or *bombachas,* made of a material that looks like the "sponge bag" worn by Edwardian dandies, and fitting closely round the ankles, but for the rest he wore only a check shirt and an old khaki windbreaker. He was barefooted, and, most disillusioning of all, he didn't have a horse. He was merely a herdsman, he explained, not a cowboy. The word *gaúcho,* in fact, is applied, both as a noun and as an adjective, to anybody living in the state of Rio Grande do Sul.

The Estância dos 3 Capões near by—the name was executed in iron scrollwork above the gateway—did something to restore the romantic coloring. The bunkhouse was furnished with benches covered with hides or sheepskins; a blackened kettle was suspended over an open hearth and a row of *cuias* and *bombilhas* stood on the mantelshelf. A group of *gaúchos*—with horses—were getting ready for a roundup. They too hardly looked like Douglas Fairbanks. They were unshaven and had bad teeth: one of them wore a maroon pullover riddled with holes, and another an old army tunic. But their *bombachas* had elaborate stitching down the sides and were tucked into soft leather boots with big, circular spurs attached to them. They wore wide flat hats with straps hanging under their chins, check shirts and knotted red kerchiefs round their necks. In their wide leather belts, with square silver buckles, they carried revolvers and long knives in ornate metal sheaths. Suspended from their waists were *rebenques,* clublike riding crops made from the penises of bulls and covered with leather. Some of them wore *ponchos* or *capas* of dark blue lined with scarlet—like the cloaks of Life Guardsmen. Others had them neatly rolled behind their saddles, which were placed on top of several blankets and at least three sheepskins. Hanging from the saddles were tools for splicing and cutting wire, and oiled rawhide lassos. One of the *gaúchos* also had a *bola*—a rope tipped with three metal balls, which used to be flung round the hoofs of running steers to topple them to the ground. But he never used it now, he told me. "It breaks too many legs. Besides, *senhor,* the cattle are all tame nowadays. When I was a boy they were as wild as the buffaloes of the American Wild West."

There are thirty million of these cattle, according to one estimate. Many of them are the descendants of the "Creole" cattle which the *bandeirantes* from São Paulo discovered wandering in vast wild herds when they first entered the region in the early 1700s. No one seems to know for certain where they originated, but most likely it was from animals which had escaped from the old Capitania of São Vincente after 1532 and later from the Jesuit missions on the left bank of the Uruguay River. They were hunted by the early settlers much as the bison were hunted by Buffalo Bill and his contemporaries. The tongues were specially prized, and it was common practice for a *gaúcho* on the trail to kill several steers, simply for their tongues, and to leave the carcasses to the vultures.

Now the herds are branded, and though the *estâncias* are of vast size they are demarcated by wire fences. Most of the cattle I saw in this part of the *pampas* were mongrels, but in some of the *estâncias* the stock had been improved by the importation of Herefords, Devons and Jerseys, and the French Charollais, which are becoming increasingly popular.

The Estância dos 3 Capões was a symbol of a social and economic revolution that has been taking place in the *pampas* country. It was one of the hundreds of private *estâncias* that have been acquired in recent years by big monopolies like Anglo-Frigorífico. The big colonial-type house was empty except for the *gaúchos'* bunkhouse, the kitchens, where a caretaker and his family lived, and a couple of rooms kept furnished for the Anglo-Frigorífico buyers when they were visiting. It must have been an impressive mansion in its time—not so long ago either, for it had been wired for electricity. There was a fine tiled hall, a stone staircase and huge fireplaces in all the rooms. At the back were an orchard and a poultry yard, a water tower and the ruins of a small slaughter-house. The house was approached by a long avenue of eucalyptus trees.

When the *gaúchos* returned from their roundup the wood fire for the *churrasco* was lit on the crumbling tiles of what had once been an Italian garden. While we were waiting for the strips of mutton to cook (speared on stakes) one of the *gaúchos* drew his revolver and took pot shots at the statues of classical gods and goddesses and at the grottoes with their images of the Virgin and Child. "It's the only chance we get to use a revolver now," he said wistfully as he returned it to its holster.

He was a tall, rangy man with a skin like old leather, the most punctilious of the *gaúchos* in matters of dress. But he seemed to sense that in this part of the *pampas* at any rate the old-type *gaúcho* would soon become like his counterpart in the American West, an anachronism. His heyday coincided with that of the small *charqueadas,* which, like the one once attached to this particular *estância,* have mostly been swallowed up by big monopolies like Anglo-Frigorífico.

The process of salting and drying meat in sun and air was probably derived from the Quechua Indians of the Andes, brought to the Argentine by the Spaniards and then carried down to Uruguay and southern Brazil. *Charque,* in fact, is a Quechua word—the American "jerked beef" represents a corruption of it—and it designates a process which the Indians applied to various kinds of meat.

I shall never forget my first sight of *charque* outside the Anglo-Frigorífico plant at Pelotas. Row upon row of wooden horses and hanging over them what at first I took to be dirty, yellowish-gray dishcloths, flapping and swaying in the breeze; acres and acres of them like a surrealist version of the Field of the Cloth of Gold. Close up, I saw that one section, several acres in extent, consisted entirely of transfixed hearts, as if it were the site of some Aztec sacrifice.

Almost equally bizarre were the mounds, over ten feet high, faced with rolls of lungs, and weighing three hundred tons apiece, in which the strips of *charque,* like petrified sacking, were subjected to further processes of drying and salting. I managed to tear off a strip from one of the heaps: it was gritty with brine, tasted like very salty bacon, and was tough as leather. It keeps almost indefinitely. Less than fifty years after the arrival of Pedro Alvarez Cabral in 1500, Brazil was already exporting salted meat to other parts of South America; and the production of *charque* became one of the great colonial industries. When the big monopolies arrived on the scene it was still sufficiently important for them to devote to it a considerable part of their resources. They had obvious advantages over the old *charqueadas*: bigger capital and greater shipping and marketing facilities for one thing; but above all, superior equipment and organization. They reduced the wastage, which had been as high as 40 per cent of cattle at each killing in the *charqueadas*, to about half that figure. Even so, the *charque* process remains a wasteful one. One of the English overseers at Anglo-Frigorífico told me that 440 pounds of fresh meat were reduced to an average weight of less than two hundred pounds. He pointed to one of the stacks and said, "That represents a whole herd—good plump Herefords; I remember them well."

Charque, in consequence, takes second place to canning; and as far as the export trade is concerned, refrigeration is rapidly becoming more important. The day will come, when, with the laying of roads and railway tracks, refrigerator trucks and freight cars will carry fresh meat all over Brazil. And when it does, the old-style *gaúchos* will probably disappear.

I had always sworn that I would never enter a slaughterhouse. Meeting the cattle on the *pampas*, where they seeem to belong as naturally as the *quero-quero* birds, had strengthened my resolution. As luck would have it, when I was in Pelotas Anglo-Frigorífico were handling a large Israeli order, and when I learned that this meant that the killing would be carried out and supervised by a team of rabbis, my sense of the bizarre got the better of me.

My heart sank when I saw the herds waiting their turn in the large corral just outside the gates of the plant. Contrary to what I had always understood, they showed no signs of restlessness; they were grazing peacefully, though I at least could already smell the blood. Even when they were driven in a long column through the first of the water tanks they seemed puzzled rather than frightened. It was only when they found themselves crowded in two parallel alleys, divided into sections by trap doors, that they began to panic, struggling to escape, bucking and leaping, urged on by electric goads. I stood with one of the overseers on a catwalk from which I could see both the advancing columns of cattle and two pale-faced black-bearded rabbis, dressed in long clinging white overalls and tight-fitting white caps like those worn by surgeons, one of them grinding a long knife behind an iron screen, the other, knife in hand, standing impassively in the middle of the killing floor.

The first pair of steers were now directly below me, in the last compartment but one. As if they were being subjected to some monstrous practical joke, sprays of water suddenly shot out at them, and to my horror they shuddered and lifted their great toffee-colored eyes toward me, not appealingly but (far worse) merely noting my presence with that automatic flicker—expecting nothing—that I had seen in the eyes of prisoners behind bars. It was as much as I could do not to leap into the compartment below to fling my arms round the shaggy, dripping necks.

Now, slipping and slithering as it struggled to get away from the goad, the foremost steer was driven into the last compartment. Another appalling practical joke as the floor gave way beneath him and he was flung on his side, legs protruding. Quick as lightning two men in long rubber aprons tied the legs together, the rear rope was attached to a pulley and the steer was swung out, upside down, into the center of the killing floor. It opened its mouth to bellow its protest but before any sound came another man had slipped a noose round the mouth and forced the head back. The rabbi passed his free hand over the throat, poised the knife over it, paused for a fraction, then brought the knife across with two or three powerful sawing motions. A gaping door had opened in the steer's throat, through which blood poured in a thick, red stream. Immediately it was swung away from the killing floor and out into the plant behind, tongue hanging out, chaps falling away from the face. The whole operation had only taken a few seconds, and after the knife had descended the animal had not even twitched.

Already another steer was swinging out into the center of the floor and the rabbi, white face expressionless, was running his thumb along the blade of his knife. Again the quick sawing movement, again the river of blood. And so it went on and on as the animals, lunging and bellowing, were driven to their last undignified scramble. It was the assault upon living dignity that shocked me more than the actual killing, which was as quick and merciful as any taking of life can be. In every case death was instantaneous and the rabbis never made a mistake, ignoring the blood that poured down their overalls and flecked their beards, taking it in turns in the center of the floor or honing the knives behind the screen.

By the time I had seen the sixth throat gape I had had enough. I left the catwalk and went on into the plant. A few yards behind the killing floor the dead animals (I still could not bring myself to call them carcasses) came sliding, one after another, along a rail, as if in a giant wardrobe. A hole was made in the chest of each and another rabbi, immensely dignified in spectacles and a flowing gray beard, plunged his arm, encased to the elbow in a plastic sheath, inside the body to check, as the Mosaic law enjoined, that no part of the lungs adhered to the ribs. If he was dissatisfied the animal was rejected. In any case only the forequarters are considered "clean." It made no difference as far as the plant was concerned. Its work went on remorselessly, inexorably, as if its only purpose was to carry the degradations of sprays, goads, trap doors and knives to their last possible conclusion by rending, tearing and grinding away the last vestiges of mortality.

The long line of animals traveled slowly on, with a short pause every half minute or so while the various groups of workers, barefooted, carried out their tasks. The floor was awash with blood, vomit, urine and feces, still steaming. The smell of death, in spite of the constant spraying, pressed on one's nostrils. Another stop, and the hide was pulled halfway off. Another, and the operation was completed; the hide slithered down a hole in the floor to be washed and treated somewhere below. Next stop, and electric saws hummed; soon the feet and the head had gone, to be dispatched for further processing, the severed head with its great glazed eyes looking like a stage property for a performance of Bottom's transformation. The carcass—white and glistening, undoubtedly a carcass now—traveled on. The electric saw hummed again, and it was split down the middle; now it was merely two sides of meat.

On and on, like an assembly line in reverse. In one section miles of intestines were being sluiced in warm, bloody water. Another section consisted of rows of inflated bladders and oesophagi, the one circular in shape, the other oval, both blood-flecked—grotesque travesty of a balloon shop at carnival time. Here another rabbi was at work, blowing up lungs with an air hose and scrutinizing them to make sure they had none of the forbidden flaws. Only when all the Mosaic injunctions had been observed were the half-carcasses stamped in Hebrew and sent on to be packed for transport in the refrigerators of an Israeli freighter.

By now I was able to push the horror of the execution floor and the bloody space behind it into a corner of my mind. The snowy tripes might almost have been lengths of muslin and the girls handling them, in their white overalls and caps, assistants in a haberdashery store. I experienced only a passing qualm when I saw other girls with scissors in their hands snipping the hair off tails (to be used in the manufacture of house painters' brushes) and the finer hair from the insides of ears (to be used—a trade secret, this—for camel's-hair paintbrushes and fetching about six dollars a pound). The piles of bones and horns were merely raw materials, as impersonal as wood or metal. Hardly a scrap was wasted: even the blood was dried, and the ribs were ground and sold as protein meal.

The carcasses in the refrigerator rooms, where the workers wore huge rubber gloves and folds of canvas wrapped round their boots, and where heaters were attached to the scales to keep the mercury from freezing, were nothing but hunks of rock. But the ginger-colored gallstones, carefully guarded in the laboratory, were treasure-trove, worth almost three dollars an ounce, for they are exported to China and the Far East as amulets and aphrodisiacs and are much in demand by Oriental fire-swallowers, who hold them in their mouths—whether for magical or scientific reasons no one seemed to know. As for the sections where monster stewpots gobbled up crates of peeled vegetables, where oceans of broth basted a million meat balls, where huge vats seethed and bubbled— savory smells and jolly women cooks almost turned them into outsize versions of one's favorite eating house.

Almost. When at the end of it all I was handed a tin of corned beef with a label depicting the head of a plump red steer with curving horns, it all came back to me and once again I saw the shaggy body yanked up by the rear legs, head lolling, neck swelling, and the thick red stream pumping over the killing floor. The tin with its cozy label seemed the ultimate indignity.

Back in the town there was an atmosphere of tension. Knots of people stood at the street corners talking and gesticulating. Shop- keepers kept dashing out to the pavement. Radios blared from every open doorway and window, and nearly everybody, whether on foot, bicycle, horse or donkey, carried a transistor set glued to the ear. I thought revolution had broken out, until I remembered that today Brazil was playing Mexico for the World Cup. A moment later there was pandemonium: fireworks exploded, dogs howled, everybody went mad. Brazil had just scored a goal.

That night I dined on eggs and salad in one of the restaurants; I stuck to a vegetarian diet for a week. There was a long table near me decorated with flags on little stands. A few moments later the dinner party entered—several men with bald heads, black mustaches and navy-blue suits and four lovely girls wearing coats with fur collars. The beauty queens again. When Miss Rio Grande do Sul caught sight of me she stared at me unbelievingly, then turned her head quickly away. She looked a little peaky—the tour- ing and junketing no doubt—but her eyes were brilliant and she was far more beautiful than any of the others. She was perhaps

a little too thin, I thought, to become Miss Brazil, though I hoped
I was wrong.

One of my objectives, as I traveled westward from Rio Grande
(for I had gone on until I reached the southernmost tip of Brazil)
was to find the wild ostrichlike birds which the Brazilians call *emas*,
and which, I had been told, wander about in flocks in this
part of the *pampas*. I had still seen nothing of them when I
approached Livramento-Rivera, where the wandering frontier between Brazil and Uruguay was demarcated by breast-high pillars.

The countries met like the confluence of two rivers whose waters
mingle but still retain their distinctive coloring. The rolling *pampas*
were the same: there were the same herds of cattle, sheep and
horses and there were *gaúchos* on both sides of the frontier. But
there remained that astonishing power of human beings to register
the minutest differences of upbringing, tradition and culture.
Somehow I could always tell who was Brazilian and who was
Uruguayan.

The hyphenated name of the town was itself a symbol of the
blending and of the separateness. The boundary line between the
two countries runs across a fine, rectangular, tree-lined central
praça and Livramento is on the Brazilian side, Rivera on the
Uruguayan. A marble column marks the exact spot where the fron-
tiers intersect, announcing in Spanish and Portuguese that in 1943
the presidents of Brazil and Uruguay had inaugurated the "Praça
Internacional" and the "Plaza Internacional." There are no customs barriers between the two halves of the city. Both currencies
are acceptable in the shops and hotels, and many of the city's affairs
are jointly administered.

The streets immediately surrounding this central *praça* maintained a kind of neutrality. They were those of a *pampas* township
almost anywhere in South America, farm wagons and pony carts
outclattering the noise of cars and jeeps, rows of horses hobbled
outside the stores and bars, gunshops and leather shops, outfitters
selling *ponchos, capas,* windbreakers, check shirts and woolen goods,

gaúchos riding out on week-long roundups with provisions and cooking utensils stacked behind their saddles. The *gaúcho* dress was almost universal except for professional and business men. One young man was so resplendent in gleaming black boots, silver spurs, scarlet neckcloth, a leather band decorated with brass studs round his hat, and a dramatic check jacket that he even looked a little like Douglas Fairbanks. I asked him to stand still while I took a photograph. Several other *gaúchos* gathered round; they were laughing heartily. *"Não tem cavalo!"* ("He has no horse!"), they cried; and the young man slunk away, muttering. One of the *gaúchos*, surprising me by his knowledge of English, explained, "Teddy-boy *gaúcho!* He rides a motor bike!"

One didn't have to go far for the different national characteristics to assert themselves. On one side of the Praça Internacional the children played only football; on the other side they played strange Spanish games with bat and ball as well. And the farther one penetrated in either direction the more noticeable the differences became. On the Uruguayan side there were restaurants which served *paella* and ornate pastries, antique shops which displayed fans and lace mantillas. The old women were proud and upright, their heads covered in black shawls; the young ones wore earrings and flashed black eyes. The policemen were dandified in blue uniforms, peaked caps and white belts, cuffs and gloves, and they controlled the traffic from white-painted boxes like miniature bandstands. The houses were square and white, with wrought-iron gates and balconies and curly iron bars at the windows.

As one went deeper into the Brazilian side, things became increasingly drab: streets of one-story houses, the yellow stucco stained and moldering, the few old buildings, arches and pediments dimmed by neglect, and in place of the Spanish *bravura* a kind of good-natured seediness.

I had still not seen any *emas*. But one night I attended a party at the home of Livramento's leading doctor, a portly Pickwickian character who received me with a Churchill-size cigar in his hand and wearing a smoking jacket. Among the guests was a charming and cultured Brazilian family of Basque origin, the father a rancher and wool dealer. While we were listening to a record of a *gaúcho* song which lamented the passing of the wild herds and the days of the *bola*, I asked if the *emas* too were a feature of the past. "It's not always easy to find them," the rancher agreed. "They travel considerable distances and you might look for days and not see them—then suddenly they are at your back door. Tomorrow we will go looking for them."

Mother, father and daughter called for me at my hotel early the next morning. To my surprise we headed for the airport. "You forget the distances," my host said. "We have seven *estâncias,* but they are so widely separated that the only way of keeping in touch with them is by plane."

A four-seater Piper Cub was waiting for us on one of the runways. We climbed in, and a few moments later the *pampas* were whirling below us. A strange landscape from this angle, green and brown like a plastic relief map: flat grasslands (there is no rice in this part of the *pampas*) dotted here and there with clusters of farm buildings, clumps of eucalyptus and water pools like the broken bits of a mirror, and crisscrossed at intervals by the low stone walls. The herds of cattle, mostly red Herefords or black Aberdeen and Angus, also looked as if they were made of shiny plastic. From his height their movements were practically indistinguishable; and the mounted *gaúchos,* threading their way in and out, seemed infinitely slow as if moving in a dream. Even when we swooped down close and the herds separated exactly down the center as if the shadow of the plane had driven a furrow through them, they still seemed in slow motion. The horses looked only a fraction faster, their manes gently rising and falling, tails and hoofs slowly lifting, and flank and shoulder muscles undulating in a poetry of movement as if they were taking part in a ballet. The sheep, their legs invisible, were like scuttling wood lice. And then, what at first I took to be dusty bushes blown about by the breeze, as we swooped closer I saw to be birds with broad, turkeylike backs, long, jerky, gray necks and ungainly legs. *"Emas!"* my host shouted. "Don't worry, we'll get a closer look at them later on!"

A few minutes later we landed on the *estância*. I saw a long, white stone bungalow with a tiled roof and a rectangular tower at its center. It was surrounded by a perfectly kept box hedge. A veranda with easy chairs stretched the whole length of the house, and wide, green-shuttered windows looked out onto it. The lawns were cut out of the *pampas,* coarse and springy, but beautifully mown and rolled, and shaded by shrubs and weeping willows. Creepers with big violet, starlike flowers festooned the pillars of porch and veranda. There was a magnificent tiled swimming pool with a springboard and summerhouse at one end.

Inside, the floors were of Brazilian hardwoods scattered with glossy black and white hides. In the living room a log fire was burning in a huge cowled fireplace. There were settees, armchairs and rocking chairs, bureaus and sideboards of polished jacaranda. The two tiled bathrooms contained porcelain baths and showers behind rose-colored plastic curtains.

The *capataz* of the *gaúchos* lived with his wife and family in a stone house, comfortable and well-furnished, on the other side of the compound. It contained an office with a small telephone exchange: telephones were installed, he explained, at outposts placed at intervals on the huge estate, so that he could keep in touch with his *gaúchos* on their rounds.

The *sota* (assistant) *capataz* measured up at last to my schoolboy idea of what a *gaúcho* should look like: a handsome figure over six feet in height, with a brick-red complexion and a black mustache, his boots, *bombachas* and wide-brimmed, flat-crowned hat all black, a scarlet kerchief at his throat, a *poncho* with a scarlet lining over his arm, and a long *gaúcho* knife in a beautifully chased silver sheath in his belt. His horse was a glossy black thoroughbred with a white forehead.

He took me to the pens, where the sheep (mostly pedigree Romney Marsh) were about to be dosed. They were driven down a gangway, their mouths were forced open and the *sota capataz* inserted the nozzle of a stainless steel instrument and pressed the handle to release the medicine.

There were also two magnificent fifteen-month-old pedigree Hereford bulls, short, massive, with fleecy white foreheads, which my host had bought on one of his visits to England. The herdsman treated them as if they were rather sulky children who had to be humored. He was an old man, his *bombachas* patched and darned, his feet in carpet slippers. When I congratulated him on the appearance of the bulls he grasped my hand; his hand felt as hard as horn. "Yes, *senhor*, there are *emas* here," he told us. "Last night they broke one of my fences." He spoke without resentment. "They are the *gaúcho's* friends, *senhor*," he explained. "We don't interfere with them more than necessary: if we did, who would deal with the snakes?"

We mounted a jeep and drove into the *pampas*. Half an hour later we saw the *emas*: there were seven of them, pecking at the ground, their necks bent like lengths of rope, their bodies like gray feather dusters, their rumps, at the ends of cabbage-stalk legs, white as if they were wearing underpants. They were smaller than ostriches, and not as graceful-looking as emus, though they were similar in appearance except that they had longer beaks and bigger (but equally flightless) wings. Their correct designation is "three-toed rhea."

The jeep approached cautiously, then suddenly accelerated, but not suddenly enough, for in a flash the birds were off, streaking across the *pampas*. In motion they looked for all the world like eccentric old ladies, all feather boas and bits and pieces, but they had an astonishing turn of speed, and could, my host told me, outpace most horses. In addition, as we found when we gave chase in the jeep, they could suddenly change direction, zigzagging like forked lightning. They are quite peaceable; but if cornered by a horseman, I was told, they will turn and charge. Most of the *gaúchos'* horses, however, have learned to side-step these attacks.

Ironically, when I reached the airport the following day to board my plane back to Pôrto Alegre, half a dozen were foraging in the long grass at the edge of the airfield. They broke into a gallop and ran parallel with the plane as it taxied along the runway, until we had soared upward and they were no more than gray dots on the vast expanse of the *pampas*.

The radio on the plane was broadcasting a commentary on the World Cup match between Brazil and Spain; passengers and crew sat tense and silent. In Pôrto Alegre the shops were stacked with fireworks in readiness for another victory celebration. When I strolled into the *praça* outside my hotel Miss Rio Grande do Sul, wearing a turquoise sweater, was posing for photographers. She gave me a very odd look this time. I shared the plane back to Rio de Janeiro with an Australian trade delegation which had been visiting the state, and two of the organizers of the Students' Union. The Australians seemed more bewildered by the economic complexities than optimistic about trade prospects. The students were tense and excited: they were attending a meeting of delegates from many universities and were seeking an interview with the Minister of Education to try to persuade him to postpone examinations until the dispute had been settled. Rio de Janeiro lay ahead, and, after Rio, the Atlantic, Europe and home.

10

DEPARTURES

It didn't take me long to realize why the student delegates had been so excited. The smell of revolution was in the air. The deterioration since my last visit was unmistakable. Inflation had taken a startling turn for the worse. The official exchange for pounds sterling and dollars was even more unrealistic. The private exchanges on the Avenida Rio Branco were openly offering higher rates.

The breakdowns in the electricity and water supplies were more widespread and frequent. The condition of the roads had worsened, and in the side streets the culverts were broken and it looked as if the refuse hadn't been collected for weeks. It was clear now that the student strikes were carefully planned and co-ordinated, and a report had just arrived that in Santos workers in several factories had made common cause with the students. There were riots in Rio against shortages and soaring prices: sugar, for example, had suddenly and mysteriously disappeared from the shops. There were rumors that some of the shortages had been engineered by one of the factions in the government itself as a stick to beat their rivals with, and others, that the whole situation was deliberately fomented in order to bring the President, João Goulart, into disrepute so that someone more amenable could be put forward as the "saviour of the nation," or so that the generals could take over.

This time there was no revolution. Once again the country somehow stumbled out of the crisis. But nothing was solved.* I have had
letters from friends in the northern cities telling me that practically
every street is now crammed with the starving and the homeless.
The ragged armies, moreover, are increasing daily and spreading
farther and farther afield. Friends from cities in the south, which
have never before had a refugee problem, tell me that they wake up
to find that they have been invaded overnight. A Brazilian econo-
mist has asserted that well over 70 per cent of the population are
living below subsistence level.

There are some, of course, who try to mitigate the worst of the
conditions. I had been told, for example, during my first visit to
Rio of a priest, who, after a fire had destroyed part of one of the
favelas, had set about raising funds for the construction of a block of
flats—and a visit to this *favela* was one of the pieces of unfinished
business I had set aside for my return to Rio. The priest was away,
but one of his social workers, a pretty gentle creature trying to hide
her aristocratic origins under a shabby mackintosh, offered to take
me there with a mutual friend.

The arrangement was that the three of us should meet outside
the church, but owing to some misunderstanding our friend did not
turn up. The *favelas* are patches of waste ground where squatters
have settled without permission from the urban authorities, paying
no rates and therefore receiving none of the city's facilities. They
are virtually outside the law and the police never enter them unless
a serious crime has been committed. I had heard of several cases of
visitors who had been attacked by gangs, stripped, robbed and as-
saulted and thrown unconscious into the streets outside. Perhaps,
I suggested, we had better postpone our visit until we could organize
a larger party? "It will be all right," the social worker told me.
"Senhor Júlio knows we are coming."

"Who is Senhor Júlio?" I asked.

* And now there has been a "generals' revolution." Whether it has really
solved anything is another matter. G.P.

"The chairman of the Favelados' Committee, a man to be reckoned with."

The *favela* stretched up a hillside, the huts and shacks clinging to the clefts and gullies as if they had been tipped out of a refuse lorry. Two small Negro boys were waiting for us. One of them ran ahead to inform Senhor Júlio of our arrival. The other guided us through an intricate network of alleyways, catwalks, ladders and steps cut into the hillside. The open drains, in which dead rats floated, were bridged in some places by planks with handrails of lead piping. In others we had to jump, praying that we wouldn't slip: planks and handrails alike were coated with a paste of yellow slime. The huts were piled, one above the other, on every available patch of ground and constructed of every imaginable material. The heaps of garbage were chest-high in spite of the hens, the small ginger pigs and the black and white goats.

Senhor Júlio's bungalow at the top of the hill was a surprise. It was made of mud and plaster, freshly whitewashed. The door was painted green and there were chintz curtains at the windows. The inside walls, too, were plastered and whitewashed and there was a composition flooring. The *sala* contained a table covered with a white embroidered cloth and adorned with a vase of artificial flowers, a dresser full of glass and china, straight-backed chairs and armchairs and a sheepskin on the floor. Several pictures of the Amazon and one of Saint George killing the dragon hung on the walls. In the bedroom was a double bed with a silk coverlet, a wardrobe and a dressing table. In the kitchen were a cooker, a refrigerator, and a shower with hot and cold water, all of them operated by cooking gas.

The house had been built and fitted by Senhor Júlio himself. He was a tall, handsome Negro with a long, bony head and large, penetrating eyes. He was dressed in a pair of blue serge trousers and a white sports shirt. His wife, a young, pretty Negro woman wearing an apron over her flowered frock, unlocked the dresser, proudly displayed the best china and served us coffee and homemade cakes. Senhor Júlio was polite but by no means affable.

"The English *senhor* no doubt has heard many tales of the *favelas?*" he said, fixing his eyes on me. I agreed, a little too eagerly, for he frowned and said, "And, as he is a writer, no doubt the *senhor* is anxious to add to them?"

It took me five minutes to convince him that I was not in search of sensational copy.

"It is true," he said, "that terrible crimes are committed in some of the *favelas*—though not, I assure you," and he frowned again, "in this one—but no worse than anywhere else. Some people seem to think that we *favelados* are outcasts, scum. We are not. We are civilized Brazilian citizens—as you can see." And he looked round him with satisfaction. "We live in the *favelas* because everywhere else houses and rents are too expensive. But in *this favela* we live orderly lives."

"If you do not have police protection," I asked, "how do you manage it?"

"We organize our own *vigilantes*," he said.

"What other work does your committee undertake?"

"We interview applicants for building sites, and make sure that undesirables don't arrive at night and set up their shacks secretly, and we see to it that people don't overcharge for the use of their land."

"Their land? I thought the land didn't belong to anybody."

"It doesn't. But we allow squatters who have been here for some time to charge a small rent for any bits of land they can spare."

"How do you manage without any of the city services?"

"My committee is organized into sections—one in charge of the water supply, another in charge of sanitation and so on."

"Do you have much sickness?"

"Not as much as you would think, *senhor*. There is some dysentery of course and an illness we call '*favela* ague.' As you have seen, our sanitary arrangements are primitive and we are very overcrowded."

"How overcrowded?"

"There are fifteen thousand people living in this *favela* alone," Senhor Júlio replied grimly.

"Perhaps the *senhor* doesn't realize," he added, "that approximately a million of the inhabitants of Rio de Janeiro live in *favelas?* And this, I assure you, is one of the best. As you see, we are high up. In the northern part of the city some of the *favelas* are below sea level; there the air is not easy to breathe."

"Do other *favelas* have committees?"

"Most of them."

"Do the various committees get together?"

"Not yet. But our priest is trying to promote some sort of cooperation."

"And the new flats?"

"Yes, you must see the new flats."

He got up, took a silver-handled umbrella from a corner and led the way out. On the way down the hill he took us into several of the shacks. Senhor Júlio's next-door neighbors were a Negro family from Bahia: the mother, big and buxom with a yellow bandana round her head, two little girls in gingham frocks with red ribbons in their hair, and a boy of about ten wearing dungarees and a baseball cap, the father a laborer on one of the building sites in the city. The hut was a ramshackle affair, but there were chairs and beds, a radio and a vase of artificial flowers on a shelf, and once again that puzzling picture of Saint George and the dragon. The kitchen was no more than a hole dug in the hillside, but it contained a cupboard filled with crockery and cooking utensils and a cooking-gas stove.

In another hut I spoke to a young man who was away from work with an attack of *gripe* ("grippe"). A dark suit hung on a nail by his bedside. He was a clerk in a commercial office, he told me; but he was married and had two children, and it was only by living in a *favela* that he could make ends meet.

Everywhere there were attempts to impose some kind of gaiety and dignity. Olive-oil tins filled with flowers or cactus plants hung outside most of the huts, and there were even minute fenced gardens containing a few vegetables or a banana tree. On many of the window sills parrots or cockatoos perched, and other birds were kept in cages. Washing was spread over roofs, verandas and fences, though I found it difficult to imagine how it could dry clean.

That it did I learned when a bevy of secondary-school girls appeared, in their usual spotless uniforms picking their way through the mud and into the huts, taking care not to splash their white socks and patent-leather shoes.

The block of flats at the foot of the hill was an ugly building of greenish-brown cement, but the accommodation it dangled before the eyes of the *favelados* must have seemed palatial. The standard apartment, designed for a family of five or six, consisted of a *sala*, two bedrooms, a kitchen, and a lavatory with a shower; a broad concrete ramp zigzagged up to the roof, where each family was to have a space for washing and hanging out their laundry. The main structure was there, but the walls were unfaced; there were no window frames, doors or fittings of any kind. The only inhabitants were three goats. Senhor Júlio scowled when he saw them, and rushed forward brandishing his silver-handled umbrella. He succeeded in driving two of them out, but the third broke away and dashed up the concrete gangway. Senhor Júlio raced after it. On the sixth floor it leaped onto the balcony. To my horror it jumped off and I expected to see it dashed to pieces, but it landed neatly on the balcony of the floor below and trotted down the ramp and out into the *favela*.

"We must organize the children to keep watch," Senhor Júlio said when he rejoined us. "If this kind of thing happens the place will be a ruin before it has been a building."

"Where are the workmen?" I asked.

"There are none," Senhor Júlio replied. "Work on the flats stopped six months ago. We do what we can in our spare time, and when he is here the priest spends several hours a day with mortar and trowel. But there is much still to be done."

"What has gone wrong?"

"There was money—from the United Nations Organization, I believe—but the priest was told he could only have it if he guaranteed that the *favelados* would vote 'correctly.' He has refused to accept political blackmail. Now he is trying to raise funds from other sources. But it looks as if it will be many years before we are finished."

Senhor Júlio conducted us to the lane leading from the *favela*. He shook hands. "I hope," he said, "that the English *senhor* has learned that, though we *favelados* are outside the law, we live as decent law-abiding citizens who try to better their lot."

A tall, gaunt figure, leaning on his umbrella, he watched us go. We were just turning the corner when I remembered one other question I had meant to ask. I ran back. "Excuse me, *senhor*," I said, "I wonder if you mind telling me your profession?"

He smiled for the first time. "Here," he said, "I am beyond the law. Out there, in the city, I am a policeman. Brazil is a strange country, is it not, *senhor*?"

I was staying in a big, dark hotel downtown, facing Botafogo Bay, still respectable but with the air of having been stranded, like a whale, high and dry above the tide race of modern Rio. Convoys of trams clattered past, and the *lotações*, or buses, their exhausts pointing skyward even in Rio, screeched to a halt at the request-stops. The cars and taxis roared past in a never-ending stream. The din became so familiar that when, an hour or so before dawn, it died down to a mutter, I would wake up suddenly and strain my ears as if the world had come to an end.

Sometimes I would get up, dress, and wander into the Avenida Beira-Mar. A mist would shroud the Sugarloaf and the islands in the bay and veil the tumble of the waves, which seemed to stir and grumble as if they took their cue from the muted traffic. It was the hour when the oddities of the Big City were abroad: a late reveler washing his shirt in one of the fountains; an old Negro woman curled up on a seat, singing hymns; an elderly athlete in knee-length shorts, prancing on the curbside; a group of drunks playing football with an empty beer can among the bulldozers and cranes on the site of yet another development project. Then quite suddenly, as if the sun had drawn them out of the earth, the cars would be hurtling past once more and, as the mist dispersed the waves, islands and peaks would crowd close, throwing their jagged lines across the scene like the splintering of a windshield. As the sun rose higher, the smart ladies of Rio would descend from their limousines and exercise their poodles and dachshunds in the gardens of the Palácio do Catete or along the broad parkway, lined with palm trees, which runs down the center of the Avenida Beira-Mar. Sometimes a band would play, or some military ceremony would take place at the foot of the monument to Admiral Barroso: rattling of drums, sounding of trumpets, much saluting and heel-clicking, and soldiers in cerise tunics with white trousers, caps and gloves.

Sometimes I wandered through the older quarters of the city—islands of astonishing calm. Along the Rua do Ouvidor and the Rua do Rosário, for example, which were spanned at intervals by slender bronze arches from which street lamps were suspended, where cars were prohibited, and where jewelers and smart dress shops occupied the ground floors of low eighteenth-century houses; along the Rua Paissandu, darkened by palm trees with smooth, regular trunks like concrete pillars, almost as tall as the neighboring skyscrapers; through the Cosme Velho district and the Largo do Boticário, with their high colonial houses. Many of Rio's artists and writers lived in this area, side by side with old-style aristocrats. I visited one beautiful mansion, the home of a famous poetess who was also the descendant of a family once powerful in the councils of the emperors. It was crammed with mementoes of John VI's stay in Brazil and of the courts of the emperors Pedro I and Pedro II, with figurines of saints from Minas Gerais, examples of pre-Columbian Indian pottery, and relics of slave days, including a grim-looking branding iron with the family's monogram, and (bizarre contrast) a solid-silver crown and scepter worn at carnivaltime by the slave "lord of misrule."

After lunch I would take my *sesta* in my dark, anonymous bedroom. I fancied I could hear the breathing of Rio's millions around me, and yet at the same time I felt completely isolated, like a creature alone in its burrow in a hill honeycombed with burrows.

There was an abrupt awakening on the afternoon when Brazil

was playing Chile for the World Cup—the match that would clinch the championship. I slept through the opening stages: the voice of the commentator coming at me from all sides merely had a soporific effect. But suddenly the commentator was yelling "Goal!" and a thousand voices took up the cry. All the doors of the hotel were slamming and people were rushing up and down the corridors, shouting, crying and cheering. I could hear a stampede of feet somewhere outside my window, so I got out of bed and drew the heavy curtains. I found myself looking out onto the balconies of a block of flats built round three sides of a quadrangle. I was just in time to see the backs of the inhabitants—many of them like myself in pajamas and dressing gowns—disappearing into their flats to listen to the resumed commentary.

A few minutes later they came pouring back onto the balconies, shouting "Garrincha! Garrincha!"—the name of the great player who had just scored another goal. The children leaped and shrieked, leaned over the balconies and threw lighted squibs and crackers to each other; their elders leaned round the partitions to shake each other by the hand. Streamers, confetti, and scraps of paper torn from telephone directories floated down. To and fro, this way and that, along the three sides of the block and on twenty floors the columns of cheering, shouting people rushed. It was like looking inside an anthill that had gone haywire in the face of some crisis. And then, as the hoarse, quivering voice of the commentator started up again, they disappeared as quickly as they had come.

So it went on, with the excitement mounting and the tumult growing as Brazil continued to score until at length she had won by five goals to three. This time the shrieks, yells, cheers, catcalls, whistles, hooting lasted for a full ten minutes. Traffic throughout Rio came to a standstill as drivers stood up, leaning on their horns, and passengers danced on roofs and bonnets; windows were shattered by several explosions, and a number of people lost their eyebrows; the gutters were knee-deep in streamers and confetti. Next day the newspapers brought out special editions devoted to blow-by-blow descriptions of the match, paeans of praise, prayers of thanksgiving, photographs, biographies, and *obiter dicta* of the players. The economic crisis was relegated to the back page.

In Bahia I had missed the Negro *candomblé* ceremonies. But in Rio there is a variation of the cult, called *macumba*. The difficulty was finding an authentic meeting—one that had not been rigged for tourists. I had the good fortune to meet a well-known woman writer who had written studies of the various African cults in Brazil and who herself belonged to a genuine group. She was unable to take me herself, but her brother, who also belonged, agreed to do so.

First I had to be presented, in order to obtain his approval, to the *Pai-de-Santo*—"Father of the Spirit (or Saint)"—who was in charge of the *terreiro,* or "meeting ground." We drove to a suburb on the northern outskirts of the city, down cobbled, unlighted side streets and stopped outside a brick, two-story villa. The *Pai-de-Santo* was a soft-spoken and dignified mulatto of about forty, wearing a sports shirt, gray flannel trousers and a very smart pair of sandals. He led the way to a long room built onto the back of the house, very much like an English parish hall. He introduced us to his wife, the *Mãe-de-Santo,* a plump, impassive woman, also mulatto, and their daughter, a slight, pretty girl of sixteen, with big, dark eyes, and a smooth skin, ivory slightly tinged with olive. "Tomorrow," her father said, putting his arm round her shoulders, "my daughter will become a daughter of the Spirit." The girl winced. Her mother gave her that odd look of curiosity mingled with compassion that an older woman gives a younger when she is on the verge of some important experience. Half a dozen other women, black or mulatto, were hard at work getting the hall ready.

The ceiling and rafters were draped with lengths of paper, red, white, blue and yellow—"to represent the elements"—and on a side table were dishes of powder of the same colors. On other tables were arranged the musical instruments for the ceremony—drums and tom-toms, draped in dark cloths, calabashes, *maraccas,* bells, double triangles and metal bars. A pair of swords, one short, one long, lay on a shelf. Accouterments of a particularly sacred nature were hidden behind curtains in little alcoves. There was a larger alcove, or altar, on the platform, brightly illuminated and crammed with wood or plaster images, brightly painted, lavishly dressed in silk, velvet and tinsel, and surrounded by lilies and sprays of fern. Most of the figures were of haloed saints, crucifixes round their necks. Among them was Saint George, with a red cross in his shield, standing on a plinth composed of the dragon's coils. I told the *Pai* of the pictures of Saint George I had seen in the shacks in the *favela*.

"You must not believe it," he told me, "when people describe *macumba* as a pagan religion that only pays lip service to Christianity. It is true that some of the priests criticize us, but others give us their blessing. As you see, these are Christian saints, but they have a special significance for us because our own African gods have merged into them. In Saint George, for example (and sometimes in Saint Anthony), we can also see Ogum, the god of war and of iron. Similarly we identify Xangô, the god of thunder, with Saint Michael here in Rio de Janeiro, and with Saint John and Saint Peter in other parts of Brazil. You will see here, too, images of Saint Jerome, Saint Lazarus, Saint Barbara, and other saints, all of whom have their equivalents among our old African gods. Though of course," he added rather hastily, "the Christian saints transcend them all. But may I ask you, *senhor,* if you know anything of our African mythology?"

I admitted my ignorance.

"The main story will not take long. For most of the African slaves in Brazil the Lord of the Skies was Olorum, a being without form who manifests himself only through secondary gods or *orixás*. The chief of these *orixás* was Obatalá, the Sky, and Obudua, the Earth, who became the parents of Aganjú, Land, and Iemanjá, Water. Aganjú and Iemanjá also mated, and they had one son, Orungã. Like Oedipus in the ancient Greek myth, Orungã fell in love with his mother, and one day when his father was absent he tried to violate her. As he pursued her she fell down dead—and immediately her body began to swell. From her breasts flowed two rivers that formed a great lake, and from her womb sprang fifteen gods.

"You will understand, *senhor*, that when the slaves were told that they must be converted to Christianity they saw in the God Almighty of the Bible their own Olorum and in the Virgin Mary something of their own Iemanjá, while Obatalá was transformed into Christ Himself. And, as I have said, those fifteen gods who issued from Iemanjá's womb (among them Ogum and Xangô) became identified with the saints. It is some of these, *senhor*, who will manifest themselves tomorrow night."

I pointed to two other figures, one male, one female, reddish-brown in color and with Indian headdresses.

"Those are the Indian gods, Sereia do Mar, Queen of the Sea, whom the Negro slaves identified with Iemanjá, and Caboclinho dos Matos, god of the chase—or Oxossi in our African mythology. In the *macumbas* of Rio, you see, there is a synthesis of Negro, Christian and Indian beliefs. I do not really approve of these Indian intrusions. I come from Bahia myself, and I regard the *macumbas* as corruptions of the Bahian *candomblés*. But their pure form is not acceptable in Rio, though in this *terreiro* you will see the closest approximation. I obtained the permission of my own spiritual *Mãe* in Bahia to establish it, and once a year I go back to her for purification."

"These are all gods or saints you have shown me," I said, "but doesn't Satan figure in your theology?"

He regarded me gravely for a moment, then said, "Come with me, *senhor*, I will show you." He led the way out of the hall, along a corridor and down a flight of steps into a cellar. Behind a row of guttering candles were two black figures, a large female one and a smaller male one with necklaces of red beads round their necks, both grinning ferociously. "Exu and Leba—the Evil Ones," the *Pai* said in a whisper. In front of them was an enamel plate on which lay the bodies of two black hens; bottles of beer and wine (symbols of demonic possession) stood in the corner. "You have been privileged," the *Pai* told me when we had returned to the hall. "There are few apart from initiates who are allowed to see Exu and Leba. But you have listened with respect to what I have had to tell you. Tomorrow perhaps the good spirits will speak to you."

When we returned the next evening the hall was packed. The majority of the audience were Negroes or mulattoes, including a number of quite small children, but there was a sprinkling of well-dressed white people. The *Pai* had reserved seats for us in the front row. I felt uneasy, and as so often happens my discomfort found a physical focus: there was a hole in my right sock and my big toe was rubbing against the leather of the shoe.

On the platform stood about twenty men and women facing each other and forming a semicircle. The women ranged in color from olive and coffee to coal black, and in figures from the statuesque to the emaciated. Most of them were in their thirties or forties, except for the *Pai's* daughter and a grandmotherly-looking Negro woman of about sixty-five, with white hair and gold-rimmed spectacles. They were wearing red dresses with floral patterns, gathered at the waist and flounced, and red bandanas, with the exception of the *Mãe*, whose head was surmounted by a kind of yellow turban and who in addition had a yellow silk shawl with a long fringe draped round her shoulders. Their legs were bare and they wore sandals on their feet; some of them were also wearing aprons over their skirts and lace-edged cloths slung over their shoulders.

The men included several pure Negroes, including one with the handsome bony features and graceful neck of his Sudanese ancestors, another fat and round like a cooking pot and one of those gangling Negro youths who look all wrists and kneecaps, as well as several mulattoes. But some were white: a tall burly man in his fifties, with broad shoulders, a bald dome and white "side-wings" above the ears; another a little younger; an elderly man with a long furrowed sheep's face and a clipped gray military mustache; a dapper little man with long chestnut-colored hair; and a young man in his twenties, very pale, with big doelike eyes. They wore red shirts, or white shirts with red sashes, white trousers, and sandals or canvas shoes—and in some cases the mysterious cloths over their shoulders.

The *Pai* was also dressed in scarlet and white, but instead of a shirt he wore a loose-fitting tunic and trousers of silk. He was seated just below the platform behind a drum (now undraped), with the other members of the orchestra grouped round him. When he was satisfied that all members were present he beat a roll on the drum, the other musicians quickly took up the rhythm, and he began to sing. His voice was vibrant and powerful, but pitched high in a kind of monotonous keen. Then there was a pause. The musicians struck up a different rhythm, and the whole audience rose to their feet and sang with great fervor—the children included—what was recognizably a hymn. I was puzzled to find that I could not distinguish a word. I turned to my companion and whispered in his ear, "What language is this—a local dialect?" "No," he whispered back, "it is Sudanese; the words and rhythms of all these hymns and prayers have been handed down with hardly any alteration from the first slaves." A small Negro girl of about nine, standing on my right, her frizzy hair tied in a large red bow, turned her head, frowned at me and sang with great lustiness, her shrill treble rising above all the other voices, as if to reprove me for my ignorance.

This pattern of solos from the *Pai* and hymns from the audience continued for about half an hour. Then the candles were lit in all the alcoves, and jugs of water and bowls of fruit and other food were placed on a cloth at the front of the stage while a Negro woman of tremendous proportions and astonishing agility prostrated herself before them, bringing her forehead to the floor, then swaying back to a sitting position and chanting a blessing or thanksgiving. The food and water were then returned to tables, well clear of the center of the stage, and the proceedings entered a fresh phase during which a dialogue of prayers and responses was conducted between the *Pai* and his congregation. He would lean forward, chanting and beating out the rhythm on his drum with great deliberation, and fix his eyes on the congregation as they replied, the bond between them strengthening every moment—and at the same time the semicircle of men and women on the platform began to sway to and fro, with heavy trancelike movements. As the women's flounced skirts swung I saw that they were wearing long lace-trimmed Victorian-looking drawers.

This stage lasted a long time, so long that I was myself lulled into a kind of trance, and hardly noticed that the rhythms had increased in tempo and urgency and that the movements of the dancers had become more frantic and agitated. When the platform exploded into action it came as such a shock that my impressions have remained chaotic and I can't guarantee that I am reporting the rest of the proceedings in the correct order or detail.

It began with one of the women, a slender mulatto of about thirty, letting out a bloodcurdling shriek. She began to whirl round and round at incredible speed, until at last she crashed to the floor, where she lay moaning, flailing her arms and kicking her legs (the point of the long drawers was now apparent). The other women crowded round her, holding her down, cradling her head in their arms, very gentle and solicitous, as if they were assisting at a childbirth. They took off her apron, and then removed her head scarf, which they bound tightly round the upper part of her body, just below the breasts. She was helped to her feet. A helmet was placed on her head, and a sword in her hand. She stood for a moment, dazed, then she opened her lips—and my blood curdled as a weird, high-pitched cry issued from them. It was the voice of Exu, one of the evil spirits. And then, most grotesque touch of all, a lighted cigar was placed in her mouth, and, puffing steadily, sword upraised, she began to walk about the stage, with odd jerky movements. The lace-edged cloth that had hung over her shoulder and which had also been removed was now laid on the floor in front of her and the others on the platform came forward one by one and knelt before her. The congregation in the body of the hall was absolutely still. There were beads of perspiration on my companion's forehead; the eyes of the little Negro girl stood out like electric-light bulbs.

The orchestra started up again, the rhythm faster and even more urgent. The *Pai* had handed over his drum to another musician and was now standing on the platform. This time it was the turn of the pale-faced young man. His convulsions were even more violent and were succeeded by a series of spasmodic, jerking movements, and then the voice of Leba, the other evil spirit, came from his mouth in an unearthly wail. He too was fitted out with helmet and sword, and a lighted cigar (designed, like the black hens sacrificed the previous night, to propitiate the spirit) was thrust into his mouth, and he too received homage. Then both of them, man and woman, began stalking about the stage, uttering their weird cries, while the others made way for them. At one point the woman removed the cigar from her mouth and held it behind her back; the lighted end rested on a bare shoulder blade, but she showed no sign of having felt it: the *Pai* darted forward and gently unfolded her arm, guiding the cigar back to her mouth.

The evil spirits having taken possession, it was the turn of the gods, each summoned by his or her own complicated rhythms, prayers and chants—and each uttering a characteristic cry. The bald-headed white man, for example, after contortions so vigorous and prolonged that the *Pai* had to come to the help of his attendants, became Ogum, god of war, strutting about the stage with shoulders hunched forward, arms dangling, face screwed up like that of an angry gorilla, and uttering weird grunting noises. The dapper little man danced for a long time, but was apparently finding it difficult to achieve the climax of surrender. The *Pai* returned to his drum, nodded to the other musicians, and they struck up an entirely new rhythm, monotonous yet horrifyingly compulsive. The congregation gasped and whites of eyes rolled in terror: it was, my companion explained, the *ijexa*, "a rhythm which no spirit can resist." It achieved the desired effect, for suddenly the little man with a wild cry fell back into the arms of his helpers, his body heaving and shuddering, his chestnut-colored hair falling over his face, the necklace swinging to and fro, the light of the candles glinting upon its swaying crucifix.

In most cases the visitants manifested themselves not only through

their special cries but also through special symbols and regalia—
taken from the alcoves and shelves, which had been concealed behind curtains, the previous evening. Thus one of the women wore
a crown with a fringe of beads, another held an elaborate arrangement of mirrors in her hand, two had their faces completely concealed in black cloths and were guided by helpers, and the *Mãe*
emerged from her convulsions with her hair hanging down the
front of her face, and hobbling on a stick.

At one stage the *Pai* called upon the grandmotherly old Negro
woman, who had been acting as one of the *ogaus,* or attendants.
Apparently she had not expected the summons and did not welcome
it, for she pleaded with him for several minutes, but at length she
gave a sigh and allowed some of the other *ogaus* to remove her
head scarf and apron. The orchestra struck up. The old woman
passed quickly into her convulsions as if her frame was accustomed
to them by long years of experience, but they seemed to tax its
strength and for several minutes afterward she trembled and moaned
feebly.

On another occasion the *Pai* came to the front of the platform and
beckoned to someone in the congregation. A short but very round
and solid Negro woman of about forty, wearing a tweed skirt and
woolen jumper, came forward and climbed onto the platform. Soon
she too was twirling round and round as the drums beat and the
chanting rose and fell; she had surprisingly tiny feet, which were
accentuated by very short ankle-socks; they seemed to twinkle beneath the great bulk like the pivots of tops. Then she heeled over
to be caught and held, thrashing about like a stranded whale, as
the attendant *ogaus* tied the scarf beneath her mountainous
breasts.

When the turn of the *Pai's* daughter came to act for the first
time as the instrument of the spirit to whom she would thus be
consecrated for life her seizure was of exceptional violence. Her
body arched and curveted like an eel, and in spite of her slight build
the *ogaus* had difficulty in holding her. Then when the spirit
"took possession" she raised her head, and her shrieks, wild and

thrilling, sounded as if they had been torn from her entrails. Memories of classical myth flashed through my mind—Pan and Syrinx, the Bacchic rout, the mysteries of Eleusis, and ravished Philomena.

Eventually all the spirits associated with this particular saint's day had descended into the bodies of their devotees, who now grouped themselves in front of the altar, once more in a semicircle, still maintaining the characteristic stances and expressions and uttering the cries of their respective "hosts."

The large woman in the tweed skirt and jumper, however, detached herself from the group, tottered to the edge of the stage and in a plaintive voice called out to someone in the congregation. A homely-looking woman in a coat and hat bustled forward. The initiate pointed to her ears, muttered, "Hurting me, hurting me," and leaned forward like a child waiting to be kissed, while her friend gently unscrewed her earrings and placed them in her handbag. Then, making little whining noises, the woman on the platform pointed downwards as if to say, "Oh, my poor feet." And her friend bent down, removed her ankle-socks, put them too in her handbag and returned to her seat, very matter-of-factly, as if the two of them had just had a housewifely chat. The woman returned to her place in the group by the altar.

But now the *Pai* once more stepped forward and surveyed the congregation. They watched him intently, absolutely silent. Then he beckoned to several men and women. They came forward, paused at the foot of the platform to take off their shoes, and ascended the steps. Their eyes were fastened hungrily on the spirits of the gods, in their fleshly habitations. But suddenly the *Pai* held up his hand; slowly he turned back toward the congregation and beckoned. A murmur of surprise ran round the room and I turned to see who it was who had been singled out. Then I found that my companion was nudging me, and I realized to my horror that the *Pai* was beckoning to me. In a daze I got up. "Take off your shoes," my companion whispered. My consternation increased. I had just remembered the hole in my sock.

When I took off my shoes and ascended the steps to the platform my big toe felt as big as a football. I tried to curl it up inside the sock so that it would not show. Hobbling on the side of my instep, as if I were a cripple, I was conducted by the *Pai* round the semicircle in order to receive the blessing of the spirits. Each spirit, as I was halted by the *Pai*, uttered its distinctive cry. In some cases the cry was short and sharp; in others it lasted for several seconds as if some particularly urgent communication was being attempted. When I stopped in front of the girl, that strange rending cry rang out again, shrill and vibrant. I turned my head aside; I felt embarrassed.

There was no relaxation of posture or expression among the possessed. I looked directly into their eyes, but there was no answering flicker. The platform reeked of the sickly sweet perspiration of the men and the sour smell of hysterical women. I was filled with a sensation of mingled irritation, uneasiness and distaste, partly the result of concern lest the ridiculous contretemps with my sock might be interpreted as lack of respect (though nobody seemed to notice), partly because I felt that with my hobbling movements I must be as grotesque a spectacle as anybody else on the platform, and also no doubt because my nerves were jangling from contact with the forces, whatever they were, that had been released.

At any rate I was glad to get back to my seat and to watch the other members of the congregation making the rounds of the embodied spirits, putting me to shame by the wholeheartedness of their response. When the last of them had left the platform, the orchestra struck up, the audience rose and began singing something that sounded more like a conventional hymn. I thought that this marked the end of the proceedings and I made ready to go, anxious by now to get into the fresh air and under a clean black sky. But my companion pulled me back, and a moment later the singing stopped and everybody sat down again. The *Pai* beat out an entirely new rhythm on the drum and a whole new series of chants and counterchants began. The tension again mounted and at last, when I thought I could stand it no longer, one of the white men on the platform let out a shriek and once more fell to the ground, writhing and heaving. When he was finally helped to his feet he was deathly pale, his shirt was stuck to his body, and it was as much as he could do to remain on his feet. One of the *ogaus* wiped his forehead and removed the insignia he had been carrying. The gods had begun to leave the bodies of the faithful.

This stage of the proceedings lasted as long as the first part. The convulsions were even more violent and prolonged, and after them both men and women were weak and trembling. The dapper little white man had to be held for several minutes, his body sagging from the waist like a broken doll's. The girl's face was pale and tacky like a candle, and there were black rings round her eyes. Her mother, in her own habiliment now, but herself a ghastly yellow color, helped her away and we could hear her vomiting somewhere behind the stage. I myself was so exhausted that I could not focus properly and everything became blurred and confused. I know that at one point a toast was drunk to Ogum, presumably before he returned to his normal self, but I cannot recollect at all clearly. The bizarre and the unexpected persisted to the end. One of the women (it was, I think, some little time after she had recovered from her trance) suddenly began leaping and dancing about the stage, laughing and chattering in a high-pitched girlish voice. She had decided, apparently, that she was with child by the god who had inhabited her. She rushed to and fro, tugging at the sleeves of the other women, announcing the glad tidings and receiving their congratulations, given with indulgent smiles, gravely and seriously. At the end of it all, the *Pai* conducted further prayers and hymns and the congregation dispersed quickly and quietly, with the solemn, closed-up expressions of those who feel they have undergone a "purgation of the emotions."

It was only right that my last impressions of Rio should be visual ones. I traveled northeastward, along the road that zigzags upward to the Serra da Estrêla, past deep valleys, their sides clothed with what my eye, trained by earlier custom, accepted as grass, but which on closer inspection revealed itself as giant trees packed as close as blades of grass; past other slopes where the trees swept down like sloping rain, with no visible means of support. In the distance, dominating everything, was the jagged stub of the Dedo do Deus, the "Finger of God"—and round it other stubs, some bare, some with a thick fur of green on their summits, others with merely a dab of green as if a giant's trowel had transplanted a clod of earth.

On beyond Petrópolis—where an official sat in the entrance hall of the Emperor Pedro II's summer palace behind a mound of felt galoshes and unerringly fished out a pair of the right size—and toward the Serra dos Orgãos the landscape became even more baffling, a chaos of tumbled rock and mountain smoking with foliage and mist as if an earth-quake had just taken place. My eyes tried to find a pattern, but these mountains jutted this way and that; they didn't form a range; it wasn't even possible to speak of "summits" or "peaks" for there was nothing so conclusive; they simply stopped, snapped off like broken teeth. By the time I had reached five thousand feet I had abandoned all hope of forming a coherent pattern in my mind's eye: those fantastic contours must remain forever elusive.

Back in Rio I drove along the Avenida Beira-Mar, past Flamengo and Botafogo beaches, through the Botafogo Tunnel and on to Praia do Leme and then along the Avenida Atlântica. The white skyscrapers of Copacabana seemed to have edged closer to the beach and the breakers to have grown more restless since my last visit. Beyond Ipanema and Leblon the road was hemmed in by a towering rock face on the right, and on the left the sea thundered and swirled through caves and galleries below it. Another road, blasted out of the solid rock, brought me to the Lake Rodrigo de Freitas, its shores overshadowed by Cantagalo, Cabritos, and farther to the northwest, by the Serra da Carioca.

I made my way, twisting and turning, to the Alto da Boa Vista and Tijuca Forest, where the last emperor of Brazil loved to ride and picnic. Here too were mountains all around, soaring and swelling as if they were clouds kneaded by the wind: Tijuca Peak, the

Bico do Papagaio ("Parrot's Beak), and the granite hump of the Pedra da Gávea.

On again to the Corcovado range. Below me lay the panorama of Rio. Slopes and valleys, cascading with blue-green vegetation, scattered with pink, white and terra-cotta houses, and the *favelas* trailing like creepers down the gullies. The complicated crisscross—like a map of the moon—of avenues and roads and alleys with the traffic streaming along them like ants. Spires, roofs, towers, and the skyscrapers like clusters of white rock. The Jockey Club and race track like the board for a child's game. The cartwheel of the Maracanã Stadium, where Garrincha and Pelé and his fellow footballers had won their spurs. The city cemetery, its tombstones glinting like chips of quartz. The vast expanse of Guanabara Bay, with its myriad inlets and islands, tilted up now, flat and luminous like the sea in Brueghel's *Fall of Icarus,* the skyscrapers of Niterói quivering through a golden haze, and above me the Christ of the Corcovado, his arms outspread. Again I had failed to register any coherent pattern, but my eyes pricked as if with shafts of light. They too, I felt, were beginning to grow new dimensions.

It was not quite the end. I thought it was when I boarded the plane for Europe at the Galeão International Airport. I had decided to plunge straight back into my old world, not to subject whatever was stirring within me to the whittling away of a long sea voyage. But at Recife the plane came down for its last refueling before the Atlantic crossing. I stepped out on to the tarmac, and immediately the heat of the northern tropics closed round me like warm cotton wool. I felt the interminable jungles, as if I were standing at the edge of a green furnace. I could smell the muddy waters of the Amazon, the dirt and decay of the northern cities, the rotting palm thatch of the huts and the sweat of emaciated brown bodies.

This, I thought, was the reality. This was the real Brazil, in spite of the skyscrapers, factories and machines of the south. This, as challenge, fulfillment or defeat, was Brazil's future. This was where the raw material of humanity in its continuous struggle with the forces of Nature was to be found. This, moreover, was the reality as far as I myself was concerned. It answered to the chaos of hopes and desires I had brought with me when I first sailed into the Amazon—a century ago, it seemed to me now. I was still not certain whether during the course of my travels through Brazil and through the countries of my mind it was seeing or feeling that predominated. Or did the two function now side by side? Perhaps the impressions that had poured through my eyes had worn fresh channels and planted in them new shoots of life. Perhaps one day a new flora and fauna would startle and delight me. Somewhere in the heat of this jungle lay the essence of human experience, the regenerating heat of a new Brazil. And this was something I could not see, but only feel.